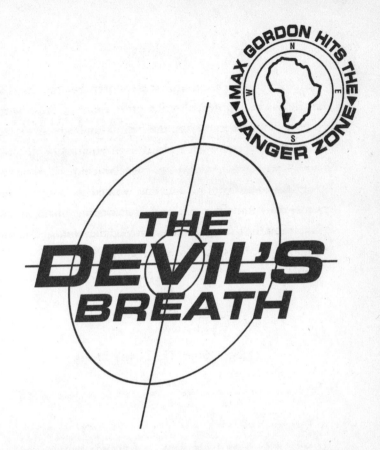

MAX GORDON HITS THE DANGER ZONE

THE DEVIL'S BREATH

DAVID GILMAN

PUFFIN

PUFFIN BOOKS

Published by the Penguin Group
Penguin Books Ltd, 80 Strand, London WC2R ORL, England
Penguin Group (USA) Inc., 375 Hudson Street, New York, New York 10014, USA
Penguin Group (Canada), 90 Eglinton Avenue East, Suite 700, Toronto, Ontario, Canada M4P 2Y3
(a division of Pearson Penguin Canada Inc.)
Penguin Ireland, 25 St Stephen's Green, Dublin 2, Ireland (a division of Penguin Books Ltd)
Penguin Group (Australia), 250 Camberwell Road, Camberwell, Victoria 3124, Australia
(a division of Pearson Australia Group Pty Ltd)
Penguin Books India Pvt Ltd, 11 Community Centre, Panchsheel Park,
New Delhi – 110 017, India
Penguin Group (NZ), 67 Apollo Drive, Rosedale, North Shore 0632, New Zealand
(a division of Pearson New Zealand Ltd)
Penguin Books (South Africa) (Pty) Ltd, 24 Sturdee Avenue, Rosebank,
Johannesburg 2196, South Africa

Penguin Books Ltd, Registered Offices: 80 Strand, London WC2R ORL, England

puffinbooks.com

First published 2007
1

Copyright © David Gilman, 2007
All rights reserved

The moral right of the author and illustrator has been asserted

Set in Monotype Sabon
Typeset by Palimpsest Book Production Limited, Grangemouth, Stirlingshire
Made and printed in England by Clays Ltd, St Ives plc

British Library Cataloguing in Publication Data
A CIP catalogue record for this book is available from the British Library

ISBN: 978–0–141–32302–2

*For my mother whose stories opened the door to
her child's imagination. And in memory of my father
who gave his son the spirit of adventure.*

DANGER ZONE: AFRICA

Select a location **NAMIBIA**

BEWARE! Deadly Beasts!

In the Namibian desert, you are never far from danger. Behind every rock and round every corner, lies a deadly threat.

1. **Spitting cobras**
2. **Wild hunting hyenas**
3. **Charging elephants**
4. **Black scorpions**
5. **Stamping wildebeest**
6. **Prowling lions**

KEY FACTS

AREA:
- Total 824,292 km²
  318,261 sq. miles
  (34th largest country)
- Water (%) negligible

CAPITAL: Windhoek
(22° 34' S, 17° 06' E)

CURRENCY: Namibian dollar (NAD)

BUSHMEN

The San Bushmen are hunter-gatherers and are the oldest inhabitants of southern Africa, where their ancestors have lived for 20,000 years. They make their homes from wood that they gather and survive by hunting antelope and seeking out fruits, nuts and roots in the desert.

Many Bushmen were forced off their traditional hunting grounds by cattle-herding tribes and European colonists and now live in areas that are unsuitable for hunting and gathering.

HOW TO SURVIVE IN THE DESERT

- Make sure you tell someone before you set off
- Bring plenty of water, rations, shelter material and a first-aid kit
- Prepare to kill or be killed
- Never go alone. Take a companion
- Always expect the unexpected

1

The killer, like many assassins, came in the night.

The distant, echoing boom of gunfire and the lazy but deadly arc of machine guns' tracer rounds seeking out their target across the windswept countryside would help hide his presence. And tonight would be one of his easiest assignments. His victim was a fifteen-year-old boy, so he was in no doubt as to the success of his night's work.

He checked his watch. His timing was good. He was in position. First choice: make it look like an accident – a broken neck. Second choice: a shot to the head and dispose of the body. It made no difference to him. The wind had veered from the east to the north – there was a colder bite to it and he thought of the soldiers lying out there on the waterlogged ground. They would not have slept for days and, with almost constant gunfire and the demands of patrolling, exhaustion and the cold would have eaten into them. Not him, though; his zipped roll-neck was mohair and his topcoat a padded Timberland (no external Gore-Tex to make any rustling sound) and his Rockport boots were waterproof. It was good kit that kept his muscles warm and ready to move in that split second when speed and agility were needed. The killer's random thoughts eased away the remaining few minutes until his target would appear.

The steady chattering of the soldiers' machine guns, a couple of kilometres away, was a comfort to him, the staccato rhythm like music to his ears. The ground-sucking crump of mortar fire and the thud of distant artillery blended in his senses. Some of his happiest days as a soldier had been spent killing, but nowadays he offered a more personal service in his lucrative trade of murder. He was being paid impressive money for this job – so, whoever this kid was, someone badly wanted him dead. He checked his watch again, and then eased a 9-mm semi-automatic pistol from his waistband – better to have it ready.

Out in the darkness, a few minutes away from where the killer waited, fifteen-year-old Max Gordon jogged along the thin strip of tarmac. His dad had been right in sending him to school here; these past three years had built up his strength and agility, and he'd decided to enter for one of the junior triathlon contests: extreme sports were the real test of nerve and skill. Next year there would be a Junior X-treme Competition in the French Pyrenees and Max wanted to compete in the downhill mountain-bike race, snowboarding and wildwater kayaking – every one a big adrenalin rush. He knew it was ambitious, but he had the stamina and physical strength now. These extra late-night training runs were paying off. Although it was nearly pitch black, especially when the North Atlantic weather fronts roared in from the coast, there was always enough ambient light to see the tarmac ribbon guiding him around the dinosaur-like boulders.

His breathing settled as he locked into a perfect pace. Across the landscape firepower criss-crossed the night. Explosions were much further away and parachute flares jigged ineffectively in the sky as the buffeting wind swept them away. But he was safe where he was. The commandos and paratroopers were in a designated training area and were no threat to him here. Another four kilometres on the loop back and he'd turn for home, have a hot shower and then bed.

Then he heard a sound that didn't belong. Instincts focused his senses. A soft metallic click – about twenty metres ahead. There was a curved bowl worn away into the hillside, probably made by animals seeking shelter over the years, and that's where the noise had come from. Max knew there shouldn't be any soldiers about here and caution slowed his pace. The wind had shifted slightly, to dead ahead, and that was why he had heard the noise. Like a car door being pressed gently closed. Or an automatic pistol being cocked. He knew that sound well enough.

In less time than it took to think, he veered off the road and into the gorse, putting on a turn of speed and feeling the needle-sharp foliage scratching his legs. Just as he glanced back, a shadow moved from behind a sheltering boulder and then disappeared again. Whoever was out there knew what he was doing, and there was no doubt in Max's mind that the shadow was after him.

He pounded across the dangerously uneven ground, risking a twisted or broken ankle. A fall would put him at the mercy of whoever was chasing him, but he had no choice – he needed to put distance between himself and his pursuer. Arms pumping, eyes streaming with tears from the cold, he glanced around and saw the blurred shadow coming at an angle towards him, but it looked as though the man's bulky clothing was slowing him down. Max was heading straight into the military danger zone – the terrifying crackle of gunfire ahead of him was louder than he'd ever heard it before and the lethal stream of bullets scythed across the sky; he ducked instinctively from the ripped air above his head.

Another quick look over his shoulder told him that the shadow had gone, but then Max lost his footing. Stumbling, he fell; his arm scraped granite and flint, and the raw pain made him yelp. He rolled and scrambled to his feet again – but now in almost complete darkness. The machine-gun firing had stopped; the artillery and mortars had fallen silent. He was running into a black void where the low, ground-hugging fug of smoke stung his eyes and the acrid taste of cordite burned the back of his throat. It was like the aftermath of a massive fireworks display – except these fireworks could rip you apart. He realized, too late, that he'd underestimated the shadow pursuing him. He thought he could outrun him but the man had cut behind him, keeping himself out of sight, and Max could still hear the thump of his feet, getting closer now. Desperation powered him on, his feet came free of the gorse and found a scratch of track through the bracken. Sucking in as much air as his lungs could bear, he ran blindly onwards. The whiplash of a bullet cracked past his ear, followed almost immediately by the sound of the gunshot from behind him. No doubt now – his pursuer was out to kill. Max felt his legs give a little, but that was the ground falling away into a dip. And the man behind him was getting closer, homing right in on his target like a heat-seeking missile.

Max ducked and weaved and then he almost cried out in fright as the night sky exploded. A criss-cross of tracer tore low across the sky, and a part of his brain told him that these were fixed-position machine guns, sweeping arcs of fire. Thousands of rounds a minute were perforating the darkness, less than a metre above his head. He was in what the soldiers called 'dead ground', a belly dip in the earth where bullets couldn't reach him, only now the ground was rising again.

Thoughts raced through his mind. Run? Fall? Crawl? Too late. He had to make a run for it. As he reached the crest he felt a powerful thud into his back as the killer tackled him, and the weight carried him, face down, into the gorse and bog. Max squirmed and fought until he'd twisted his body under the man, who then sat on his chest, pinning Max's arms with his knees. The pain bit into his biceps but he couldn't buck the man off.

The dull glint of the pistol nestled next to his face reflected the crimson gun flashes and explosions around them. The assassin was catching his breath; his eyes stayed firmly on Max's face. Cold, relentless eyes. Max knew in that instant that the man had no feelings, so nothing he could say would stop him. More than anything else, the killer was irritated. He had a job to do and this kid had taken him by surprise. The boy was kicking and bucking, and he was stronger than the man had thought, but he had him pinned. He put the pistol on the ground next to the boy's face so there was no chance of him reaching it. He'd break his neck, that'd save him the bother of disposing of the body. A bad fall against these rocks would look like an accident.

Max was gagging, losing consciousness as the man's hand palmed his face sideways into the stench of the bogland sludge. Lights were flickering in his head – explosions of pain – but he didn't know whether it was him dying or the army's firepower above him. The killer held Max's head with both hands, ready to twist and snap his neck.

And then suddenly it felt as if a tremendous gust of wind swept the man from Max's chest. It whipped him away, but, as it did, something splattered across Max's face. It wasn't the cold sting of rain, it was warm – the man's blood. Sitting on Max's chest he'd pushed himself above the skyline and exposed himself to the machine-gun fire. One round in three was red tracer, and there was a lot of red tracer tonight. It smashed the killer's body, pulverizing bone and muscle, the rounds burning his clothing.

For a moment Max was numb. This was a surreal glimpse into hell. He got to his knees, felt for his throat and gulped in air, tasting the dull, metallic stench of blood. He had to get out of here. The noise was deafening now. He gazed, mesmerized, across the black void in front of him, like a rabbit caught in the headlights of a car, unable to move, watching as the red fingers of death swung back towards him.

A shape loomed out of the darkness and what felt like a lorry smashing into his chest knocked all the wind out of him as his back thumped into the ground. Barely conscious, he was aware of fleeting images: the feel of the rough material of a soldier's camouflage jacket, the dim sight of his white-edged eyes in a face streaked with camouflage cream beneath his helmet, and the far-off sound of his voice yelling 'Cease fire! CEASE FIRE!'

Max sank into a black, silent, bottomless pool.

2

Despite its name, Dartmoor High wasn't a normal secondary school. It sat above the snowline on the northern edge of Dartmoor National Park, built into the rock face like a small, medieval fortress. Nestled into the ancient granite of Wolf's Head Tor, it was believed to be the site of an outpost of Rome's XX Legion when they fought for and secured ancient Britain.

The Victorians originally built Dartmoor High as a prison for the criminally insane, believing that society would be better off if the prisoners were locked away in an isolated spot. After a few terrifying nights spent alone with the inmates in such a bleak place, where one's imagination turned the wind's howl into an evil, supernatural moan, even hardened warders refused to serve there. Eventually the inmates were institutionalized in slightly more humane conditions elsewhere.

After a chequered history, it finally became a private school that concentrated on vigorous physical pursuits and no-nonsense education.

*

A hundred years later it was still a boys-only school. Some of the former pupils had gone on to become explorers, soldiers, pilots, pioneering doctors, MI6 officers and successful businessmen; there was even a well-known rock-star who had studied there. They all benefited from the self-reliance that Dartmoor High gave them. Pupils came there from all over the world, and it was now regarded as an exclusive school, catering for twelve- to sixteen-year-olds. Although it seemed to have a fearsome reputation that scared a lot of the new entrants, they soon found the staff to be firm and fair, and they discovered the excitement that this kind of adventure-training school offered. The emphasis was on the boys themselves proving that they were cut out for it. If they weren't, they could always go to other schools. Once they'd adapted to their new surroundings, most would rather stay at Dartmoor High, despite the howling wind, the blistering cold winters and its close proximity to one of the military's biggest training areas, than go anywhere else.

But being hunted down and killed was not on the curriculum.

Max's cuts and bruises were treated by Matron. It may have been a boys-only school but the headmaster recognized the need for some kind of female role-model, so there were a couple of women on the staff. Right now, Max wished his mother was around to give him a hug. Tears stung his eyes but he tried to be brave and pretend it was caused by the antiseptic Matron was putting on his arm. Matron murmured a few comforting words about there being no shame in crying, and that no one would know. Max didn't care about anyone knowing, he had cried for ages when his mum died, four years ago, and he couldn't help some tears now, but once he put it in perspective and took some deep breaths to calm himself down, he felt better. He was alive. Marks – ten out of ten.

Once Max had been checked by the school's on-call doctor and had given his statement to the police, he learned that it was a paratrooper who'd saved his life by hurling him to the ground out of the way of the machine-gun fire that had killed the assassin. The army had been in the training area for two weeks on a live firing exercise, and by chance the eagle-eyed soldier saw Max being chased and, without time to stop the firing, hurled himself at the dazed boy, saving his life.

Everything else was a mystery. 'I've spoken to the police, Max; they don't know who the dead man is. Not yet, anyway,' Mr Jackson, the school principal, told him. Fergus Jackson didn't have the look of a traditional school headmaster. He seemed to live permanently in corduroy trousers, hiking boots and a woollen round-neck sweater. Max sipped the hot chocolate someone had given him as they'd moved through to Jackson's study, a big room with a blazing fire in a massive granite fireplace. Multi-coloured rugs cushioned the slate floor and well-worn, creaky leather chairs and sofas were arranged around the fire.

Mr Peterson, Max's housemaster, was also in the room, looking more worried than usual. His appearance was that of a rather ineffectual bookkeeper. He had floppy hair and wore spectacles, and he always seemed to be deep in abstracted thought. This appearance was deceptive: he'd led a vigorous life, climbing the world's highest mountain peaks in between teaching boys geography and white-water canoeing.

The attack remained a mystery. There was no obvious reason for anyone to try to kill Max. 'Do you think it could have been a random attack?' Max asked. 'Y'know, some kind of nutter who crawls out from under a stone whenever he feels the urge?'

'From what you've said, it seems he was determined from the start to kill you. Otherwise, once you'd run he could have simply got himself out of there and disappeared into the night,' Jackson answered.

'How did you realize it was an ambush?' Mr Peterson said.

Max recalled when he'd heard the sound of an automatic pistol being cocked, a moment indelibly impressed on his memory.

Every school holiday, the boys could stay on at school and take part in various activities, such as an expedition to climb Ben Nevis, a canoe trip, or even bear watching in Canada; but if they were really desperate they went home to their parents. It was a school rule that families had to be seen at least once a year, otherwise Mr Jackson and the staff would never have a breather. Max chose to see his dad every time. He loved it. He always had. Tom Gordon was a . . . well, Max wasn't a hundred per cent certain what his dad was, to tell the truth, but it was something along the lines of a hydrologist-geologist-archaeologist, who travelled around the world. He found underground wells in the deserts and helped Third World villagers get a clean supply of water; he uncovered hidden cities and identified lost civilizations; he scuba-dived off exotic ocean reefs, searching for lost wrecks. No wonder his dad urged him to go to Dartmoor High – he wanted his son to be as resilient and capable as he was. Life should be an adventure, he always told Max, but you had to be equipped to go on the journey. It was brains as well as physical fitness that were needed.

It had been eighteen months ago when Max had heard the oily slide and click of metal against metal as his dad's hands cocked a 9-mm Browning pistol. Max had never been that scared before or had ever seen that look in his father's eye. It chilled him. It made him feel that the smiling, warm, loving father he'd always cherished had a cold place in his heart that was as deep as glacier ice.

For the summer holidays that year he'd joined his father on a dhow from Zanzibar, sailing down the east coast of Africa. His dad was taking a break from his work, showing Max a spectacular reef that teemed with sharks. Beneath the calm, gentle swell of the Indian Ocean the sea was thick with them. However, on the eighth day, pirates had roared up alongside them in a rigid raider boat, its high-powered outboard engines enabling it to catch up easily with the lumbering dhow. The modern-day cut-throats had a good intelligence network, gathering the gossip around the harbours as to who was sailing where. They were known to attack yachts and kill their crews. The dhow's crew was terrified by the half dozen men, each brandishing an AK47, that virtually indestructible workhorse of the gun world. Max's dad had ducked down into the cabin and came back a few moments later, just as the first of the pirates clambered aboard, his gold-capped teeth glinting as he laughed at the terrified crew. Max's dad had quickly stepped forward, grabbed the man's neck with his left hand and squeezed a pressure point. The pirate was immobilized, his gun clattering to the deck; at the same time Tom Gordon fired twice into the pirates' boat's fuel tanks – the shock wave from the tremendous explosion made Max reel. The pirates bailed out and Max's dad pushed the terrified captive pirate over the side. It had all happened in a matter of seconds. Tom Gordon shouted a command in Arabic and the dhow swung away, leaving the screaming pirates clambering on to what was left of their boat.

'Dad! What about the sharks?' Max finally managed to choke out.

'They should have thought of that before they set out to murder innocent people,' his dad replied, still grim-faced but, unlike everyone else, unshaken by the incident. Then he'd smiled, and he was the same old dad Max loved, though now he realized that there was a lot more to his father than he had ever known. 'They'll have a transponder linked to their mates back on shore, but by the time they get here we'll be long gone and out of range. They can cling to the wreckage until then.'

The memory lingered a moment longer, before Max realized that Mr Peterson and Mr Jackson were still waiting for him to answer the question.

'Oh . . . sorry. I heard the man who tried to kill me cock the weapon; it was something I'd seen and heard before when I was with my dad.'

Jackson and Peterson looked uneasily at each other for a moment.

'Max,' said Jackson a little hesitantly, 'we've tried to contact your father, but . . . well, we're not sure where he is.'

'He could be anywhere,' Max said. 'Maybe you should try the organization he works for.'

Jackson paused, trying to decide whether he should tell Max what he knew. It was Peterson who broke the silence. 'We have. It seems . . . he's gone missing.' Max barely noticed Jackson's look of disapproval at his geography teacher's lack of tact. 'Best you should know,' Peterson said.

Gone missing. That had an ominous ring to it. Under any other circumstances Max wouldn't have been too alarmed – his father was often out of radio or mobile phone range. But now? 'It's been more than a week since he made contact with anyone,' Jackson said.

Max nodded, thoughts flooding his mind as he tried to think clearly and picture what might have happened to his dad. 'Where was he?'

'Namibia.'

Diamond country. Namibia's coast ran for thousands of kilometres along the south Atlantic. Vast tracts of land were off-limits because there were diamonds waiting to be picked up. Max's dad had told him about Namibia before. A huge triangle of a country, bigger than France and the UK put together. Away from its mist-shrouded coast was an arid, brain-sizzling desert and scrubland. The Okavango swamps with their crocodiles lay to the east in Botswana, Angola was north, beyond the Kunene River, and South Africa lay to the south. There was a lot of game: lions, elephant . . . but what else? Max's brain couldn't put it all together. His dad must have been injured, or worse. If an assassin had come in the night for Max, whoever wanted him dead must have captured or killed his father first. Why?

Jackson's voice interrupted his thoughts. 'Naturally, if this wasn't a random attack on you, then we have to assume there's a connection.' Max nodded. What would Dad want him to do? 'In the circumstances, Max,' Jackson went on, 'we think we should go to the vault.'

The vault. That was where you heard voices of the dead. Max had known a couple of boys whose parents had died – they'd been taken down to the vault. Every pupil had his own key, kept in Jackson's safe, which unlocked a deposit box in the underground chambers of Dartmoor High. The vault was fireproof, bombproof, everything-proof, because it was cut into the granite hills on which the school was built. When a parent died, it was a legal requirement that a guardian be nominated to look after the boy, and that information was in each boy's deposit box. Sometimes there were personal letters, mementoes, and usually a legal document that gave a lawyer's name for his inheritance – if there was one. It was also a condition of attendance at Dartmoor High that each parent left a digital recording for their child. Jackson believed that if tragedy struck, the comforting voice of a parent was just about all a boy had left to help him cope with the trauma.

Voices from the dead. Going to the vault was so final.

Matron tapped on the door; Jackson nodded for her to come in. 'We thought we'd do that tomorrow, Max,' Jackson said.

Matron was carrying a glass of water and a pill holder. 'The doctor reckoned you should get a proper night's sleep. Help you deal with things.' Matron offered the sleeping pill to Max. 'It's only a mild sedative. OK?' Jackson assured him.

Max nodded, took the pill and a gulp of water and gave a reassuring smile to Jackson, Peterson and Matron.

'Good boy,' Matron said.

'We don't want to cause any alarm, Max, so, as far as anyone else is concerned, you strayed into the Danger Zone and took a tumble. Are you all right with that?'

Max nodded.

The moment he was outside the study, Max spat the tablet out. He'd tucked it under his tongue and pretended to swallow it. It wasn't that he didn't trust anyone; he just wanted to keep a clear head and think this through. That's what his dad would want him to do. That's why he'd sent him to this school in the first place.

Max's room was big enough for a single bed, a small table used as a desk, a chair, a bookcase, a trunk for personal bits and pieces, and a single wardrobe. It may originally have been built as a prison cell, but now it offered enough space to have the essentials – but no luxuries, not even a television, though there was one in each House's common room. There were four Houses at Dartmoor High: Eagle, which Max belonged to; Wolf, Otter and Badger.

Max lay on his bed. He realized he might be facing the starkest moment of his life. If his dad had been killed, he was an orphan. No, he just didn't believe that. His father was too resourceful, but no sooner had this positive thought arrived than another one chipped in. Nobody is immortal and if they, whoever they were, had killed his dad then they must have taken him by surprise. Ambushed him. As they had tried to do with Max.

Max let out a deep, troubled sigh. He had escaped; maybe his dad had, too.

He turned his head on the pillow, his eyes gazing idly at his desk and bookcase. Something wasn't right. He looked again. Things weren't exactly where they should have been. A small pile of textbooks was nudged across the desk at a different angle. He always had them in a certain place because he liked to rest his left elbow on them when he wrote his essays. And that Cook Island figurine of a war god was facing slightly away from the window when it should have been gazing directly across the moors. What else had been moved? Bits of stone from the ruins of Aglason in Turkey where Alexander the Great had attacked across the mountains; a rock crystal found in the Himalayas which had a glint of some magical light in it, said to be from the cave of an ancient mystic; the amber teardrop from Russia which a hundred million years ago had encased a wayward insect in its resin. All bits and pieces his dad had given him. Now Max's senses sharpened. Letting his gaze sweep across the room, he realized that someone had pulled books away from the wall, checked them and put them back a bit too neatly. He knew the artefacts were not in exactly the place where they should have been because, despite the obligation to keep his room tidy, there was always a faint layer of dust noticeable on any flat surface. Max wondered what on earth the intruder had been looking for.

There was a knock on the door. 'Max?' It was Sayid, whose mum taught Arabic at the school. Max let him in and closed the door quickly behind him. Sayid was his best friend.

When Max's father had worked in the Middle East, Sayid's

dad had been killed by terrorists and Max's dad had pulled strings to get Sayid and his mother, Leila, into Britain. Max was never sure what the connection was between the two men, except that they had worked together, and it seemed that Tom Gordon owed some sort of debt to the Khalif family. Max's father explained that Sayid and his mother needed a safe place, well out of harm's way, and he told Max to keep an eye on the new boy. Max did exactly that, but now Sayid had been there long enough and didn't need looking after any more.

'The whole place is buzzing, Max. The army, the police coming and going. What's going on?' Sayid whispered quickly.

'I went for a run and decided to get a closer look at the guns.' Max shrugged.

'You can be gated for that! No more Saturdays in town for months.'

'Yeah, I know, it was stupid. The firepower was awesome, though. The whole place was shaking.'

Sayid looked over his shoulder at the closed door nervously and Max could see something was up. 'Max, you'd better tell me if there's anything else. I'm your mate, yeah?'

'Yeah, 'course. It was nothing. I broke a school rule. Big deal.'

Sayid gave him a disbelieving look and then pulled a crumpled envelope out of his back pocket. 'Sorry this got a bit mangled, but I didn't want anyone else to see it.'

'What?' Max asked, because Sayid still looked as though he knew there was something going on.

'This is addressed to me,' Sayid said as he handed over the letter. The envelope was open but there was another one inside with one word written clearly – MAX. Sayid shrugged. 'Your dad obviously wanted this to get to you without going through the usual channels. It came in this afternoon's post – I couldn't find you.'

Max nodded. His father had used the one person in school whom Max could always rely on in a tight corner. He ripped the envelope open – and on the piece of folded paper inside there was, again, only one word. FARENTINO.

Max knew what his dad wanted him to do.

Sayid waited patiently.

Max took a deep breath. 'Sayid, listen. My dad's in trouble, he's gone missing . . .'

'Bloody hell! Where?'

'I'm not sure, but he was last heard of in Africa, and this note he sent you confirms that he's trying to contact me. He's laying a trail for me. Sayid, listen, mate, you've got to keep this to yourself. I mean, things are pretty bad . . . I didn't just wander into the Danger Zone tonight. I was running from a bloke who was trying to kill me.'

Sayid Khalif knew the gut-wrenching fear that assassins had brought into his own life. Only he and his mother had survived an attack in Saudi Arabia, and if Max and his dad were targets then he felt the fear as keenly as Max. 'I won't say a word, promise.'

'Not even to your mum.'

'Especially not Mum, she'd be frantic for you and your dad.'

'Thanks. Right, well, I reckon that once I've opened my box in the vault tomorrow morning I'll be off. My guess is, Dad has left me another clue in there.'

'You leave school, and Mum'll find out your dad's missing.'

'No, Mr Jackson will tell everyone it's compassionate leave, that Dad's sick or something. Don't tell her the truth, Sayid, I'm already putting you in danger by telling you.'

'I could come with you.'

'No you couldn't. Besides, I'll need someone back here I can trust. Can you sort something out computer-wise, a decent code system or something? Then you can act as my back-up.'

When it came to computer science and technology, it was Sayid everyone turned to. He'd come close to causing a major scandal and a national security alert when he hacked into the Ministry of Defence's computer system which the government had paid hundreds of millions to create. Their computer analysts had chased Sayid through a labyrinth of code and almost got to him, before he led them down a dead end with a trapdoor and self-destructed his whole program. Had they caught him, the repercussions would have been enormous: a fourteen-year-old kid from Saudi, inside the heart of the British Defence security system! Only he and Max knew about it. That was a secret worthy of real friendship.

'I'll be here. I'll set up a rerouting system so any message you send will be hard to trace.'

'Make that "impossible to trace", Sayid. My life might depend on it.'

3

The vault was one hundred and thirty-three steps below the ground floor. It was amazingly dry and damp-free because the granite walls were so thick and the warm air from the geo-thermal heating unit was channelled into the school from beneath here. Mr Jackson stood back a respectful distance as Max opened his safe-deposit box. The envelope inside was security-stamped and tagged with a tamper-proof clip. Max tore open the envelope. Inside was a USB memory-stick MP3 player that would hold his father's message. Max's passport was there, a credit card with a PIN and account number and what looked like a couple of thousand pounds in cash. There was also a lawyer's letter, which stated that Max's father had few assets other than the country cottage in France; his dad always rented a furnished apartment during his brief stays in London. All of which, Max realized, meant he was pretty much broke and that Max's legal guardian was to be someone in Toronto whom he had never heard of – Jack Ellerman. Max looked again at the packet that held the envelope with the money and credit card. But if Dad was stony broke, what was all this about? Then he saw the symbol on the envelope: a small drawing of an Egyptian hieroglyphic – the jackal-headed figure of Anubis, god of the underworld. Underworld. Hidden from view. His dad was sending him a message to hide the contents of the envelope. Max pushed the money and the credit card under his jacket and then turned. Mr Jackson was right behind him, had he seen Max hide the envelope?

'Everything all right, Max?'

Max held up the USB player and the letter. 'Seems Dad's broke and he's sending me somewhere I really don't want to go.'

Mr Jackson put a protective arm around Max as he read the letter from the lawyer. 'I see. Well, that's why we hold a parents' contingency fund. We'll arrange that ticket for you. But there'll be enough in your school trust fund to cover the rest of this term, we wouldn't force you to leave. We can make a plan, Max. A lot of the boys have bursaries to be here.'

Max smiled gratefully, but shook his head. 'Once I've heard Dad's message I suppose I'd better do as he asks.'

They started their long walk up from the vault – ascending from the underworld – and Max remembered that Anubis was also the Egyptian god of the dead.

Max said his goodbyes to Sayid and his mother, then Mr Peterson drove him to the station for the London train. Three hours later, he was in London, a modest-sized rucksack on his back with everything he needed – which was little more than a change of clothes. He'd listened to his dad's voice on the recording three or four times, but it was only twenty minutes' worth. There were no clues, no hint as to what his dad might have expected to happen to him. It was mostly about Mum and how much they'd always loved him, and how his dad hoped that the school had been the right choice . . . how much he missed Max. It was all a bit vague. But his father's secret message on the envelope made Max extra cautious.

When Max got off the intercity train, he turned as if making for the Heathrow Express platform, but then he cut around a fast-food stand and backtracked, towards the short tunnel that led to the taxi rank. There was a long queue but he lingered for a while, casually watching to see if anyone was following him. Then he moved quickly back inside the building and went down to the tube station. He kept looking; there didn't seem to be anyone familiar, but then he saw a man in his twenties – quite scruffy, possibly a musician or art student, listening to his iPod. His rough-cut hair and worn clothes blended in well, but Max noticed that he was wearing a pretty expensive-looking watch, which he checked frequently. Max suddenly realized that he had seen him hanging around the Heathrow train platform.

Max squeezed into the carriage and the iPod man, using another door, got into the same one.

His senses now sharpened, Max looked up and down the carriage, through the connecting doors. He noticed a middle-aged woman, quite smartly dressed, her expensive fashion bag over her shoulder. Max realized she had been about ten places in front of him in the taxi queue.

Someone must be after something he had. But what? Why would they have tried to kill him on Dartmoor if he had something important they wanted? It made no sense. Not yet, anyway. The important thing now was to make sure no one followed him to his father's contact.

When the train arrived at Charing Cross Underground station there was the usual push-and-shove as those on the crowded platform tried to get on board. Max watched. iPod Man was trying to observe him, looking sideways so there was no direct eye-contact. And Smart Bag Woman was doing the same. Half a dozen people managed to squeeze in just as Max pressed towards the doors and the throng on the platform. The doors were closing when he shouldered his way through, and as his feet touched the platform he turned and saw the man and woman push their way out. So, they *were* following him; it wasn't a figment of his imagination. However, he'd already thought of a plan. As he stepped on to the platform he dropped his rucksack between the sliding doors so that when they closed they immediately sprang open again. In that instant he plucked the bag off the floor and edged his way back inside. He was strong enough to push aside a couple of heavier men; that was one thing about Dartmoor High, they made you use every muscle in your body – maybe it was so as to deal with travelling on the London Underground.

As the train pulled away he saw the look of surprise and panic on his watchers' faces. He'd beaten them. How many more were there to get past before he could reach Farentino?

He made his way to Trafalgar Square, and outside the National Gallery he jumped on a tour bus full of foreign tourists and took a seat upstairs in the open-topped Routemaster. It was too cold for most people, but he wanted a clear view to see if he was still being followed – besides, he didn't mind the cold; he was used to it.

As the bus made its way along the Embankment, the

Thames seemed to be flowing faster than the traffic, so he jumped off, sprinted up the steps near the Courtauld Institute, dodged across the traffic snarled up in the Strand and into the fringe of Soho. At last he felt sure he had put enough distance between himself and whatever teams of watchers there might have been.

By the time he'd walked up towards Soho Square he'd listened to his father's message again. Dad had always been so open with his feelings when they'd been together. Fathers and sons were always going to fall out at some stage, Dad told him once, but Max should understand that, no matter what happened, he loved him with all his heart. So, Max reasoned, if his dad was usually open about how he felt, why was he saying so little on a recording which he knew would be played if something happened to him? Perhaps it was because he feared someone else might have listened to it first – if that was the case, was there a hidden message Max hadn't picked up on yet? He didn't know, but he'd keep listening until he had exhausted that possibility.

Soho Square, its edges planted with shrubs and trees, made a welcome oasis among the city buildings. There were office workers grabbing a quick coffee or a sandwich as they took their lunch hour; a couple of people sleeping rough hogged the benches, while pigeons ducked and bobbed as they hunted for crumbs from the sandwich-eaters.

Max skirted the square, then cut across it diagonally. He was as certain as he could be that he was no longer being followed. He approached a black, high-gloss-painted door, which was crammed unobtrusively in between two other old buildings. One, the Zaragon Picture Company, was an independent film-making company, the other the head office for a wine merchant. Max checked the small brass plaque on the black door – *Farentino* – to make sure he'd remembered the location correctly; it had been a couple of years since he was here last. *Farentino*. That's all it said. No description of what business was conducted there. He pressed the intercom and told the voice that answered who he was. The door clicked open and he stepped into the quiet, safe world of his father's most trusted friend.

Max could smell the musky odour of the animal's skin. It seemed so out of place in the well-furnished rooms of Angelo Farentino. The animal pelt had never been properly cured, but it served its purpose of protecting the bundle of hand-written notes from the elements. As Max let his hands feel the texture of the animal skin and the papers it protected that he had just been given, Farentino paced back and forth, his expensive Italian shoes making hardly a sound on the marble floor. Max wanted to devour the words on the pages – they were his father's field notes – so he skimmed across them, desperate to learn any information about what had happened to him in Africa.

'Your father knew something was very wrong,' Farentino said as he paused to pour himself a glass of red wine. 'He always sent his notes by email and a disk copy by courier. This . . .' he wagged a finger at the bundled papers, 'this is . . . extraordinary!'

Angelo Farentino was not a man to be taken by surprise. For thirty years he had been a publisher of books on environmental issues, and Tom Gordon on his travels had helped draw attention to many of the most damning ecological disasters across the world. Max kept reading. The notations were neat but in places looked as though they were written in a hell of a hurry. '... *evidence of heavy machinery* ... *borehole excavations should not be in this location* ... *all indications are* ...' Some of the pages were torn, denying the reader tantalizing conclusions that Max's father had made.

Farentino sat, his arms resting on an antique walnut table, his fingers nervously fidgeting. 'Max. I fear for your father and he is obviously frightened for you. That's why he gave you so little information. He knew he could trust you to use your brains and not show anyone anything. Which is why he sent you to me.'

'And this Canadian, Jack Ellerman? I've never heard of him.'

'Fictitious. To throw anyone interested off the scent. So, I'm going to send you to very good friends of mine in northern Italy. You'll be safe there until I can help you find your father.'

Max gazed at his father's papers. They were pockmarked with grime and grubby from dirty hands; some of the pages were stuck together and in one place an ugly brown stain crept like a squashed lizard across the paper. 'Is this blood?' Max asked.

Farentino shrugged. He wasn't sure, and even if he were he wouldn't admit it. Max took another bite of the pizza Farentino had ordered in and sipped the peach smoothie the Italian was so good at making. Despite everything that had happened, Max was hungry and knew he had to keep his blood-sugar levels up if he was to concentrate and make any sense out of all this. 'Dad sent his notes, wrapped in a gazelle skin, across two hundred kilometres of desert and wasteland in the care of a Bushman.'

'That's right. The Kalahari Bushmen are nomadic, they're the last indigenous people in Africa to live like that, and your father must have established a rapport with them. The Bushman took these notes to a farmer who runs a wildlife sanctuary, a sort of private game park, and who is, I suppose, someone either your father or the Bushman knew.'

'And he sent them to you.'

'To a literary agent I use in Johannesburg. That was the instruction Tom, I mean your father, had written. Max, he was so far out in the wilderness, there was no communication. There are so few people out there. He saw something he shouldn't have, is my guess.' Farentino averted his eyes.

'What?' Max asked him.

Farentino shrugged and gave a small, non-committal gesture. 'Maybe it's nothing. No, maybe it is.' He hesitated, but he knew this was no time to hold back. 'The literary agent I used. His office was destroyed by fire and he was badly injured. Yesterday. The same day you were attacked.'

Max let that sink in. Obviously a big effort was being made to stop any information about Max's dad or what he'd discovered getting out.

'Who knows about these notes?' asked Max.

'No one else. I'm not letting anyone know anything until I can work through them. Trouble is, the gazelle skin has sweated acids into the paper. It's going to take weeks for us to separate the pages.'

'Are there any clues at all in what Dad wrote?' Max asked hopefully.

'We haven't found anything extraordinary yet; they're so incomplete we can't make much sense of them.' Farentino sipped his wine. 'But the place the Bushman delivered them to is hundreds of kilometres away from where I thought your dad was working.'

'Is anyone looking for him?'

Farentino winced; he unwrapped one of his expensive cigars, rolled it in his fingers, sniffed it. Max waited. Farentino was wary of answering.

'Angelo, tell me.'

Farentino appeared to weigh up whether he should. He looked hard at Max and then made up his mind.

'No one is looking. Not really. I have tried to do what I can. The Foreign Office has asked local police and game rangers to keep an eye out.' He dabbed the cigar between his lips in a small, nervous gesture. Max knew there was more to come and he felt a tightening in his stomach muscles. Maybe the pizza hadn't been such a good idea after all.

Farentino opened a file on the desk and showed Max some corporate reports and press clippings concerning an international exploration company called Shaka Spear Exploration. Every picture featured a man as big as an international rugby player – in fact he looked like a Maori, except that his head was shaved and he wore a topknot of hair like the Chinese warriors Max had seen in the movies. 'That's Shaka Chang,' Farentino told him. 'His father was a Zulu, his mother Chinese. He has connections that would make the President of the United States envious. He has a fearsome reputation as a corporate businessman, but he also has an incredible track record for helping the underprivileged, so he's pretty much untouchable.'

Max gazed at the man who controlled one of the biggest exploration companies in the world. In none of the pictures was Shaka Chang smiling. 'Namibia has massive deposits of diamonds. Is that what Dad was looking for?' Max asked.

'No. A dam is being built there. It has created much controversy. Not everyone is happy. Ecologists are trying to stop it. It will create a massive hydroelectric scheme and bring a lot of wealth to the country. It'll be worth billions. Shaka Chang is behind it.'

'If the dam is already planned, what was Dad doing there?'

'That I am not sure about,' Farentino replied anxiously. 'From what I understand, it will not only flood ancient Bushman burial grounds but will have a huge impact on Namibia's unique ecosystem. So he was searching for aquifers.'

'I don't know what that means,' Max said.

'Think of deep underground layers of rocks . . . like maybe a honeycomb of rocks. All those nooks and crannies contain fossil water. Water can be more precious than diamonds out there, and if your dad found any subterranean rivers or these deep deposits it could cause Mr Chang a huge headache.'

'Then that's why Dad got his notes to you. If this Shaka Chang is as powerful as you say, then maybe he thought Dad might have sent something to me. That's why they tried to kill me. That's why someone searched my room.'

Farentino shook his head. 'It's possible. But we have no idea what they could have been looking for. Do we?'

'No,' Max said.

Farentino looked at Max, probing his eyes with his own. 'Max, did your father leave any kind of clue, any message, anything at all to tell you what he found out there? Anything?'

Max scanned the information in his brain. If he had doubts or suspicions, or if there was anything he had not yet uncovered, then he should tell Farentino. So why didn't he? Something told him to keep his thoughts to himself. Trust no one. Not even Farentino? No one. Not yet.

Max almost squirmed at his complete lack of trust, but these were extraordinary circumstances. 'Angelo, Dad might still be alive. And if there's a chance of that, then I'm going to help find him.'

Farentino raised his eyes in silent prayer. 'Yes, I was afraid of that.'

Max shuffled the pictures of Shaka Chang. One of them slid from under the others. It was an aerial photo of a fort in the wilderness in what looked to be Africa. Behind the fort was a massive lake or swamp. The boulder-strewn ground to the front was softened by an open plain. The whole place seemed formidable – well, that made sense, it was a fort, after all.

Farentino fingered the photograph. 'That is Shaka Chang's headquarters in Africa. He has private accommodation there. That line you can see in the desert is an airstrip; the river and lake are crocodile-infested. No one goes in, or comes out for that matter, unless Shaka Chang says so.'

Max felt a sense of evil about the place. 'It looks really menacing.'

'Yes. Namibia used to be called German South-West Africa. It was their territory. The fort was built before the First World War.'

'Does it have a name?' Max asked.

Farentino went quiet for a moment. There were stories about that place that chilled the blood. 'They call it Skeleton Rock,' he answered quietly.

Max watched Farentino's face. It was as if his eyes were the portals to his secret thoughts. Max's intuition was correct. The Italian was nodding, almost imperceptibly, to himself. He had reached a decision.

'Max. There are matters I must discuss with you. There are things you should know about your father.'

An hour later, heavy with the burden of what he had just learned, Max used the credit card that his father had promised was secure to book a flight. There was a direct flight by Air Namibia from Gatwick, but if the people following him expected him to try to reach his father, they would be watching that flight. Finally Max had one last favour to ask of Farentino, and it was not going to be an easy one, but the Italian pulled it off in record time.

They drove to the airport as darkness was falling. Max sat quietly. There were no more questions to be asked. Farentino had explained his mother's death and passed on the burden of secrecy that surrounded his father's work. It made Max even more determined to find his father.

Max promised Farentino that he would stay in touch as

best he could, but warned him that any information he sent would be through a third party and would carry a webmaster's name – *Magician*.

Farentino berated himself loudly for letting Max out of his safe-keeping. His only consolation was Max's assurance that he'd have gone anyway; at least this way Farentino knew about it and would be in London whenever Max needed help.

At Heathrow's Terminal 3 Farentino hugged Max and kissed his forehead, which Max managed to bear without too much squirming. He gave his new friend a hug – he felt a bit more grown up now and there was a nod of acknowledgement and respect from Farentino.

Max pushed his way through the bustling terminal, trying not to look too obvious as he scanned the crowd for anyone who stuck out. The people who had followed him earlier didn't seem to be anywhere in sight. Luckily, the large number of passengers made it easy to pretend that he was simply deciding where to go – which was partly true. He checked his watch. Time was getting tight now. The Air Canada desk was in Zone D. He joined the business-class queue for Toronto. There were only a couple of people in front of him and as he waited he glanced around again – and his heart suddenly thudded and an invisible fist walloped him in the chest as he saw Mr Peterson, his geography teacher from school. He could barely hide his shock.

Max tried to settle his breathing, but there was another feeling now, a physical pain which he knew was fear. Mr Peterson was on his mobile phone and half turned his back as Max saw him. Max kept his head, not giving in to the impulse to stare at him; instead, he let his gaze sweep across the crowd in case Peterson used his peripheral vision to watch him. Peterson. He liked him. He was a great teacher. And there he was, part of the conspiracy to track Max down and kill him.

The check-in clerk called Max forward, which snapped his mind back into gear. Max handed his passport and ticket across the desk, but the crawling in his stomach wouldn't go away. Mr Peterson had been at the school for only a few months. He would have known Max's daily schedule and he was probably the one who searched his room. Who was paying Peterson to betray him? Max didn't have time to think about it. 'Oh, this is an economy ticket.' The check-in clerk smiled.

Max knew that, of course. He was gambling that, if he played ignorant, the cheerful-looking woman would check him in anyway. 'I'm really sorry. I didn't know.' He grimaced. 'I've never been on a big plane before,' he lied.

She quickly tapped her fingers on the computer keyboard. 'Oh, that's all right. I'll check you in here. I bet you're really excited.'

Max nodded enthusiastically.

'Any luggage?' she asked as she gazed at the screen.

'No, just my backpack.'

She asked him a few security questions and then packaged the ticket, his passport and boarding card together. 'I've given you a window seat. Enjoy the flight.' She pointed down the hall. 'Security and departure's down there. Have a really nice time in Canada, Mr Lawrence.'

Max thanked her and turned away. Peterson was still there, but he'd moved a bit further down the concourse. He must have been satisfied that Max was on his way to Pearson Airport, Toronto, to stay with his new guardian, Jack Ellerman, because he snapped his mobile shut and turned on his heel, his job done. Max felt a sense of relief, but he still had to get on that plane for South Africa without being spotted. There might be others in the terminal looking for him.

The Toronto plane left at 21.30. The Virgin check-in desk for Johannesburg was in the A Zone, and that plane left at 20.05 and they were already boarding. Max had to get to the gate in time, and if he didn't do it in the next fifteen minutes his whole plan would be ruined. He quickened his pace, dodging through the crowd, and then he saw another boy about his age. He too wore cargo pants, a sweat top, trainers and a lightweight fleece. His hair was a bit longer than Max's and his shoulders weren't as broad – Max had done a lot of white-water canoeing in the swirling waters of the River Dart and that had built up his arms and back muscles – and although Max had never seen this boy before, the North Face orange-coloured fleece identified him.

The other boy's eyes were looking at the crowd ahead of him and then they locked on Max. The boy changed his small rucksack to the other shoulder and as they drew level each nudged the other's shoulder. It was barely a couple of seconds of contact but in that time, and with a mumbled, 'Sorry, mate,' they passed each other. And in those moments, Martin Lawrence, the son of one of Farentino's clients, exchanged the ticket, passport and boarding card for those in Max's hand. Martin was happy to get a free trip to Canada – snowboarding was great at this time of year. Max now had his own passport and ticket for South Africa that Martin Lawrence had used to book him on to the South African flight. The two boys looked very similar, close enough not to cause any suspicion from a busy check-in clerk.

So far, so good. In eleven hours he would land in South Africa and be a lot closer to finding out what had happened to his father. It had been a gruelling twenty-four hours and he wouldn't care what movie they were showing on the flight. What he needed was sleep.

Outside the terminal, Peterson waited a few moments as a car approached the pick-up area. iPod Man and Smart Bag Woman were inside. Peterson climbed in. 'He's on the Toronto plane. Let's go.'

As the car edged slowly into the night traffic, an Airbus 343 bound for Johannesburg roared down the runway. Max, settled in his seat and wrapped in a lightweight airline blanket, saw London's lights shimmer below him, a seabed of diamonds. He was asleep by the time the plane gained its cruising altitude, and as the ground slipped away, dreams were already troubling his exhausted mind. Juggled images of a hostile environment in an unknown country vied with a deep-rooted sense of dread about the forbidding desert fortress, Skeleton Rock.

4

Adrenalin had scoured Max's body over the past twenty-four hours, putting him in an almost constant state of physical alertness as his mind responded to the 'fight or flight' hormones banging through his system. Despite the fatigue, he had slept badly. Unfolding thoughts of his father and the responsibility Max now carried excited and scared him.

Farentino had painted only a fairly broad picture of what his father did, but nevertheless it explained where his father's strength and courage came from. How did a graduate scientist end up fighting pirates and ambushing smugglers of endangered species? Or hacking his way through impenetrable jungles to find the source of a rare plant that could cure desperately ill people without letting the huge, profit-making drug companies exploit it?

Tom Gordon's own sense of adventure helped, but the government had trained him. He wasn't a spy, but his job came close to it – and in some ways what he did may have been more risky. He took on dangerous people who flouted international law. He had been field-trained by the best and, given the incident with the pirates off the coast of Africa and the way his dad had dealt with them, Max had an idea Special

Forces might have been involved in that training. His father had a privileged 'go anywhere' freedom, checking on rogue countries to see whether they were breaking or contravening international law. He met Max's mother in South America when she was researching the damage caused to the environment by illegal logging in the rainforests. Within a couple of years they realized that governments around the world were often turning a blind eye to major illegal scientific and ecological issues. Trade agreements and mutual interests corrupted everyone.

His parents' integrity made them not only important contacts but also many enemies. They challenged big business, brought executives to trial and forced many illegal companies that endangered the environment to close. Mention the names Tom and Helen Gordon to anyone in science and ecology, and the brave, pioneering trouble-shooters were quietly acknowledged as being fearless. Anyone threatening the well-being of the Earth with dangerous activities was their target. But eventually Tom and Helen resigned from government service because politics interfered with their work. They joined a small but dedicated group of people, privately funded, who moved across international borders, helping those who wanted to make a positive contribution while exposing and bringing to court those whose greed caused misery.

Max quickly made his way through Johannesburg International Airport. He moved swiftly down the concourse, past planes on the apron, their nose-cones almost pressing against the terminal building – big, fat geese masquerading as peacocks, their brightly painted tail fins flared out behind them.

The first thing he had to do was contact Sayid and warn him about Mr Peterson. Flipping open the TriBand mobile, he waited as it connected to the local server and then he began texting. Thinking of Sayid brought the time-frame into focus. Was it only yesterday he had left his school and taken the train to London and put this whole plan into action?

'OK,' Sayid had told him, 'you'd better take this.' His friend had handed Max his new mobile phone. 'I've swapped the SIM card, it's clean. I don't know where you're going to end up, but if you really think there's someone out to kill you and your dad, odds are they'll have a trace on your phone.'

Sayid explained that if Max texted him, the program he had created would scramble the message. Text was quicker and safer than voice. Sayid would then unscramble the message at his end, once the signal had been bounced in and out of European servers. With any luck the bad guys wouldn't twig that Sayid was his contact; at least not for a while. The biggest problem would be if Max was out of range of any signal. The best Sayid could offer then was for Max to use a landline, take a chance with uncoded speech, and Sayid would rely on his computer to disguise the download.

Max checked the text. `Peterson followed me 2 airprt. Also thnk he searched my rm. Dont trst him. Rpt: Dont trst Ptrson.`

Twenty minutes before Sayid received Max's encrypted text message, he was pounding, tired and wet from a strenuous cross-country run, up the broad granite staircase to his room. The boys always ran as hard as they could across Dartmoor's demanding terrain because they had the time to themselves from when they crossed the finish line until the evening meal was served in the oak-timbered hall.

His trainers squelched from the bog sludge, so he leaned against the wall and pulled them off, preferring the sensation of the cold stone beneath his feet. In that moment of silence he heard someone talking, and sounding quite exasperated. The voice was coming from Mr Peterson's room. As he got nearer to the closed door he could clearly hear Peterson's voice; it was obviously a telephone conversation. Sayid made sure no one else was in sight and pressed closer to the old door.

'. . . I told you he never got to Toronto . . . I don't know how he managed it! . . . and I don't want to keep going over it . . . no . . . no, the boy at the airport must have been a friend, he's not a pupil here . . . None of that matters. We've lost him and I'm really worried about it now . . .'

Then a few muffled words were said that Sayid could not hear. Peterson had probably turned away from the door, perhaps he was pacing back and forth across the room, as his voice was unclear at times. Then Sayid picked it up again.

'. . . well, obviously South Africa . . . and if he knows or finds out what his father discovered . . . yes . . . yes . . . we must do what we can . . . I feel responsible. Do we have any people over there? Anyone we can use? Good . . . put them on alert until I can find out more . . .'

Sayid dropped a shoe. The noise it made was not particularly loud but it was enough for Peterson to stop talking. Sayid ran as fast he could on tiptoe along the corridor to his room, and as Peterson yanked open the door he was already around a corner, out of sight. Peterson looked up and down the corridor and saw no one, but he could not fail to notice the wet footprints and the globule of black mud on the floor. The footprints went straight towards Sayid Khalif's room.

Peterson weighed up the risks. Had the boy heard anything? He stepped back into his room. If he confronted Sayid now, it might trigger the boy's suspicions that Max was heading into serious trouble.

Max's connecting flight to Namibia landed a couple of hours later. Windhoek's airport had only a small building for its terminal, but South African Cliff Swallows nested there, and White-rumped Swifts swooped across the building's panoramic windows giving a view of the harsh scrubland that lay beyond the runway. A dozen or more kilometres away, a malevolent-looking black cloud rolled across the horizon like a giant rain-filled tumbleweed; a sudden storm, prodded on by forked lightning, dumping its much-needed rainwater.

The rolling weather front reminded Max of home. Dartmoor was a remote and sometimes dangerous place, but this huge expanse of wilderness could swallow him up and no one would know.

Max suddenly felt very alone and, if he was honest, scared. The flight to Canada would have landed a few hours before he reached South Africa. If the people following him had watched the airport in Toronto and had seen his look-alike arrive, would that have been enough to fool them? If it hadn't, maybe they had figured out where he was heading. He was about to check the mobile phone, to see if Sayid had sent any messages, when his eyes caught the fleeting blur of a swift as it swooped to catch a flying insect.

The bird probably saved his life.

As he turned to watch it, he saw two men heading towards him who looked as though they wrestled crocodiles for a living. One had long hair and wore a bush shirt and khaki shorts; his squashed-nosed face sported a scrub beard. A scar across his cheek separated the whiskers – a white slash against his sun-baked skin that the beard failed to conceal. The other was pure Hollywood. Tall and broad, his chest like two concrete paving slabs that his T-shirt could barely restrain. His close-cropped hair and pilot's dark glasses could have got him work for any top fashion magazine. Instead, he and his partner, ex-South African policemen, were hired killers.

Max didn't have to think twice about their intentions. He ran for the nearest door and they followed, dodging the few remaining passengers. Max pushed through into a 'Staff Only' area, a long corridor with wire cages to one side and a solid concrete-block wall on the other. He heard the thump of the door as the men came after him. He risked a glance over his shoulder – the men were too big to run side by side along the narrow passage, so one of them ducked off to his right and clattered on to a metal spiral staircase that corkscrewed down through the cages which, Max realized, were for storing luggage waiting to be loaded on to aircraft.

Scarface was almost on him. Max felt him snatch at his neck and the man swore, missing him, as Max stretched out an extra pace. But there was nowhere to go, and within a couple of seconds Scarface would grip him with those huge hands. Then Max saw the downward-twisting rollers used by cargo handlers to slide heavy cases to the loading area below. Max dived, his backpack now on his chest like a belly board.

The rollers rattled as he hurtled downwards. The man behind him shouted something in a foreign language and kicked the wire-caged wall in frustration. He would have to retrace his steps to the stairs. Max hit the curved stainless-steel barrier at the bottom of the chute. It flipped him over. He rolled, hugged his bag to his chest, vaulted over the low barrier and ran straight into Mr Hollywood, who wrapped his muscled arms around him. 'Got him!' he yelled; his expensive capped white teeth smiled as they chomped down again and again on a piece of well-chewed gum.

He was too confident. Max threw his head back, giving himself just enough leverage, then slammed his heel down, as hard as he could, on the man's ankle. It was one of the most painful self-defence tricks he had learned. Mr Hollywood shouted out in pain and dropped his chin in disbelief, as Max whipped his head back up, connecting with the perfect jawline. He heard the teeth shatter and a mumbled, agonizing choking sound. Max knew the man had probably bitten his tongue half through. The shock and pain weren't enough to stop him though, and he lurched at Max, who rammed a shoulder with all his strength beneath the gasping man's rib cage, as if he were tackling a rugby opponent. It rocked Mr Hollywood back on his heels, the momentum forcing his legs against an overweight suitcase: he lost his balance and tumbled helplessly backwards towards the stainless-steel rim of the chute that moments earlier had flipped Max over. It sliced into the base of the man's skull. Blood oozed around his T-shirt and his eyes rolled back into his head. Air bubbled through what was left of his smashed mouth. He wasn't very handsome any more.

Max pulled his backpack over his shoulders and ran down through the loading bays. Where was everyone? This must be a cargo and luggage holding area, so no one would be here unless they were loading. He had been lucky so far, he knew that. Where was Scarface? He heard an engine grunt behind him, and as he turned a forklift truck accelerated straight at him. Scarface had the pedal to the floor, diesel fumes spewed out and the two metal loading shafts were rising to chest level as Scarface operated the hydraulic lever. He meant to skewer Max like a kebab. Max spun around and ran – but there was nowhere to go. He was in an alleyway of cargo. Crates and boxes were stacked high on each side and pallets supported all kinds of material. Industrial generators were housed next to domestic refrigerators; construction pipes and electric cabling shared a stack with crated household goods. Max ran as hard as he could, but there were only forty metres left and then Scarface would crush him against the end-of-alley shelving.

Max looked around desperately. Was there a chance he could climb up and pull something heavy down on to Scarface? That wouldn't work; the forklift had a protective cage over the driver. Then he realized what he had to do – his only chance. He turned and faced the beast of a machine, now only a few metres away. He couldn't dodge to one side, Scarface would twitch the wheel and crush him against the metal shelving. He stood his ground, like a matador waiting for the charging bull. Scarface was momentarily perplexed, but didn't care. The two giant blades of the forklift's arms were now at chest height. Max made a grab for them, barely hanging on as the well-worn metal slipped under his grip. If he couldn't climb up, he would go under the wheels. Like a gymnast on parallel bars, he swung his lower body and hooked his leg over one of the shafts.

Max straddled the blade and hung on, his body almost within touching distance of Scarface. He sat as square as he could, staring down Scarface, who had not taken his eyes off him. The beard parted – a grin of victory. He would smash Max into the end shelving. Max glared at him. He was drawing on his last strength and energy, and he had to keep this sociopath's attention focused. Max swore and shouted, and then spat as much spittle as he could manage out of his dry mouth. Scarface stopped smiling. The urge to kill Max was foremost in his mind, and impact was imminent.

Then, suddenly, Max swung under the metal shaft, clinging on with his arms and legs. In that moment Scarface realized that Max's body had been blocking his view. He threw an arm up in self-defence, but it was too late. The forklift slammed into the end shelving. A hundred lengths of copper tubing that had been stacked there now reacted to the impact and rocketed forward above Max's arms and legs and into the unprotected Scarface. A dozen lengths of pipe, as lethal as a hail of arrows, slammed into him. Max was shunted off the forklift and into the shelving below the remainder of the copper tubes, which spilled from the shelf and clattered over him.

Bruised and winded, he fought free and climbed from under the pier of metal. Scarface was either unconscious or dead. Copper spears punctured his arms and chest, pinning him to his seat. The forklift's motor had stalled.

It was suddenly very quiet.

Max needed a drink.

Back in the terminal building, Max had his face over the water fountain, swallowing as much as the feeble spurt would allow. A young woman, dressed in bush fatigues, tanned and looking as though she lived and breathed Africa, had come up behind him. He thought she must have been about seventeen. Her bright smile and blue eyes looked even more stunning because of her short, sun-bleached hair. She was lithe but strong looking, like an athlete, and the shorts that reached halfway down her thighs were evidently worn for practicality rather than fashion. A couple of grease marks, ingrained dust and dirt suggested that she used them as a hand-wipe whenever necessary. Max was caught unawares, and his heart was pounding, not because she had startled him, but because of the way she looked.

'Are you Max?' she asked.

'Yes,' he finally managed to answer, wiping a dribble of water from his chin.

'Sorry I'm late. Had a problem with a fuel line. Come on then.'

She turned away.

'Hang on a minute,' he called after her. He wasn't going to be treated like a puppy – and after the last twenty minutes he was not going to follow anyone anywhere, no matter how appealing they looked. She stopped and waited. 'I don't know who you are,' he said, realizing this might be a set-up.

She gazed at him. 'I'm Kallie van Reenen,' she answered. 'He said you'd be cautious. That's good out here – it might keep you alive.' She raised an eyebrow. Was that enough information?

'Who said?'

'Mister Farentino.'

Max nodded and fell into step with her. And wished she weren't so attractive.

When they left the terminal she took him to the other end of the airport apron, where private aircraft were parked. Safari companies often flew their clients from here, and local farmers used it as their nearest parking area for the city. Farentino had warned her that Max was on his way, and as it was her father to whom the Bushman had delivered Tom Gordon's animal-wrapped field notes, she was the starting point for Max's journey.

The outside temperature was a shock. Sweat gathered around the waistband of his cargo pants and soaked a long stain down the back of his T-shirt. Max knew he would acclimatize quickly, as he had done before on trips with his father; but his body was also coping with the stress he had been through. He edged into the shade of a hangar and watched silently as Kallie did her pre-flight inspection on an old single-engine plane that looked to be well past its sell-by date. But he remembered his father telling him about these old bush-bashers. They were as solid as they come, and every aircraft had to have a vigorous on-going maintenance and airworthiness certificate, so he took some comfort in that.

Kallie checked the propeller, making sure there was no damage to it; then the flaps; she ran a loving hand along the struts and then, finally, clambered on board. Max was edgy, expecting police cars to come screaming up any minute. But nothing happened.

He checked the phone. The message from Sayid on the blue screen was brief: Peterson nos where u r.

Max grimaced. Thanks, Sayid, but recent events have already confirmed this.

'OK!' Kallie shouted. 'Let's go!'

Climbing into the cockpit was another step away from whoever else Peterson might have sent after him. He gratefully strapped on the safety harness. Kallie flicked control levers with practised ease, clicked the radio on, contacted the tower and was given clearance to taxi. Max had a Flight Simulator on his computer at Dartmoor High, but this old plane's instrument panel looked completely different from the F16s he tried to manoeuvre at Mach 2 on his computer screen. No target screen, no rate-of-climb dial, no radar. With a bit of thought he could identify the basic instruments as her fingers moved to the master and alternator switches which turned on all the electrics for the plane. Stuck to the instrument panel was a somewhat tattered, postcard-sized, laminated board. The laminate was bubbled in places, and the heat had frayed the edges into brown crackling. Half a dozen words were typed on it: *Rather Too Many Pilots Forget How It Goes.*

'What's this?' he asked, as she eased out the throttle lever, slowing the plane so that it was barely moving, waiting to take up position for take-off.

'Oh, my dad. He worries. He taught me to fly. But you know what dads are like. Don't want you to make mistakes if they can help it.' She hesitated, noticing the shadow that flickered across Max's eyes. 'Sorry, that was thoughtless of me. Under the circumstances.'

He shook his head. 'It's OK. Honest. My dad's the same.'

She smiled. 'It's a reminder. A whatchamacallit. When the words trigger things . . .'

'A mnemonic.'

'That's it.' She pointed at the capital letter for every word, each a stab at a pilot's memory. 'R – Radios on. Rudder check movement; T – Trim elevator to take-off position, throttle tension and set for start; M – Mixture rich, magnetos on; P – Pitot heat – that's in case there are icy conditions, not much chance of that today; F – Fuel select for tanks, flaps set for take-off; H – Harness secure, hatches closed; I – Instruments, check temperatures; G – Gyros set to the compass heading, gear selected down and three green lights.'

Max knew he would have trouble remembering the reminder, let alone what it stood for. Before he could think of anything sensible to say, Kallie's voice changed to a monotone, concentrated answer as she responded to the instructions from the air traffic controller's voice in her headphones. The old Cessna 185 rattled like a supermarket trolley full of empty tin cans. Kallie eased in the throttle, gave Max a reassuring smile – which did little to help his nerves – and then the plane lurched forward, centred on the runway's white strip. Suddenly they were rumbling towards the horizon. Max watched the airspeed indicator climb from 60 to 65 miles per hour – the plane was ancient enough for its dial not to show aeronautical knots – the rev-counter touched 2550 revs and Kallie pulled the plane up into the sky, straight at the high hills that were far too close to the end of the runway for Max's liking. The long, gradual climb took forever, and the plane rocked a little. She smiled at him. 'This kind of heat can make things tricky in the air.'

She seemed confident enough that they were going to clear those fast-approaching hills.

'Would you keep your eyes on the road,' he muttered.

After half an hour he could barely hear himself think. The plane's engine was deafening, like having a petrol-driven lawnmower sitting on your lap, and there was only one pair of headphones, which were clamped over her ears. They were cruising at 130 miles per hour, the vast expanse of the country below them etched with the occasional never-ending line of a road. Max tried to take an interest in the mountains to the east, their slopes furthest from the westering sun now cloaked in shadows and dust haze. But he was feeling rotten.

'Not long!' she shouted. 'Only a couple of hours!'

He was uncomfortable. His backside ached. The old seats were like the old-fashioned tubular chairs they used to have in the school's assembly hall, and he could not see above the instrument panel. How could you land when you couldn't see the ground?

The plane wavered gently, its nose and blurring propeller pointing slightly above the horizon, as it seemed to balance precariously. The altimeter was marked in feet, and the needle nudged marginally past the '2' mark. Two thousand and a bit feet. Then the plane dropped into some sort of hole in the sky. The engine surged, Max's stomach almost came up into his throat. 'Turbulence!' she yelled again. 'Happens all the time!'

He felt grubby from not having showered since he left Dartmoor; the long-haul flight's food sat somewhere in his stomach like a ball of clay, and the noise and heat from the engine were scrambling his brains. And the attack at the airport had left him decidedly shaky. Airsickness started to coil around his throat like a clammy hand.

She glanced at him. 'You going to puke?'

Embarrassed beyond belief, he nodded.

'Stick your head out the window!'

He pushed out the Perspex side-window the fifteen centimetres its hinge allowed, and thrust his head out into the cold slipstream that buffeted his face. And then he vomited. The airline's pre-packed dinner disappeared beyond the tailplane, free from the confines of his stomach. He wished he could be free of this plane. But it was a long way down – as the dinner showed him.

He decided to keep his head outside the cockpit. With any luck he might freeze to death. That would save him the embarrassment of facing Kallie again.

What a way to make a first impression.

Brandt's Kraal Wilderness Farm was a jewel in the scorched landscape. A small, underground spring-fed waterhole, about a quarter the size of a football pitch, and surrounded by palm and willow trees which created a cool haven. The ramshackle house was a huge, original Victorian bungalow with a deep veranda running all the way round it. Tired white paint covered the decorative finials running along the veranda's lintel. Rust, time and the desert had taken their toll of everything he could see.

Kallie swooped the plane once across the farm, fifty metres above the battered galvanized roof, and then side-slipped expertly and landed close to the house. Max was thankful to get his feet back on terra firma. The heat sucked his energy from him. A couple of cross-bred dogs eased out from the dark beneath the house, which he could now see was built on low brick piers, and their deep-throated growls warned Max.

She soothed them. 'Easy, boys. Come on.' They went happily to her, tails wagging lazily. Now confident that Max was no threat, the dogs sniffed his hand as he looked around him. The water obviously provided a vegetable garden, and drinking for livestock. These people were as self-sufficient as they could be. And where there's water there's wildlife, and that in turn brought hunters. A raptor circled lazily, high above the water. Ominous. Vulture-like.

'It's an African hawk eagle,' Kallie told him as he shielded his eyes. 'Plenty of birds here for it, and some small game as well. I hate to see the songbirds get taken but . . . well, that's how it is. Getting killed out here is a daily occurrence. For animals at least.'

'Are your parents here?' he asked, expecting the formality of introductions and preparing for long explanations as to how he was feeling, why he was there, and how hopeless his task might be.

'Divorced. Dad's got a newer plane than the old Cessna. He's taken clients up west and north. Lot of birders come out here. It pays OK.'

'So you stay here alone?'

'I do the bookings, keep the place going. Got a few helpers for the heavy stuff; and there's a town about an hour away. It's pretty convenient,' she said.

'I thought this was a wildlife farm. I don't see any,' Max said as they reached the shade of the veranda.

'Used to be. It went bust thirty years ago. We kept the name.'

'And where's Mr Brandt?'

'He died a hundred years ago. This used to be a watering hole for cattle drovers, and Brandt had this place then. We kept that name, too. There didn't seem much point in changing it. People round here don't like change.'

People? Max could scarcely believe anyone lived within a thousand kilometres of this place.

It was a blessed relief to lie in the cool water that slopped nearly over the edge of the old cast-iron bath. The discoloured water came from the same source as the watering hole, the underground spring, but it was tepid, not icy as it would have been at home.

Kallie knocked on the bathroom door. 'When you're ready!'

A simple bed, covered with a mosquito net, stood in the middle of what was a room obviously belonging to a sportsman. Pictures and trophies were everywhere: swimming, rugby, shooting, hockey, football. It was Kallie's brother's room.

'Johan's away at boarding school. Look, you're going to need better clothes than what you've got. You're about the same size, so I've dug out some of his stuff.' Lightweight khaki shirts and shorts were on the bed, well worn but still serviceable.

'How old is Johan?'

'Seventeen, same as me. And you?'

'Sixteen, nearly seventeen,' he lied. He was big enough, he decided, to get away with it, and he wanted to impress her. She looked at him and turned away.

'We need to eat – and talk. Get dressed.'

She had this casual way of telling him what to do. He didn't like it, but he figured that people who lived out here didn't have much chance to hone their conversational or social skills. He dropped the towel from around his waist and climbed into her brother's clothes.

By the time he sat on the veranda, which she called a *stoep* – an Afrikaans word – the sun was setting, light bleeding gently away, giving up the land to cooling shadows. Night comes quickly to those latitudes, and by the time food was brought to the table the sky was black. Beyond the water and trees, low on the horizon, the yellow full moon edged upwards. It was a wonder of such uninhabited places that Max had experienced before. Crystal-clear nights, free from the light-pollution of city and town, gave the stars a water-like clarity – so many, the sky glistened with them. And Max never ceased to wonder that this moon, so close that it seemed he could step to the edge of the world and touch it, had known the footsteps of mankind.

One of the farm workers lit a paraffin lamp and the night bugs and moths hovered, attracted by the deadly flame.

Max ate his first decent meal in a couple of days. It was

basic meat and vegetables and had been cooked by a servant, a woman with a slight pallor to her skin, almost apricot colour, and what looked like Mongolian features: high cheekbones and narrowed eyes. While Max chewed, Kallie explained. The woman was a descendant of the Bushmen, nomadic hunter-gatherers whose way of life was virtually extinct. Two hundred years ago, colonists and black tribesmen alike hunted them like animals and, although the Bushmen never owned land – a concept alien to them – in more recent times the areas in which they hunted had been taken by the government and they themselves herded into a reserve. It sounded similar to the story Max had heard about the Native Americans.

'Over the years my father did what he could for the Bushmen,' Kallie told him. 'They're very special, not many people understand them, and their language is extremely difficult to learn. It's all about clicking the tongue against your teeth and the roof of your mouth . . . different sounds, different emphasis. Sorry, that doesn't explain it very well, does it?' She turned and spoke gently to the old woman who had served them food. Max thought they were sweet-sounding, rhythmic words, and he could hear the different click sounds. The woman nodded and moved away, her eyes averted.

Kallie saw his interest.

'Don't stare at her, Max. Staring is rude in Bushman culture.'

'Sorry,' he muttered. 'I don't know much about the indigenous people here.'

She was silent for a moment. 'Y'know, the Bushmen are trapped – their souls are in a kind of hell for them. They are

God's creatures, as close to the red dirt as the animals that wander over it. Now we tell them they have to live in settlements, or reserves, but when the rains come and the lightning chases the clouds, then they have to go walkabout. Their spirit is out there in the desert. You put one of these people in prison, he dies, and if they stay out here, many die of hunger and thirst. Climate change, poaching, indifferent rainfall and the twenty-first century – it's all stacked against them.'

She gazed at him, searching his face, and he felt the blood ease into his cheeks. He looked away. There were so many questions he wanted to ask her – about herself – but that too was probably ill-mannered.

'Why are you here?' Kallie asked.

'What do you mean? Because of my dad. Why else?'

'I don't know.' She looked out across the dry grassland. 'This country kills a lot of people, Max. Maybe you should expect the worst.'

'I like to take a more positive outlook on things. I think my dad's alive.'

'Fair enough. Y'know, it was because my father had always done what he could for the Bushmen that one of them brought those field notes here. He left his family out there to do that. My father was the only white man they could trust. That's the only connection we have with whatever has happened.'

'And I appreciate your help in bringing me here.'

She looked away, and after a moment he followed her gaze. The old woman had taken a lantern and gone into the willow trees by the water, where she beckoned someone there to join her. A Bushman boy of about thirteen stepped out. He was slightly built, with an open, appealing face which smiled easily. He dipped his head in respect for the old woman. The only clothing he wore was a loincloth, embroidered with simple red and blue stitching. He carried a quiver of pencil-thin arrows and a short hunting bow over his shoulder, and in his hand a spear. He nodded as the old woman spoke to him, and then he looked up to where Max and Kallie were sitting.

'He was the one who brought your father's notes, four weeks ago. Long before Mister Farentino contacted us. He's been here ever since.'

'Here?' Max asked. 'Does he work here now?'

The boy stood, unmoving, silhouetted against the enormous moon. Max watched as its soft glow embraced the boy and encircled him protectively.

'No. You don't understand,' she said. 'He's been waiting for you. He says it was written you would come. You're some kind of ancient prophecy.'

5

The Bushman boy's name was !Koga, pronounced by drawing the tongue away from the roof of the mouth – at least that's how it sounded to Max. *Cl*oga was the best he could manage; he thought it sounded as though he was clucking at the hens, back at the school's farm. There is no history of writing for the Bushmen so Kallie wrote '!Koga' – showing Max that the '!' was the European way of expressing one of the many click noises used in the Bushman language. 'He speaks some English,' Kallie told him. 'His family helped a geologist for a couple of years.'

Max shook hands with the boy, who glanced away shyly. 'He told my father there were rock paintings in the caves,' Kallie continued. 'I don't know where, but I reckon about three hundred k's from here. No one I know has ever been there. The paintings, so he says, show your arrival. He wants to help find your father.'

!Koga remained silent, his eyes watching the horizon. Max was uncertain. This could be a wild-goose chase. The middle of nowhere was a dangerous place to be chasing flights of fancy.

'Look,' he said quietly, hoping not to offend the boy,

'pictures of me on cave walls sound a bit dodgy. Maybe my dad told him I would come, maybe !Koga or his family drew them – y'know, part of their storytelling folklore or something.'

Kallie pulled a face. 'I wish that were true, but the !Kung Bushmen don't have a history of rock painting. The last ones discovered were a thousand years old.' She nodded to the boy, who turned back towards the cool shade of the trees by the waterhole. 'Don't ask me how they know some of the spooky things they know – but I trust whatever it is they're in touch with. Call it ancient wisdom; call it spirits of their ancestors – whatever it is, a lot of Bushmen have got it. He'll take you as far as he can, back to his own people, wherever they are. Anyway, they're the ones who last saw your dad.'

Max only wanted to save his dad; cave paintings and prophecies felt as though they were going to get in the way. But could he afford to risk not going along with the very boy who had delivered his father's notes?

As he crawled under the mosquito net that night, his father's face was the last thing he saw as he tumbled into fitful sleep. At first he was troubled by images of being chased, of being cornered in dark passageways, of being held under water, suffocating – all reflections of the day that his unconscious mind interpreted in its own way. But gradually he slipped past the monsters and settled into a deep and restful slumber.

When he awoke, the first shards of light were breaking up the sky. Stretching away the sleep, he realized he was feeling great. And he was starving. He could smell coffee and fresh bread. It was pre-dawn cold so he pulled on a lightweight jersey and made his way to the kitchen table.

The old woman nodded at him, unsmiling, and said something he did not understand, so he nodded back, and within minutes a hot tray was taken from the old wood-burning stove's oven; corn cakes and sausage were slid on to a warm plate and then the sizzling sound of three eggs being fried filled the kitchen. In less than a minute the plate was put in front of him. Not exactly the kind of health-conscious breakfast he was used to, but out here, he guessed, you ate what you could.

By the time he had wiped the plate clean, the sun was dazzling the windows. Kallie came in and poured coffee into one of the tin mugs. 'You ready to go?'

He nodded, uncertain what she had in mind. 'I'd fly you on further, but I can't. I'm going up to see my dad, he needs supplies. He's extending his safari, that's north-west from here.' She picked up her coffee and went back outside. He realized she meant him to follow her.

An ex-military, long-wheelbase Land Rover stood ready in front of the farmhouse. Its bodywork still sported a faded camouflage pattern. Two shovels were strapped to the bulkhead, a canvas cover was stretched across the skeleton frame of the vehicle; a dozen jerrycans were secured in the back, with another two in special holders on each side of the headlights, and a whip aerial's three-metre length quivered in the barely noticeable breeze.

'Most kids out here can drive round the farms by the time they're ten or eleven, what about you?'

Max nodded. His dad had taught him when they were on one of their holidays, but that was in a small, battered old car. This brute of a 4x4 might be beyond his skills. 'Sure,' he said, 'but I've never driven in the desert before.'

'It's mostly scrubland. If you hit soft sand you drive slowly; if you get stuck you deflate the tyres. That's the low-ratio gearstick for when it gets really tough.' She leaned across the Land Rover, pointing out the equipment. 'There's a foot pump, shovels and these sand channels.' She patted two metal runners, a couple of metres long and half a metre wide, strapped on the side of the Land Rover. 'My guess is you're heading for grassland and then maybe the mountains. This thing'll take you anywhere, just don't tip it beyond thirty degrees or you'll roll it. There's water in those jerrycans and diesel in these.' Max took all this in, determined to put a brave face on the daunting task. Twenty metres away, !Koga waited, squatting on his haunches, watching.

'I've packed a few days' dried food, but you won't starve.' She looked towards !Koga. 'Not with him.' Kallie gave him that look again. Gazing right into his eyes. This time the blood didn't rush to his face. He felt confident. No point kidding himself or anyone else, he decided, not out here.

'I lied when I said I was nearly seventeen. I'm not. I'm fifteen,' he said.

'I know. I checked your passport when you were asleep. Sorry about that, but I wanted to make sure you were who you said you were. You're crazy, you know that, don't you?' she said.

He nodded.

'But if it was me . . . I'd be doing the same thing.' She smiled. And for Max that was warmer than the sun already climbing in the sky.

'Time to go,' he said.

Max wrestled the steering wheel. Over the past few hours he had tested the engine's power, had made a mess of the four-wheel-drive settings, got it sorted, pushed himself and the machine and was bombing along a semblance of a track, red dust chasing him. !Koga sat next to him, a firm grip on the dashboard, smiling at the thrill of it. Kallie had told him that !Koga spoke some English, but so far the boy had not said a word. Maybe he was as caught up in the moment as Max. Heat, speed and a humming engine were intoxicating.

Max eased off the accelerator: this was still what they called a road out here, but a surface of loose stones on a hardcore base was giving way to off-road conditions. Low scrub began to obscure the way ahead. As keen as he was to strike out and find his dad, he had to make sure he got there safely, and that meant he had to use his brain as well as his muscle.

Before he left the farm, Kallie had spread out an old, creased and sweat-stained map, showing him landmarks along the way to Skeleton Rock – of which there were precious few. Buffalo Boulder, Snake River – a twisting dried-up river bed; Dancing Grass Valley – where a permanent breeze from the mountains swayed feather-topped savannah grass; Lightning Tree – the remains of a giant baobab, blackened but still standing after a mighty storm had rolled across its arid valley.

Grid references and map bearings would be his lifeline and he could plot a course using the fixed compass clamped to the dashboard.

'You see rain anywhere – on the horizon, in the mountains – you take extra care,' she warned him. 'We get flash floods that'll tear you and that Land Rover to bits. One minute it's a dry, safe place, and the next there's a wall of water roaring out of nowhere.'

As if Max didn't have enough to worry about, now a rain storm could kill him.

Fear can destroy a man, his dad told him once, but knowledge dispels fear. Equip yourself with as much information as you can, lessen the odds against you and then you have a chance. Don't give in to fear. It's all in the mind.

Words, echoing.

OK. He had done all that his dad had taught him. This wasn't a jaunt across Europe or America, where he could tap a number into his mobile phone and get help; there was no phone signal out here. Kallie had given him her radio frequency, explaining that most of the farmers used radios to help each other across these vast distances, so if he got himself into trouble at least there was a chance of summoning help. Though how long it would take to reach him was anybody's guess.

The sun was at its zenith, beating down fiercely. Mirages appeared on the horizon: illusions of upside-down mountains, trees that weren't there and broken ghost images of animals. Nothing moved. The furnace-hot air whipped across the top of the canvas cabin, trapping them. Time to stop.

Max eased down a couple of gears and bumped through the scrub and into the dry, waist-high grass. He eased the Land Rover under shade-giving branches, pushing aside low-growing acacia trees. Within moments of switching off the engine and getting out to stretch, a shadow swooped low overhead. For a second he thought it was a bird of prey, but as the darkened shape slipped across them the sound of an aircraft engine broke the silence. It must be Kallie, he thought, on her way north. But instinct warned him not to raise his hand and wave. The plane banked away. It was a different type of aircraft from Kallie's, and in a tight turn it circled to fly over the area again.

Whoever it was, they were looking for him. The old Land Rover's camouflage blended easily into the tangled acacias and high grass. Max and !Koga moved deeper into the shade and squatted together as another growling roar passed over their heads.

He cursed himself. It was probably his own stupidity that had brought his pursuers on to him so quickly. He had been showing off, driving the Land Rover to impress nobody but himself and maybe !Koga. The dust trail could have been seen for a hundred kilometres from up there.

The plane turned again, clockwise this time – from the east – watching for shadows that shouldn't be there. Max did not move and the rush of noise went by again. He was certain there was nowhere for the plane to land, so perhaps they were spotting for men on the ground. Yes, that made sense.

Once the plane was far away towards the horizon Max grabbed a pair of binoculars from the cab, clambered on to the top of the Land Rover and balanced on the steel roof-supports. He could see across most of the landscape. The plane had not swung back again. Was it looking for a landing place? He traversed the horizon. Nothing. A couple of kilometres away, a small herd of giraffe were feeding, their thick tongues rolling out to eat thorny branches from the higher trees.

A small kick of dust alerted him. Was that a rhino pushing through the bushes and grass? Sweat stung his eyes. He squinted through the glare and heat haze. Then one of the giraffes swung its neck and started galloping with its awkward gait. The others followed. It was no rhino that had spooked them. A pick-up truck, with half a dozen men in the back, rolled and jolted slowly across the difficult ground. And the men were armed.

Max ducked involuntarily. Then, realizing that the plane could not have spotted him, otherwise the pick-up truck would be heading straight for them, he peered again through the tinted lenses. The truck was several kilometres away and was moving obliquely away from them. Max slithered down and checked the map. His dust trail must have told the pilot his direction of travel. The armed men would be in a position to cut him off if he stayed on his intended route.

He had to find another way. As he scoured the map, !Koga was on the ground, scuffing the dirt with a stick, then putting down stones and twigs. He crumbled dried leaves, keeping his fingers together so that the bits fell in one place. 'Max,' !Koga said quietly, speaking for the first time. Hearing his name spoken gave Max a sudden sense of companionship. He crouched next to the Bushman boy, who was pointing to the model he had created. 'Here,' he said, touching the gravel he had sprinkled, and raised a finger. That was to be the first place they must reach. !Koga then indicated the other places in turn – the crumpled leaves, the upright stones, the twisting scratch in the dust. And each time he pointed, he raised another finger. Four fingers, each objective in that order.

Max understood immediately, creased the map back into another fold and searched for the places that !Koga had made on the ground. The foothills of the mountains were boulder-strewn, then the mountains themselves swept down to a grassy plateau. The contours on the map took his eye down to the twisting river. Max smiled and put his hand on the boy's shoulder. They were in this together and !Koga was the best person to have with him. Max felt great. How could he ever get lost out here with his new-found friend? His confidence surged; another three hours to nightfall and they would easily make camp in the foothills.

And then he made the second mistake of the day. He underestimated his opponents, and it nearly killed them both.

Max drove through the tall grass, his eyes fixed on the distant rise of mountains. He would rejoin the track, drive for two or three kilometres and then find an entry point to the foothills for what looked to be an arduous drive across bumpy terrain. Concentrating hard so as not to have any mishaps before he reached the road, he failed to see the dust drifting in the sky over his shoulder. He was within metres of bursting through the low trees and shrubs, up a small rise in the ground, before joining the track. He pulled the gear lever down, floored the accelerator and the Land Rover surged up and on to the road. Max swung the wheel, shifted a gear and nearly died of fright as a black pick-up truck grated alongside, colliding with the Land Rover. Metal screeched and he heard shouts from the men in the truck as they tried to regain their balance.

The pick-up had been travelling at some speed and failed to see Max's camouflaged vehicle as it lurched out of the undergrowth. Just as well. There were three men in the back, all armed, and if they had seen the Land Rover, Max and !Koga's blood would now be soaking into the dust.

For a second the two vehicles grated metal against metal, jostling side by side. Max glanced desperately across at the gunmen. The driver was wrestling with the steering wheel, just as Max was doing. The men in the back were thrown down. One of them had been standing against the roll bar, clutching a radio handset in his fist, and that wire was broken as the man fell and rolled. The image fed information to Max's brain. They had lost radio contact!

The vehicles clashed again, and Max felt the Land Rover sliding, being pushed dangerously close to tipping over the rim of the road and back into the tall grass. The steel sand ramps strapped to the side saved them from serious injury. The gunmen's 4x4 had ripped the ramps away; now they slid under its wheels and for a few vital seconds took control out of the driver's hands. The pick-up was riding a two-metre skateboard. Max heaved the steering wheel over and the bull-bars on the Land Rover's nose clipped the rear of the pick-up, spinning it around. However, the driver did an amazing job of turning into each successive spinning skid, giving the men in the back a chance to clamber to their feet.

There was a gap between the pick-up and the edge of the

road, and Max headed straight for it. The pick-up truck was parallel again; snarling faces in the billowing dust; shouts above the noise of the tortured engines. One of the men steadied himself with one hand and levelled an AK47 straight at them. Sweat stung Max's eyes, the windscreen glare blinded him momentarily, the Land Rover's engine was screaming and he could not get another ounce of power from it. The gunman couldn't miss. They were dead. Why hadn't he fired? The man screamed. Blood smothered his chest as he fell into the other men. Confused, Max turned to see !Koga holding his metre-long hunting bow, now free of its lightweight shaft. It was a killing shot, taking the gunman in the heart.

The Land Rover got past the pick-up, whose driver was trying to respond to one of his men screaming and shouts of panic from the others. !Koga's face was expressionless. Kallie had told him enough about the Bushmen for him to know that they did not relish killing; that there was no anger in a kill. Life was taken only when it meant survival. The Bushmen did not kill for sport. No matter how harsh their life in the desert, no matter how many times !Koga had killed to eat, Max felt sure he had never harmed another human being before.

Max nodded at him, hoping that simple gesture would convey everything he felt; knowing it could not.

Max had to get them out of here. The pick-up had fallen back, giving him a few vital extra seconds before the expected gunfire found them. The men in this pick-up were the second search party; the spotter plane had been working two teams on the ground. Why hadn't he thought of that? Berating himself served no purpose. !Koga pointed ahead. 'Animal path.'

Where? Max could see no sign of anything. Then a slender line that broke the edges of the scrub caught his eye. It was no different from back home, when the Dartmoor ponies moved across the land. Over the years the animals' nomadic journeys squashed any growing thing underfoot and created a scar through the heather.

Max gripped the steering wheel and yanked hard. The Land Rover took the ground well. They rocked and rolled, their shoulders banging against the door frames, but the old vehicle clambered up the stone-laden slope like a mountain goat. Max looked back. The men in the pick-up had sorted themselves out and the 4x4's defiant wheelspin told Max that they were coming for him again. Max had a good lead, at least four hundred metres, but he was losing sight of the game-path that guided him. !Koga gestured, his hand curving, showing Max the twisting route.

The boulders were small, about the size of three footballs in a carrying net, but their edges were jagged. They could hear them scraping underneath. Then it felt as if someone was throwing stones at them, a clattering dull thud against the sides, like hailstones on a roof. But microseconds after the imagined pebbles stung the Land Rover, the flat crack of the AK47s chased the bullets. Canvas ripped, jerrycans spilled their precious cargo and the throat-catching stench of diesel filled the cab. The hessian water bag hanging on the outside of the door exploded as one of the bullets narrowly missed Max.

The gunmen had stopped. The Land Rover had a higher ground-clearance, so the pick-up could not follow. Those men knew this was not the place to be stranded – without a radio and with one man dead, they were already at a disadvantage. To risk damaging their vehicle beyond repair was a risk too far. All Max had to do now was get across the ridge, so temptingly close, which would put them out of sight and range. And then keep going.

The men were aiming badly, failing to consider the rising ground in front of them, so their shots fell short. With a surge of acceleration Max pushed them over the top and out of harm's way.

Except that in that last, crucial moment, the Land Rover suddenly jolted to a dead stop. !Koga was off-balance – he was looking back, watching the men. His head whipped forward and cracked against the dashboard and he groaned, slumping forward. Max floored the accelerator, but all he could hear was the screaming engine. They were wedged, straddling a broad, flat boulder, and the wheels could find no purchase.

Max checked !Koga. He was unconscious. Max had to get the Land Rover free. He piled out of the cab, clambered on to the canvas roof and started to rock the vehicle backwards – pushing his weight down, trying to give the back wheels some grip. The gunmen were still a long way down the hill, but their firing had stopped – because the 4x4 driver was clambering upwards towards Max, a pistol in one hand and a hunting knife in the other. This was personal. The man stumbled, cursing his clumsiness and the pain as his shoulder slammed into a boulder. But rage powered him on, his eyes fixed on Max. His prey.

Max was defenceless, the man less than ten metres away now, and Max could hear him grunting with exertion and see the sheen of sweat on his face. The man's gun hand hung limply at his side – he had caught it a punishing blow on the rock – but the knife he wielded would be enough to do the job. The man slashed at Max's feet and the tough canvas slit as if it were tissue paper.

The driver's injured arm stopped him from clambering aboard, but there was no way Max could keep his own balance on such a flimsy roof. He needed a weapon. The radio aerial! It was in a pod-like bracket on the rear bulkhead. The man slashed again and spittle shot from his lips as he snarled in frustration, but Max jumped over the cab, found his footing on the spare wheel that was locked on the bonnet and jinked to the left as his feet hit the ground.

The driver had chased him but he was on the far side of the Land Rover, near the right-hand headlight. He would have to come all the way back to reach Max, who had reached the aerial and had both hands pressing down on its base. He twisted it free from its locked position and held what was now a three-metre-long metal whip. The man lunged, but he was a couple of metres away. Max slashed at him and the stinging metal cut across the top of his neck and shoulder. He cried out, but then snarled and spat even more, like a tormented scrapyard dog. If he ducked beneath Max's swinging arc he would gut him like a fish.

Max was well balanced – a slight bend in his knees, his feet edging up on to his toes, waiting for the rush of his opponent. His fists were clenched around the aerial's base as a warrior would hold a double-edged sword. The driver waited, Max watched his eyes; the man stabbed forward, but that was a feint – he intended to swing his arm back and plunge the razor-sharp blade into Max's stomach. Max yelled, giving himself a surge of energy, ridding himself of the last vestige of fear, and whipped the aerial across his body – left and right and back again. Welts of blood suddenly appeared on the driver's arms, chest and face. An almost surgical cut suddenly ran from above his left ear, down across his face and on to his neck. He was blinded. Max stepped back, nausea welling inside. He had caused the man serious injury, it felt terrible, and his feeling of guilt almost made him lower his guard. A voice shouted from his own mind – *He was going to kill you!* Max recovered and tightened his grip, but there would be no further attack – the man was defeated. He fell, picked himself up and went down the hill at a stumbling run, blinded by blood.

Max's efforts on the back of the Land Rover had rocked it free, and it had slid off the flat-topped rock. He threw the aerial into the back. They needed help and the radio was their only means of contacting anyone. Kallie. He would radio Kallie. She would send the police, or the army, anyone. Max felt the icy fear of being completely out of his depth.

But as the physical exertion of coaxing the Land Rover diagonally down the reverse slope of the ridge focused Max's panic, his doubts swept away like the dust behind him. He would radio for help, but he was not going to stop. He would find his father. The bouncing Land Rover jolted !Koga. Max was steering with one hand and holding the Bushman's shoulder with the other, keeping the boy's head from banging against the dashboard. By the time they reached the flat road !Koga's eyes had opened.

'What happened?' he asked.

'We won!' Max shouted. He laughed, though the steering wheel had a life of its own and demanded less celebration and more concentration as they lumbered across the uneven ground. !Koga smiled and said something Max took to be the Bushman equivalent of 'Let's get out of here while the going's good.'

They were on the cooler, moister side of the hills, which offered more vegetation, the reason why animals trekked here. The boulders gave way to gentler ground with the hills to one side; they were now in a valley, heading towards the guardian mountains. As the ground levelled, Max let the tension ease out of his hands – he had been gripping the steering wheel until his knuckles were white. With a backward glance and the thought that it would take their attackers at least an hour, probably longer, before they contacted the other group, he allowed himself a sigh of relief. Fear had dried his mouth and he was parched, but he made a deal with himself to stop and drink only when they were in the lee of the mountains, which had already lost the sun and which would offer them safety and shelter. A good vantage point, a safe haven for the night, was all he wanted now. And that drink.

As they drove towards the mountains, now purple in the evening light, he gazed in wonder at the amphitheatre which lay before him. Perhaps this was a small corner of the Garden of Eden. He could not know its beauty concealed a treacherous place of death, where bones of the dead already lay.

A satellite link between Shaka Chang and his man in England beamed their voices across the thousands of kilometres between them. Things were not going as planned. There was

73

no friendliness when they spoke, only irritation that the simple task of eliminating a boy was taking so long. Chang was on the first level of his desert fortress. It was a proper fort, huge and square, with battlements, like the French Foreign Legion had had in the Sahara, only this one had been built by a deluded German count in the nineteenth century. He had imagined himself to be a king and he built the castle as a fortress. It was impenetrable, riddled with underground chambers, escape routes, cellars, dungeons and a gravity-fed water system from a deep well. Unbeknown to the count, the castle lay on a fault line that a future owner – Shaka Chang – would develop into a mini-hydroelectric power supply. One day, the count told his wife and children he was going for a walk to admire the flowers along the riverside boulevard, and his wife realized that he had finally gone mad. There were no flowers, no boulevard and, by that night, no count. They found his blood-smeared, silver-topped cane next morning. She and the children went back to Bavaria, to the cold, the snow and everything she had missed, including the count's wealth, which she inherited. The fortress lay empty until the First World War, when the German Army took control. A bitter war of extermination was levied against the indigenous people and the fortress's reputation for housing mad and then cruel people was embedded.

And ten years ago Shaka Chang moved in.

He made it a modern outpost with every conceivable luxury. Now he stood in a vast room. Deep, cool shadows created an almost permanent chill, so there was no need for air-conditioning. The view from the panoramic window encompassed desert, mountain and an area of wetland, almost swamp-like, which seeped away from the reed beds at the river bank. When animals came to drink, there was no greater observation place in southern Africa. It also gave him a view of the crocodile sandbanks, where he liked to watch them bask and glide like assassins into the still waters to feed on unwary victims. Not all the prey were four-legged animals. A salutary lesson for all to see – anyone displeasing Shaka Chang made a serious mistake.

The driver who had led the chase earlier had been summoned. With one of his men dead, and himself still bleeding from Max's whipping, humiliation competed with the physical pain that had been inflicted on him. The driver was thirsty but dared not ask for water. It had been a scorching day. He would have given just about anything to slide into the cool water of the infinity swimming pool that lay like an oil slick across the black marble floor and dropped into the sky at the edge of the big window. He waited on Shaka Chang's pleasure – and prayed it was not going to be his displeasure.

Guards stood at the entrance as he awaited his master. He shifted nervously from foot to foot, his slashed T-shirt, encrusted with blood, stuck to his dust-caked body and by now the cuts were itching furiously. Chang, by contrast, was dressed in a cotton shirt, hand made of the highest-quality materials in Jermyn Street, London. He reached for a bottle of water, the condensation on the blue glass clinging like frost. His tailor always cut the shirts loose enough so as not to stretch across Chang's muscular frame, but nothing could deny that bulk and power. Black slacks and calfskin slip-on shoes completed the effect of a modern businessman –

immaculate taste and informal appearance which stamped his authority.

To one side, in one of the darker corners, another man hovered, barely visible, which was the way he liked it. He was quite opposite in physique and style to Chang. Small and skinny to the point of being gaunt, with a grey pallor to his skin, Mr Lucius Slye never went outside unless he had a big black umbrella to shield him from the sun and glare. Secretly, he was known as Mr Rat to everyone who knew him, though they would never say it out loud – he was too dangerous. His pinched face, his pointed, sniffy, twitching nose and threads of hair pulled back across his balding head gave him a definitely rat-like appearance. A buttoned-collar black shirt, black suit, black shoes and socks heightened his anaemic appearance. But he was essential to Chang. At every minute of every day he knew the status of Mr Chang's widespread business interests. A PDA never left his hands – his whole world was held in that electronic aide. And now as Chang spoke to his man in England, his gaze never left the wretched face of the driver. It was hard to tell whose eyes were more frightening – Chang's deep brown pools of mystery or Slye's soulless grey portals.

Chang spoke calmly as he gazed out across the vastness that was a small corner of his empire. 'This line will only be secure for a few moments more,' Chang said as he trickled water into a glass, 'so what do we know?'

The voice from England was as clear as if the man was in the room himself, the speakerphone creating a slight echo within the confines of the fortress's stone walls. 'He's a smart boy, and he's tough. The training at school has given him a certain resilience. And he can look after himself. But . . .' The man hesitated, he was buying time. After all Max was on Shaka Chang's territory now; he would know how resilient Max had been. The man went on, '. . . what we still do not know is whether he was given clues to where his father has hidden the information he discovered, or whether he is simply trying to find his father. Either way, obviously, that evidence must never reach the authorities.'

'And definitely no indication in England as to what might have been discovered. You have checked?' The veiled threat in Chang's voice was unavoidable. If the man in England had missed something as vital as Max leaving the explosive information with anyone in authority and was on nothing more than an escapade to rescue his father, then Shaka Chang's latest multi-billion-dollar deal might already be compromised. And Chang's man in England would have precious few hours left to live.

'He does not have the complete information. I would have found out,' the disembodied voice confidently assured Chang. 'He needs to be stopped *before* he finds out more. I shall continue to do what I can from here.'

Chang nodded. 'Wait,' he instructed the man on the phone.

Then he turned and faced the driver. The man flinched.

'Where are they?'

The driver tried to swallow, but his mouth was too dry. His voice croaked. 'East of Camel Rock, they crossed into the valley. They could hide in those mountains for days, sir.

We did all we could, Mr Chang. The pick-up, it just couldn't follow them over that ground. But they won't get far, their Land Rover is finished. I can promise you, sir, they won't be going anywhere. And we tried to . . .' Chang raised a finger. Enough. He did not want to hear any more excuses.

He spoke again for the benefit of the speakerphone. 'I do not think we need worry about this boy. He has gone into the Valley of Bones. If the lions or snakes don't finish him, then the elements will. I think the matter is closed. None the less, keep searching for his father's evidence. If we can locate it, well and good; better if we could destroy it rather than run the risk of *it* destroying our plans.' Chang touched a button, disconnecting the link. He turned and gazed at the driver, who bowed his head, desperate not to meet Shaka Chang's eyes.

'So. You let the boy escape?' Chang said quietly.

Max had clawed the Land Rover up a gentle incline, eased it on to a scrap of a track and stopped under an overhanging rock. Trees and bushes shielded them from the valley below, so Max decided that this was as safe as they could get.

But his sense of success quickly soured. Bullets had punctured the jerrycans of diesel, and if he was lucky he could drain off half a can at most. The provisions box had somehow broken free during the chase and could be anywhere, many kilometres behind them. Worse still was the loss of water; those jerrycans had been on the front of the Land Rover and the initial collision with the 4x4 had pierced them. All they had now was a couple of water bottles between them. !Koga pointed to the way they had come. A persistent dribble of black oil followed to where the Land Rover was now hidden. Those boulders had ripped out something vital. No water, no food, and now no vehicle.

'We need help,' Max said as he locked and secured the radio's aerial in its base. He flipped on the power switch; battery life was crucial, so it had to be used sparingly. There was no gentle hum of life from the radio, the warm-up lights didn't come on, there was no hiss or crackle through the headset. Then he spotted the neat hole drilled into the front of the radio set. He yanked the radio towards him and peered behind it. A flared mushroom of torn metal told him that a bullet had punched the life out of their only means of communication. The frightening reality of a bullet's damage struck home. If either of them had been hit . . .

'No water, no food, no transport, no radio. I think we might be in a spot of bother,' he said.

The shadow of night and a below-freezing temperature settled quickly. They needed warmth and nourishment. 'We'll light a fire and eat whatever is left,' he told !Koga. 'You think we're safe enough here, for tonight at least?'

!Koga nodded. 'Those men would not follow us. There are lions and hyena out there. Tonight is all right. Tomorrow . . . tomorrow will be hard.' If !Koga thought it was going to be hard, Max realized he was in for a tough time. !Koga gathered kindling while Max found a few tins of food that had not been shaken free during the chase. OK, so tomorrow would be tough – but that was tomorrow's problem. He shivered, but he told himself it was because of the night air, not his fear.

Max built the fire: kindling, small twigs, then heavier wood. It was so dry it flared the moment he put the flame to it from a cheap plastic lighter. His dad had taught him the benefit of carrying a small emergency pack when heading out into the wilds: waterproof matches, a fishing line, hooks, a beta light – bits and pieces that could mean the difference between life and death, should anything go wrong. But Max had left Dartmoor High in a hurry and had not expected events to strike so quickly. The fluid-filled plastic lighter was a substitute bought at Windhoek Airport, along with a toothbrush and a tube of sun-block. He would need to protect himself in the severe heat, and if the English cricket team smeared sun-block across their faces when they played, then he felt no qualms about the warpaint effect. But cleaning his teeth might have to wait.

They surrounded the fire with rocks. They would need the warmth these generated during the night, but Max was careful to use only heavy, solid stones. Softer rocks such as shale could explode when exposed to heat.

The evening meal was not a great success. They picked at the food, despite their hunger. Maybe the tins were old or perhaps it was the lack of salt but, whatever the reason, it tasted and smelled like dog food. Max decided they needed to cheer themselves up. A hot drink would combat the cold night air and ease the stress of the past few hours – it would also help wash down whatever it was they had just eaten. Using some of the precious water, he made instant coffee, squeezing in half a tube of condensed milk that had miraculously separated itself from the missing box of provisions. He let !Koga drink first and watched his smile of satisfaction as he sipped the hot, sweet liquid. !Koga passed the mug back.

'Tomorrow we hunt. We must eat real food,' he said.

Max nodded. His survival depended on !Koga now. He hated feeling helpless but knew he had to stand back and let the Bushman boy lead them to safety. He watched as !Koga carefully laid out his handful of arrows.

From a small wooden tube !Koga spilled out cocoons he must have collected some time before Max had met him. After carefully selecting two larvae and returning the others for safekeeping, he picked the grubs from their cocoons, rolled them between his fingers until they cracked, then smeared the liquid just below the arrow's metal point. Each arrowhead had a small, torpedo-shaped joint made of bone that connected to a reed collar which held the tip to the shaft. When the Bushmen shot an animal, the impact allowed the joint to separate arrowhead from shaft, leaving the poisoned point in the animal and the re-usable shaft on the ground. Then they tracked the animal until the poison weakened it sufficiently for them to kill it with a spear or knife.

Max held one of the arrows close to his face. He felt a fascination with the small metal point. It made him want to run his finger across the tip, testing its sharpness. !Koga snatched his wrist and, with what Max took to be a gentle admonition, took the shaft back. The boy clucked helplessly at the white boy's ignorance.

Don't touch !Koga's arrowheads, whatever you do. Kallie's warning came back to Max. *The poison is lethal, it'll kill you.* The Bushmen, experts at using venom on the arrows, chose certain plants to extract their poison, as well as scorpion and snake venom, but they preferred the larvae of the chrysomelid beetle, something that looked like a ladybird and whose larvae could be found buried beneath dead trees. There is no known antidote to this poison. Nosy, adventurous schoolboys from England would be dead in minutes if they so much as scratched a finger on an arrowhead.

Tomorrow, then, they would hunt – and begin their most serious test of survival. They would enter a hostile world on foot, with no weapons other than the knife Max carried and !Koga's lightweight spear, bow and arrows. Max gazed into the fire, the flames shapeshifting, mesmerizing him as they snared his thoughts and gave life to the shadows – a macabre dance of imagined creatures.

Tomorrow seemed frighteningly close.

6

Far to the north-west of the Valley of Bones, beyond the hundreds of kilometres of red sand dunes that lay, scallop-like, towards the coastline, Atlantic fog sucked in by the intense temperature inland shut down any flying Kallie's father had planned for the next few hours. It would pass in due course, and the tourists on the bird-watching safari were quietly thankful for this respite from the scorching sun.

Ferdie van Reenen was a big man, with a wild beard and a battered face from being a boxer in his youth. He had survived war, flood and famine on his farm, but it would be his daughter Kallie who would break his heart one day, when she grew older and left home. But until that happened she could also raise his blood pressure. He was due to fly his clients further north, to the Kunene River on the Angolan border. His twin-engined Beechcraft Baron could do the trip comfortably with its fifteen-hundred-kilometre range, and he was all set, now that Kallie had delivered the additional supplies he needed. She had also delivered the news about Max and !Koga.

Van Reenen secured the luggage net in the back of the plane. His voice was as rough as old desert boots, and distinctive: a mixture between a Dutch and a German accent.

'That was a stupid thing to do, my girl. Helping that boy will bring trouble down on our heads, you see if it doesn't!'

Kallie ticked off the final item on the supply manifest; she always kept accurate records for the farm's accounts. Legend had it that when her father served in the South African Air Force, he could fly a Hercules C130 transport plane through the eye of a needle at three hundred knots, upside down and with a full cargo; but money and income taxes presented a bigger challenge. And so, at times, did his daughter.

'Pa, don't start.'

'Start? You fly to Windhoek, you send him off with my old Land Rover, my *favourite* Land Rover . . .'

'Pa, it's the *only* Land Rover.'

'Exactly. I cherish that thing. That's not the point. He's just a boy!'

'He's fifteen,' she interrupted.

'A boy!' he insisted.

'When you were fifteen, you spent three months in the bush hunting, you rounded up five hundred cattle for your father . . .'

'It was a thousand head of cattle. Never mind me! He's an English schoolboy who has probably never even seen the sun, and he'll fry out here. And now he's gone off on a scatterbrained expedition to try and find his father, who is nowhere to be seen or heard of!' Ferdie van Reenen angrily wrenched the securing rope tight. Kallie stayed quiet; there was little point in going head-to-head with her dad. 'Do you have any idea what this would mean if anything happened to him? We helped him. We sent him out there – probably to die!' her father spluttered.

'I sent him out there. Me. I made the decision.'

'Wrong one to make!'

'He's got diesel, water, food – he can reach any of the game lodges by radio if he gets lost or if the Land Rover has any problems,' she replied.

'The Land Rover is in perfect running order. That's not the point! We will be the ones dragged into court. Accessory to stupidity will be the charge, as well as accessory to careless abandonment, or accessory to manslaughter, or accessory to something! Father missing. Son missing. My daughter's brain missing!'

Kallie took a deep breath. Her father's life was stressful enough, trying to keep two planes, a farm and a struggling safari business going. The Beechcraft had been bought with a big loan from the bank, and any mishaps or drop in business could push her father into bankruptcy. 'Pa . . .' she touched his arm, 'you taught me to fly when I was twelve, I've been able to look after myself for a while now . . . believe me, this boy would have gone off on his own if I hadn't helped him. And I think he's capable of handling things. He's a tough kid. The man from London called, asking if I could help. I picked him up, I did the best I could for him. He thinks his father is in trouble. !Koga thinks he's been sent by the Great God to be with his people . . .' She stopped; she could hear herself making matters worse.

'The Bushman was still at the farm?' he asked.

She nodded. 'He wouldn't leave until "*the fair-haired boy came who was sent to be with them*". That's what he said. Pa, you know they have a sixth sense about these things. What could I do? Say no? Tell him to go home?'

Her father pulled up his coat collar. He hated the damp. He hated not flying. But he loved his daughter. He looked at her, the moisture from the fog clinging to his beard. Then he shook his head. 'No. He sounds a brave boy.' He kissed her cheek, turned towards the airfield's building and pointed a finger at her. 'But when this weather lifts, you fly straight back to the farm. Enough is enough. Understand?' She nodded, and he put his arm around her. 'Good. Come on, buy your old man a cup of coffee. God, I hate this weather.'

Kallie returned his hug and fell into step as they set off for the airfield clubhouse. She wanted to make radio contact with Max, to see if he was all right. She was responsible for helping him, she knew that; but now she felt like a big sister towards the English boy. And, from her experience, brothers always got into trouble.

A low-pressure weather front had moved across the North Atlantic, tumbled across Ireland and then punished the Devon coast with torrential rain. Dartmoor High's granite walls kept the elements at bay, but during storms like these, when the clouds hugged the high ground and enshrouded the school, the long, low-lit corridors and stairwells created an almost sinister atmosphere. And shadows seemed to move when they shouldn't. It was all in the imagination, Sayid told himself as he skulked along, hugging the gloomier side of the corridor's walls. Since he had sent the message telling Max that Peterson knew where he was, there had been no contact with his friend. And there had been no chance for Sayid to eavesdrop again on Peterson, so yesterday Sayid had taken matters into his own hands. He needed a piece of equipment from a specialist shop in London that he could buy on the web. And for that he needed a credit card, and there was only one place where he could find one: his mother.

Sayid had been brought up with a strict code of behaviour, and theft and dishonesty were considered 'heinous crimes' according to his mother and his late father. He had had to look up the word 'heinous' in the dictionary to know how seriously they viewed such things. But Sayid had no choice but to use his mother's credit card illegally and order what he needed. His mother would have done anything she could to help Max, but then she would have asked why he needed this particular device, and then he would have had to explain that he wanted to bug Peterson's phone; his mother would have thrown a wobbly, and matters would have got totally out of hand. He had six weeks before his mother would discover the item on her credit card billing, so he would worry about the consequences when the time came. By then, he hoped, Max should have returned safely. It wasn't that he hadn't tried another way of doing things, either. He had tried to hack into Peterson's computer, but the granite walls, as well as Peterson's firewall, stopped him. Sayid soothed away his guilt over the card. There had been no choice. Not if he was to help his friend.

He had to discover who Peterson reported to, so that he could relay that information to Max and Farentino. But how to get into Peterson's locked room was another problem altogether.

Shaka Chang could buy anything he desired, but he could not get the information he needed from Tom Gordon. The scientist had outwitted Chang and hidden the vital evidence which could ruin Chang's plans for good. He comforted himself with the thought that the scientist was no longer of any consequence; Tom Gordon would not be telling anyone anything. But Chang had a grudging admiration for the boy who had set out from England. Max Gordon's determination could prove more troublesome than he expected. Once his men had driven him and the Bushman boy into the Valley of Bones, Max had held little interest for Chang; now he began to wonder if he had been too hasty in that dismissal. If by some absolute fluke the boy survived, and if, as he suspected, the boy's father had somehow told him where to find the information that was so very damaging – then he should not underestimate the emotional strength of anyone trying to save a loved one. Not that Shaka Chang had ever been loved. Feared and loathed, yes. Love was too difficult and complex an emotion to analyse, but he did recognize it as a driving force in others.

Mr Slye, ever aware of his master's desire to be in total control of any given situation, muttered that perhaps it would be prudent to double-check on the boy's survival. Chang agreed. 'Send them back again. No excuses. Find either the boy's body or, if wild animals have had him, his remains.'

'And if by any chance they track him down and he is still alive . . .?' Slye asked. He would never presume to offer a complete answer to any situation: suggestions were complimentary to his employer's intelligence; a solution without one being requested, impertinent.

'Kill him on sight. Either result will be a satisfactory outcome, Mister Slye.'

'The men who failed before? Should I order them to hunt down the boy?'

'Yes. But lessons must be learned.'

Mr Slye dipped his head slightly in obedience and acknowledgement. 'How very wise, if I may say so, sir.'

Chang sighed. Slye's brazen pandering was, in many ways, repulsive, but in this lay his value to Chang. Absolute obedience and a mind that Chang recognized as being one of the most devious, informed and manipulative he had ever known. Chang gazed for a moment at the weasel-like body. If only Slye's teeth had not been so pointed and he was more photogenic, he would have made a first-class politician.

The driver who had led those failed hunters was already being taken care of, and the example made of him would be witnessed at first hand by the others. Chang believed lessons should often be taught with a sharp slap on the wrist, so to speak. A little pain never hurt anybody, was Chang's motto.

He stood on the huge balcony. Thirty metres below him, the fort's gates opened. This would be an excellent start to the day. A juicy slice of melon melted on his tongue. He forked another piece into his mouth from the bowl of chilled mixed fruits that he always had for breakfast and gazed indulgently at his beloved crocodiles by the river. He loved to spoil them. So much so that he had decided to give the monstrous creatures a morsel for breakfast. The driver.

He watched as the small motorboat chugged out into midstream. The crocodiles on the sandbanks lifted their snouts. Who needed guard dogs when any intruder would have to get past them? The screaming man, held firmly by the very men who had accompanied him in the pick-up, was

89

unceremoniously bundled over the side, and the vessel beat a hasty retreat; those crocs could overturn a five-metre boat with ease. The floundering man was very much the centre of attention as half a dozen crocodiles powered towards him. How nice to be wanted, Shaka Chang thought as he squelched a ripe grape between his teeth. He turned to Slye. 'I do hope he doesn't give the crocodiles indigestion – they are a protected species.'

Finally the horrifying screams stopped. The churned water settled. Chang nodded to a white-gloved servant: he would have his coffee now. A low rumble of thunder groaned across the horizon; perhaps there would be some rain in a couple of days. Either that or it was the crocodiles' stomachs, dealing with their breakfast.

A cool breeze, or even a full-blown storm, would have been welcome so far as Max was concerned. He and !Koga had set out at dawn, heading for the distant mountains, but within a couple of hours the temperature was already over forty degrees Celsius. !Koga reckoned they could reach the foothills of the peaks by that night if they moved quickly enough and if they were lucky in the hunt. It was the 'moving quickly' that Max was struggling with. Bushmen can chase down a wounded buck for a whole day before they finish the kill, but Max was struggling to breathe the lung-searing air after a couple of hours, and they were only walking.

He had been keen to travel later in the day, but !Koga warned him that this was when the predators would be hunting and, even though Max was a good runner, he did not have the speed or strength of a lion or a leopard.

The Valley of Bones had been formed millions of years ago. Some force of the universe had flung a meteor into this wasteland, and the impact had thrown up jagged mountains and shattered the Earth's crust into fractured veins of gullies and crevasses. The dry scrub and acacia survived only because of the seasonal rains, but if they failed, then the vegetation withered even more. Mud holes and surface roots provided moisture for the grass-eating animals, while they in turn fell victim to the carnivores. It was a hellhole of heat, dust and death. The depression from the meteor's impact created a huge frying pan, and Max was in danger of dehydration. What helped save him from heatstroke was an ex-army floppy hat his dad had brought back from Iraq, though he never told his son what exactly he had been doing there – another secret. The hat helped keep at bay the brain-frying sun, but it was thirst that would shut him down – and probably drive him crazy – if he did not get some fluids soon. Max felt queasy, his blood seemed to be boiling, a surging wave of nausea gripped him and he was losing control. His mind began to wander. Everything in front of him was a blur. All he was doing was putting one foot in front of the other, but now even that was proving difficult. He had put a smooth pebble in his mouth to try to keep saliva going, but that had not helped and, despite promising himself to be frugal, the last of the water had already trickled down his dust-parched throat a couple of hours earlier. The frightening reality of the wilderness was worming its way into him like a tick burrowing under his skin. He had to shake off the fear. He had to be strong. But what he had to have was a drink.

!Koga glanced back and saw Max on his knees, his face

dust-caked, his breathing coming hard. A few paces, and he was back with him, coaxing him under the spindly shade from an old hag of a tree. !Koga placed a hand on Max's shoulder and smiled – a look that was all innocence yet totally reassuring. Then he stepped away and began scuffling through the dust.

One of the stunted trees had a hollow at its base, worn away either by the weather or by animals. !Koga cupped his hands and dug in the sand at the tree's base, and he kept scooping sand away for the best part of twenty minutes. Then he took a narrow, hollow reed from his animal-skin pouch which looked like a soft-sided quiver and, after easing the ruler-length reed into the hole, began to suck. Max remembered one of the boys shoving a length of hosepipe into the petrol tank of a teacher's car and siphoning off enough fuel to use in his scooter. But he had no idea what !Koga could find in the sand with a thin piece of hollow reed.

After five or six minutes !Koga took another reed from the pouch and came back to Max. He said nothing, but he put his fingers under Max's chin, gently teasing his head backwards. He put one end of the reed in his own mouth and the other on Max's lips. Max felt water trickle down into his mouth. !Koga had drawn up a mouthful of water and was feeding it to Max, denying himself the first pleasure of slaking his thirst.

Max nodded gratefully, immediately feeling better, and !Koga went back and began the process again.

It took another hour before !Koga had enough water to fill the small water bottle they carried. The Bushmen depended on tubers and other plants for their water supply in these arid places, but when these were scarce they had to find a *sipping hole* – a place where some boulders and hollow trees allowed dew to accumulate and seep beneath them.

Max felt the strength return to his body from the invigorating drink. Now the mountains did not seem so far away. How !Koga could draw water up like that he didn't know, but he had a faint, uncertain memory from a science class about something called capillary action.

There was still no sign of anything to eat, though !Koga spent most of his time gazing down, looking for spoor. If they did not find food here, it would be a cold, hungry night spent on the mountain – and it seemed unlikely that there would be anything to hunt up there. Max knew he would grow progressively weaker in these conditions. And then he would falter. Nature shows no favour. He would be the one eaten by hyena or lion.

The hours passed in the near-silence of the valley. There was the occasional scream of an eagle and sometimes a rattle of pebbles as something, probably a small animal, dislodged loose stones on the slopes. !Koga had picked up speed, but Max kept pace as the Bushman loped effortlessly ahead. Max realized that the air was cooling; the mountain peaks on the western side of the valley would soon protect them from the blazing heat because the sun was slipping lower in the sky. !Koga suddenly crouched down in the bleached scrub and slowly raised a hand. Max crouched as he covered the last few metres to join him. !Koga pointed through the brush. Max couldn't see anything. Then a slight movement caught his attention. A small buck stared at them from about twenty metres away. Its skin shivered, shrugging at a bothersome fly.

Warily it kept its head up, not feeding on the poor offering at its hoofs, looking cautiously towards them. It had not yet picked up their scent.

!Koga eased an arrow on to his hunting bow. Max gazed at the beautiful creature. The large, liquid eyes distressed him. They were going to kill this beautiful creature. Another reality check. This was about survival. There was no pre-packed, plastic-wrapped cut of meat on a chilled shelf around here. If he were at home and they had told him to go and kill a lamb, to slit its throat, he would have become a vegetarian overnight. Here, this creature was going to give him life.

The buck jolted and ran as the arrow plunged into its flank, near the heart. Max could hear its hoofs clatter across the rocky surface and caught a glimpse of a white flash – the erect hairs along the buck's spine – as it bounded away. It was a springbok, which could leap more than three metres in the air from a standing position. !Koga did not hesitate. In a few strides he was where the buck had quivered in uncertainty, moments ago. It was important to identify that particular animal's hoof print. Bushmen would often spend hours chasing their prey, and they needed to make sure they were following the right animal. !Koga was on one knee, his eyes scanning the ground. Retrieving his arrow shaft, he glanced over his shoulder to make sure Max was following.

'Come! It's good!' A skilled hunter could keep his family and clan members alive and !Koga's joy at his success was not to be diminished by any queasy feelings Max might be experiencing.

!Koga sprinted away. Max may have been fit, but he was not in the same league as this seemingly undernourished boy.

Revitalized by the drink, however, he pounded after the Bushman, determined to give a good account of himself; also, he didn't want to let !Koga down.

A small pride of lions, three females, two cubs and a male, had their sanctuary on a small outcrop of rock beneath acacia trees that clawed their way out of the ground. The lions were three kilometres downwind, and though the air barely moved, they had caught the scent of the distressed animal, and another smell – human beings. Only once before had they killed a man but the taste had stayed with them – as sweet as warthog and much easier to kill. They were unafraid of the man-scent that stirred them from their slumber. This was their territory and there were intruders. In addition to the wounded animal there was now the bonus of man-flesh. If there was a kill to be had and they failed to hurry, hyenas and vultures would get the best pickings. Leaving one female to care for the cubs and the male to saunter down at his leisure, the two other females began a slow, loping run. The pride would eat that night.

The slow-acting poison finally weakened the young springbok and it lay, helpless, on the ground. Max, grunting with effort, arrived in time to see !Koga slit its throat. The poor beast gave a single spasm and died. !Koga offered his knife to Max.

'Can you skin?' It seemed less of a question and more of a challenge and Max felt it keenly. Bad enough that the Bushman boy was going to keep them alive by his hunting skills; was this a taunt? What exactly could Max contribute?

He nodded, ignoring the home-made knife !Koga offered, and pulled out his own fifteen-centimetre bush knife.

!Koga expertly made a small incision into the springbok's belly; then, using his thumb, he eased the skin aside, being careful not to contaminate the meat by piercing the stomach. !Koga's deft movements allowed him to ease out the animal's gut, which slithered and slopped on to the sand. He reached into the cavity and cut away the heart and liver; this was his by right: the hunter who made the kill chose the best pieces for himself. It was not a selfish act, but one of practicality. The hunter needed endurance for stalking and the strength to run for many kilometres after wounded game; heart, liver and tongue were rich in fat and protein. But once a Bushman had made a kill, no one in his family or clan would go hungry – they shared everything. Max was struggling to do what was expected of him. The groundsman at Dartmoor High used to shoot rabbits, and Max had seen him skin those. It seemed a fairly straightforward process, but Max did not know where the entry point for his knife should be on an animal this size. !Koga took his hand and good-naturedly guided it, showing him where to place the point of the blade. But then the Bushman stiffened.

'What's wrong?' Max asked.

!Koga was looking back along the valley, his eyes squinting in the glare, his head turned a little as he listened. A sudden flurry of air, a small dust devil no taller than the boys themselves, scurried and died. !Koga waited and Max, deferring to his bushcraft, stayed silent. He couldn't see or hear anything that might be a cause for alarm. !Koga whispered, 'We must go quickly now.'

Fear sharpened Max's senses. He scanned the valley again, but there was nothing to indicate impending danger. By the time he looked back !Koga had cut a strip of skin from the springbok's leg and fashioned a pocket to carry the heart and liver. Max obediently took the meat thrust into his hands as !Koga tied it fast with strips of sinew, as a butcher would tie a joint of pork. Creating a sling, he pulled it over his shoulder like a bag. Then he grabbed Max's arm. 'You run hard?'

'What?'

'There.' He pointed to rising ground, beleaguered with boulders fallen from the higher peaks. 'We run, we cannot stop. You run that far? That hard?'

Max gauged the distance; that had to be at least a kilometre. The sandy ground would make it heavy going, and there would be an almighty scramble to get up among those boulders, to shield them from whatever it was that had spooked !Koga. 'Piece of cake,' he lied. The boy did not understand. 'OK. Yes,' Max told him.

'Do not make noise. No shouting. You fall down, you do not cry out. You must be quiet. Yes? Understand?'

'I understand,' Max replied. He did not know why !Koga was giving him such precise instructions, but his instincts told him not to question them.

!Koga grabbed one of the springbok's horns. Max grabbed the remaining back leg and hoped !Koga wasn't planning to drag it all the way. They humped it for a couple of hundred metres, straining in the heat and stumbling with their unwieldy burden, leaving a clear blood trail. When they reached a clearing, !Koga nodded. 'Here. Drop it.' Without waiting for Max to ask any questions, he turned and ran. Max was going to struggle to keep up. !Koga darted and jumped like a gazelle, running flat out across the broken floor of the valley towards the boulders. The ground, shattered from millennia of the Earth's pressures and contortions, now had gaping cracks in it, anything from a few centimetres to more than a metre wide. Max's leg muscles ached – it was impossible to find any rhythm in this crazy race against time. A sprint, a jump, then a weaving run, suddenly another small chasm to get across. He did not have !Koga's agility, but he had a grim determination to reach their objective. Just don't trip and tumble into one of those crevices, he kept telling himself – that would be a one-way ticket to hell. He jumped. Sweat stung his eyes and the heat sapped his energy, but he stayed focused on the receding figure of the Bushman boy. Bloody hell! He was leaving him well and truly behind. He urged himself to put more effort into it, but his mind was a bigger challenge than the hard going. It badgered him, taunting his efforts. *You're too tired for this. You'll cripple yourself if you fall, then what good will you be to anyone!? Just stop for a breather and a drink. For a moment.*

The lions had picked up the pace; blood scent from the kill filled their nostrils, but the dead springbok was not their primary target. It was the shuffling, ungainly gait of the humans that attracted them. And one of the humans had stopped, flapping his hat to cool his face. To them he was an animal in distress, weakened by heat and exhaustion. Vulnerable. The perfect target. The lionesses were in attack position; one of them moved to block any chance of escape while the other hurtled forward in an timeless display of killing efficiency. The human had his back to her; her gaze never faltered. She charged and leaped. Her huge claws raked his back, her jaws clamped on his neck, crunching through his skull and spinal column.

He was dead before he hit the ground.

The other human was screaming in fear.

7

The twin-engined Beechcraft Baron lifted off smoothly from the runway. The fog had cleared and Ferdie van Reenen was a happy man again. The sun was shining, he was flying his plane, and there were paying guests aboard. He waggled the wings in farewell to Kallie, who waved from the airstrip. The only unsettled feeling he had as the plane banked and one of the passengers gulped aloud in anxiety was that his daughter would disobey him. 'Listen, you get even a whiff of trouble, or you see any dodgy characters lurking around, you get hold of Mike Kapuo. He's a good bloke and he won't stand for any nonsense on his patch.' She had agreed, of course. Kapuo was a good cop, but his 'patch' was, in truth, hundreds of thousands of square kilometres. Kapuo had shut down a lot of wild-game smuggling and he policed the Walvis Bay docklands with a tough, personally trained crew. His police force had to deal with rough customers from all over the world but, as good a cop as he was, Mike Kapuo was four hundred kilometres south of where Kallie stood, watching her father fly into the blue.

She had promised her father she would fly straight home, but that malfunctioning fuel line was still causing trouble, so he had reversed his decision and insisted that she stay until the mechanics had given her old Cessna a clean bill of health. Kallie wasn't too frustrated. At least that bought her a few hours to try and contact Max by radio again and to speak to this Sayid in England. Maybe Mike Kapuo was worth a call as well. Any major accident would eventually be reported to the police, though of course bodies tended to be eaten by animals or birds if left undiscovered for very long. Why wasn't Max answering the radio?

Inside the small building that served as a stopover for some of the flying safaris, Kallie ordered a cold drink and pulled the old-fashioned plastic phone towards her. The single landline ran all the way up from the coast, so this would give her a chance to phone England. Tobias, the barman, always seemed to be smiling, a smile as cheerful as the luridly coloured T-shirts he wore. He subscribed to the African philosophy of *ubuntu*: that there was enough for everyone, that sharing was the civilized way to live. But free phone calls to England did not qualify under that category. He gently pulled the phone back across the bar counter.

'Tobias, come on, man. One phone call.'

'And how do I explain it? No.'

'You can put it on Dad's tab.'

'Me? Charge your father for that? I don't think so.'

'He never checks the account, I do.'

'And I'm the one who would be cheating him. No.' Tobias wiped a damp cloth across the top of the counter, even though it did not need cleaning because he wiped it every other minute. Tobias liked things to be right.

Kallie avoided the damp spot. 'It wouldn't be cheating.

Not really. Only a bit. Look . . . we book the call through the operator and then she can phone back and tell you how much it costs. I will then pay for the call and you give me a receipt. How does that sound? It's a really important phone call, honest.'

Something didn't feel quite right, but Tobias couldn't put his finger on what it was. He nodded in reluctant agreement. Kallie lifted the receiver and gave him a look which said that the call was private and how about he let her get on with it? Tobias moved to the other end of the bar.

In the privacy of his room Sayid opened the padded envelope, peeled back the cover of the small plastic package inside and held the button-like piece of silver on his fingertip. It was no bigger than the battery in his watch, but if he could get it into Mr Peterson's phone, it would give him a chance to trace whoever Peterson called. His mobile phone blared out the *Mission Impossible* theme. The screen told him it was an unknown caller.

'Hello?'

Kallie's voice crackled a bit. 'Sayid?'

'Yeah,' Sayid answered warily.

'My name's Kallie van Reenen.'

She explained who she was as quickly as she could.

'Kallie! Wait a sec!' Sayid said, as soon as he realized the importance of her call. He quickly plugged his mobile into the back of his laptop, danced his fingers across the keys, effectively scrambling her voice to anyone who might be listening in.

'OK. The line's safe. Have you heard from Max?'

'No. You?'

'Nothing. Where is he?'

'I don't know. I'm going to have to call the police, I should never have helped him.'

Sayid knew it was no use shouldering blame. 'He'd have gone anyway.'

'That's what I told my dad, but I'm not so sure I believe it any more.'

'Kallie, the police couldn't find Max's dad, they're not going to find Max. And for all I know, the publicity may alert whoever could be involved. But I've discovered something that I don't think Max knows.' As he was speaking he slid open his desk drawer, pushed his hand underneath it and pulled away a letter that was stuck to the underside with Blu-Tack.

He went to the door, checked that no one was hanging around outside and then closed it again.

He spoke more quietly. 'Are you there?'

'Still here,' Kallie said.

'A letter came yesterday. It was from Max's dad. I've got it.'

'How? Didn't the headmaster or whoever check his mail?'

'His dad sent it to me. He's done it before. As if he didn't trust anyone else. I checked the postmark, it was sent almost a week earlier than the last one. So Max went to Africa with only the information he had.'

'Where was it posted?'

'Walvis Bay, Namibia.'

'Walvis Bay.' She sounded thoughtful.

'Is that important?'

'I don't know. It's the biggest port here, and there's a heck of a lot of shipping comes in and out. What does it say?' She could hear a faint rustle of paper on the line, as if Sayid was holding the letter in his hand.

Sayid kept going to the door and checking the corridor; he did not want to be overheard or interrupted, especially if Mr Peterson was on the prowl. If there were people trying to stop Max from finding his father, they would be scanning for calls – Sayid would not be able to talk for long. No matter how clever Sayid was in the short term in scrambling the voice print, sooner or later they – whoever 'they' were – would break his coding. 'There's not much time. They might be monitoring my phone signal, but here's what the letter said.' Sayid read out the letter Max had never received. '"Max, remember Egypt? Seth causing problems here. I found his secret. Leopold will meet you at Eros. Leave now. Get out, son. There's not much time. I love you. Dad."'

'Almost like a telegram,' Sayid said. 'The statue of Eros is in Piccadilly Circus. This Leopold was obviously going to take Max somewhere safe. But he never showed.'

Kallie had listened carefully, appreciating Sayid's concern over how long they had spoken. 'Do we know who Leopold is?' she asked.

'Not sure. I know his dad had a field assistant. A German or an Austrian guy who knew his way around Namibia. Odds are it's him.'

'And who's Seth?'

'I looked that one up. Max and his dad used to go off all over the place during summer hols . . . Egypt was a favourite.

Seth was the god of chaos. Something to do with living outside the universe as we know it. This wasn't a neatly typed letter, it was scribbled in pencil . . . just like the one Max got before he left. That's all I know, except that there's a teacher here called Peterson and I definitely know – I mean for sure – that he followed Max and is up to his neck in all of this.'

'So Max's father was warning him. He didn't have access to a phone, so he had to scribble a note. Then he must have got someone to post it, because if it was postmarked Walvis Bay, there are tons of phones around there. He must have known someone ruthless, like this Seth figure, would try and hurt Max. OK . . .' Her thoughts tried to join up the pieces of the puzzle which didn't make much sense, other than Max's father was obviously warning his son. Only it wasn't OK. This was far more serious than simply a boy looking for his father in the wilderness of Namibia.

'He was supposed to come here, Sayid. London has nothing to do with it. It wasn't Eros's statue, it was Eros Airport, Namibia. And this Leopold guy was supposed to meet him, but didn't.'

Sayid's voice interrupted her thoughts. 'Kallie, I have to go. Keep in touch, will you? I reckon we're the only ones who can help Max survive this. Text if you can.'

'That's difficult, Sayid. No masts out here, unless you're near a city. Phones are pretty rare as well. OK. I'll do what I can, this end. Look, if there's anything really important you can leave a message here with a guy called Tobias. He can always get the flight shed to radio me. And you'd better watch out for Peterson.' She gave him the telephone number and replaced the handset.

Tobias was standing at the end of the counter, wiping glasses and examining them for blemishes. He glanced at Kallie, who was sitting quietly. 'Trouble?'

'Maybe. If a kid from England phones, get word to me, will you?'

''Course I will.' He handed over an old plastic-lined vacuum flask. 'It's a long, hot flight home. I've made you my special Desert Buster Ice-Cold Special. It's on the house.' She barely heard him, but his voice broke her concentration. 'Just don't shake it up too much – it's an old flask.'

'What? Oh, right . . . thanks, Tobias.'

She climbed off the stool and made for the door with the flask under her arm.

The phone rang. Tobias answered. 'Hello. Yes . . .' It was the operator. '. . . that's right, we made the call . . . it was how much? To a mobile phone? It was *how* much?!' Kallie was at the far end of the room.

'Kallie!' Tobias yelled.

'Put it on my dad's tab! I've got no cash,' Kallie shouted behind her as she pushed through the door and was out of sight. *That* was the one thing Tobias had not taken into account: Kallie having no money.

She faced a tough journey, flying more than three hundred kilometres, against prevailing winds, to Walvis Bay. She needed to speak to Mike Kapuo in person. No matter what her father thought, she was now well and truly involved in Max's well-being. Obviously there were vicious people out there, intent on preventing him from finding his father.

If only she had known this before, she would have . . . would have what? Stopped him? Helped him? Max was going to do whatever he felt was necessary. She headed for the hangar where the old, sand-blasted Cessna sat. One of the mechanics was closing the engine cowling, and when he saw Kallie he smiled and waved. All fixed.

Kallie van Reenen cursed herself for letting Max go alone. Her only comfort was that !Koga was with him.

Max wanted to scream. The lioness had given a flick of her neck and shaken the already limp carcass. She turned away, dragging the remains back to where it would be eaten. Max was in his own agony. He had followed !Koga, going flat out, and then he had fallen. His thigh slammed into a rock. It dead-legged him and he was helpless. As he tried to clear the hurt from his mind and bite back the scream that would have helped relieve the pain, !Koga was at his side, dragging him almost brutally into the shade and cover of a boulder.

Below them in the clearing, where they had dumped the springbok's carcass, two men had appeared. Both carried rifles and they had been moving fast, running hard across the valley. How had they tracked them so quickly? Max remembered that the Land Rover had left a trail of oil, like the springbok's blood, for the men to follow. From where the stricken vehicle was abandoned any good tracker would have found them. The men had stood for a moment, looking towards the area where Max and !Koga had run, but they were unable to spot the boys. Then one of them had taken off his hat and fanned the heat from his face. The sand-coloured lioness was less than ten metres away from him by then. She had extended her stride and silently attacked. The second man, a further fifteen metres away, searching for tracks, turned as he heard the impact of the lioness crushing his friend's body. His was the scream that had echoed down the valley, bouncing from rock face to rock face. He fumbled with his rifle, but then the second lioness appeared and began her run. He turned, yelling and swearing, clawing at the rising ground, trying to outpace the lioness.

If the man's nerve had not broken he might have survived. The springbok kill was between him and the second lioness, and she was more interested in the bloodsoaked animal than in him. But his panic alerted her. She could not resist her natural instincts; like a cat with a mouse, she pursued the doomed man. There was a brief moment, like being involved in a car crash, when time slowed down, creating a sense of unreality. The man had spotted Max, who had stood up on the other side of the clearing, the pain in his leg forgotten. In his final moments of life the man screamed for help from the boy he had come to kill. 'Help me, boy! For God's sake help me!'

Max shouted as loud as he could and threw a hefty stone towards the attacking lioness – a futile gesture: it fell too short for the lioness to even notice. The man scrambled backwards. The big cat had momentarily glanced towards Max when he yelled at her, and he looked right into her amber eyes, Boy and Beast, held for a fraction of a second in time. But her prey was at her feet. It was over very quickly.

Max felt his stomach heave. The savagery of these last few moments, seeing the men torn apart, was too much. He gagged and vomited. His mind was clear: he knew he had to escape, but what he had just seen he hoped never to see again.

!Koga was silent. The lions were feeding, vultures appeared

by the springbok carcass, and hyenas snapped bone and tore flesh in a voracious feeding frenzy.

The boys turned away, climbing towards the rising peaks, away from the Valley of Bones.

Max followed !Koga's every move as the rock face became more difficult. Neither had spoken since the lionesses' attack. Max felt the granite rasp his fingertips as he struggled for a grip, but he didn't mind the rock's bite. A strange feeling had been growing within him. It was difficult to explain, but if his dad had been with him he would have understood without the awkwardness of explanation. The events of the past few days, and in particular the slaughter of those men, had created a hard-edged resolve in Max. Before, he had been determined to see things through and to give his all in trying to find his dad, but now he knew he could face anything that came his way. He could respond to the moment, drawing upon a deep resource that had grown within him. His mind insisted on trying to analyse it, but he told it to shut up. There were more immediate things to think about, like scaling these mountains. And for once his agile mind, that liked nothing better than to complicate his feelings, did as it was told.

The cave beckoned like a sanctuary, offering shelter from the day's heat, still clinging to the rocks. The boys had been climbing for some hours, edging along the narrow pathways made by animals; higher and higher they went until the valley floor was in the far distance, disguised by heat shimmer – a mirage lake. !Koga reached the cave mouth first and extended a hand to Max, pulling him over the edge of the huge flat area that was the extended floor of the cave. It was time to rest, and they rewarded themselves with a sip of the precious water. Above their heads, an overhang gave them protection from the sun and the view was as if they were floating in a balloon. Now they were this high, Max could see an undulating landscape, a mixture of hills, scrub plains and saw-tooth mountains, stretching out as far as he could see. It was not very different from where they had journeyed already. The land was unrelenting in its harshness. He pulled the binoculars from under his shirt; sweat-stained and covered in dust, the lenses needed a bit of spit and a wipe. Once he had them clean, he scanned the horizon. The panorama yielded half a dozen dust devils scuttling across the plain; the horizon was murky with heat haze, and another of those small rolling cloud formations journeyed slowly across the skyline. It was too far away to bring any quick downpours, but Max hoped it meant that waterholes were being replenished somewhere ahead.

Sharp-pointed mountain peaks to the east were tipped with darkening red from the setting sun. Max thought they looked like crocodile teeth tinged with blood. He told himself he would have to stop creating such gruesome images, but he had to admit the mountains did have an animal-like quality, and they were certainly not as gentle or mysterious as the Dartmoor Tors back home. The moment the sun set, he caught a flash of green on the horizon, a play of light as it dipped beneath the edge of the world; then it was gone, leaving only a blood-red line.

!Koga stood watching the sun disappear. Max caught himself studying the young hunter for a moment. Dust covered his skinny frame and his eyes were red and sore from the day's journey. Max reckoned a strong wind would lift the Bushman boy off cliff, he seemed so light. But !Koga had been tireless, he had never complained, he had put his life in danger for Max; he had hunted and killed with great skill. He had been patient with Max, explaining that the land spoke, that it breathed and felt pain. Max understood that it was the boy's inherent connection with this brutal place that had saved their lives. And now he sat, watching the sunset pull the cover of darkness over their heads. !Koga was a primitive boy in a primitive landscape, and Max now understood that this was not a derogatory expression, it was in him, too. He had touched on something so basic, he couldn't describe it. But it was a good thing. It strengthened rather than weakened. It was, he suspected, the core of his own humanity. So few of these Bushmen survived; he knew he was privileged to be with !Koga, and now he felt a bond with the boy that was akin to brotherhood.

He touched !Koga's shoulder, and the boy turned. He looked sad and gave only a hint of a smile in recognition of Max's gesture.

'What? What's wrong? We did well today, it was a hard day, but we did well,' Max told him.

The boy nodded and looked towards the ever-darkening sky. !Koga said something Max did not understand, a clicking sound. '*Gauwa.*'

Max shrugged. 'I don't understand,' he said.

'It is the god who takes the father's light. It is darkness. It is *Gauwa*. It is the time when there is spirit of the dead.'

'The night time? You mean the darkness?' Max asked him.

Clearly, !Koga was saddened by the loss of the sun. Despite their experiences of the day, and the knowledge that the fear and the killing were part of life for !Koga, losing the sun caused him . . . what? Max wasn't sure. It was something like grief, he supposed.

Max pointed to the east, across the mountains whose peaks now held the dark in varying degrees of blackness. 'Tomorrow. Yes? The sun. That is where it will come tomorrow.'

The boy nodded, he knew that. But there was still a sense of abandonment. The temperature dropped below freezing and Max felt it keenly. The cotton shirt and trousers he wore offered little protection, and they were also showing signs of wear and tear. The five-centimetre needles of the camelthorn bushes ripped clothes and skin with equal ease. Max had cuts on his arms and back and his shirt looked as though someone had taken a razor blade to it. !Koga, wearing only a loincloth, showed no sign of the cold, and the few old scars on his back and arms proved that the boy had learned his lessons about avoiding the thorn trees. They needed a fire, and quickly.

Max had a bruise the size of a cricket ball from his fall, but it was the loss of the plastic lighter that concerned him more: it had been shattered when his thigh hit the rock. He showed the fragments to !Koga, but the boy seemed unconcerned. From his pouch he took out a small cross of softwood and a narrow stick with a notch cut in its end. He secured the wooden cross on the ground under his foot, then, holding the stick between his palms, twirled it until the base smouldered.

Max had tried this once or twice when he went camping, and it needed dry moss or lichen to get a spark going, something he always struggled with in the dampness of Dartmoor. !Koga's finger went back into the pouch, and fluffed out a small piece of tinder, what looked to be part of a bird's nest – dry leaves and grass. Holding this to the base of the stick so it caught the heat, he gently blew on it until there was white smoke. Easing it under the bits of stick Max had foraged from the hillside, the fire crackled, putting a smile back on !Koga's face.

It was only when the fire was well and truly alight and !Koga had buried pieces of the springbok beneath the hot embers that Max realized where he was. He was standing in a domed cave which stretched back another twenty-odd metres into darkness. Ridges of granite of a similar length ran along the floor of the cave, almost like stepping stones, to reach the flat surface of the walls. !Koga had said nothing, but when he nodded at Max's realization, Max knew this was where the boy had planned to bring him all along. !Koga gathered a fistful of burning twigs and held them up so the light crept into the recesses of the cave.

The shadows from the flames danced across the walls of the cave, illuminating rock paintings: swathes of ochre-painted animals, hunters and their stories. It was the place of the ancestors, the place of the spirits of the dead.

The prophecy.

8

The walls showed the story of the First People. It was their beginning told in pictures, an unfolding tableau of the creation of the Bushman and the hunt for the mighty eland whose horns, even in its death throes, could impale a man. Skeletons of eland and lion had been found in the desert with the lion skewered on the eland's horns. The reverence for the eland, the biggest of all antelopes, the size of an ox, was at the heart of the Bushmen's existence – and their survival. It was the subject of their dance, their music and their paintings. One of the Bushmen's creation stories was that the insect-god Mantis created the world, and it was the eland he chose first to inhabit it: eland, the most noble of antelope with the strength of a giant, tender with its family, caressing them with lips and tongue, confirming and reassuring, like a mother with a child.

As Max followed the story, !Koga was at his shoulder, holding the burning sticks, pointing to the drawings, explaining in his own language what the pictures meant. And although Max could not understand the words, the soft incantation of the story lulled him, allowing the drawings to take on a life of their own. The shadows gave them energy, making the tableaux move along the wall. Lion and giraffe, antelope and baboon, hyena and snake: the family of the wilderness was there.

The ghost-like hunters ran, killing the eland which would give them life; they danced in praise and thanks. Through !Koga's lilt Max could almost hear them chanting. Figures twisted and turned, some lay down, ochre-coloured blood coming from their noses, in the trance dances that emphasized the supernatural link between Bushman and eland. !Koga was telling him all of this with small gestures and rolling eyes. He curled his fist in front of his stomach, twisted it, showing it like a knot of energy that crept up out of the body. The pictures and the mime made simple sense.

Bushmen mothers suckled their children; more men, themselves like stick insects, gave chase after another antelope. Max heard the words '*Gauwa*' and '*Gao!na*', images explained their meaning – the setting and rising sun.

The embers flickered, the shadows drew a curtain across the scene. Max caught a glimpse of something at the back of the cave, a drawing that did not belong with the others. It was of Anubis, the Egyptian jackal god of the underworld; but this time the figure was more in keeping with the others on the wall – like the Bushman drawings. The jackal's body pointed to the left, deliberately directing the viewer to look deeper into the darkness.

'Max,' !Koga whispered. As if his name was a statement, a matter of simple fact. There was still enough light to see the drawing of the boy, a white boy, shown in white pigment, with yellow hair. !Koga pointed at the drawing and at Max. 'Max,' he said again. Like the images of the ancient hunters, he was shown running. To where? The frieze went on – carefully etched drawings, painted and shaded on the granite, became another story. A crocodile's jaws, blood-tipped – these were the mountains Max had seen. A stumbling figure – no spear-wielding hunter this, but a ghost-like man, leaning on a staff. At the end of the man's pointing finger was a multi-pointed star, highlighted in charcoal and chalk. As Max traced the figures on the rock wall, a flurry of scratches symbolized a tangle of thorn trees, brittle and stark, but they sheltered what looked like a dove, its wings extended, lying on the ground. Max didn't know what that meant. The next drawing showed him a gaping hole, swirling like a whirlpool, and what seemed to be a cloud hovering over it. Now Max was confused. The simplicity was lost on him. But he understood the final figure. Its image stabbed pain into his chest as he reached out and touched it. The figure of the man with the shining star at the edge of his hand now lay on the ground, an etched line of red drawn from his leg. With awful certainty Max knew this was his father and that he had been injured. Was he lying out there, helpless? Max didn't know. 'Oh, Dad,' he whispered, 'where are you?'

The burning brand !Koga held dimmed as the flames died down. He touched Max's arm, wary of disturbing his thoughts. !Koga gestured to the final scene depicted on the rock face. The fair-haired white boy's wraith-like figure seemed to leap across the void, and with him came a dozen or more Bushmen with women and children. It looked as though they were leaving a group of others, who lay prone. Its meaning seemed clear: Max was leading Bushmen survivors away from . . . what? Obviously from some kind of great danger, and clearly something Max's father knew about.

Max had often watched his father unfold a field book and sketch his surroundings, then use a small box of watercolours to capture birds on the page. It was not that unusual for field scientists to be proficient artists, sketching flora and fauna, and Max was convinced that this is what had happened here. This was no prophecy, daubed hundreds or thousands of years ago, this was painted by his dad only weeks earlier.

!Koga smiled and nodded. To him, the drawings *were* the prophecy.

He gestured that they should return to the light and warmth of the fire and eat. Max nodded, hoping !Koga could not see the tears in his eyes. He signalled !Koga to go back and, as the boy's shadow blocked the fire's flames, Max hunched down in the darkness, and silently wept. Not since his mother had died had he felt such helplessness and despair. He lingered inside his own dark place for a few moments, then gritted his teeth until he felt his jawbone ache. This wasn't grief, he told himself. It was self-pity – either get rid of it or go home. Turn around. Get !Koga to lead you all the way back, climb on a plane, return to friends at Dartmoor High, tell the police about Peterson and then leave it to them. If that was the option, he would have no part of it.

The meat had cooked in the embers and, despite the charcoal taste, which reminded Max of one of his dad's barbecues, the food nourished them. 'Did my father send you here?' Max finally asked.

!Koga shook his head. 'My father.'

'Your father told you to come to this place?'

'Yes. I did not know it was here. My father came to us, he had been gone a long time, and he gave me that thing which I took to the farm.'

'The skin? With the field notes?'

'The writings, yes. My father is old and he was tired because he had run for many days. And there were others before him. They brought the writings to my father and he put them in my hands. There was no food and no time for him to hunt. He ran all the time. He was very tired, and sick, but still he ran.'

Max tried to put the pieces together. Max's dad needed him to come to this cave, to tell him where to go, so he had sent word through the Bushmen, and eventually !Koga became the messenger and Max's guide. Like a whale's song in the ocean, the message had reverberated across the wilderness, and the Bushmen had understood and carried it onwards until finally Max had arrived. He watched !Koga eating, quick to avert his eyes when the boy looked up. He knew so little about !Koga. All Max's attention had been on himself, his father, his problems, the how-tos and whys and wherefores. Somewhere out there, !Koga's family roamed while their son honoured his father and did his duty in bringing an unknown white boy towards his own father, who had drawn these pictures which seemed to have convinced the Bushmen that he would help them somehow.

The day's exertions finally claimed them and, before the last of the meat was eaten, they curled up next to the warm stones around the fire and slept.

*

A deafening crash snatched Max from his scattered dreams as a lightning strike hit the mountainside opposite. The boys were on their feet in seconds, alert for any danger, but, realizing it was only a violent storm, they moved to the mouth of the cave for a better look. A flurry of wind scattered the fire's cold ashes; the moonlight shaped and reshaped the black rolling clouds, and the air was heavy with the threat of rain. As another lightning strike illuminated the mountain across the valley, Max could see a swarm of shadows scurrying in terror.

'He-who-sits-on-his-hands,' !Koga said.

Max didn't understand, and then looked more closely. The lightning's brief and intense floodlighting showed him more than a hundred baboons scurrying for shelter. Baboons! !Koga meant baboons. However, before he could watch them any longer a cloud tumbled down the mountain behind the boys and smothered them in a grey fog. The air chilled quickly as the wind tugged at the cloud, tearing it from the cliff face. Max held out a hand, feeling the damp air, wanting the rain, but none came; only a dew-like residue clung to the rocks. And then the brief swirling assault ended. The rolling storm passed and they were left with the crystal night sky and the first edging of dawn. The baboons had fled into the crocodile-toothed mountains.

Once again the vastness was silent.

Max gazed out into the night. The never-ending land crept into the darkness, beckoning him, daring him to enter.

An enemy in waiting.

The stench of disinfectant almost made Kallie gag. Being used to the unsullied air of the desert, the impact of the confined police station, with its claustrophobic corridors, noisy holding areas and humanity shoved together in close proximity, made her skin itch. This was a world she never saw in the wilderness. She tried to keep her eyes averted from arrested men shouting abuse at their captors or women screaming through their drunkenness; cage doors rattled closed, a cleaner mopped the floor and Mike Kapuo finally guided her through this maze into the sanctuary of his office.

His once-starched shirt, now crumpled and sweat-stained, refused to stay tucked in his waistband, and his efforts to confine it inside his trouser belt failed. It always had; even when he was a boy at school, his shirt had had a life of its own and hung like a tail. Mike Kapuo was a bruiser who liked his food. He was a tall man whose belly hung over his trousers; his sausage-size fingers made the big handgun he carried look like a child's toy. Despite his bulk, though, he could move fast when occasion demanded, and he had boxed for the police service until he was nearly forty years old, a record for a heavyweight. That was where he first met Ferdie van Reenen; they were opponents in the ring, and Kallie's father was the man who had stopped him from becoming the champion by knocking him out in the fourth round. They had been good friends ever since. Nowadays Kapuo left the more physical demands, such as villain-chasing on foot, to younger men. At fifty-seven years of age he should already have retired, but he loved the job and his staff loved him, even though he could be a hard taskmaster. Only the criminals were distressed by his staying on in the CID. Kapuo cared about people being hurt by the callous and self-serving attitudes of others.

'You shouldn't be down here at this time of night,' he told her.

'Where else would I find you?'

He smiled. This was one determined girl; if he had been out on one of his deep-sea fishing trips, she'd probably have swum out to reach him if there was an important enough reason. And for her to be here, it had to be important.

'You weren't just passing by, then?' he teased.

He poured her a cup of coffee which resembled river mud but was hot and tasted sweet, which was exactly what she needed.

'Your dad OK?' he asked. It wouldn't be the first time Kapuo would have had to help Ferdie van Reenen. The last time Kallie's father had tackled a gang of poachers – he went after them with a vengeance and a shotgun – he had got himself badly hurt. If Kallie hadn't got to Kapuo and he in turn had not reached Van Reenen, the poachers would have got a lot worse than the few years in jail they'd received.

'He's fine. He's up at Kunene with some birders.'

'Uh huh.' Kapuo waited. She was sipping the coffee, first looking at him, then letting her eyes gaze away around the untidy room – not that Kapuo thought it was untidy. He knew where everything was.

'I think I've got a problem,' she finally said.

'More of a problem than my lousy coffee?'

'Worse.'

She hesitated. He waited.

'I think someone is trying to kill a boy I know,' she said carefully.

He looked at her. Kallie van Reenen was her father's daughter and, like him, would never say anything just for effect. 'And why would you think that?'

'Because I think they've just tried to kill me as well.'

Lucius Slye was an orderly man. He insisted on making his own bed in the morning because the servants did not fold the sheets correctly at the corners. His toothbrush, razor, hairbrush, toothpaste tube and hair gel – to keep his thinning hair from leaping from his scalp in a frenzy of static the moment he stepped anywhere near the hi-tech equipment – were all neatly laid out next to his spotlessly clean washbasin. Neatness, tidiness, orderliness, cleanliness and attention to detail were exactly what Slye needed in order to function. He did not have the emotional resources of Shaka Chang which enabled him to adapt to any changing situation with animal cunning. No, Mr Slye needed a controlled environment in which to function at maximum efficiency. Which is why he hated loose ends. And ever since the Gordon boy had been in Africa, loose ends were squirming like a basketful of snakes, not that he had ever seen a basketful of snakes – he would probably scream and faint if he did. Like many cruel-minded men, Slye was a coward at heart.

He had suggested that Shaka Chang might just consider following up the failed attempt on Max's life at the airport with an attack on the Van Reenen farm. But Chang had said no to that. That would attract far too much attention. At least the airport violence could be thought of as a personal attack, a mugging that had got out of hand. Chang did not want to complicate matters by causing harm to outsiders.

'Let events unfold, Mister Slye,' Chang had told him. 'The wilderness or our men will finish off the boy.'

But they hadn't yet, had they? Mr Slye was a good employee and he knew he needed to relieve some of his master's burden – because Chang *was* his master; he held the power of life and death over him. Chang, Slye believed, had enough to worry about. There was the massive hydroelectric scheme that would generate billions of dollars; there were the illegal drug shipments coming in from all over the world through Walvis Bay, and then there was the not-inconsequential matter of the destruction of the natural habitat and the thousands of people who would probably die as a result of Chang's plan. And that is why Mr Slye had taken it upon himself to remove one of the loose ends – Kallie van Reenen.

She had taken the boy from Windhoek Airport and equipped him for his journey. Slye had tracked her northwards to the remote airfield where she met her father. He had left with a safari party so he was not involved, but his informers had told him of the girl's flight plan filed for Walvis Bay. That was a long way from home. She had information she should not have, that was Mr Slye's conclusion. It had not taken much to ensure that one of his local men fixed her plane, guaranteeing it would crash.

Most satisfyingly, he had heard her Mayday call over Skeleton Rock's radio transmitters.

Even more gratifying was the sound of an explosion and the girl's scream. Mr Slye was convinced that Kallie van Reenen must have crashed in the middle of nowhere. In the unlikely event of the crash site ever being found, an investigation would conclude that her old plane was simply not reliable enough.

In the meantime, hyenas and jackals would dispose of her remains.

He flipped open his PDA and ticked off one item on his list of things to do. It read: Kill Kallie van Reenen.

Kallie had done her pre-flight checks as always, but when she took off she thought the engine sounded ragged. She had pushed in the throttle, gained take-off speed and hauled the plane into the sky.

Within an hour she knew she was in trouble. There was the unmistakable smell of avgas, the engine shook violently in its mountings, followed almost immediately by a loss of power. The aviation fuel was flooding the engine compartment at just about the same time as her brain flooded with fear at falling out of the sky. Fire was her immediate concern, so there was no point in trying to restart the engine. The Cessna 185 was known among pilots as a tail-dragger, difficult at take-off and landing; if she managed to land without power, she was going to need all her skill to come out of it in one piece. The plane's nose dropped, the propeller whirled of its own volition, nothing more than a windmill. Her training kicked in. Calmly but urgently, she banked the plane into the start of a sweeping arc, away from the rocky hills piercing the dunes ahead, all the time looking for a suitable landing site. She flicked the radio dial to the emergency frequency: 121.5 megacycles. 'Mayday, Mayday, Mayday,' she called. The international distress signal sounded unreal, coming from her own lips. It was something she had never expected to say. 'This is Victor Five, Bravo Mike November . . . Mayday, Mayday, Mayday . . .'

And then there was a bang and she was spattered with fluid. She yelled in fright, wiped her eyes clear and brought the plane back under control as best she could. No more time for Mayday signals, she had to get the plane down.

Without the comfort of any response from her radio message – there was a real chance that there was no one close enough to hear her cry for help – she gave one last shout for help, giving her location as best she could, and felt her stomach churn as the plane dropped in a swallow-like curve towards the ground.

The wind whistled through the cockpit, the death of the engine eerily shrouding her in its silence. She was losing altitude rapidly now, the plane was shaking and the vibration shuddered into her arms through the controls. She got her airspeed down to eighty knots, which was near perfect for gliding. A needle-thin strip of track drew a line in the sand in the far distance, and another led for several kilometres to a remote farmhouse. She swooped and curved through the sky, using the configuration to bring the plane lower and lower, trying to get it into the correct landing position. It was tricky and dangerous; she needed to apply the plane's flaps in the moments before landing, and if she misjudged her rate of descent and final approach she would end up careering off the track. Once the flaps were down, she would be totally committed to the landing. If it was deep sand down there, it would suck in the wheels and cartwheel the plane – and that would probably kill her. She side-slipped the aircraft, allowing it to remain at a reasonable speed, and by watching the relative motion of the intended point of touchdown through the windscreen she fine-tuned the rate of descent. Whatever the outcome, she knew she would be alive or dead in less than a minute.

A final banked curve, the controls juddered, she levelled out, eased the nose up, shoved the flap levers down and felt the wheels bounce.

The wheels skidded across the hardened surface and she guided the trusty old plane to a final standstill.

Silence.

Then she heard the sound of metal creaking: the engine cooling down.

She sat for a moment, letting her relief at her survival wash over her. And then she laughed. She had brought a crippled aircraft down safely in some of the most frightening minutes of her young life, and she was covered in Tobias's Desert Buster Ice-Cold Special.

It was the flask that had exploded. She licked some of it from her face. It tasted better than at any other time she could remember.

Mike Kapuo listened carefully to her story. She told him everything that had happened since she had picked Max up at Windhoek Airport, why he was in Namibia and then finally recounted her own terrifying experience.

'You're certain it was sabotage?'

'Yes, I thought I didn't recognize the mechanic when I went back to my plane. The fuel injectors had been loosened – they came away after about an hour's flying – and a piece of the braided pipe had been replaced with a length of plastic tubing.'

'So what? I've done the same with the fuel line on one of

my old cars. That's not proof of sabotage or attempted murder.'

'Yes it is,' she insisted. 'Avgas melts plastic. It was enough to get me up into the air, and then it was only a matter of time. If the injectors had not rattled loose, then the pipe would have melted. It was double insurance to bring me down.'

He nodded without saying anything. She was streaked with dirt, grained in from her journey into Walvis Bay on the back of a farmer's pick-up. Kapuo knew the after-effects of trauma; she would need food and rest.

'We'll talk tomorrow. You're coming home with me.'

'Mike, I can't.'

'Yes you can. I'll have someone go out and look at your plane, and we'll thank the farmer who brought you in.'

'You do believe me?'

'Yes, I do. I saw an inter-departmental report about two men being severely injured at Eros Airport the day you picked up this Max Gordon boy. They were known hard men, who hired themselves out for any unpleasant work that needed doing. We've also had a report on this boy's missing father for a few weeks now, but initial searches gave us nothing. We figured he was either dead or dying. You know how it is out there.'

'Max's father sent a letter to England from here, in Walvis Bay. And this guy he works with, someone called Leopold, he was here as well,' Kallie told him.

Kapuo hesitated, debating with himself how much he should tell her. How much might his friend's daughter know? Kapuo folded his jacket over his arm and eased her out of the office. 'You need a hot bath and some of Elizabeth's cooking. We'll tackle this whole thing tomorrow morning.' His wife's food and a decent bed for the night would bring the girl down to earth a little. Lower her defences.

If she had useful information, he could pass that on to the man in England who was hunting the boy and his father.

9

The chilled night cramped their muscles, and for a long time Max had lain, staring into the cave's void, knowing his father had been there and had left a message. Only the exhausting anxiety of not knowing what that message meant finally sent him to sleep.

!Koga shook him awake and, as he rubbed what little sleep he had from his eyes, gestured Max to follow him to the mouth of the cave. !Koga pointed, smiling contentedly. '*!ko-gnuing-tara* – the Dawn's Heart,' he said.

Max looked. Low on the horizon was a fat ball of light. Max had seen that star before. Where? Years ago when they were in Egypt, his father had woken him early, wrapped him in a blanket and taken him out into the cold desert dawn. He pointed. 'See that light? That's Jupiter.' Max realized that's what the drawing in the cave meant. His father was pointing to the 'morning star' – the planet Jupiter, the Dawn's Heart. Telling him where to go: east, beyond those mountains. Max smiled. The dawn swept away his self-doubt as the storm had blown away the clouds of darkness.

Max ran with renewed energy towards the rising sun. Spears of light shot through the ragged mountain peaks. His long strides kept up comfortably with !Koga, whose feet seemed barely to touch the ground. The grass was still sparse, barely ankle-deep, but it made the ground softer underfoot and running easier. They had clambered down the slope from the cave and pushed hard to reach the opposite mountainside, whose sweeping grassland curved up to embrace massive, sculptured boulders. The baboons had raced for the safety of the rocks during the night's storm, so as they drew closer !Koga slowed the pace. The last thing they wanted was to burst unannounced into a baboon colony's breakfast; their curved, razor-sharp canines could inflict lethal wounds. !Koga stopped as Max caught up with him. They were halfway up the mountainside, a thousand metres from the summit, where the jagged teeth barred any entrance. Down at this level the ground undulated, and if they stayed on course they could skirt the mountain range using these lower slopes – but they had to negotiate their way through the baboons.

A gateway through the boulders led them to a three-sided bowl in the hillside: a small amphitheatre of grassland and trees, which offered shelter from severe storms and a collection point for any precipitation. Max and !Koga stood in silence. To reach the far side they would have to walk for at least a kilometre through what looked like a couple of hundred feeding and grooming baboons. The boys had not yet been noticed. 'Walk slowly, yes?' !Koga told him.

'You bet,' Max said, licking his lips nervously.

Although they were scattered across the grassland, the baboons were in family groups; at various points big male baboons stood guard, watching over their females and offspring.

'The big baboons . . .' !Koga indicated them with a lift of his chin.

'The males?' Max asked.

'Yes. They come for you, they run at you, like attack . . . you stay. Stand still. They want to see if you a threat. OK?'

'Oh yeah, I'll invite them for tea while I'm at it.' !Koga seemed uncertain about Max's sarcastic answer, so he reassured the Bushman boy. 'I'll close my eyes and think of England. I won't move.'

From somewhere ahead came a sound like a guttural dog bark. One of the guardian baboons had sounded the alarm. A sudden ripple of fear ran through the troop; youngsters ran to their mothers, but it was not the boys' presence that had frightened them. The baboons crouched, looking up. A shadow drifted across them. Max searched the sky. A martial eagle had stepped off a high peak and glided into a thermal. The warm morning air carried him easily across the gathered baboons, but he was still too high to swoop and make an attack on any vulnerable youngster. !Koga tugged at Max's arm. This was a good time to make their way through the distracted baboons.

After a few minutes the huge eagle, showing first its dark-brown back feathers, then its speckled white chest, curved lazily in the air and drifted away. Perhaps it had spotted easier prey further down the valley. Max reckoned it was big enough to take a small antelope, so a young baboon would certainly not have posed a problem for the winged predator, which could strike with stunning power. Its talons could pierce a skull, biting deep into the base of the brain, causing instant death. Then it would carry the prey to its nest and dismember the carcass, tearing out the intestines, severing the head and limbs to be eaten. The baboons obviously knew the ominous reality of the raptor's shadow.

The danger passed, and now Max and !Koga were in the midst of the baboons. One of the males stood on its hind legs, watching them from a distance; the others returned to their nit-picking duties while the youngsters played in a chattering, raucous rough-and-tumble. A huddle of boulders lay in Max and !Koga's path; baboons scattered as they approached. Some of the rocks were scooped out, worn down by centuries of weather and baboon activity; now they acted like the granite drinking troughs Max knew from Devon. A distant memory, Devon: gentle, forgiving Devon, where the enfolding hills nurtured the traveller into meandering pathways and fields, where the wildest creature likely to be seen might be a barn owl looking for fieldmice. Max's mind wrenched back to reality. The baboons had stopped whatever they were doing and were watching them.

!Koga crouched at one of the basins; his hand tickled the water and brought it to his lips. 'It is from the storm. It tastes good.'

Carefully they edged closer to the water. Would the baboons fiercely protect their invaluable resource or let them share it? Max pulled off his bush hat and peered down at his reflection. The shadow of the boulders above the drinking rock blacked out the sky, creating a mirror-like image on the water's surface. He gazed down at himself. The reflection that stared back looked nothing like the boy who had started his quest only days earlier. His fair hair was tufted and streaked with dirt – who needed hair gel when days of dust and sweat did the same job for free? He was different – leaner, gaunt even, and the caked dirt made him look older. His eyes were red-rimmed from the sun's glare, and his tears of the previous night had washed a couple of tracks in the grime. Beneath the dirt a tanned, weather-beaten face glared back at him. He looked like a wild man. And maybe now he was.

Without another thought he dipped his cupped hands into the cool water and drank thirstily. Then he pushed his head under, scratched his fingers through his hair, and rubbed his face. As he pulled free of the rock pool a baboon took fright and fled, chattering. Maybe Max was more acceptable as a dirt-clogged creature from the bush. He knew he had not contaminated a drinking hole, other rock faces spilled water as baboons leaned forward and sipped. A young baboon sitting in a rock bowl gazed back at him like a boy in a bath, then dragged one hand over its head, spiking its own short hair, punk-like. Max pulled the binoculars from his shirt to stop them banging against the rock and put them down next to him on his bush hat, as he took another luxurious wallow.

Lifting his head clear, he snorted dust and mucus from his nose. He would never take water for granted again. It was sobering to think how much of the precious liquid he wasted at home. He gazed out across the curved hillside. Watching the baboons was a momentary diversion. Max sensed their caution at his presence, but they did not seem to register any threat.

!Koga's gleaming, dripping face emerged from another pool. 'Max,' he said quietly.

Following his gaze, Max saw that the punk baboon had stolen his hat and binoculars. Max tentatively reached out towards it, but it jumped back and scurried into another's arms, where they hugged and gazed warily at him. Max needed those binoculars. He stepped carefully towards the youngsters. A bark warned Max. He turned. A big, heavily built male was stalking towards him. Its front paws supported muscled shoulders and the mane of long hair around its neck and shoulders made it look even more threatening. It was a metre tall and the dog-like muzzle snarled as it barked again. Max stood still, sensing the ripple of tension in the animals around him. The baboon bared its fangs. Max saw !Koga slowly ease an arrow into his bow. 'Don't kill it, !Koga. It'll be OK.'

'I don't know,' !Koga replied. 'Maybe not. He is the leader. Others will attack if he does.'

Max glanced around. !Koga was right. The warning bark had alerted other males. The strict hierarchy of the baboon troop meant that the older juveniles, often acting as scouts for the troop, rallied when the danger call came from the leader. Other males stayed with their families but were nevertheless alerted.

Max reassured !Koga. 'We'll walk away . . . slowly.'

Once in a while Max had come across kids at school who were stronger than he, and there was always the odd bully to contend with. Despite best intentions, some kids just had to exert their dominance, and Max had had a couple of scraps at school. There was Baskins and Hoggart, two of the older boys. They got out of hand at times. If they weren't looking for a scrap with someone else, they would rough and tumble each other. Whatever the outcome, it meant a few bruises, but this baboon with its razor-sharp teeth was way above the Baskins and Hoggart league – this was the equivalent of a knife-wielding, streetwise kid with a very bad attitude. If there weren't something to hand for self-defence, then a fast sprint for self-preservation brought no shame. Only Max would never outrun this bruiser. He flinched as the baboon coughed another bark and with a snarl charged to within four metres of where Max now stood with his back to the rocks. The other baboons began to join in, their screeches and threats sounding like a badly out-of-control football crowd.

'Next time he will really attack,' !Koga shouted, bringing attention to himself from the other young males. The height of the boulders offered some immediate sanctuary, but that would be short-lived once the frenzy spread. It was not much of a choice: an attack would come sooner or later.

'I want a chance to get out of this, !Koga. We walk slowly, and then we run. All right?'

!Koga gazed at the confident boy who stood unflinching before the baboon's agitated aggression.

'We'll run like hell, !Koga, once we reach those rocks over there. You ready?'

!Koga nodded and eased his back along the boulders, watching the gathering juveniles, who were eager for combat, once their leader attacked. Almost shoulder to shoulder, the boys edged away. Within moments, one of the juvenile males broke ranks and charged. The screaming, indignant bark of the leader barely stopped the young baboon before it reached Max – who smelled its fetid breath and saw the ragged spittle hanging from its lips. It was an image momentarily frozen and Max realized, as he gripped the hunting knife in his fist, he would fight for his life if need be.

Together, the boys eased away from the advancing baboons

– it seemed like a small army was gathering around them. It was a hundred or more metres before they could reach the rocks, allowing them to put on a turn of speed. The rocks would divide the advancing baboons and give the boys a chance of reaching the flatter, wider plain beyond the fringe of the mountains.

Eighty metres: females and younger baboons were screeching, knowing there was danger, uncertain as to where it came from . . . seventy . . . Max and !Koga glanced behind them: the ground was uneven but, providing they did not fall, reaching the rocks looked possible before an attack. Should they risk turning their backs and run now? Fifty metres: the juvenile baboons were making darting attacks against both boys, another big male baboon took up a flanking position; this was going to be a concerted attack when it came and the experienced males would lead it. Thirty metres: and it was still too far. Max looked across to !Koga. The boy shook his head. They were not going to make it after all.

'Get ready, !Koga, we have to go for it now!'

Max sensed the quivering anticipation in the startled looks of the baboons and felt his own energy gathering to explode. Then suddenly a shadow swept across them all.

The shrieking peaked. The commanding voice of the leader barked above them all and the baboons were unleashed. They surged towards Max and !Koga, who were helpless. Blurred images – fragments of his mother and father – slammed through Max's mind. He saw !Koga level his spear in readiness. This was it! A fight to the death. He sucked in air to scream his defiance.

But the horde swept past them, jostling them, the juveniles

now taking the lead, scouting ahead, leading the troop to safety beyond the place of exposed danger.

A reprieve!

Max and !Koga reacted instinctively and ran with them, pounding across the ground, immersed in the baboons' hysteria. They were safe amidst the panic. The blackness fell across them again, but it was not the shadow of the hunting eagle. The darkness belonged to a far more dangerous creature.

Five hundred metres above the desperate baboons, the silent predator rose higher on a thermal spiral. On huge, featherless wings stretched across a skeletal frame, like those of a prehistoric pterodactyl, it whispered through the sky. The glider's Perspex cockpit, an all-seeing eye, held Shaka Chang, the body-hugging cocoon tight around his muscular frame. Each day he would fly, an observer of his world around him. Slye had tried to contact the men sent to kill the boys, but their radio transceiver responded with a lion's rumbling growl and the sound of it being scraped across the ground. They could only imagine that a lion was scuffing it like a plaything as Slye's voice called vainly in the wilderness. Chang was indifferent to the men's fate and this morning's flight served only to acquaint him with the terrain from where the boy, a suspected enemy, might emerge – or where he had perished. Chang liked to know everything about those who were trying to interfere with his plans, and ultimately he trusted only his own eyes.

Chang gazed down at the fleeing baboons. He thought he saw a shape, different from the others, but the warm air scooped him upwards and obscured his vision. He heeled the glider around again and swept low across the broad, sloping mountainside, his glider chasing its shadow across the ground. The baboons clambered into rocks, seeking shelter from the perceived threat. Chang twisted left and right, searching for the figures that had caught his eye. Nothing. Only terrified monkeys – no different, he thought, from most of the human race, content to move across the barren expanse of their lives in herds of mindless obedience. Once again he banked into the thermal and felt the surge of nature's power lifting him above and beyond the mountain range. Power he could control.

On the far horizon, cumulonimbus, the king of clouds, gathered a storm-threatening army. Even Chang would not venture into that awesome turbulence. It was like a nature god, and any intruder would be tossed and ripped apart by the contained force the clouds held. Stacked like multiple atomic explosions climbing sixty kilometres high, their bonds would finally be broken and would release tonnes of rainwater, flooding the landscape below, then Shaka Chang's dam would restrain the power of that water. And that control would give him command of life or death over the whole region.

Everyone needed water. Diamonds and gold were mere trading commodities, crystals and metal made glorious by the vanity of man; but he would still take them when they were thrust into his hands as payment for releasing the life-giving energy he had entrapped. But before that happened, those self-same rains would carry out the first step of Chang's plan. They would scour the Earth's underground caves and fissures, carrying a plague of death, to destroy human and animal life for thousands of kilometres. Governments would then give even more for Shaka Chang's unsullied water. And all that could stand between him and domination was a fifteen-year-old boy and the knowledge he might hold. And it was only that boy's power over him that caused Shaka Chang a moment of doubt.

Satisfied that the harsh landscape below offered but a meagre chance of survival for anyone foolish enough to challenge it, he eased the glider towards the heavens. Two hundred kilometres away, he would swoop from the sun like an all-powerful god and descend to earth, returning to Skeleton Rock, the earthly home of a celestial warrior. The bringer of chaos and destruction which were the instruments of success.

The rains were coming soon.

Sheltering under the lee of the rocks, !Koga and Max kept their faces turned away from the silent hunter. Who could be flying a glider out here? Was it a wealthy farmer indulging a hobby, or was there a more sinister reason for the silent approach? It was not worth risking being seen, and they hoped they had not been. Once the quivering wings had lifted the slender body across the mountains, the boys broke cover and ran. The baboons, still terrified, offered no threat. And provided the glider did not return, they were free to run as far and as fast as their legs could carry them into the distant scrubland and the safety of the trees.

Max and !Koga pushed themselves onwards; Max was convinced that, if his father's cave message had shown them the way, there would be other clues waiting somewhere ahead. They ran across open savannah flecked with thorn trees, moving deeper into more shaded areas. Soft-topped grasses undulated, their feathered tips touched with dust and sunlight. It was getting too hot to move at this pace, and Max slowed to a walk, but !Koga urged him on: he would crouch and, with extended thumb, point out animal tracks to Max, explaining that predators had also sought shade but were far enough away not to pose any immediate danger. Finally !Koga knelt and placed his hand in a darkened blemish in the sand: the remains of an old fire. 'They are near.'

'Who?' Max asked.

'Those who helped your father. My family.'

When Mike Kapuo took Kallie home, Elizabeth, survivor of thirty-two long-suffering years as a policeman's wife, hugged her, let her soak in a hot bath, and then fed her the usual scrumptious meal that she always managed to feed to her family. Two sons, a daughter and now grandchildren, not counting waifs and strays like Kallie, all sat around the big kitchen table next to the solid-fuel stove that Elizabeth Kapuo refused to be parted from, even though they sweltered in the summer months. It was as comfortable a family home as anyone could wish for, and Kallie was envious. The pain of her own parents' divorce had never left her. Her father was like a modern-day buccaneer. He was a free spirit who would die for his family, but getting him to stay at home was impossible. Kallie had grown up quickly, and being stuck out on the farm gave her a stubborn strength, but while she was wrapped in the warmth and friendliness of the Kapuo family, she allowed herself to relax. Finally, unable to swallow another morsel of food, she gratefully fell into bed.

She woke up the next day with dawn still an hour away. Suburban sounds had roused her from fractured dreams. The house still slept and, as she made her way towards the kitchen to make coffee, she walked past a room whose door was slightly ajar, as if the latch had not caught; a shaft of light cut into the passageway. There was a gentle scratching sound which she could not identify. She carefully opened the door wider. Mike Kapuo obviously used the room as an office. The desk lamp was still on and papers and files were evident – Mike had probably been working late. A cat was licking itself on the desk, its claws gripping the sheets of paper beneath it. That was the scratching noise Kallie had heard. The cat had obviously spent a comfortable, undisturbed night under the warmth of the lamp. But then Kallie's movement at the door made it leap from the desk in fright, scattering papers across the floor.

Kallie muttered under her breath. Why hadn't she just minded her own business? She scooped up the papers and tapped them together into a tidy pile, but as she went to put them back on the desk she saw a name typed on a sheet of paper and the air suddenly became even colder. 'Tom Gordon: Missing Presumed Dead'. It was a police search report, dated a couple of weeks earlier. She scanned the single sheet. It was a cursory read, full of police-speak jargon; a pseudo-formality that police forces all over the world adopted, as if the clunky language made it all the more serious. She didn't care, she kept reading. It had obviously been a search conducted with limited resources, which would have made it virtually impossible to find anyone presumed injured in the thirstland.

She thumbed through the rest of the papers. At least a dozen sheets had something to do with Max's father. It took her only a few moments to realize that the papers the cat had spilled belonged in a folder that had been left open on the desk. She went to the door, quickly checked that no one was moving in the house, eased the door closed again and got down on her knees. She spread the sheets out on the floor, angling the lamp down.

The folder was like a detective's case-file. Description of the missing man, reports from search teams, the one-page summary she had just read, a photocopy of the area searched. There was nothing that seemed to offer any new evidence or information about Tom Gordon. She put the papers back together and put the file back on the desk. As she did so, her fingers touched another file, closed this time, but with the edges of photographs showing. She opened the folder. The black-and-white pictures were of a man's body being pulled out of the harbour. Click. Click. Click. Photo after photo taken by a police photographer. The victim finally ended up on his back, the feet of the policemen, just in frame, turned away from him. They had done their job now. It all had the cold, calculating feel of distant emotions, of routine. Of matter-of-fact death.

A square of official information had been glued to the top left of the picture. Date and time when the photos were taken; the name of the police photographer, and finally the name of the deceased (if known).

It was.

Leopold. Anton Leopold.

And someone had scribbled a reminder to themselves on a Post-it note, stuck to the inside of the folder. The pictures of the dead man were bad enough, but the message made her feel physically sick: 'Tell Peterson'.

Thousands of kilometres away, the mists of Dartmoor settled, refusing to move until the next weather front shifted them with a hefty gust of wind. Life was going on as normal for Sayid despite his frustration at not being able to get into Mr Peterson's room to bug his phone. Having practised on his own room's door lock, he had learned how to tease the tumblers and open it, but Peterson's door had a more efficient lock and he failed in his attempt to pick it. If only everything were electronic, he would have had it hacked and opened in minutes. What was the good of progress if these archaic door-locking devices were still around? He kept the small transmitter tucked in his pocket in case he saw Peterson leave his door open. He would need less than thirty seconds to slip the bug into the telephone's casing.

After Kallie's telephone call, Sayid sent an email through to Farentino, using the name Magician, just as Max had instructed him, ensuring his own identity could not be traced or revealed. He told Max's protector what he knew – which was precious little. There was the information about Eros in Namibia; that someone called Leopold was supposed to meet Max; that someone powerful was going to cause chaos out there and that Max . . . well, Max was totally alone and could not be contacted. Sayid also told Farentino that a local girl had helped Max move north-east. And that was all he knew. Sayid decided not to mention Mr Peterson until he found out more for himself – he desperately needed to get that bug into his telephone.

Sayid walked determinedly along the corridor to check once more if Peterson had left his room, giving him another crack at the lock. Thoughts of Max weighed heavily on his mind when suddenly Peterson's voice echoed along the granite walls. 'Sayid! One moment.' Sayid stopped in his tracks, caught completely off guard by Peterson's stealth. One minute he wasn't there, the next . . . 'Where are you off to, Sayid?'

'I was . . . er . . . I was . . . I went to see Mister Simpson about the details for next week's cross-country run,' he lied quickly, clutching the transmitter in his pocket.

'Mister Simpson is supervising homework. You know that.'

'Yes, sir. I lost track of time. Anyway – he wasn't there. Obviously . . . because he's . . . as you say . . .' It was all getting very lame, but Peterson seemed not to notice.

'I want to talk to you. I think my room might be best.' And he walked the few paces past Sayid and opened the door that Sayid had tried so assiduously to break into.

Given Mr Peterson's appearance of being clumsily attired, as if whatever came to hand became the clothing of the day, there was a surprising formality to his room. The books were neatly stacked and, from Sayid's first glance, seemed to be in order of category: geography, history, biography, caving, mountaineering, English literature. The desk was composed of two doors, balanced at each end by a couple of two-drawer filing cabinets as a base, so there was a great amount of space for the tidily stacked papers and the big map that lay, spread out, across it. Boots (wiped clean of mud), trainers and cross-country sandals sat on a shoe rack. It was a small room, kept under strict control. No television, but a digital radio and

CD combination, and a set of wireless headphones hooked on a purpose-made stand. Classical music CDs nudged language discs, which in turn nestled next to a wide variety of contemporary music.

'What?' Peterson asked, as Sayid looked around his room.

'It's a heck of a tidy place, sir.'

'I suppose it is. I don't see it that way. To me it's . . . ordered. When you're climbing, you need to know where every bit of kit is, sometimes in a hurry. It's less stressful knowing where things are, as I learned when I was in the army.'

'I didn't know you were in the army, sir. I thought you climbed mountains before you became a teacher.'

Sayid's brain was racing. If Peterson had been in the army, was he still connected somehow? He had read that some ex-soldiers worked in security or as mercenaries. What if someone had paid Peterson to arrange the attempt on Max's life? Sayid had to work hard to keep his imagination under control. He was in the room, and that was all that mattered. Now he had to keep things rolling until he could find a way of getting the small transmitter into Peterson's phone. He edged around the room. A cordless phone sat on one corner of the desk. The slide-off battery compartment on the handset might not offer enough room for the bugging device, but the base unit would serve just as well. Better, in fact, because the phone signal would go through there from the handset.

While he tried to think how to pull it off, he studied some watercolours on the wall, which weren't badly executed. One of them held Sayid's attention. It was of a mighty snow-covered peak – higher than those surrounding it. The setting sun bruised the sky, absorbed by the snow. Peterson noticed his interest. 'Mount McKinley,' the teacher told him.

'Alaska,' Sayid answered.

Peterson smiled and nodded. His geography teaching hadn't fallen completely on deaf ears then. He poured water into a kettle. There were two mugs, two spoons, sugar and milk, all to hand.

'Did you climb it?'

'Yes.'

'How high is it?' Sayid said, buying time.

'Twenty thousand three hundred and twenty feet – the north peak is a few hundred less. I still think in feet when it comes to mountains.' Peterson was making coffee for them both without asking if Sayid wanted any.

'Why not take pictures, sir? Why paint them?'

'Ah, well. Anyone can take a photo. Painting requires a certain eye, a certain attitude, I suppose it's almost a kind of meditation. You sit there, get absorbed by the subject . . . it's a skill I don't have.'

'Then you didn't paint these?'

Peterson handed Sayid the mug of coffee, studied the map on his desk for a moment, and turned it slightly so that Sayid could see it more clearly. It was a map of Namibia.

'No, I didn't. Max's father did.'

Max's father! Max had never mentioned to Sayid that Peterson knew his dad, and Sayid was certain that, if it was true, then Max certainly didn't know about it. And if that was the case, why wouldn't Max's dad have told him? Peterson had to be lying, trying to draw Sayid into giving information. It was sinister. Peterson was studying him closely and Sayid suddenly felt that the geography teacher was a lot more than he seemed.

'Max never went to Canada.'

'He didn't?' Sayid hoped his look of surprise was convincing.

'Has he contacted you?'

'No, I thought he was just getting over everything. Y'know, the attack and his dad . . .' He shrugged, there was nothing more to add.

Peterson tapped the map. 'I know he's in Namibia.'

Sayid gazed at the outline. It looked huge and empty – blimey, Max, just where are you? Sayid had to string this out as long as he could. 'Namibia,' he muttered as if he wasn't sure where it was.

Peterson smiled. 'Namibia. You know where I mean.'

'Oh yes, sir. I just can't believe he's there. I mean, why Namibia?'

Peterson watched him for a moment. Sayid felt as though he was being scanned by a magnetic resonance-imaging machine. Peterson's eyes seemed to go right through him. Sayid felt his stomach quiver. Peterson was starting to scare him, yet he had said nothing threatening or ominous.

'I want to find Max,' Peterson finally said. 'I want to help him. I believe he's in grave danger and I know people who can get to him, who might just save his life. He's out there in the wilderness and he's not equipped to survive. Whatever you can tell me will help him. Do you understand?'

Sayid nodded. These 'people' were probably the ones hunting Max right now. Sayid remembered the last text message Max had sent him. *Don't trust Peterson.* 'I wish I could tell you something, sir. Max is my mate, but . . . well, I just don't know anything.'

Before Mr Peterson could ask any further questions a sudden commotion exploded in the corridor. Two boys ran past at full tilt, yelling, followed by a terrific bang as they knocked over a bench and a picture above it. Baskins and Hoggart, the two boys who were always scrapping, were making a ruckus along the corridor.

Peterson strode to the door and shouted: 'You boys! Stop that! What the hell do you think you're doing?'

Baskins and Hoggart had given Sayid the chance he needed. He grabbed the phone's cradle and turned it over. The base had four small screws holding it together; although he had come prepared with a watchmaker's screwdriver, there was no time to undo them and slip in the tiny transmitter which now stubbornly refused to be held by his fingers as he searched for it in his pocket. The shouting outside stopped, there was a muted apology from the two boys, and Peterson told them to get back to their dorm. He was only a couple of dozen paces away now and heading back in. Sayid saw there was a small gap in the base beneath a plastic hook which the thin transformer cable could be wound around for storage. He finally teased the elusive bug from his pocket and dropped it into the hole. He would just have to hope that it would work.

No sooner had he turned the phone right side up and pretended to turn his attention back to the map of Namibia, than his mobile phone rang, making his already-stretched nerves jump. He flipped it open as Peterson came back into the room. Sayid couldn't take his eyes off the words on the blue screen.

'Something important?' Peterson asked. It sounded innocent, but Sayid knew it was a shorthand way of asking if the call had anything to do with what they had been discussing.

'Oh, er . . . just my mother . . . she's trying to find me. I was supposed to have extra lessons.'

Peterson seemed to accept the inevitable. 'All right, Sayid, get going. But if you hear from Max, I'd like to know. We'll talk again later.'

'Yes, sir.'

Sayid got out as fast as he could and ran for his room. Peterson had already picked up the handset and was about to make a call. Now the bug was in place, Sayid needed to get his computer up and running to organize the trace.

And there was another reason for hurry. The text message was from Kallie. Only six words, but they meant that Max was in a much more dangerous game than Sayid had realized. He had to erase the message in case Peterson appeared like a ghost and snatched the phone from him. He looked at the text again: `Leopold dead. Peterson knows. Max missing.`

Three points on the compass – Max, Sayid and Kallie.

And none of them could know that Max was only hours away from death.

10

The night brought ghosts.

Silver shadows flickered through the bony limbs of trees, making the dry grass flicker like will-o'-the-wisps. The moonlight played with the breeze, teasing Max's imagination as he sat diligently on guard duty. The boys were vulnerable to night predators, so while one slept the other kept watch. Max yawned, opening his eyes as wide as he could, and stretched away the fatigue that clawed at him. The moving shadows were enough to frighten him into wakefulness for a while, but even fear must ultimately yield to exhaustion. However, his drooping eyelids flew open again when a jackal's high-pitched, wavering call came from somewhere nearby. The slight breeze brought the twittering cries of a distant pack of wild hunting dogs. Perhaps they had made a kill somewhere.

Max's senses had been sharpened by enduring the wilderness. He now noticed small things, like a change in the breeze, where shadows offered some concealment and where there might be a sipping hole for water. Animal smells would carry on the faintest movement of air and he had learned to distinguish the different trails of antelope, hyena, mongoose and wild dogs. At every opportunity !Koga had shown him the tracks and scratch marks the animals made, though Max knew that, no matter how hard he scoured the ground, he was never going to be an expert like !Koga, who could recognize different species of birds from imprints in the sand. The Bushmen hunters could identify everything, from an ant's track upwards. And it was no textbook learning. !Koga knew things because he had seen them, touched them, tasted and smelled them, just as Max had learned to climb mountains and kayak the white water. As he had come to understand the lethal danger and dizzying fear of a rockfall and the smashing, intolerant water that held him under when it flipped his kayak, so had !Koga spent every day of his young life in touch with this wilderness.

Now, like !Koga, Max faced each waking hour in survival mode. No one else in the world existed except for the two of them. Thoughts of his father were like heat-haze mirages, an illusion. They would become reality only when Max saw and held his father. 'Live for today' took on a completely new meaning when life was so precariously balanced every hour.

'!Koga!'

Max heard the stampede start out of nowhere. Panic. Beasts in turmoil. Then he smelled the dusky odour of the animals and was momentarily uncertain where they were coming from because the deceptive light obscured their direction. !Koga knew instantly. The small herd of buffalo, maybe twenty or thirty of them, was confused, first charging in one direction and seconds later churning the dirt in another.

'Lions!' !Koga yelled and pulled Max away, running on a parallel course to the charging mass. 'They split herd!'

It was like a kind of madness. The grunting, heaving buffalo, themselves deadly and now terrified, and the boys running in the choking dust. Buffalo crossed their path, almost trampling them. They dodged and weaved, !Koga's voice being drowned by the thunder of hoofs. Max lost sight of !Koga, then saw him again, over on the right now, skirting the heaving mass. Max tried to reach him; the other boy had turned, still running, looking back for him. Max raised a hand but doubted whether !Koga could see it. 'I'm here, keep going! Keep going!' His voice impotent, his throat dry.

A buffalo was suddenly alongside and barged against Max, its tough hide rubbing his arm for only a fraction of a second. It was going so fast that it was past him before he could evade the shove. He twisted, falling into the sand, but rolled instinctively, praying that he wasn't in the path of another beast. Disorientated, he searched desperately in the darkness. The moonlight now sat on top of the mini dust storm, an eerie half-light that drew a line between earth and sky. No more than fifteen metres away, a lioness seemed to surf the silver wave as she rode the haunches of her victim and then sank below the surface again as she pulled it down. The herd came together again, moving on in another direction. The sounds of the kill faded and the stench of offal that had momentarily filled Max's nostrils was behind him somewhere in the darkness, and the yelping hyenas took their place in the hierarchy.

Max ran as best he could between the low-hanging branches and then he saw !Koga. The boy sat, nursing the back of an injured leg, looking as though he had been spilled out of a cement mixer.

'You all right?' Max asked when he got to him.

'I fell.'

'Me too. Is your leg broken?'

!Koga shook his head. 'A buffalo stood on me.'

'That was bloody clumsy of you,' Max said as he hauled !Koga to his feet. The boy carefully tested his weight. Nothing was broken, but it was very painful – several hundred kilograms of buffalo using you as a doormat, even if it pressed you into deep sand, was going to hurt for a while. What caused !Koga more distress was his broken bow. His pouch, the quiver, all had been smashed. Only the spear remained and !Koga used it to help balance himself.

Max put his friend's arm over his own shoulder and supported him as he hobbled along. His eyes scanned around them, watching for any shadow that might change into something more tangibly dangerous than his imagination. 'I hope your family haven't gone on their hols or anything, I could do with a bacon sarnie, or some beans on toast, even a Big Mac wouldn't be a bad idea . . .'

'Why are you talking stupid things?' !Koga smiled.

'Because I'm fed up of being scared to death and eating lizards.'

!Koga said nothing. They kept going, putting the lions' bone-crunching sounds far behind them.

Max had survived another day. One day at a time. Each footstep. Each thought. Closer to finding his father and his secret. He was confident he would win through. If all was fair in the world, he would have a decent crack at pulling it off. But nature did not understand fairness any more than !Koga comprehended a Big Mac.

No matter how skilled or lucky Max had become in his

survival, nature always struck when least expected. It would not be a crushing buffalo or the steel-like claws of a lion that would plunge Max into death.

Nature was sneakier than that.

As daylight came !Koga seemed to be moving more easily, and although their pace had slowed, they made good progress, leaving the mountains shimmering in a heat haze.

'There is a waterhole – small, enough for us. I know where. We must go there. We must drink.'

They had filled the small canteen at Baboon Hill, as Max now thought of it, but they had already drunk most of the water. !Koga was right, they must find water wherever they could.

A couple of dozen meerkats stood watching their progress from a safe distance, uncertain about the two upright apes that scuffed through the dust. Deciding to play safe, the meerkat whose job it was to warn of danger squeaked his alarm and they all turned tail, showed their backsides to the intruders, and ran for safety to their sand burrows. Max had been mooned before, but never by so many at once. He couldn't help feeling it was one for the record books and a story the boys at Dartmoor High would enjoy. It was hard to imagine life back home right now. He could not allow his mind to drift either, wondering if Sayid was trying to contact him, or whether the triathlon team had been chosen, or whether Mr Peterson was still at the school or had done a runner, once Max had evaded him and his people. He had to stay focused on where he was. Lack of concentration could have serious consequences.

After a few hours !Koga muttered something and gestured towards the horizon. Max searched the distance but whatever !Koga had seen eluded him. 'I don't see anything, !Koga.'

'Behind those trees, by the boulders. You see?'

Max scrunched up his eyes once more against the glare. Once, when his father had taken him on a trek through a German forest into the hills, he had taught him to find the way forward by looking at something in the near distance, then to find another further on, and further on still, then the eye identified distant objects more easily. Max let his eyes settle on a gully about three hundred metres away, then a clump of thorn trees at five hundred where the ground rose, and finally settled on a ravine marked by an untidy rock formation.

Vultures.

They hunched on the boulders, barely moving. Waiting.

Another two hundred metres beyond that, he saw a movement. Two long, pointed, symmetrical horns were swaying towards him, an animal's distinctive black-and-white face beneath them. 'Gemsbok,' !Koga said.

Max knew it was a big antelope, but it seemed too tall, in fact its head must have been almost two metres off the ground. !Koga smiled but said nothing, and he began limping towards it. Max looked again, his hands cupped around his eyes to shield them from the glare. He waited patiently, just as !Koga had taught him, and then he realized that there were men carrying meat and the antelope's skin. It was a hunting party returning home. !Koga's family.

*

Within an hour Max and !Koga reached a settlement. Beehive huts were being built by women, and children played and laughed in the sandy enclave of grass, shaded by giant camelthorn trees and half enclosed by the gnarled white stems of smaller shepherd's trees with their bushy green leaves. These half-dozen temporary shelters would serve as home for as long as the Bushmen wished.

The hunters had already arrived and the butchered carcass was being hung in chunks and strips on poles to dry. As !Koga and Max moved into sight, everyone stopped what they were doing. An old, prune-faced woman, wrinkled by more than half a century of living in the harsh sunlight, called !Koga's name, as if announcing him to everyone else. Max stayed where he was as !Koga went forward and was greeted, first by the men and then by the women. But everyone's eyes were on Max. !Koga was nodding and smiling as he spoke, and he turned and looked at Max. Then they fell silent. Max hated being the new boy at a party.

'I'm Max Gordon,' he said. But no one moved, spoke or even smiled. Then an old man, skinny as a rake, puffing away on a carved wooden pipe, rubbed a leathery hand across his stubbled head and said something. A murmur went around. A couple of kids had started to play again, but the women gathered them into their arms. Something important had just happened and Max was not certain what it was. The old man moved up to Max, stood in front of him, nodded, as if he knew him as an old friend, then placed a hand on Max's shoulder and spoke gently to Max's eyes. Max felt embarrassed, but the old man continued to talk, keeping his hand in place. After half a minute Max felt calmer, almost as if his mind had latched on to the soothing words without needing to know what was said. The old man took Max's hand and led him like a child towards the group.

!Koga said, 'You have seen the dream paintings. The old man is . . .' he searched for the words, '. . . *BaKoko* . . . he can cure sick people.'

'A medicine man?'

'No . . . I cannot explain.'

'You mean a shaman?' Max asked.

'I do not know that word. *BaKoko*. He can see the dreams. He can change into animals. Leopard. Eagle.'

'A shapeshifter?' Max said. He had seen enough films and read enough stories to know that humans do not change into animals without someone else's imagination. 'OK, he's a shaman. He is respected. I understand that.' Max decided diplomacy was better than disbelief.

'He knows the cave. He has seen the dream,' !Koga said.

Max almost groaned aloud. How could he tell them the cave paintings had been made by his dad to show him which direction to take, to find whatever it was he had to find? He could not bring himself to shatter their illusion. It was probably one of the few hopes these people nurtured.

They settled Max by a small fire, as guest of honour. The fire's ashes had long settled in the sand, but embers still smouldered. A group of men squatted nearby and !Koga sat opposite him. Tensions ebbed, the children played again, and the women returned to their hut-building. A woman was beckoned. She carried an ostrich egg. She knelt down and scraped away the top embers of the fire and fitted a narrow reed into a small hole in the top of the egg, then, pushing and turning a small blade into the base of the egg, blew into the straw. The yoke bubbled out into a battered tin bowl that the woman held beneath it. She then eased the slithering yellow into the embers of the fire. In a few minutes she turned it and cooked the other side. It looked like a big, fat naan bread Max used to order at his local Indian restaurant, about the size of a large dinner plate. He was suddenly ravenous. The woman broke the big omelette, which was quite firm, and handed half to him and half to !Koga. Max hesitated. His mouth was watering from the smell, but he did not want to deprive others of their food. This was definitely some kind of treat. He noticed, though, that !Koga was scoffing the food as quickly as he could. Max waited no longer. Being guest of honour had its compensations. He'd tell them about the cave paintings later.

Another half-dozen hunters entered the camp. They carried only small game caught in snares, but the older man at their head, who was warmly greeted by !Koga, looked towards Max. A woman gave the hunter something to drink, but the man never took his eyes off Max.

A small delegation formed: the shaman, this new hunter, !Koga and a few others. They came towards Max, who stood, respectfully, and waited. They shook hands, formally.

'I am this boy's father,' the hunter said, touching !Koga's shoulder. 'I have sent him so he might bring you to us.'

'You helped my father.' Max felt a quiver in his stomach, he was standing before the man who might have been the last person to have seen his father and who could help him.

'He is gone,' the hunter said.

'Where?' Was he being given hope?

'It was a place of death.'

Max felt his heart might burst out of his chest. Did the hunter mean his father was dead?

Max waited, barely able to stay silent. The hunter said something to !Koga and the others. They seemed to be in agreement. !Koga's father touched Max's arm, suggesting he sit in the shade. The men squatted and Max cushioned himself on the sand. The hunter asked a question of !Koga, placing his left hand beneath the elbow of the other, his fingers dangling like legs, making an image of an animal. What was the word that described that animal?

'Giraffe,' !Koga answered.

His father nodded. 'We tracked giraffe and in the place where the earth bleeds we killed him. It was a long chase, our poison took a long time, and then !Gam, one of our best hunters, he pushed his spear into its heart.'

'Is that the place of death?'

The hunter shook his head and indicated the camp. 'Four days from this place our people . . .' he showed six fingers, 'they die.' He put his fingertips into his mouth. 'They drink. And they die.'

'Was my father with them?'

'No. He saw our people die. He saw the men.'

'What men?' Max asked, sensing the danger lurking in the hunter's story, which of necessity had to be repeated to the others in their own language.

'White men, black men . . . far away. Your father followed, but he gave me the book of papers. I put them in a skin, we take them to a white man we trust. Many days. Many.'

'Was that Van Reenen?' Max prompted him.

'He is known as Van Reenen.'

'So where is my father?'

The man fell silent, either unable to answer or uncertain how to do so. Max pulled out the folded map. It was even more worn than when he started out from Kallie's farm. He pointed, just wanting them to look and, hopefully, to understand.

'Was it here? Here? Where? Can you tell me?'

The map meant nothing to any of the Bushmen. In the past there had been those among them who had been induced by promises of payment, liquor and food to help in the white men's war. They had gone to track and help kill an enemy the Bushmen did not know. They would have understood the story of the map, but they had long since died.

The hunter shook his head. He cut the air with the edge of his hand, showing direction. 'Four days from this place. The earth bleeds.'

Max did not understand.

'It is a place where there is water if you dig,' !Koga explained. And he confirmed what he said to his father and the others. So, it was a kind of watering hole or underground water supply, Max reasoned.

'Your father, a good man. He was afraid.'

'Afraid? My dad? I don't think so.'

'He was a brave man, but he was afraid. When he saw our people.'

So Dad was tracking down men who had killed Bushmen. Was that it? Max asked himself, what had he seen that scared him?

'Was my father on foot? Did he walk?'

'No. A truck, with the other white man.'

'There was someone else with my father?'

'Yes. I do not know him.'

Max knew that whenever his father had worked in southern Africa previously, he had engaged the services of Anton Leopold. That must have been the man with Dad, he realized.

The old man had barely stopped talking and !Koga listened for a long time before translating, speaking as if he were the voice of his father. 'Your father had an injured leg. But he was strong. He and the other man, they went away together after he gave me the papers which I brought to my son, who is young and who could make the journey, and who could speak to the whites. He took them to Van Reenen. That is all I know. But we were told you would come.'

Max gazed down at the map. The best he could hope for was to determine just where he was and the direction travelled that brought him there. North from Kallie's place, then pushed eastwards by the gunmen. After that they had moved north-north-east to the cave, and then east again from his dad's drawings. Given that he and !Koga had not gone in a straight line, the direction seemed clear on the map. Another four days' walking would take them to where the Bushmen died. There was nothing on the map to indicate where that might be. The Bushmen had their own names for places. So if he continued on this heading, it might eventually lead to his father. Or to further clues.

!Koga's father reached his hand out to touch Max's face. Max didn't flinch. The hunter's hand caressed his cheek for a moment, and he gazed at him. He whispered something barely audible, but everyone heard and muttered some kind of agreement.

Here we go again, Max told himself. This had something to do with the cave paintings, he was sure of it.

'Is this about the cave?' he asked !Koga, who nodded.

'Look . . . maybe it's not as it seems,' Max said tentatively. !Koga did not understand. 'I mean,' said Max, 'perhaps those drawings were done by someone else. Like . . . my dad, maybe.'

'Your father?'

'Yeah, like a message.'

'Your father could not have done those things.'

Max looked at the hunter. 'I think this has gone far enough,' he said. 'My dad did those pictures to try and show me where to go.' His voice was edgy.

None of the Bushmen showed any reaction. Then the hunter took Max's hand and held it between both of his. He seemed very sad, as if he was saying goodbye. The group turned away, but !Koga had reacted to the gesture from his father and said something that sounded angry. Throughout their whole ordeal so far, Max had never heard !Koga sound so upset. The men stopped, spoke to !Koga, soothing him with their words.

What the hell was going on? Max could only stand and watch their body language and listen to the tone of their voices. Once again !Koga raised his voice, but the old men just shook their heads and, with a final, almost pitying glance towards Max, went back to the others. !Koga stayed, kicking the dust, venting his own frustration. Then he too turned away.

'Hey. Hang on a minute,' Max said.

!Koga turned to face him, and Max saw there were tears in the boy's eyes. Max went to him.

'!Koga, what's up? Did I say something to upset everyone? If I did, I'm sorry.'

The boy shook his head.

'What then?'

'It is not for the telling,' !Koga almost whispered, as if unspoken words were wild creatures needing to be caged.

Now Max knew he must have made an almighty blunder. '!Koga, you'd better tell me cos I'm going to need help here. I'm going to need your father to take me to this . . . this "place where the earth bleeds".'

!Koga shook his head and turned away.

Max grabbed his arm. 'Tell me!' He loosened his grip. The two boys stared at each other.

'They say it was known you would come,' !Koga said, and then he paused before averting his eyes. 'And they said it was known that, when you came to us, then that was the time you would die.'

Max couldn't quite take that in for a moment.

'I'm going to die? Well . . . we all have to die. And we've been close a few times these last few days . . . Oh, come on, !Koga. You can't always believe in that stuff.'

!Koga interrupted him, touching his arm, gesturing to the encampment. 'Here. You will die here.'

Max took in the scene. It was probably the safest place he could be. A domestic gathering of huts, food being cooked, children playing, the sound of laughter. He was amid the gentlest and happiest people he had ever experienced. He was safe here.

'They're wrong,' Max assured him.

'No. They said you would die here.' There was a different look in !Koga's eyes. 'And that I would kill you.'

11

Kallie van Reenen left the house while everyone else was still sleeping. She felt wretched. The photos of the dead Anton Leopold and the note to Peterson confirmed that Chief Inspector Mike Kapuo, the man she and her father trusted, was connected to those hunting down Max. Not wanting her absence to initiate a search, she left a scribbled message telling Kapuo that she had gone into the city for a few hours and that she would return to his office later that morning. She knew she could not simply disappear, she had to see this through, so she mustn't arouse his suspicions.

Only Thandi Kapuo was awake when she left, and Kallie convinced her quite easily to let her use the girl's mobile phone to send an urgent text message to Sayid. Fourteen-year-old Thandi was currently grounded by her parents and no one was speaking to anyone, so helping Kallie was one way of getting back at her parents. Kallie felt some sense of relief that she had at least managed to warn Sayid about Peterson and his connections.

By the time she reached the docks, the port was busy. Shipping containers were stacked high, and cranes plucked them one by one and dropped them on to the backs of waiting trucks. Released air brakes hissed like steam engines urgently wanting their power set free. With a shift into gear, the long-haul trucks eased away to take their cargo to its final destination.

Kallie unfolded the photograph she had taken from Kapuo's file. It was a picture showing the location where Anton Leopold's body had been found. It took her a couple of hours, but she finally orientated herself and found the place. She looked at the photo again and saw that his body had been moved gently by the tide so that it was caught against a ship. She knew about prevailing winds which could push a plane off course, and tides did the same thing to anything afloat. The photograph was date- and time-coded. She checked her watch – about an hour and a half later in the day than when the picture was taken. The tide would have shifted quite a bit, but she could make allowances. The deep-water harbour would also have had a lot of shipping moving through the port, so the ebb and flow of the displaced water would have influenced where the body ended up, although there was no way she could ever work that out. She would stick with the tides, she decided.

''Scuse me, can you tell me when high tide is?'

The man with a clipboard, talking into a two-way connected to an overhead crane, had just guided a container down from ship to shore.

He looked at her, liking what he saw. She was attractive. The flying cap shielded her eyes, but he could see they were blue with a fleck of green, and she had a great smile. Maybe he was in with a chance.

'Why would you want to know that?' He smiled at her.

'My dad is buying me a kayak.'

'Lucky girl. But you should be over at the marina, not here.' The man couldn't take his eyes off her. There was a squawk on the radio which he ignored. Good-looking girls usually gave the likes of him a wide berth. 'You have to be careful out there. Tides are fast. And what with the trawlers over there and the seals, well, they bring in the sharks. You don't want to get tipped into the water. You shouldn't be wandering down here, either. Harbour's a rough place.'

Kallie glanced around. Dockside workers were coming and going, forklift trucks ferried smaller crates around. She was sure that if anyone tried anything, there were enough people around to help.

'I'm just checking the place out, there's a lot of shipping out there. All a bit scary.' She was unsure whether the look of worry on her face conveyed the right degree of helplessness.

'Yeah. It changes all the time. There's usually a couple of metres between tides. Look, I've got my break coming up, why don't we go and have a cup of coffee and I'll tell you whatever you need to know.'

'Thanks, but my dad wouldn't like that, I don't think.'

'Well, maybe you don't have to tell your dad everything you do.'

'He'd find out anyway.'

'You think?'

'Yeah. He's head of police here,' she lied easily. She could barely keep herself from laughing aloud at the look on the man's face. 'But thanks anyway.'

She walked past him as he managed to mutter, 'No problem.'

The quayside was one and a half kilometres long, divided into eight berths for the big ships. Kallie walked its length; every berth was full except for the one at the end, and two tugs were busy fussing and nudging a big container ship into place.

If Anton Leopold's body had been found, or at least photographed, at the time the police said it was, it must have bobbed down the tide from one of these furthest points. A chain-link fence topped with razor wire stopped her getting any closer to the ship being edged against the quayside. This berth had its own unloading facility; a massive shed acted as an on-shore warehouse and she could see containers stacked inside. On the far side of the shed, a barrier, manned by an armed guard, was the only way in or out of the facility. An emblem was painted on the roof of the warehouse, identifying the company: a cobra, its fangs bared, entwined itself around a spear, which she recognized as an assegai, the short, broad-bladed stabbing spear used by Zulu warriors in their many wars. On each side of the spear was the letter S. She caught her breath. SS – *Shaka Spear*. Chang's company owned the facility.

A shadow appeared. Kallie turned. The man she had spoken to minutes earlier was standing a few metres behind her. She had boxed herself in – the wire fence behind her, stacked containers to her left and, to her right, the sea.

Now the man had an unpleasant smile – his tongue licked his lips nervously. 'So, you're more interested in Mister Chang's ships than in me.'

The big ship had been nudged against the quayside. She looked up at the name bending across the curved stern: *Zulu King*. Shaka Chang owned the shipping line and the warehouse, and he was bringing in hundreds of containers. If Anton Leopold had seen this, had it aroused his suspicions? Had he found out what was in that warehouse, or in the containers? As thoughts raced through her mind, the man reached out and caught her by surprise. Twisting her around, he dragged her into the stacked containers' dark alleyway. She struggled, but he clamped his calloused, oil-smeared hand, as rough as sand, over her mouth.

'You can scream as much as you want when I'm finished with you,' he growled.

The stench of his breath made her want to gag. She dropped her shoulders, reached behind her, dug her nails into his face and eyes, and then rammed her heel down his shin into his instep, just as her dad had taught her. The man yelled in pain, but still he kept hold of her despite her struggling. Words of warning slammed into her brain. She was isolated, crying for help probably wouldn't bring anyone within earshot, not in dockland. She sank her teeth into his hand, yanking his wrist down as she did so, and, as she held his arm as tightly as she could away from her mouth, screamed: 'FIRE! FIRE!'

He tightened his grip on her but she kept screaming, 'FIRE! FIRE!' And then she did what her dad had said might be the last resort in attack, she willed herself to relax every muscle in her body and collapsed in a heap. Even strong men could lose their hold on a dead weight. She had to be ready to roll clear when she hit the ground. She went down; the sudden lack of resistance took the man by surprise and he failed to hold her.

She rolled. He stumbled over her, fell forward and tried to stop himself from slamming into the nearest container. His hand partially broke his fall, but he banged his head on the harsh, ribbed metal. It was enough for Kallie to break free, get to her feet and run.

As she raced back into the sunlight, three or four men were running from one of the ships being unloaded. In a split second she knew that if they were hostile she would plunge into the freezing water and take her chances with the current and the sharks. But as soon as they saw her, one of them shouted, 'Where's the fire?' A quayside blaze could be deadly serious, especially with a ship riding high out of the water, less than thirty metres away, its fuel tanks nearly empty except for highly explosive fumes.

Kallie pointed towards the containers and, as they went past her, she ran as hard as she could in the opposite direction. She wanted to get as far away from the danger and violence as she could. At least in the wilderness savage animals could be identified.

Max had spent the last few hours trying to come to an understanding about what !Koga and the others had told him. He had inherited his father's sense of practicality, of not believing in any waffle or mumbo-jumbo about seeing the future, trances or seances or just about anything that he couldn't experience directly. Scientists liked to prove things, and if the data and research added up, then the results were duly accepted – up to a point, or until someone else came along with a better argument. But his dad had also taught him to respect other cultures. Emotional belief was a powerful force to be reckoned with and, if !Koga and the others believed that the *BaKoko*, the shapeshifter, could take on the form of animals, then Max was going to have a hard time convincing them that there was no reason on earth why !Koga would, or should, kill him.

These were just thoughts. What Max needed was to take action, and if some crazy guy's vision was distancing the boy who had helped him this far, then Max had to press on alone. All day the Bushmen had gone about their business in the camp, but !Koga had also stayed away from him, keeping himself to himself, obviously as troubled about the prophecy as Max was confounded by it. So Max had decided he would make his own way from the camp. He only needed a general direction to follow, and the sun's journey across the sky would give him that. And his watch; without !Koga's instinctive sense of direction, he would use it to navigate his way onwards. It used to be his father's and was Max's prized possession. If Max held it horizontally so that the number 12 pointed towards the sun, then the mid-point between that and the hour hand would give him the north–south line.

He was ready to go. He would steal provisions. He had identified where the women stored water in empty ostrich eggs, and the dried meat hanging in strips would keep him going for a few days. He realized he could not simply wander off; he needed a way out of the camp. For the past couple of hours he had moved casually through the area, behind the grass huts, near where the children played, and had skirted the hunters, who now slept in the heat of the day.

There were two ways he could strike out – the first through the gnarled shepherd's trees, which were low enough to obscure the upright figure of someone moving away. A hundred metres or so from the camp, the trees were less dense and he would have to sweep around the far edge of the settlement. He caught himself thinking that what he was actually doing was not continuing on his journey but escaping from a threat of death. Were the Bushmen so unconcerned about him moving around because they knew he would not get far? How had he changed from being helped to get this far, being thought of as part of some prophecy to a – the word seemed stupid, but he could not stop his mind from thinking it – a sacrifice.

There was a second option for a way of escape. The trees behind one of the huts had been cut down to form the framework for its grass coverings, so there was a bare patch of land which he would have to walk across with the stolen provisions; but once he reached the trees, a mound ran almost sixty metres to the right, then fell away into a narrow gully. He could crawl or crouch behind the embankment and then make a run for it when he got into the deeper ground. It would have to be in daylight, probably at the hottest part of the day when everyone was sleeping. He couldn't be sure if the hunters would go out again, but he wasn't going to hang around to find out. Moving across the open space would be a bigger risk – but sometimes big risks paid off, provided everything had been taken into account.

He sat with his back against the embankment, letting the mottled shade cool him as he thought through his options. Tomorrow might be too late. He decided to go that night –

hoping the gully would run further than he could see. He needed distance. He needed darkness.

His eye caught a movement at the edge of the trees and he froze. !Koga stood ten metres away. Max had been concentrating and had not heard a thing. The boys stared at each other, !Koga stepping quietly, almost cautiously, closer. Max waited. !Koga held his spear, but there was no sense of immediate threat. 'Max,' !Koga spoke barely above a whisper as he made a delicate gesture with his hand. 'Come here, Max.'

'You following me?' Max smiled, hoping his voice sounded casual enough, but his back muscles tightened. How long had !Koga been there? Why had he followed him into the half-light of the trees? Why was !Koga slowly raising his spear? He was closer now, no more than five metres away, and Max had not moved, mesmerized by the effortless grace of the boy's walk.

!Koga stared, unblinking, then, like a bird dipping to snatch a grub, his shoulders dropped, turned slightly and the spear cut through the air. Max barely had time to duck; he swivelled, the lethal projectile a few centimetres from his head. He fell, supporting himself with one hand as he hit the sand. The spear thudded into the tree where only seconds before he had leaned, but now a twisting, coiled cobra, fully three metres long and as thick as a man's arm and with a flared hood the size of an open hand, was pinioned by !Koga's spear. It must have been seconds away from striking the unsuspecting Max.

'Bloody hell! You gave me a fright,' he managed to splutter. !Koga chopped the snake's head off, letting the writhing mass squirm in the dirt as he pulled his spear free, still treating the poisoned head with respect.

The unchanging laws of nature allowed Max a moment of gratitude towards the boy who was still his friend; they gave him the few seconds of life where, crystal clear, the etched tree trunks, the bloodied spear and the smiling Bushman froze like a picture snared in a digital frame.

Max grinned, pushed himself out of the sand and felt a sudden hot pain on his wrist. He looked down at the most primitive member of the Arachnida – scuttling, black and yellow, a fourteen-centimetre scorpion that had just stung him.

He staggered back a pace, more as a natural reaction than any great fear. 'It's OK,' he said. And laughed. After a monster of a cobra had nearly sunk its fangs into him, this was nothing. There was barely a mark on his wrist. No swelling appeared, no inflamed skin. Not initially. Then pain started at the wound site, alerting Max that perhaps this wasn't something to be laughed off so easily. Acid-like heat burned inside his veins.

!Koga took his arm, looked at the wound, brought the end of his spear down on the scorpion that was scuttling away, and called Max's name. Max didn't respond. !Koga broke the shaft, put a piece of wood in the crook of Max's elbow, and forced it closed. That would help slow the poison. Max thought he had sweat in his eyes because !Koga was slightly blurred, yet Max's body felt paper-dry; the sensation that seared his arm and into his chest made him feel sick. Neurotoxins were flooding into his system. Something that felt like a claw wrenched at his stomach muscles and, as a wave of light-headedness swept over him, he sank to his knees.

He felt !Koga trying to pull him up, and the boy was saying something, but he couldn't hear him. He was going down, further. He could see the grains of sand now, !Koga's face next to his, slapping him, shouting, mouthing words he could not hear.

Then the boy ran.

Alone, Max heard sounds within his own body. His heart thumped, like a boxer's glove beating him on the side of his head. He mustn't stay here, it was too dangerous. He had to move. *Come on, legs, come on, gotta go*, he told himself. But his body wasn't listening, it was fighting the poison that attacked his vital organs, disabling his central nervous system like a computer virus worming its way deep inside and destroying all essential data.

His throat was closing, the air unable to reach his lungs. He felt a strange sensation. Men were carrying him, honey-coloured men with narrow eyes and leathered hands. Tree branches' shadows fluttered across his eyelids like swarming butterflies, then an old man – where had he seen that old man before? – was pushing his fingers into Max's mouth. Maybe he was trying to get air inside. Pain knifed through him, putting intolerable torsion into his muscles, closing down his windpipe. If he had been in a city, doctors would have realized that he had had an unusually rapid reaction to the lethal venom and would aim to neutralize the effects of the over-stimulation of his autonomic nervous system. They would have put him on an intravenous drip and administered a solution of calcium gluconate over ten to twenty minutes to help decrease the muscle pain and cramps; they would have sedated him for the convulsions that now racked him and put drugs into him to stop his heart failing, which it was now doing. The doctors would have known that death would usually occur within six hours if they weren't quick enough.

Out here, life was not available by prescription.

Help me, someone whispered in his darkening mind. *Help me, don't let me die*, said the disembodied voice. *Mum? Dad? Where are you?*

Like a spider touched by fire, his body curled in a final spasm, turning in on itself, his consciousness sending blackness as the only comfort against the indescribable agony.

A final thought, like the devil laughing: by saving his life from the cobra, by making him fall into the sand, !Koga had killed him.

The prophecy was true.

His heart stopped.

His lungs failed.

Max Gordon was dead.

12

'I know we might be showing our hand, but I think we should do it,' Peterson said into the phone. He listened, frustration biting into his normally controlled manner. 'Farentino *must* know more about this whole matter . . .'

One floor down, six doors along, Sayid watched the sound waves on his computer screen; the spikes of Peterson's voice rose and fell. Sayid's dual-core processor computer handled its workload with efficient ease. As Peterson spoke, a digital voice recognition system, which Sayid had downloaded and tweaked, recorded what he said. The software wasn't state-of-the-art or bi-directional, so Sayid couldn't hear what the person talking to Peterson was saying, but if Peterson was drawing Farentino more closely into the equation, then Sayid would have to warn him.

'We can't just let the boy run free out there. I need more help.' Another interruption. Then Peterson sounded threatening. 'I want this boy. You owe me. I need information. I'll put my own people on to him, but I believe the situation is worsening.' Then, after what was obviously a momentary reply, the line cut dead.

Sayid watched as the peaks and troughs flatlined. A few

keystrokes later, thousands of numbers began to spin from top to bottom of the screen as the system searched for the telephone exchange and then the individual number of the person Peterson had called. Access Denied. Restricted Exchange. An encipher and decipher process was installed at the other end of Peterson's conversation. It was designed to provide a non-intrusive presence when the cryptographic equipment was in an open-conversation mode. So someone pretty powerful was shutting down any possibility of tracing the call, as well as encoding and decoding whatever Peterson said to them. To hell with that. Nothing was restricted so far as Sayid was concerned. It was going to take a long time, but he would track them down.

Farentino may have been isolated in his own world of specialist publishing, but his instincts were sufficiently honed to know when something was not right. He watched the street for any signs of unusual activity. A flashed warning had pinged on his computer screen from Max's unknown friend: Be careful. They might be watching you. Now he gazed out of the window, glancing at office workers and tourists as they sauntered across and around the square. There was no one who struck him immediately as being out of place but, if they were on to him, then Farentino was already one step ahead. The game was too important to lose. He had his exit strategy planned. He unwrapped a Montecristo cigar, taking pleasure in its aroma and texture before heating the tip with a match: it was going to be a case of holding his nerve and playing it out until the final moments, before making his escape. It would take at least half an hour to smoke this fine Havana cigar – more than enough time to alert friends – important friends. He just hoped that Max had found his father's secret before it became necessary to run, because then there was a risk – infinitesimal, he acknowledged, but a risk none the less – that could suddenly escalate; and if Max was still alive, then an all-out effort would be made to finish him before he discovered the vital information that Tom Gordon's enemies craved. Farentino gazed out through the window. He blew a smoke ring. They were not on to him yet. There was still time.

Once Kallie had escaped from the docks, she returned to Mike Kapuo's office as she had told Thandi she would. The senior policeman smiled when he saw her and gestured for her to wait outside the room. A steady stream of officers was coming and going, so she sat patiently until he beckoned her in from the hard bench she was occupying in the hallway. Sitting amid the hubbub of the busy police headquarters gave her time to think things through. Could Shaka Chang, or people who worked for him, be involved in Anton Leopold's death? Had Leopold been killed while he was with Max's father at the docks? Maybe not. Leopold saw something he shouldn't have, then? Max's father had sent his assistant to Walvis Bay – that's where the letters to Max were posted. Why? Because Max's dad was either injured or close to discovering another piece of the jigsaw puzzle, part of which lay at the docks. Yes, that made the best sense, because !Koga's people had taken the field notes from way up north, and that's where Tom Gordon was – somewhere. Perhaps Max's father did not even know that Leopold was dead. If Shaka Chang's company was doing something illegal in connection with shipping, then he was bringing something into the country that he shouldn't, and that something might be what this was all about.

'Kallie, come on in,' Kapuo called.

She settled down as he poured coffee for them both and settled himself back into his swivel chair with a sigh of unburdening his feet from the weight they had to carry. 'You were out of the house early,' he said casually, watching her over the rim of his cup.

'I can't sleep in, you know what it's like once you've lived in the bush. Cities don't agree with me. I had a good walk and looked at the shops when they opened.'

'Uh huh. You didn't buy anything, though?'

'No, don't really need much.'

'First girl I've ever heard say that.' He smiled.

'Mike, I've been thinking.'

'That's a bad sign in my household, it usually means I'm going to be dragged into something I don't want to be dragged into. Go on.'

'Anton Leopold is dead, isn't he?'

Kapuo was too old a hand to show any surprise that she had found out and he wondered if it was just a guess.

'Why do you think that?'

Kallie couldn't admit she had seen his report in his office at home because then he would know that she might have seen the note about telling Peterson. 'Because you haven't mentioned him once and I told you that he was here in Walvis Bay. So, I presumed the worst. I guess you didn't want to upset me.'

Kapuo nodded. 'Yes, he's dead. He drowned. He was found

in the harbour. We think he got drunk and fell in.'

'What did the post-mortem say?'

'Why are you asking? Don't you think that's all a bit gruesome?'

'I'm interested because of Max – not that I can do much about it,' she added quickly.

'He had traces of prescription drugs in him – sleeping pills and anti-depressants. That and the booze wasn't a great idea.'

Kallie nodded and lowered her face to the cup; she had to hide her eyes in case Kapuo noticed her alarm. She knew plenty of men who worked in the wilderness, some of them with a liking for strong liquor; but no one needed their senses dulled by either sleeping pills or anti-depressants – that was for people living in the rat-race cities. Anyone hoping to survive in the bush needed their wits about them, and the sheer physical exertion of being out there was enough to make anyone sleep like a baby.

'Was he on a doctor's prescription?'

Kapuo realized she had thought it through quickly and that she was not someone to be fobbed off with any glib explanations.

'He wasn't local.'

'But he must have had his pills on him, that way you could trace the doctor who prescribed them.'

'No, he didn't. They must have got washed away when he drowned. And before you ask, we haven't traced any family doctor in his background – not yet. He didn't have a definite base he worked from. He was a freelance who acted as a geological guide for visiting mineral exploration people and scientists. People from universities, things like that.'

'He was well thought of, by the sound of it,' Kallie said. 'I mean, serious people like Tom Gordon, well, they're not going to hire anyone with problems, are they? Their lives might depend on someone like Anton Leopold.'

Damn. This girl was interrogating him. She was building on his answers and taking a logical line of questioning. She was making a case out of it!

'Kallie, what am I going to do with you?'

'I'm going to fix the plane, then go home.'

'You came to me for help.'

'I think maybe I panicked. Your imagination can get out of control when your engine fails.'

'So now you're saying no one was trying to kill you?'

'No, I don't think they were. Sorry, Mike, it sounds a bit hysterical, doesn't it?'

'What about the fuel injectors and the plastic pipe that melted?'

'The injectors could have worked loose, I suppose, and the plastic pipe might have been put there by an inexperienced mechanic. It's just that, the more I think about it, the more I convince myself that I overreacted.'

Kapuo had the kind of penetrating look that made it difficult not to wilt when it settled on you. 'I have to decide whether to tell your father or not. It's my duty as a police officer but, more importantly, as his friend.'

'Dad told me to come to you in case I felt in danger. All right, I did, but I think maybe I was wrong. And if you tell him all of this, he's going to abandon his safari, lose clients, lose money, and have his reputation as a first-class guide questioned. Dad'll drop everything to come home and be with me. Don't do it, Mike. Please. I can deal with what's happened.'

'You've got yourself involved in something bigger than you think. A dead man, a missing scientist and a boy running loose in the wilderness. I've had requests from people in England who have powerful connections, asking me to keep them informed about anything unusual happening in relation to Tom Gordon.'

'So you don't think Anton Leopold's death was an accident, then?'

'I never said that. Your imagination is running riot again.'

They stared at each other. Kallie could play the unblinking game despite the turmoil boiling inside her, but she lowered her eyes in submission. There was no point antagonizing Kapuo, who would decide whether he would be happier sending her home and so getting her out of the way, or insisting that she stay with his family until her father could return.

'What kind of thing *am* I involved in, and who are the people in England?' she asked.

'I can't tell you that. Let's just say that what happened to you worries me.'

Mike Kapuo fell silent. He had spent hours being tormented about Kallie van Reenen's story. First of all, he believed her story about the attempt on her life, and her denial these last few minutes convinced him that either she knew more than she was saying, or she had discovered something new. And she was right about one thing. If he told her father, he would throw up everything to get back to her. But if one attempt had been made on her life, would her father be in any position to help? He could put her in protective custody, but sooner or later he would have to justify his actions. If the press heard about a girl being held for safekeeping, then this whole 'missing father and son' incident could be blown sky-high. How to keep tabs on Kallie was his dilemma.

Kallie could tell he had made a decision. 'I think I can trust you to go home and leave us to try and find the boy and his father.'

'Thanks, Mike. I will.'

'Damned stupid English kid. As if we didn't have enough problems trying to find his father. OK, I'll get someone to take you back to your plane and have one of our air division mechanics sort out your engine.'

Kallie gave him the best smile she could manage without sagging in relief.

Mike Kapuo had reasoned matters through. He knew exactly how he would keep an eye on Kallie. This mechanic would plant a tracking device in her plane, and between that and radar alerts he would know exactly where she was. He convinced himself he was not using her as bait, but rather that, if she knew anything she should not, then Kapuo would have a chance of getting to her – before she got hurt. Though if her father ever found out what he had done, the two old bulls would lock horns. Blood would be spilt.

13

Death was a vacuum. For a nanosecond it was suffocatingly quiet, as still and silent as a crypt buried deep beneath the oldest, biggest church imaginable, a place so noiseless that, if a million people screamed at once, they would not be heard. Air did not move. Thought did not exist. Sensation was diminished to a moment so fleeting, it was impossible to experience it.

And then a surge of thunder, like a confused and violent wave breaking on a shallow reef, hurled him into a void.

As his heart stopped, Max's mind reverberated through consciousness, travelling beyond the speed of light and sound, as if seeking a portal in space where it should merge, make contact with whatever it was in the great unknown.

Starbursts of light, like the very best firework display in a matt sky, suddenly inverted and became pock-marked black speckles. Then that too suddenly vanished and became . . . nothing.

Max's brain told him he was drowning, that he had fallen, for it was now a sensation of tumbling through this invisible force. No time to think, no moments to recollect what he had read once: that when you die, there are welcoming spirits singing heavenly music reaching out to guide you onwards and upwards. This was a white-water ride in a black sea of fear.

His instinct for survival fought against this overwhelming sensation but, like drowning, the moment came when he could struggle no longer, and finally he surrendered. It was a moment of being instantly fearless, incredibly calm. A beautiful warmth enveloped him as he floated. There was no pain, nor was there fear; instead, he had the simple desire to bathe in the comfort and safety of whatever it was that soothed him. In that moment of surrender, his mother's face touched his own, her hand stroked his cheek, her lips kissed his eyes; he smelled her hair and a breeze of a whisper told him he was loved. That his pain was over. That he should sleep. That she was always with him. Always had been.

An echo of a memory, of what was his own voice, softly called to her. *Mum, I missed you so much . . . I love you, Mum . . . I knew you weren't dead . . . I knew . . . can we go home now . . . ?*

There was no answer. The gentle night carried everything away and left him as still and unmoving as a deep underground pool of water.

Time does not exist in death. Max stayed in darkness until something flickered. Wisps of fire, then brighter light, a pyramid of flames. Shadows broke the glowing heat. Muted sounds, a chant, ebbed and flowed.

The shaman plunged his fingers into a pouch of powdered herbs, their source known only to him. He forced them into Max's mouth, the sticky mess adhering to the boy's gums, sitting under his tongue and, through his salivary glands, entering his system. Everyone moved away as the shaman placed his hands on Max's stomach and heart. When Max's heart stopped, the shaman pulled a huge eland skin across them both, ushering them into darkness.

Within two minutes, Max's heart thudded, as laboured as an old engine trying to start. *BaKoko*, shaman, shapeshifter, forced a liquid concoction down Max's throat; Max choked, then vomited, and finally slept, embraced like a child by the wizened old man.

More than twelve hours later, Max's eyes opened. The canopy of stars greeted him, and stick-like shadows chanted and shuffled around a big fire. Two men held his shoulders, another two his arms and legs, !Koga was one of them, as the shaman curled his fist and ground it into Max's lower stomach. He worked his fist up below his sternum, and Max felt a lump that became a ball of energy. It rose, through his belly and into his lungs and heart, and blood poured from his nose. The men dragged him to his feet, pulled him towards the flames and carried him around the fire as the chanting increased and the blood kept flowing. He was part of a trance dance which lay at the heart of Bushman culture – the Dance of Blood.

Another journey began.

His shadow-form raced through the night, across rock and sand; his eyes saw everything. The moon was high, its pale imitation of day etched the land. Animal-like, he sped across a plateau, its edge reaching into space. Max paid no attention and leaped from the precipice. Whatever form he had taken on the ground had changed, and now he could fly. He soared, glided across canyon and ravine, dry river beds, trees and hills. The dream was reality. A supernatural energy possessed him, an inhuman instinct coursed through him. Arms were wings, his feet curved talons. He felt the night wind and let some unknown guide possess him.

A mottled canopy nestled across the ground, filtering shapes of trees, disguising their hidden secret. It was the dove. The dove beneath the trees that Max had seen in the cave.

He cried out.

A screech, like an eagle's cry, echoed through the emptiness.

Max was dancing around the fire alone, his head back and mouth open, though that primal shriek was silent. The others watched him. His eyes focused on their hazy images. Suddenly exhausted, he sank to his knees. Hands lifted him, laying him on a grass mat, then covered him with cloth and skins for warmth. The shivering fever had started. It would be hours before he regained consciousness.

!Koga sat with him, bathed his head and face with precious water, and wondered where his friend's spirit had travelled.

Through a shadowland of dreams, Max vaulted time, soaring through extraordinary landscapes, and then lay dormant as waves of colour lapped across his body. Throughout it all, in various guises, was the jackal, Anubis of the Egyptians, weighing his heart on the scales of heavenly justice to see where his spirit should be sent. Then, as a running dog, it paralleled Max's every move, and changed again into a watchful creature, sitting by a roaring fire in the night, dancing with the flickering images. Never an enemy, always a guide, the dog-creature watched, unperturbed by Max's unconscious confusion. But deep within the cave of his own mind, Max knew instinctively that the jackal would guide him.

For two days !Koga sat with the fever-ridden Max. The Bushman boy had selected a branch from a wild currant tree from which they made their bows, and had patiently shaped the curve he wanted. As he fastened the gut string and tested its pull, Max groaned and eased himself on to one elbow. His mouth was clammy; the dried blood had been washed from his face, but its metallic taste coated his tongue.

Max eased the stiffness from his muscles. His arms were covered in dried mud; his torso and hair were also caked. He stood up uncertainly.

'Your skin. It was burning,' !Koga said. 'I put mud on you. It is good, it will protect you.'

Max took the water-filled ostrich egg !Koga offered him. A small mouthful at first, with which he rinsed his teeth and throat and then spat out. It felt as though he had cleared a tonne of muck, and then he drank greedily. The encrusted mud had dried into what felt like a second skin; his shorts were tattered, his nails broken; his muscles still ached from the spasms of the fever and the contortions from the Dance of Blood. But he felt strong. Stronger than he ever remembered. The Bushmen watched him and he gazed back, seeking out every face, looking into their eyes. He was saying a silent thank-you to them all, and they seemed to understand, nodding at first and then breaking into smiles and laughter. The shaman, *BaKoko*, gestured him towards the tree's shade.

'*BaKoko* stopped the poison,' !Koga told him as they walked across the compound. 'He gave you medicine, only he can do this. It was he who brought the blood from inside you.'

'I think he may have given me some kind of hallucinogenic weed, they can lock you up at home for taking that stuff,' said Max.

!Koga showed no sign of understanding, so Max smiled and put his arm around his friend. No need for that to be explained.

As they sat with the other men, who kept a respectful distance from the shaman, they ate food the women had prepared. Strong-tasting eland meat, some root bulbs cooked deep in fire embers, and a mixture of some kind of cornmeal that Max did not recognize. It made no difference, because he was famished, and the food disappeared quickly. All the time he ate, the *BaKoko*'s words simmered like steam from a boiling pot, a steady low murmur of storytelling that !Koga could only translate in fits and starts. But the essence of the old man's words was clear. The Bushmen still believed Max's arrival was foretold, that his journey demanded courage and that he was brought to them so that the snake might strike, that he would fall, that the scorpion would sting and that the great darkness would come upon him. It was meant to be. He must understand that this world they lived in was a dream, that few could be shapeshifters, that as he understood more of what now lay within him, he could use the creature he desired to guide him through danger. If Max allowed the thoughts to take hold, he could experience the essence of any animal. This was a rare privilege and carried with it a responsibility to be used wisely – if it was not, the force that had now been set free within him would devour him.

All of this the old man explained until the sun skimmed the top branches of the trees and the shadows deepened. Finally the old man nodded to !Koga. The boy presented Max with the hunting bow he had made while Max lay unconscious, a sheath full of arrows and a small pot of deadly poison for the arrowheads.

They had made him a hunter. Honoured by their gesture and humbled by their care for him, Max solemnly accepted the gift. Across the flat wilderness the sun retreated. The shadow raced like a tide, smothering everything before it. Max caught a shimmer of movement through the trees, at the edge of darkness, and thought he saw a jackal's eyes watching him.

Max and !Koga ran: steady, loping strides through the night. Their lungs burned for the first hour and leg muscles tightened, but then they pushed through any debilitating thoughts of pain or discomfort and settled into a comfortable pace. Once their breathing eased, their efforts were almost silent as their feet padded rhythmically into the sand. The black-edged mountains, so far away they looked like a troubled wave rising from the sea bed, snared a dark blanket of storm clouds where frayed whips of lightning disturbed the night.

Max was uncertain where he was going. Instinct – and something else, something he couldn't put his finger on – guided him. It was as if his mind had projected a picture of the journey. It wasn't exactly clear, because it had no shape or form, but maybe it was a kind of mental radar, he explained to himself. Whatever it was, he trusted it. Throughout the night they kept up a steady pace, but it was Max who led the way now and !Koga who struggled to keep up. Dawn gave them renewed energy, the sunshine easing fatigue. Max gazed at the mountains; the plateau he saw was the same he had seen in his dream – or vision – he wasn't sure just what to call it yet; and it played back to him like a recorded film. He had flown from the cliff face, had swooped beyond the ravines and river beds to the trees. For a moment he hesitated, the memory catching him unawares, the urge to fly again almost irresistible. Max's relentless pace determined that the boys seldom spoke – both needed their energy and single-mindedness to go to the place of the dream. They travelled north and east for two days, leaving the mountains behind them, moving towards the place where Max's father had witnessed the death of several Bushmen. The last place he was seen alive.

At night they ate the dried meat !Koga's people had given them; Max refused to let !Koga hunt and light a fire. They were nearing danger and Max did not want to take any unnecessary chances. As he slept on the hard ground, no longer worried by the discomfort, his sleep was confused, his mind unable to separate scattered dreams from images of shapeshifting which appeared murky, as if seen through smoked glass. His body twisted and turned as his mind tried to find a place of stillness.

By the third day he knew he needed less sleep than usual. There was no denying the tiredness, but his rest took the form of a deep sleep for a couple of hours, and the remaining hours became a light-headed meditation. Conscious of being unconscious was how he described it to himself. But there was one image which came to him of which he could make no sense and which frightened him. It was the maw of a giant creature, its worn-down teeth covered in matted slime; it was deaf and blind and breathed a vomitous steam. In one of his visions Max stood on the edge of the creature's jaws, saw the monster's bile gush from its stomach to its throat and heard its wheezing gasp for breath as the mist rose from its depths. He knew without doubt that it was the gaping jaws of hell – a bottomless pit that sucked bodies down to be devoured. And the picture he could not erase from his mind was of falling into the churning cauldron.

When the Bushmen died at the place !Koga's father called 'where the earth bleeds', the hunting party had dug their loved ones' graves, smeared the dead with animal fat, covered them with red powder, then laid them in a curled sleeping position, like unborn children. The shallow graves faced the direction of the rising sun and their hunting bows and spears were placed beside them.

The two boys stood in the clearing; wind swirled dust cones, momentarily obscuring the burial site; then, as the wind changed direction, the haze settled and the desecrated graves could be seen. The bodies were gone and only their scattered weapons remained. Some were broken, others seemingly tossed aside. This was not the work of wild animals digging up the corpses.

!Koga wandered to the clearing's fringe. Who, in such a desolate place, would dig up and take away the bodies of his people? Max looked in each grave; there were no clues as to who was responsible, so he gathered the weapons, put them in a neat pile and waited for !Koga. While Max squatted on his haunches in the shade of a withered tree, !Koga went further away from the burial site, his eyes searching the ground. Finally he went down on one knee, touched his hand to the dirt and walked back to Max.

'There were two vehicles.' !Koga nodded to one side of the clearing. 'Those who came first went from here towards the rain mountains.'

Max followed him to the other side of the clearing. He could not see any signs as to who might have been in the clearing before them. There were no animal tracks, no scratches from hoofs or claws, but !Koga had spotted the faintest of indentations.

'The others,' he said, 'they went towards the salt pan.' That meant searing unwelcome heat, but a vehicle would leave tracks.

Max walked across the same ground. It took some time, but then he too saw the marks. Flat stones had been moved slightly, they no longer nestled comfortably in the hardened earth. He felt fairly pleased with himself for having at least spotted that much. He walked a few hundred metres away from the clearing, where damp lines etched the soil. These whiskers of moisture seeped up from below ground, lacing the area, and, because of the red dust, they took on the appearance of blood trails.

Max searched his memory. There was something his father had said in his field notes when he read them in Angelo Farentino's office. Evidence of borehole machinery, his father had written, which was not supposed to be in whatever area his father had been when he wrote about them. There was no evidence of excavations or tunnel digging here. But the Bushmen had taken Max's father's notes from him, and then Tom Gordon left. Where? Which direction? The natural conclusion was that he knew of a watercourse, an aquifer that seeped deep into this area; then it seemed likely he would have headed that way. But !Koga had said that there were two directions the vehicles had taken.

Confusion tangled his thoughts. He was finally getting closer to his father, so taking the wrong direction would be unbearable. It suddenly seemed faintly ridiculous to him. A western boy, without a compass, using a wristwatch for a bearing, caked in dried mud, with a primitive bow across his shoulder, standing in the middle of nowhere, without sign or sound of another living creature except a Bushman boy who squatted in the shade, waiting for him to make a decision. His father was missing, bodies had been dug up, he was lost, had survived attack, lived through deadly poison, seen images he could not describe, yet forty thousand feet above his head an airliner made its ragged white incision across the sky. Four hundred people were sitting up there while he stood in this dust bowl with a useless mobile phone in the pocket of his tattered shorts. He waved at the disappearing silver bullet. 'Hello! Have a nice holiday! Don't forget to send a card!'

He laughed at his own foolishness but quickly sobered when he saw !Koga looking at him with uncertainty.

'I'm sorry. It's just too crazy for words. You understand?'

The boy shook his head.

'No, of course you don't,' Max said. He felt slightly ashamed of his outburst and didn't know whether he should make some effort at reverence for the desecrated graves, but he couldn't think what form that might take.

Clearing his thoughts, Max suddenly knew what to do. He turned and headed for the dark mountains scarring the horizon.

'We go this way?' !Koga asked.

'Yes.'

'How do you know?'

'I just do,' Max answered. Something was pulling him, he did not know what, but it was that same deep instinct that had brought him this far. And there was something else that comforted him. !Koga was more than a guide and companion. He and Max had straddled cultural barriers, and this friendship was forged out of dangers faced and hardships endured together. Other than finding his father, there was nothing more Max wanted to do when this was all over than to help the Bushmen. He would make sure the world heard about their plight.

!Koga had told him how they were prohibited from the land they had always known and hunted; vast tracts of national parks protected animals that the Bushmen needed for food and clothing, and cattle farmers were taking most of the land that remained. !Koga's people were being squeezed into ever smaller pockets. It just wasn't right. Their way of life was almost extinct. He caught the thought and mentally chastised himself – he was making himself sound too important. There was no prophecy in those cave paintings, nothing that suggested he was going to help the Bushmen. That was a fantasy created by the Bushmen from his father's drawings.

He was simply determined to succeed but, perhaps because of those cave drawings, the Bushmen had nursed him and given him some kind of power. The same memory now flashed before his eyes. The eagle in his mind had soared and found the hidden dove. He *knew* he was going the right way.

14

Max was totally unprepared for the sudden onslaught when it came.

They had travelled all that day, rested through the night and set off again before dawn. !Koga kept checking the ground, and every few hours he told Max that the vehicle tracks definitely went towards the mountains. They reached the furthermost edge of the rising ground while it was still light. A dry river bed gave them easy access to the foothills. Max could see the sparse forest of trees in the distance but !Koga kept warning him about the cloud that suffocated the mountain top. It was now so black, it growled like a bear and the first few stinging raindrops raked them. A bitterly cold storm suddenly roared down the mountainside, as if angered by their presence. The wind hit them first, buffeting them so hard they almost fell, then a line of water, not deep enough even to cover their ankles, trickled towards them across the breadth of the river bed.

'Let's make for those rocks, in case this is a flash flood,' Max yelled, because now the wind howled venomously. Splashing through the shallow water, Max saw exactly where they should head for – the boulder was a slab of rock that stuck out like a massive diving board above the river. Within a couple of minutes they were clambering on to its broad back. Max looked behind him; where he had stood moments earlier, the water was now knee deep. Before he clambered any higher it was waist deep, and it surged around the bend, hitting the far bank, where boulders pushed it back directly towards him and !Koga. Max could see immediately what was going to happen. The water was already higher than a man, and the surge at the bend gave it a turbulent power that formed a wall of water which would strike their side of the bank, engulf the flat-bedded boulder and sweep them off.

He yelled at !Koga to run for it, but he was downwind and the boy could not hear him. !Koga was already trying to stand on the boulder, his knees bent, a hand touching the rock face for support. The water roared and, combined with the increasing velocity of the wind, it became a maelstrom of swirling rain, competing with the wind and the river as to which would destroy them first.

Max surged up the rock face, desperation fuelling his legs. He reached !Koga in time to see what was happening in the gully that channelled the water down from the mountain, above the rock they stood on. The ever-increasing volume of water churned mud and boulders in a helter-skelter ride. The bottleneck at the foot of the mountain, where it swirled around the corner to the opposite bank, increased its own resistance. As the water buffeted the bank below them, the water from that gully would take the line of least resistance. It would smash mercilessly across where they stood.

Max grabbed !Koga's arm and pulled him, but the boy resisted. 'We have to get higher!' Max yelled.

This was the first time Max had seen !Koga scared. The boy's eyes were wide and his breath came in short, gulping sounds. He was frozen with fear, looking down at the water. They would be at least waist deep when they jumped for safety, trying to reach dry land less than ten metres away. But if they didn't jump now, that distance would treble in less than a minute. !Koga shook his head. 'No water!'

'Come on!' Max was stronger than his friend and he yanked him firmly towards the edge – he could see a muddy, froth-flecked wave rising up, ready to strike.

'I can't swim!' !Koga shouted.

Max did not hesitate. 'You won't have to!' he shouted and dragged !Koga with him. They were in mid-air for a few seconds, then splashed into what, a minute earlier, had been the dry river bank but which was now chest-deep water. Max kept a tight grip on !Koga's wrist, surprised by his own strength. As they splashed into the confused undercurrent, it snatched them this way and that, but Max pushed his knees against it, ignored the bruising boulders that banged his shins, and hauled !Koga with him. As they clawed their way up on to dry ground, the wave broke behind them across the flat rock and drenched them in a curtain of water. They were wet, but now they were safe. The surging water would dissipate its own energy, the further away it travelled.

Max did not stop pulling !Koga after him until they were well and truly beyond the heaving water. Breathless, they stood and watched the water as it rolled by, now a steady stream. The rain stopped, the grumbling clouds quietened and, other than the gurgle of the water, it was quiet.

'The Mountain God,' !Koga said quietly.

Max nodded. There was no point arguing the case. !Koga had his beliefs and, after what seemed to be an intrusion on their part that caused the storm, Max wasn't so sure !Koga was wrong.

'Well, he's quiet now. Maybe he doesn't like visitors. If someone climbed over my back garden fence and trampled on the flower bed, I'd turn the hose on them as well.' Max smiled but !Koga still seemed cautious, glancing nervously towards the darkened summit.

'It was a flash flood. Look.' He pointed to the river bed. The water was lower now; somewhere downstream the ground had swallowed the river. Mud and debris scarred its path. 'And we're not going up there, so don't worry.' He put an arm on !Koga's shoulder. 'Let sleeping gods lie.'

Once they had skirted the mountain slopes, Max saw the place he instinctively knew to be their destination: a flattened area between the high grass and the treeline. The savannah grass was high enough to hide a man, but a narrow strip had been pummelled by generations of elephants as they shuffled on their endless journeys, foraging for food and water. Max scanned the area. Animals probably moved from this flash-flood area to the wetlands further north. Somewhere down there was the captured dove he had seen in his mind's eye; he didn't like to call it a vision, it was still something he could not explain to himself. What he did know for certain was that this was where those images in his head had brought him.

An eagle's screech snatched him from his reverie. He looked up at the circling bird that had swooped from the mountain's sheer face. Gazing up at the eagle, he felt a chill squirm from his chest to his stomach – it seemed the eagle was calling to him – like one eagle to another. Or perhaps it was a warning? The bird was lifted away by an updraught and a sudden flurry of wind swirled dust, forcing them to turn their faces, hands covering their eyes against the stinging sand. As the wind dropped, Max found himself facing away from the trampled grass. His peripheral vision gave him another angle, which allowed him to see a shape in the trees. It was a slightly different shade of green from the others, and a smaller shadow skirted the fringe of scrubland.

For a moment, Max thought he saw a jackal. What was it he failed to remember about one of the constant clues in this whole thing: that wraith-like figure of the jackal? His father's Egyptian stories came back to him – as well as being the god of the dead, the jackal was the guide between the two worlds. It would show the way. That made sense. Even in the cave drawings, it was the jackal's figure that had led him to the images of himself and his father on the wall.

Eagle, dust swirls and a spectre – all directed him to that one place.

The flattened grass felt like straw beneath their feet. With the high grass to one side and the low trees to the other, Max sensed a mixture of dread and expectation. The place was comforting, like a secret den he'd had when he was younger – a place where you could hide and not be seen; one of those special places no one knows about – but it also felt like a baited trap. The further they went along that elephant track, the higher the grass, the more dense the shrubs and trees.

Max stopped. !Koga had moved ahead and went down on

one knee. Max looked around him. A small flock of chattering birds scattered across the treetops. Was that a warning, or were they simply irritated by Max and !Koga's presence? Max joined !Koga and stared into the undergrowth – there was something in there – it brooded in the shadows. Something fluttered, rasping, like leaves on a beech tree.

'There are no tracks,' !Koga told him. But that didn't mean an animal could not have pushed its way into the undergrowth from another place. What little breeze there was came from behind them, so there was no apparent scent of anything, but whatever was in there would catch their scent. There were no sounds of feeding; elephants would be ripping the branches apart. What else? Buffalo were not supposed to be in this part of the country, but they had already experienced a rogue herd, the night of the stampede. Farmers had tried and failed to domesticate this most dangerous of animals, so there were still small herds scattered around. And a buffalo could wait until an unsuspecting hunter was almost nose to nose before charging and killing.

!Koga put an arrow on to his bow string and Max followed suit. Such a flimsy defence would be useless against a big animal, but it gave them courage.

Walking a couple of metres apart, they stepped cautiously into the undergrowth. The shadow was ten metres in, at the end of a broken path of shrub and low branches.

The sunlight flickered through the tree canopy; they were upon it now. Max lowered his bow, reached out to the irregular shape in front of him and touched a dried branch. He gave a tug and it fell away. Another step forward, another cut branch. That too he pulled back. Someone had cut branches down to hide whatever it was in this glade. Now his hands touched what felt like coarse string and plastic. He yanked, but it would not give. It was a net, snared over thorn branches. A camouflage net. The small, dull plastic panels fluttered differing shades of green. Max had seen plenty of these on the army training ground; an armoured vehicle's outline could be disrupted to make it very difficult to see. But now the shape behind the net was obvious.

It was a small plane.

And on its tail fin was the drawing of a dove.

The plane had been manhandled into the trees, turned, and then camouflaged. It looked as though someone wanted to be able to take off in a hurry, and that would be achieved by pulling off the cut branches and lifting the front of the netting clear of the propeller. Within moments of starting the engine, the pilot would be able to taxi forward, turn the plane on to the trampled grass, and take off.

Max and !Koga edged their way around the aircraft. The air was cooler under the trees' canopy and the netting added a lot of shade. Max felt a guilty sense of trespass; this was someone else's secret. As far as he could see, the plane was undamaged and was about the same vintage as Kallie's, so, although it was unsophisticated, with only bare rudiments for comfort, it looked perfectly serviceable. Tentatively he reached out for the cabin door latch. It was unlocked. The door creaked a little and cool air from the interior touched his face.

!Koga had moved back into the sunlight and the entrance to the trees which, from where Max now sat in the pilot's seat, looked like the mouth of a cave, with the inside of the plane and the shadows being the cave itself. Max let his fingers touch the controls, holding them in his palms like a flight simulator joystick on his computer at home. It was so silent. He felt entombed in a secret mausoleum. The unmoving dials waited for electrical current to spur them into life. Fuel gauge, airspeed indicator – in knots, not miles per hour like Kallie's – this plane was a slightly newer model. Vertical speed dial, altimeter, a row of flip switches for lights and fuel pump, warning notices to check contaminants in the fuel and to make sure the seat was locked into position before take-off and landing. A red master switch was in the off position, waiting for the ignition key to be inserted and the magnetos switched on. Ignition key. The slot was empty. Without thinking, he flipped down the sun visor and found a well-worn key with brown cardboard tag attached. An almost illegible call-sign number, faded beneath years of handling and grime, was written on the tag.

Max put the key in the ignition and turned it. There was a hum of power from the battery and the dials swung into life, like well-disciplined soldiers waiting for a command. Max quickly turned the key off. !Koga opened the other door as Max pushed the key back under the elastic band on the sun visor.

'Someone wanted this ready for a quick escape,' he said.

'There are tracks, on the grass. I think it is the same truck that was at the place of the dead.'

'That means the plane landed, the pilot met someone else in a Land Rover or whatever, hid the plane, and then they drove off again,' Max said. Suddenly he remembered the paintings on the cave wall. The dove hidden; the white man injured. This plane had to be the one his father used! It was !Koga's father who had taken Tom Gordon's notes from where the Bushmen died, and he had said there were two white men in a pick-up. Dad and Anton Leopold. So perhaps his dad had got a message from Leopold on the ground, who then met him here. Leopold would have told him about the dead Bushmen and, knowing his father, Max realized they would have driven off after the men responsible. !Koga's father had told them that the two white men went off after the other men. His father had probably concealed the plane for a quick getaway.

Max twisted in the seat to look in the back of the plane. A couple of empty plastic water bottles, a box of field rations. No clothes or luggage. Nothing to prove the pilot was his dad. There was a blackened stain which made a neat outline, showing where the small white-and-green sticker said 'First Aid'. The box itself was missing, probably taken from its mounting for the first time ever, given the dirt outline.

He clambered into the back. His fingers touched the bare metal carcass, tracing the shape of the cabin. Was anything hidden? Any clues to be found? His father had made those drawings to bring him here to *the dove*. There must be something. Then his finger found what his eyes had missed. He winced and withdrew his hand, looking at the small tear in the skin and the dribble of blood. On the edge of the plane, where the floor met the sides of the cabin, three holes were torn in the metal. The flare of impact was minimal, almost no mushrooming inwards; it was these ragged edges that had snagged his finger. He sucked the blood, then noticed the angle where the light came in. He eased out a reed-thin arrow from its quiver and placed it in the hole. The angle showed him that the bullet which made this hole would have passed between the seat and controls. The pilot would have been hit in the leg. Max bent down and realized that the dark stain on the floor was not dried mud. Beneath the passenger seat he saw a grubby edge of paper. It looked like a map.

He slid his hand beneath the seat and, as he teased it out, he heard the gentle rolling of something he had touched. Working blind, his fingers found a small glass ampoule. It was an empty morphine phial.

Max held the folded map. The words *Sector Search* were scrawled in the margin. It was his dad's handwriting. There was no doubt now that this was his father's plane.

And it seemed obvious that he had been shot.

The map's creases were even dirtier than his own map. He opened out two folds. An area was defined by boxed, faded pencil lines. Max couldn't determine just where the area was, but a dozen or more marks – small red crosses – were scattered across the map. Max unfolded another panel. His finger traced contour lines, the mountains, the rivers. The map was getting too big to read properly.

As he climbed out of the cockpit, a smaller folded map fell from the bulk of the larger one. It was a hydrology chart. Moments later, he and !Koga had opened both on the ground next to the aircraft. The bigger sheet related to Max's own map, but the emptiness of the country allowed for little detail. The north-eastern part was where the red crosses were distributed. Max traced a finger back to Kallie's area, from where he had started his journey. Brandt's Wilderness Farm was shown. It was like gliding across the country, peering down at the landscape from space. Farm names, small airfields, settlements and towns, they had all been surveyed over the years. Max worked out where they had originally been attacked when they left Kallie, their trek across the mountains, the sacred cave, the Bushmen's area. It brought him ever closer to the marked crosses. Comparing the hydrology map was more difficult. There were no place names, just the veins of water, like leaf shapes and patterns. Two or three areas looked as though the map maker had taken a blue pen and slashed a dense pattern backwards and forwards. Max realized these were the swamps. To the left of these was a dark, spider-like patch with a strand suspending it from what was obviously a big river to the north. This was a feed, and from that darkened patch the spider's legs reached out, multiple strands of water seeping into the swamps.

'I think we're about here, !Koga,' Max said as he tapped the area south-east of the spider's body.

'What are these things, here?' !Koga asked, pointing to the red crosses.

Max hesitated. 'Well . . . I think these are the places where people have died. Look . . .' And he traced their own journey until they skirted half a dozen markers. 'I think this is the place where the earth bleeds. Where your people died and where our fathers met.'

'So your father has found many dead people.'

'Yes, I think so.'

'But why did they die?'

'Maybe because of the water. These are water maps. All those thin lines, I think they might be underground streams. My father specialized in them.' Max got quickly to his feet, climbed back into the cockpit and sat staring at the radio. They needed help. People were dying, his dad was injured. His fingers reached for the on-switch. He hesitated. This was his chance to radio for assistance. He could get Kallie, the police, he could have messages sent back to Angelo Farentino. Max was on the verge of finding his father, they'd come a long way, but now he faltered.

In the stillness of the shade Max tried to picture his father and his helper manhandling the aircraft. His father, injured after someone had tried to shoot him out of the sky, and Leopold, about whom Max knew nothing. Was he a younger or an older man? He was obviously a good field man, or Max's dad would not have used him. It didn't matter. What did matter was that they had hidden the plane and readied it for a quick escape. How much power was left in the battery? Max might drain it in one broadcast. No one knew where his father was. Max could not stay at the plane, he had to keep searching. If their paths crossed and his dad got back here and still needed to escape, Max would have ruined everything. Come on, think! What would Dad have wanted? The message on the cave wall was to bring him here. Had he left the maps for him? Was that deliberate? Or were they tucked away and forgotten in the urgency of the moment? What else had he drawn in that cave? The dove under the scratchy cover, the injured man, the morning star – every picture guiding him. Then he remembered that there was a gaping hole drawn on the cave wall, like a whirlpool, with a cloud hovering over it. He jumped back down to !Koga, who was gazing at the unfamiliar landscape, seen from a surveyor's eye, of the big map.

'There is a line here. Like a snake,' !Koga said.

'Show me.'

!Koga's finger was on the coastline at Walvis Bay. The red line meandered towards the darkened area which, on the hydrology map, would have been the spider's body. 'It's a road,' Max said. 'From the coast to this area, whatever that might be. Maybe that's the route my father's field assistant took. I can't tell. Never mind that for now. Do you remember on the cave wall, there was a drawing, like a hole in the ground, a big hole, with something swirling around it?' Max grappled for a description, hoping the Bushman boy might recognize the picture he was trying to describe. 'Maybe a dust bowl, or something, y'know, a place where the wind might gather speed and twist itself up into a tornado.'

!Koga shook his head. Max knew he wasn't explaining things properly. He quickly made a model with sticks and stones, and bits of leaf and dry lichen, in the same manner as !Koga had once shown him the route they had planned to take. !Koga was part of the land, these tactile representations might carry more meaning than lines on a map.

'This is where we left your camp, where I was hurt . . .'

!Koga nodded. Max needed to understand !Koga's own ideas of where they were.

'Can you show me where the people died, the place where the earth bleeds?'

Without hesitation !Koga cleared the dirt. He scratched a line in the sand and gouged deeper scratches into the dirt to represent the ground where the water seeped. 'It was here.'

'Where are we now?' Max asked, starting to get his bearings on this dirt map.

Again !Koga drew a line away from the last markings; he pulled some grass and thorn to show the elephant tracks and the trees where they now sheltered, and he made a small stick cross – the plane.

Max made a broad semicircle around their position. 'What is here?'

!Koga seemed uncertain. Then he turned a thumb downwards, indicating different places in Max's semicircle. 'Here there are lions. Five families. They are brave lions and my people have hunted near them. To this side the salt lake is hard and takes many days to cross and there is no water and no place to go and no reason to cross it. But here we hunt wild pig and it was here that Ukwane hunted wildebeest and the wildebeest did not forgive him and lifted his head before he died and killed Ukwane. He was a great hunter. There are police at this place where the trucks stop here, it is a garage.'

'How far?'

'Five days.'

'What else?'

'Here is a place we cannot hunt. It is protected for the tourists.'

'A game reserve?'

'Yes. It was the place where we hunted, but the government said we must not kill.' !Koga's hand now swept further across. 'This place we do not go.'

'Why not, !Koga? Is it the police, or the army?' Max remembered that both the police and army, usually made up of tribes other than Bushmen, harassed the nomadic hunter-gatherers.

!Koga clicked words under his breath and shook his head, almost as if he did not want to talk about the forbidden area. 'There is death there. There has always been death there.'

Bushmen did not like talking about death. Evil spirits were real, tangible forces of nature that could take them without warning.

'Have you been there?'

'No. It is not good.'

'How far is it?' Max persisted.

'Two days – if we run like the wind –' he laughed quickly '– like you! But we cannot go to this place. It is . . . I do not know the words.'

'Is it sacred for your people? Like a burial site?' Max asked, trying to tease a more exact answer.

'No, it is not sacred. It is bad. It is a bad place.'

!Koga scooped up a handful of dirt and shaped the small hole. His hand darted quickly, gathering stones; anything sharp or irregular he pushed down into the throat of the hole; then, choosing smoother pebbles, he laid them around the edge. Finally he crumbled dried leaves and lichen, dressing the area with a softer, greener covering. 'Only some hunters have been to this place. They say there is a great monster who lives beneath the land. He breathes the stench of the dead. He tries to live with us and the animals. He is trapped beneath the ground. He is angry and wishes to be like men, but he cannot.'

If there was anything as frightening as that on, or under, the face of the Earth, then Max knew it was bound to have something to do with him finding his father. He sat quietly for a moment, then looked closely at the map, gauging the direction and distance from what !Koga had shown him on the ground. For the first time he noticed that there were still many references to place names from when the country was occupied by the Germans before the First World War. His finger took his eye across the creased paper, where he found a small, almost indistinguishable image which, if it had been necessary to check the map's legend, would have told him it represented a fort. But Max knew what the word '*Schloss*' meant. Angelo Farentino had shown him aerial photographs of the fort built by the crazy German aristocrat in the nineteenth century. The fort that now belonged to Shaka Chang. An awful moment of certainty struck him. Less than half a kilometre from the fort was a small wave-like image, neither lake, nor swamp, nor river, for it couldn't be described as any of these things. The map's writing had to be typeset even smaller than most other names because it was longer than most and it read *der Atem des Teufels* – the Devil's Breath.

That was !Koga's monster, and that was where Max knew he must go.

15

Kallie van Reenen had a suspicious mind. She blamed her father for that. He might have been a war hero but, as he always told her, the Angolan war was a bad war, waged for the wrong reasons, instigated by greed. After he had criticized the government openly they began to harass him and he moved to Namibia, away from the unforgiving South African government of the day. Now all that was over, but her father had an intrinsic distrust of bureaucracy. And as far as Kallie was concerned, when she had discovered that Mike Kapuo was involved with Mr Peterson in England, that distrust now included the police – the very people she had gone to for help. So when they took her back to her plane and the police air mechanic sorted out the problems, she logged her flight plan for home and flew to an airfield south of Walvis Bay. That at least gave the illusion that she was flying back to the farm. Five hours later, when she landed at a desert airstrip for refuelling, a fingertip search confirmed her suspicions. She found the satellite tracking device.

Half an hour later, a plane that was returning from safari and which would be sitting on the apron at Windhoek for a few days, carried the electronic tag.

The plane's pilot turned up only moments after she had planted the small transponder. 'You're Van Reenen's daughter, aren't you?' the pilot said.

'That's right,' she said, barely managing to conceal her embarrassment. Moments earlier he would have seen her acting suspiciously around his aircraft.

'If you're flying up to see your dad, better be careful,' he said, slinging his overnight bag into the plane. 'IATA's just blacklisted Namibian airspace, the relay station at Outjo has gone down. There's no ATC anywhere.'

'Oh. Right. Thanks. I hadn't heard.'

'Happened this morning. I'm heading home. The tourist industry ever hears about this, we'll all be out of work. Take it easy.' He began his pre-flight checks as she drifted away, barely able to conceal her elation at the good news he had given her.

The International Air Transport Association, which controlled everything to do with aviation, had blacklisted the Namibian government's air traffic control system. With its major relay station broken down, aircraft would not be able to see each other in the sky or land safely. And if air traffic control was not working, they would not be able to see her on their radar screens.

From now on she would fly low without logging any flight plans.

Kallie needed to contact Sayid; the best way to do that was through Tobias, and there was only one way she could get his full co-operation: through guilt.

The small airstrips in the desert and at farms had no

control towers. They were as informal as garages. Most had a fuel pump, a couple of mechanics and a shop; maybe a bar. When she landed, there was only one other plane needing refuelling and no sign of the bogus mechanic who had sabotaged her plane. She pushed the bar's doors open and strode towards Tobias, who was busy connecting a barrel of beer. The moment he saw her, he reached for the till and snatched a piece of paper. 'Boy, did you con me! Do you know what that phone call to England cost!? Your father would skin me alive if I gave him this!'

She sat on a bar stool; there was no one else in the room. 'Tobias, you nearly killed me,' she said with a straight face. Tobias's mouth opened in an unspoken moment of uncertainty and confusion. 'You remember that Desert Buster Ice-Cold Special you made me?' she said.

'Yes. There was no booze in it. Honest.'

'I know.' She waited, wanting to draw out his suffering a little longer.

'I blended the fruit and mix myself. You got sick? Food poisoning? Maybe it was something else you ate.'

'It was the old flask, Tobias. Your Desert Buster must have had fermented fruit in it. It blew up.'

'Blew up?' He was trying to picture the moment when his concoction escaped the confines of the flask. 'Did the flask hurt you?'

Kallie grabbed ice cubes from the bucket, dropped them into a glass, reached for the lemonade dispenser, and filled the glass. 'It's all right if I have a drink, is it?' she asked.

He nodded, still trying to put together how his actions might have caused her harm.

'It exploded, drenched me and the cockpit, soaked the integrated electronic circuit relay and short-circuited the solenoid on the hydraulic steering mechanism.' She said the first thing that came into her head. Tobias knew how to make every drink under the sun but nothing about aeroplanes.

'Is that bad?' he asked.

'Fatal. I barely made it. I had to report it but I didn't mention you or the Desert Buster.'

'Thank you. Kallie, I'm sorry, I had no idea a soft drink could cause so much trouble.'

'An exploding soft drink, Tobias.'

'Right.'

'In a container unsuitable for the use for which it was intended.' She remembered the words from a consumer rights report in a magazine.

'It *was* an old flask, but it was a flask, so it must have been suitable because that's what flasks are for,' he said.

Kallie realized she might have gone a bit too far in trying to con Tobias on the Trade Description Act. She needed to give him a reality check.

'I could have died, Tobias.'

He nodded gravely.

'But I didn't. So I just thought I'd come back and let you know. So you didn't worry.'

Tobias considered this for a moment. 'But I would not have worried, because I would not have known if you had not come back and told me.'

'Listen. Do you want my dad to hear about this?'

He shook his head. That was a confrontation no one in their right mind would want.

'No. 'Course not. And believe me, I have no intention of telling him.'

'Thank you, Kallie.'

'It's all right. You're a friend.'

'That's good.'

'Yes it is. And friends are here to help each other.'

'That is what I believe also.' Tobias nodded soberly, the pact of friendship reaffirmed. But he knew at that moment, in this particular friendship a gesture of recompense would be due. 'So, how much is this going to cost me?'

'I'm hurt and shocked that you think I would ask you for anything,' she said, refilling her glass. She sipped the lemonade. He waited. She shrugged. 'Only the cost of a phone call.'

Sayid was on ablution block cleaning duty. The boys worked by rota, swabbing out the showers, making sure the toilets were clean, wiping tiles, cleaning mirrors, checking if loo rolls needed replacing. No one liked doing it, and deals could be made with other boys to take over a weekly duty which interfered – not with school lessons, because that would mean it would have an abundance of volunteers – but with a much more important matter known as TT, or 'Town Time', on Wednesday afternoons. The school bus would take them to the city, where afternoon movies, coffee shops, record stores and bookshops beckoned, and where some of the older boys inexplicably spent time chatting up girls. But Sayid had volunteered to swap with one of his friends, making the excuse that he needed to build up some free Wednesdays later in the year. What Sayid really wanted was some undisturbed time to work on the mystery phone number that Mr Peterson had rung and which was proving to be totally untraceable.

Sayid had never had so much trouble hacking as he had now with the codes for the telephone exchange routing system. This was supposed to be a straightforward procurement of an encrypted telephone number. He had tried a reverse number look-up, but that didn't work because it was an unlisted number. A GUI on his computer screen had shown a London location, but then it had blanked out. Where the relay stations for the telephone connections should have flashed up in a nice big box with an orange background and *kebonged* a tone for his attention, the screen had remained still and silent. Sayid, like most hackers, was self-taught, but he had enough skills to go a long way. He had started programming with Python, then Java, and over time progressed to C, but that always needed debugging, so he updated his hardware and went back to Python. He knew he had to eventually get to grips with one of the oldest programming languages, LISP, the name derived from 'List Processing', but it needed time and experience to write properly although it was the preferred choice for artificial intelligence research. Among the cyberspace community Sayid's reputation was slowly becoming established. It was a love of programming that kept the hacker community in touch with each other. There were people in America who spent their lives underground in basements, surrounded by computers, absorbed in the endless possibilities at their fingertips. Sayid knew a few who worked in Research & Development of major computer companies and, although their names were buried deeply in code, he had sent an urgent help request to one of them. That was yesterday.

He ran the squeegee across the floor one more time: the place sparkled. He had done a good job quickly. Now he needed to get back to his room. He left the floor marker, warning that the floor was wet, propped the mop, bucket, squeegee and cleaning materials as a small assault course in case any of the teachers got nosy – they were bound to knock something over, then he could be out of his room and down the corridor in time to cover his absence.

The small figure of a whirling Dervish danced across his computer screen. This was a message from America. To connect to the message, he had to double-click on the Dervish icon. Once he had done that, a page of code clogged the screen and he tapped in a previously agreed access number. Like harpoons, these numbers shot out from the base of the screen, grabbed letters and words from the code page, rejumbled the letters and decrypted the message.

hey bro, this is your Code King Buddy. how you doin? this is big, kid. that number. forget the exchange that's no good to you anyway. doesn't mean nuthin. he could be anywhere and reroute. this number. cool. no time for guessing games. your man is high clearance. this is defense-code-scrambled. don't have a name. he's MI6. tread careful, pal. peace and goodwill. except to the bad guys.

The British Secret Intelligence Service; the words sounded like a huge pyramid of power in Sayid's head. He stared at the screen for a moment, then erased everything. If MI6 was hunting Max's dad, then he must have done something pretty serious and Peterson had connections in much higher places than your bog-standard geography teacher. Sayid tried to make some sense of it all. Max's dad was missing, someone tried to kill Max, then Peterson had Max followed to the airport. The police in Namibia were in touch with Peterson, and Peterson was asking for help from MI6. Whatever Max's dad had discovered, it had everybody scared and they were trying to stop Max from discovering his father and his secret. Sayid stopped his mind going down the wrong route. This was not an MI6 operation. The state was not involved. This was Peterson *asking* for help from a well-placed contact who would be untouchable. Peterson was owed a favour, so maybe Peterson had done dirty work for MI6 in the past. That made more sense. And it was also more frightening. How did Peterson come to be teaching at Dartmoor High? Just what kind of clout did he have to get help from a foreign police force?

His mobile rang; the screen showed it was an unknown name but the number was familiar.

'Sayid, it's me.'

'Kallie. Have you found Max?'

'No, he's still missing. I don't know whether no news is good news or not. But things are going a bit crazy.' She explained everything that had happened to her and how she was trying to keep out of everyone's sight. She was convinced that the Walvis Bay docks, Shaka Chang's shipping line and his warehouse were connected to Tom Gordon's disappearance and Anton Leopold's death. Somehow the whole mess would lead them to Max.

'Listen, Kallie, Max is my best mate, but I think you should back off,' Sayid said, beginning to realize how completely out of their depth they all were now.

'No way. Someone tried to kill me. I'm involved and this whole thing with the cops and your Mr Peterson stinks. Something's being hushed up big time and I'm going to find out what it is – and when I do, I need you to alert the British authorities, the Foreign Office or someone, because I don't know who I can trust out here.'

'I don't know who to trust either. I did a bit of illegal snooping. Peterson is getting help from MI6.'

'Who? Oh, the spooks?'

'Yeah. This is even bigger than we imagined, Kallie.'

There was a pause at the end of the phone and Sayid guessed that, like him, Kallie was trying to think what to do.

'I don't care, Sayid, I'm going ahead with my plan.'

'Which is?'

'I'm flying over the route from Walvis Bay towards the mountains. Shaka Chang has trucks shipping machinery from the docks. Anton Leopold was killed at the docks. I can't get in, but they must be bringing something out. I'll be following them.'

'That's dangerous, Kallie. They might have guns. If they spot you, you could be like a fat pigeon on a duck shoot.'

'I'll fly high enough,' she lied, knowing that over a certain height one or two of the military control towers might pick her up.

'I hate this business of not being able to stay in touch,' Sayid said.

'There's nothing we can do about that. I don't have a satellite phone.'

'No. Me neither.'

'So. That's it then.'

Her words sounded so final, prodding his conscience. 'I have to be able to do more than just sit here,' he said, regretting the uselessness of his words. Beyond all their fears, a simple fact remained: a father and his son were missing in a hostile environment. They were both British subjects and Sayid remembered his own citizenship ceremony after Max's father had sponsored him and his mother. They had been given a new life, a place of safety away from the terror of war, and he was not going to stay silent. 'I'm going to the police, Kallie. What's happening isn't right. It's just not right. I'm going to tell them everything I've found out. The cops can make a fuss of their own, and if they don't I'll go to the papers.'

'The cops might throw the book at you. And the spooks might just lock you away in a dark hole somewhere. Sayid, that's a crazy thing to do.'

'And what you're doing isn't? This way, at least one of us might get through to somebody who cares and who can do something. I won't mention you when I talk to whoever.'

'And if I get nabbed I won't say anything about you being my contact in England.' She paused a moment. 'Hey, I hope we get to meet one day.'

'Me too.'

'And Max.'

'Definitely. We can do this.'

'We're on our own then,' she said.

'No. There's three of us in this thing, and Max is strong and he's really determined about everything he does, and even if he had both legs broken he'd crawl to get to where he wanted to be. We have to be as brave as he is, Kallie. I have to tell someone.'

Those final words brought the realization that he was risking everything he had been given. And not just him: they could repatriate his mother as well. They might both be sent back to the place that had claimed his own father's life at the hands of assassins.

'Let's talk when we can,' he said.

'Sure. Good luck, Sayid.'

'You too.' Sayid switched off the phone. He had reached a point of no return.

A few minutes later, he stood outside his mother's room. He knocked, heard her call 'Yes?'

He opened the door. His mother sat, marking term papers. Sayid didn't move. She gazed at him for a moment and saw the boy's uncertainty.

'What is it?' she said gently.

Kallie gazed across the heat-baked landing strip, mentally plotting her route. There would be a lot of flying and she was tired, having already been in the air for hours. Tobias moved next to her and shared the view. He sipped a beer and said quietly, 'Tell your father. He'll know what to do.'

She shook her head, wishing it could be otherwise, knowing she could not take the risk. Her father loved her, she was in no doubt of that, but his reaction could start a small war, and she did not want to be caught in the middle.

Someone had run into a Dartmoor foal and killed it. The high moor road was not only a scenic drive for tourists but also a rat-run for villagers getting across the moor to one of the major roads. Drivers didn't usually stop when they killed an animal, be it a sheep or a Dartmoor pony, and this incident was no different. Special Police Constable Debbie Shilton closed the door of the village sub-station's small office, having arranged for the hill farmer to remove the poor creature's body. She had completed her report. The part-time policewoman had had a busy day sorting a minor dispute between two neighbours over the size of a dividing hedge, as well as giving a talk in the village hall to the local ladies' group about security in the home – not that there was much of a threat in that part of the world. There was little need for a local officer, and the police authority's budget did not stretch to having someone filling out forms about missing dogs and blocked rights-of-way, but the death of the foal saddened her. There was a callousness in some people that she could not comprehend. Leaving any animal suffering after causing it an injury was not on so far as she was concerned, and she wished that if the culprits were ever caught, the law would prosecute and make an example of them. However, that seldom happened, even when troublemakers were caught red-handed. There were times when people's behaviour sickened her. Maybe she was not cut out to be even a part-time copper.

A car driven by a woman pulled up. There was a young

boy with her. The boy looked anguished and the woman seemed scared.

'Please, officer, can you help us?' the woman said.

Shilton cast aside the momentary self-doubt; that's what she was here for, to help. Though she guessed, by the look of the young boy, that this was probably no more than a missing family pet. She smiled compassionately at Sayid.

16

!Koga had known fear in his young life. There was the time a lion challenged the hunters for the gemsbok they had brought down and he was suddenly faced with the snarling fury of a hungry lioness. He'd been so frightened that he screamed and shouted and threw stones at her, until she wilted under the hail of sharp rocks. That day had earned him respect from the other men. But it was not the fear of the lioness that had driven itself into his heart, it was the dying gemsbok. He had returned to the buck, the size of a small horse, and readied his knife. The hunter's poison had taken a long time to work, but now its central nervous system was paralysed and it lay helpless. !Koga knelt next to its head and thanked the gemsbok for allowing itself to fall victim to the skills of the hunters. He touched its soft muzzle with his hand. But he hesitated. The gemsbok's brown eyes gazed at him in a moment of unspoken affinity. !Koga, transfixed, let the knife fall to the ground. The eyes held him until the last heartbeat. And then, as the life receded from those eyes, !Koga sensed the long and lonely journey that would one day be his own death. That is what frightened him. Not death, but the journey afterwards. And that same fear had touched his heart when Max had asked that he leave him alone for a while.

Max was in the pilot's seat. The monster that was the Devil's Breath lay somewhere ahead, and he had to find the route, but something other than the desperation of finding his father gripped Max. A chill settled on him, and a silence that excluded anything that was of normal hearing. He didn't know what was going to happen. Gently, his voice barely above a whisper, he told !Koga to pull down the camouflage netting and wait by the tall grass, a final rational thought to keep the plane hidden. !Koga had looked into Max's eyes and saw death's journey begin. He could not imagine what his friend would see or where the shapeshifter of his mind would take him, but it was an unknown land and !Koga was convinced, like any hunter, that every wilderness harboured its own ferocious animals. Max's eyes began to look like those of the dying animal that !Koga remembered so well. Afraid that his friend's journey might capture his own soul and take him into the unknown, he moved away quietly.

Whatever happened when Max experienced this supernatural energy, he did not understand it. *BaKoko*, the shapeshifter, had released this ability within him, but Max thought, incongruously, that it was like learning to ride a motorbike. There was a power to hand which was scary and exhilarating and, if not controlled properly, could kill. And there was no one to tell him how to control these immense feelings. When a shapeshifter gained sufficient experience and the energy was harnessed, the actual physical shape would change. The thought of being able to become another creature was far removed from his own sense of practicality – a load of tosh, is what he would have said – until he'd had that first experience. And now he was being drawn into that power again, it summoned him from deep within his body.

Max felt he was sitting inside his own body looking out. And when !Koga teased the camouflage net across the nose of the plane, being careful that the web did not snag the propeller, everything closed down for Max. No sound, no sight; all that remained was what now seemed to be the dim light at the mouth of a cave. !Koga settled the dead branches back across the netting, deepening shade settled on the plane and arrows of light pinioned Max in the darkness of the cockpit.

He waited in silence, trying to focus his mind into a place that lay as still and as remote as a pool of water. His head nodded forward, tiredness enfolding him, a sleep-like surrender easing him away.

A shuddering wrench made him gasp. Jolted, it felt like being snatched and thrown by a mighty hand. An ice-hot force seared up his spine. It was worse than he had feared. A huge rush of energy powered him through the sky, and then he hovered silently in the air. He was higher than a skyscraper, and part of him felt quivering terror as if he hung over the edge of such a high building. His whole body shook. His cry of alarm shrieked across the sky; shadows moved on the ground and his eyes zoomed in to where a low circular mist hugged the ground. He looked over his shoulder, which was covered in overlapping layers of dense brown and grey feathers. A long way away – beyond the horizon, scrubland and low

trees nestled alongside the scar that was the elephant track –
was the tiny figure of his friend.

'!KOGA!' he yelled, but the cry that came from the back
of his throat was not a sound he recognized. He gasped, he
was unable to hover. He was a bird all right, but this time he
was no hawk or eagle or whichever raptor form he had taken
before; now he was a dove, and he had no ability to hover,
he was swooping through the air and beginning to panic; a
rollercoaster ride without anything to hang on to. But he saw
the direction he had to take on the ground. Beyond the
elephant grass, through the small forest and across the broken
plain, small plateaux rose and dipped and animal paths gave
a sense of direction for a few kilometres. Beyond the ravines
and increasing tangles of scrubland lay a ragged-edged black
hole, punched into the Earth's surface. The shape of its
snarling face would not be visible from the ground; only a
pilot or a bird would see how the land had been scrunched
and twisted from a meteor's impact, millions of years ago.
The shattered remnants of rock formed eyebrow scars, and
the slab of stone below, a broken nose. The gaping, broken-
toothed chasm exhaled a sour mist that fed the vegetation. It
was the entrance to hell and the place most feared by the
Bushmen.

The place held his attention, but when he looked beyond
the smashed earth he saw the distant glint of water. A river,
like a fat Gaboon viper, settled lazily; reeds and sandbanks
where creatures lay, unmoving. Crocodiles. Big ones. He was
learning to see things now, his head twisting, giving himself
different viewpoints, and the most obvious formation of rocks
now made itself clear. Square blocks formed a structure,

figures moved, dust rose from a moving vehicle. It was a fort. Skeleton Rock.

Max tried to turn, somehow he had to get back to !Koga, but flying was not easily mastered for a novice bird. He fluttered helplessly, as if caught in a storm, and his panic sent shock waves through the air. Another cry filled the desert sky; cruel and piercing, it instinctively terrified him. A dark shape circled high above him, the ragged edges of its wings dipping and controlling its flight. A memory flashed into his mind – baboons shrieking with fear at the shadow of a martial eagle. Now one had sighted him as its prey. Wings folded, it plummeted through the sky in perfect attack mode. Moments later, ripping talons would make short, vicious work of him. Max tried to escape; he could see the tiny figure of !Koga squatting in a tree's shade, hundreds of metres below him. !KOGA! But of course the boy heard nothing. Ripping talons slashed, a feather's breadth from Max's face, but no sooner had the eagle missed its attack than it pulled off an incredible mid-air manoeuvre and struck again. Its heel talon stabbed backwards, cutting into feather and down.

Max was falling. The stomach-churning ride was now an out-of-control tumble. But how many times had he been told he was a natural sportsman? What Max could see, Max could do. Show him the position to take on a white-water kayak, demonstrate the body angle for a downhill off-piste ski run, and Max could hold that picture in his head, and his muscle memory repeated it. Eagles went bullet-shaped in their attack dive; so too could Max. Concentration forced his panic further back into his consciousness. He felt everything change. A subtle shift of control, a tightening of his arms – or were they wings? – against his sides; the velocity buffeting his face, the ground swooping upwards and then, like air-brakes, the arm-tearing tension to slow the descent and glide into the trees. Not enough control! Branches and twigs like long-thorned fingers snatched at him.

And then blackness.

He awoke in the back of the cockpit, curled up like a jockey who's just fallen during the Grand National and knows there are a hundred steel-shod hoofs thundering towards him.

Max hauled his aching body out of the plane and stood for a moment in the warm shade. He scooped a handful of earth and put it to his nose; the earthy smell of Africa gave him a reassuring sense of being grounded.

!Koga waited nervously at the edge of the track, a look of relief on his face when Max pushed through the trees. !Koga touched the slash across Max's shoulders, as long as a hand's length. It was superficial but it stung. 'I think I fell backwards in the cockpit,' Max answered the questioning look. The truth frightened him as much as the experience; if he was mentally able to take on the form of an animal, then it was fairly certain that he could be attacked and injured or killed.

Maybe it was all in his imagination. Maybe that cut did come from falling inside the plane. At least that was one way of fooling himself.

They jogged steadily for a couple of hours, the layout of the ground imprinting itself like a three-dimensional image in Max's mind. As the sun rose higher and the heat became intolerable, they rested in the lee of a rock overhang. Max spread the maps out. The crease-marks on his own map were frayed; his father's Ordnance Survey map was more serviceable. The hydrology chart was what interested him now. By comparing his father's two maps and his own aerial memory view of the Devil's Breath, he realized that one of the blue veins formed an underground circuit from the gaping hole and travelled directly under Skeleton Rock. He wasn't sure about the hair-thin line that looped off, but it seemed the river system could also be a feed from, or was a result of, this underground water system. Max mentally chastised himself. What an idiot. He had literally had a bird's-eye view of the fort. He could have seen everything he needed to know. The river and those crocodiles acted as a natural defence, but he could have flown into the fort itself. He could have observed everything. They had to be bringing in supplies. Were they using the river for drinking water? If they were, was there a filtration plant? If so, where did they generate electricity to run it? Answers to these questions might have given him a way into Skeleton Rock.

Everything had brought him to this place, there was no doubt in Max's mind that this was where he would find more evidence of his father's whereabouts. But the memory of that last flight gave him the jitters. His hands trembled at the memory: the eagle's penetrating eyes, the talons that clawed at his face and neck. He could almost feel them closing on his chest, piercing heart and lungs, and then in those last agonizing moments of life the beak would rip him apart. It was a horror scenario. Truth was, the reason he hadn't looked more closely at the fort was because he had been so scared.

There was a part of him, the adventurous bit, that thrilled

at the idea of being able to take on another animal's form, but the reality of plunging into that half-world was another matter. For a start, it wasn't something he could just do whenever he wanted, it wasn't like taking a coat on or off, it appeared to depend on circumstances and necessity. His emotions seemed to be part of the trigger that allowed him to do it. It was something that he just couldn't analyse.

!Koga watched him, reached out and touched his trembling hands.

'Sorry, mate, must have had too much sun,' Max said in response.

'What is it we must do?' asked !Koga.

'Well, getting the SAS would be a good idea, failing that the cavalry, but if they've got another gig planned it's down to you and me, and the *me* part of the equation might be going a bit loopy. And going off your head out here isn't going to help anyone, is it?'

!Koga waited until something Max said made sense. Max traced their journey on his dad's map. 'We've come from here, I think, and we're going there, I hope. Thing is, !Koga, I've got to get into the fort. Do you know about the fort?'

!Koga shook his head.

'What about Shaka Chang? Ever heard of him?'

'No. I do not know this name. But here . . .' he touched the back of his hand on the map where Max had indicated, 'is this the place where the monster lives? Below the ground? The bad place?'

Max had tried to hide his own fear, but he could see that !Koga was getting frightened now as well. He summoned a smile for his friend.

'One good thing about being frightened is it makes you careful.'

'I would rather not be frightened,' !Koga said.

It was nightfall before they reached some high ground, a raised plateau of a hundred square metres or so. As the Earth's rim turned from crimson to gold and finally to a deep blue, darkness followed quickly, eager to exert its dominance and beauty over the harshness of day. Max lay on his back, the Milky Way so close it was almost touching his face. Of all those stars and planets, universes and worlds, he was lying here, caught up in something he could barely understand. But when the lights of the fort flickered into life a kilometre or so away, one question had been answered. They had power. So there was a generator somewhere. And there was no sign of solar panels, so there had to be a source. The river was too placid. What else could create that energy? Diesel generators might do it, but that was a huge place to illuminate and there was no familiar hum of engines.

When he awoke, the moon had shifted high into the sky and first light was already warming the air. !Koga was already awake, squatting, elbows on knees, as he gazed out towards the black pit in the distance. Max did a face wash with his hands, rubbing vigorously, forcing himself into a more alert state. 'You should have woken me,' he said.

!Koga smiled and said, 'The day will always be here. There is no need to run all the time. The day will wait. Where do we go? To the fort?'

'Not yet,' Max told him, and turned away, fearful that if he told !Koga what he had figured out, the boy would refuse to accompany him. And right now Max felt that he needed a friend close to him.

An hour later the smell of fetid vegetation around the rim of the Devil's Breath confirmed they were within a hundred metres of the gigantic sinkhole. Even though they could not yet see its depths, it appeared ready to swallow anything foolish enough to venture too close. Max felt the soggy seaweed-like goo. This place had to be a geyser of some kind, and they usually erupted on a regular basis. The question was: when? It had not happened during the previous hours when they had slept, but that damp grass and moss had not dried the previous day, so it had to blow at least twice during daylight hours.

He wished he had paid more attention to his maths and science classes at school. The subjects seemed so unengaging as he sat gazing across the Devon moorland, dreaming of other things than dry mathematical formulae. His dad often despaired at Max's poor grades and he always promised to try harder. Maths helped one to understand natural patterns and structures, his dad had explained to him. Understand maths and science, and you can figure out most things, such as language, music and culture. And erupting geysers, Max thought. Well, he'd rather be shown something than have it explained. That's why he liked going on field trips with his dad; he showed him how things worked. Besides, at school he had Sayid to help him out of tight spots when it came to cramming for exams. He had a half-decent brain, but he was lazy. There were far too many other things to do; school lessons simply got in the way. Well, now he could do with a bit of maths and geology to help figure out how often this monstrous hole was going to erupt, because his life might depend on it. And maybe this time the practical experience was not going to be much fun.

'Wait here,' he said to !Koga. 'I'm going closer.'

'That is a foolish thing to do.' !Koga muttered something under his breath which Max did not understand, and the boy gripped his arm tightly, stopping him from going further.

'I have to see as much as I can before it gets any lighter. There's not a lot of cover here – and look at those rock pools, animals will come and drink. Let's take a look and find somewhere to hide,' Max assured him.

'We should not be here,' !Koga insisted. 'I have a bad feeling, Max. This is not something you understand.'

'I don't understand a tonne of stuff, but I've got to have a look. Stay here,' he repeated.

He pulled free from !Koga's grip and threaded his way through the low boulders. His feet squelched in the moist earth, and the closer he got, the more he realized that the hole was bigger than he had imagined. Ragged projections stuck out from the sheer rock face, giving the impression of rows of long teeth lining the throat of the crater. It was still too dim to see the depth of the hole, but shadows dropped into total blackness. He heard a movement behind him. His heart walloped against his ribs, then calmed a little when he saw it was !Koga. 'Do me a favour, !Koga, when you sneak up on me, give me some warning, will you? I nearly jumped out my skin!'

'You will need more than skin when the monster sucks you into its belly.'

'If you're that scared, why didn't you stay back there?'

'Because I am supposed to protect you.'

Max felt humbled. The boy had overcome his terror to honour his obligation; the least Max could do was put on a brave face and keep his own fear under control. He smiled. 'It's not a monster, I promise, !Koga. It's just a geyser. Pressure builds up and blows water from an underground river, and my guess is, it's the source of power for the fort. It's called hydroelectric. Just like the huge dam they've built in the mountains.'

!Koga had that blank look which Max recognized as his own when Mr Lewis the maths teacher tried to explain something beyond his comprehension. But before he could explain his own limited understanding of hydroelectric power, the ground began to shudder. It happened so quickly, the boys could not move. They reached out to steady themselves because now the vibration took away the strength in their legs. And with the jarring shudder came a growl, churning deep within the bottomless pit. Max steadied !Koga as they pushed their backs against one of the boulders to stop themselves from falling. A sucking, gurgling hiss of vapour spewed from the hole, drenching everything within fifty metres, its plume at least twenty metres high. The gossamer mist settled like dew and then, with the retreating water-pressure, the plume plunged back downwards, belching air and noise as it receded. The explosion had lasted less than thirty seconds, but the power that drove up from beneath the ground rattled nerves as well as bones.

The suddenness of the eruption and the silence that quickly followed left them both mute. It took a moment for their ears to stop ringing. Max pulled a piece of something slimy off

!Koga's head, a ragged piece of weed, and presented it to him.

'A present from the monster,' he said, but !Koga was not smiling. Instead he was retreating slowly backwards, never taking his eyes from the crater.

'!Koga, it's OK. I promise. It can't harm us.'

!Koga stopped and shook his head. 'We must leave this place now. That was a warning. We are not welcome here. It is a bad sign, it is as my father told me. A bad place.'

Max knew he could not argue with a belief so rooted in nature spirits. He would never deride such strong feelings. His experiences so far had taught him that the Bushmen's secrets and their understanding of the natural world were far beyond anything he had ever come across. He deferred to his friend and nodded towards their resting place that overlooked the void.

'Come on, let's get back up there.' He turned away but felt the light touch of !Koga's hand.

'Wait. You are planning something.'

Max nodded. There was never going to be a good time to tell !Koga his plan. It might as well be now. The same dread of frightening his friend away still lingered. 'I think my father could be in that fort. If he isn't, then the people in there may know what happened to him. I reckon at the very least there have to be some clues.'

He gazed across the landscape. In an hour the sun would scorch and they would be hard pressed to find shelter, not so much from the heat as from anyone seeing them move across the ground.

'Max, if your father is in that place, how can we get inside?

The men in there might be the same men who attacked us. They searched for us and we escaped, now you want to knock on their door. Are we giving up?'

'No, we're going inside. There's a secret passage that should lead straight into the fort. At least, I think there is. Come on, I'll show you.'

He turned towards the hole, hoping !Koga would follow. When he reached the chasm's edge he held back a couple of metres, nervous of the drop despite the firm footing the embedded rock provided. He turned. !Koga was walking forward nervously, as wary as an animal seeking to drink at a dangerous waterhole. But he kept walking until he joined Max. Max extended his hand, like a nervous schoolgirl, he told himself, but knowing that he was showing !Koga that he too was frightened of moving to the edge. They steadied each other and falteringly shuffled to the edge. It was a bottomless shaft, and saw-toothed sheets of rock clung to the sides.

A fetid, quivering air breathed malevolence on them. The sibilant whisper of the unseen water beckoned them closer. Edge forward, see what lies below, see how far it is to fall. Max seemed mesmerized by its lure and stepped to the very edge, his gaze locked firmly on the black, unblinking eye far below, where the light ended and the totally unknown began. It had to be more than four hundred metres deep. That volume of water, under pressure, could blow a double-decker bus to the moon. So what was stopping all that power? How come the water never burst above the surface in any great quantity? The whole area should be a wetland.

So intense was Max's concentration that !Koga thought he was about to step into the abyss. He whispered Max's name.

Max turned and faced him. 'Follow me. I think I know what we have to do,' he said grimly.

Both boys now squatted at the other side of the crater, watching the rays shine down into the hole. Even if anyone in the fort was on look-out – and there was no reason to suppose they were – there would be little chance of being spotted. Not at that distance, and not with the glare of the sun directly in the watcher's eyes. Max pointed. About sixty metres down was another hole which looked like the entrance to a cave, almost unnoticeable. It was no more than five metres across and as high again. Around it were about a dozen smaller holes, each no more than a metre wide, punched into the rock face. 'I think that's the underground passage,' Max said, pointing to the cave-like entrance.

'You cannot know that. You cannot be certain.'

'No, but look at this.' Max opened the hydrology chart. The thin, almost inconsequential line that wriggled across the plan from the Devil's Breath to the fort could be nothing but the conduit they were now looking at. At least that's what Max told himself. 'I reckon the water gushes up, and it's so powerful it forces itself into that hole – that's like a channel and I bet it'd be strong enough to power a turbine or something closer to the fort.'

!Koga looked doubtful. He understood the force of water in flash floods, he had seen boulders bigger than elephants carried downriver, but what Max described made little sense. He nodded, not wishing to appear ignorant of something that seemed so simple to his friend.

Max scratched his head, his fingernails scraping away some of the caked dirt in his scalp. 'At least I *think* that's how it works. Something to do with ventricular power, whatever that is. I should have paid more attention in science class.'

!Koga, slightly relieved to see that not all was as simple as it appeared, felt encouraged to question the problem further. 'And those other holes?'

'Er . . . yeah. Not sure. Probably some kind of natural venting system. Y'see, I think it's so powerful that when the water surges, it wallops down that big hole and either blows back pressure through the smaller ones, or . . .' Stuck again. What else? He looked at !Koga, who now, for the first time, smiled.

'You don't know.'

'Not a hundred per cent. I reckon it has something to do with releasing pressure from the main surge.' He hesitated and said almost to himself, 'My dad would know.'

They sat quietly for some time, !Koga still wary of the monster. Occasionally he would rest his hand on the ground, feeling for the heartbeat of whatever it was that lurked so far below the surface, alert for the warning of another explosion. It was a time for silence. Like the hunting parties when they stalked their prey, they would spend hours waiting, communicating with gentle, inconspicuous hand-signals. Patience was essential. Now !Koga waited. Max would make a decision. He was the leader now, !Koga knew that. After the experience in the village and Max's ability to understand something of the monster. So he waited, remembering past victories over fear, knowing he could win again.

Max finally spoke. 'It doesn't seem as though this thing is going to erupt again. Next one's probably at the end of the day. Yeah, that makes sense, maybe. Twice a day. Morning and night.' It sounded as though he were trying to convince himself.

'We go? Down there?' !Koga hoped he didn't sound too frightened.

Max shook his head. He had already made his decision. 'I'm going. On my own.'

!Koga stood up quickly. 'No! I am not afraid!'

'No one said you were. I know I am, but I've been scared more times these last couple of weeks than I've ever been, so I can probably manage it once more.'

'I will not let you go alone. My place is with you.'

'But I can't risk us both getting hurt or captured – not now, !Koga, not after all this bloody effort.'

!Koga went quiet and shook his head slowly. He thought of the arguments he would have with his people, knowing he would be held responsible if Max did not survive.

'You cannot stop me from following you, Max. You will not know I am there. I will be the hunter tracking your shadow.'

Max touched his shoulder. '!Koga, you will always be with me. I'll carry your friendship with me. But I need you to do something else.' Max took out his father's Ordnance Survey map. 'You remember the place where the earth bleeds? And the marks my father made on his map. You know this is where Bushmen died. And all those other marks, in different places, these are places my father found. This is what he was going to report. Now this isn't enough evidence, I know that, but it's all we have right now. My father had been in all these places because of this . . .' He showed the hydrology map. 'He found what was killing your people. And maybe there's a lot more we don't know about. And I know he must have other evidence hidden somewhere, real evidence, something really concrete that can't be disputed, but I have to find him first and you have to go.' He gazed down at the vertical drop. 'I reckon I can free-climb down to that entrance, then in a few hours I'll be under the fort. !Koga, don't give me a hard time on this, I need you to take Dad's map to the police.'

'Police?'

'You said there was a police post, a few days from here. Get to them, don't give them the map, give them this.' Max undid his watch strap. The old stainless-steel chronograph was his dad's when he'd climbed Everest, twenty years ago, and he'd given it to Max for his twelfth birthday when he enrolled at Dartmoor High. Engraved on the back plate were the words: *To Max. Nothing is impossible. Love, Dad.*

He fastened the watch around !Koga's wrist. 'Give the cops this watch, it'll prove you've been with me. Tell them you know where the son of the missing white man is. But don't tell them where I am. You have to get them to contact Kallie van Reenen. Give her the map. You tell her what we've discovered. She'll know what to do. You have to do this, !Koga – to save us all.'

Max was well aware that this was almost a replay of what his father had done with !Koga's father. He had sent the Bushman on a mission to Van Reenen's farm, knowing that he had to get his field notes out while he went on searching. Fate had twisted events like a noose around a sack – Max, !Koga and Kallie van Reenen: drawn together, trapped in the same danger.

But Max felt strong. He was getting closer to his father

now – he knew it – and that would drive him on. 'I'll make a start when the sun shifts a bit, that'll give me some shade down there. I reckon it's going to be a bit of a climb.' A bit? It was going to take everything he had, by the look of it. He would have to choose his route with all his skill.

They agreed that !Koga would wait until nightfall, then he could travel faster, with virtually no chance of detection. But the night was not the time Bushmen felt comfortable. Their lives centred around the fire. This was where they cooked and ate, danced and told stories of great hunts and of gods who were animals and stars that were lovers. The warmth and comfort of the fire was as much a part of their life as the sun rising and the moon taking it away. Alone, !Koga would have to travel across predators' natural habitats. Memory maps were all he had to guide him, but the night sky would show him the way, and moonlight would warn him of shadows that moved. He would do this thing so that Max Gordon, the boy from the ancient cave drawings, could help save his people.

And because the white boy was his friend.

Max began his descent a couple of hours later, as !Koga sat nestled in the low boulders around the rim. He could watch Max's progress from there, and when he finally crawled into the cave he would return to the low plateau where they had slept the previous night. There was shade there and he would rest, before beginning his own journey into darkness.

Max was already twenty metres down, his right hand jammed into a narrow crevice above his head as he tried to find a toehold below. His weight stretched ligaments and tendons in his shoulder, but he reached out with his left hand, clawed his fingers against the uneven surface and shifted his body slightly. A sliver of rock took his weight as he swung precariously half a metre to his left; his fingers slipped as his right hand came free and the sudden, sickening drop churned his stomach as he plunged down.

'Max!' !Koga couldn't help but cry out.

Max had scraped his knees and the inside of his arm when he fell, but the drop was barely the distance from his ankle to his knee – it just felt a lot more scary than it was. Without looking back, he managed a reassuring shout to !Koga. 'OK! I'm all right!'

Controlling his breathing, he muttered encouragement to himself. 'It's fine. It happens. Nothing to worry about. Just a little slip. Nothing to get het up about. Clumsy sod.'

!Koga settled back on his haunches, heart thumping.

As often happens on a climb – or, in this case, a descent – a rhythm develops and now Max found a steady pace. The rock face was kind to him for the next ten metres as he gripped, swung, twisted and wedged his way downwards. The scrapes and cuts were stinging, but adrenalin pushed the pain to the back of his mind. Now he was feeling good, he could see his way down; spurs of rock as wicked as razor blades shafted downwards, but their edges were sufficiently ragged to allow purchase. And behind each sheet of rock, the moss and lichen offered a small comfort zone for his back and shoulders as he wedged himself in to support the next downward movement. A wet sheen covered everything, reminding him of home. Clambering down quarry walls in Devon or practising for the bigger climbs in Scotland usually meant the rock surfaces were wet, but when he did that, he

246

reminded himself, he was attached to a safety line. That's OK, a lifeline was really important when you're climbing in a rock-strewn quarry. Nothing too serious to worry about here then, he kidded himself. If he fell, he'd only fall a few hundred metres into the water, though that'd be like landing on a concrete floor. Don't think about it. The shock of falling that far would probably kill him anyway. Just imagine the lifeline is attached; that was the best thing. There, he'd already made another five metres and hadn't even thought about it.

Time condensed into seconds, that's what his attention span demanded – attention focused on every centimetre of the way, but a small voice in his head told him that he must have been on the rock face for an hour, probably more. The sun had shifted and was almost overhead now, and he still had another thirty metres to go. He jammed his hand into a letter-box slit in the rock and rested. With his free hand he wiped the sweat and grime from his eyes.

The bow and arrows were proving difficult, getting in the way when he tried to wedge his back into the crevices. He swore. He should have left them with !Koga. No matter. Another hour – tops – at this rate, and he'd be able to swing into that entrance. But now he was stuck. He couldn't turn from his back to his front, allowing a swing across the rock to grab another hold. The bow, jutting above his shoulder, was snagging. He had to get rid of it. His wrist burned as the skin was forced to tolerate more torsion with him twisting around so that he faced the rock wall. His cheekbone pressed hard against the stone; he gulped air, his free arm reached over his shoulder, grabbed the slender bow and eased it, like a contortionist, over his head and shoulder.

A small triumph and much as he cherished the hand-made weapon, he reached out into space to let it drop. As his weight shifted slightly, the crevice that held his hand crumbled. Loose, wet, shingle-like stone gave way and he fell.

He had barely time to shout. Reflexes shot into high gear and a zillion mental calculations made his arm shoot out to slam his hand, which held the bow, against the rocks. The bow string hooked over a rock and stopped his fall.

He hung, suspended from the wall, crunching his back against the boulders. Pain shafted through him and for a moment he thought he was going to fall again. The sinew on the bow flexed and the shaft bent, the supple wild raisin wood allowing a lot of give. He had to trust that the bow would hold his weight for a few more seconds. Grabbing it with both hands, he pulled himself in to the rock face. He'd definitely pulled a muscle, or maybe even bruised or cracked a rib; the pain knifed into him and took his breath away. Hanging on as best he could, he gave one last pull on the bow to help gain a foothold, and as the bow finally yielded and snapped, he managed to hold on. He could feel his nerve slipping away as quickly as the bow falling into the silent void. He clung desperately, eyes tightly shut, willing himself to carry on. No flippant humour now; no kidding with the terrified voice in his mind. This felt like the end of the world and he was frozen. Rigid.

The fall had taken him to within ten metres of the tunnel entrance. A battle raged in his head, demanding that he think. He must have dropped about five metres, no, probably more, but he had suffered no serious injuries – plenty of pain, but he was alive. Hold on. Almost there. Take encouragement and keep going. Keep your eyes open. Open them!

Someone was calling, a distant whisper that his ears refused to hear. Concentrate on the voice. Listen to the voice. The voice. Whose? !Koga. His dimming consciousness was like a dark cloud settling over him. If he blacked out now, he was finished. He was in shadow, and cool air momentarily helped keep him awake. What was !Koga shouting? Why was he stamping the ground so damned hard? For God's sake shut up, I'm hurt. !Koga, he shouted but no sound came out of his mouth.

!Koga, who had watched him fall almost out of sight into the black shadows, screamed his name. A slow-motion acrobat act showed Max twisting and turning, grabbing for support, falling further and further, whipping an arm out, the bow string catching, the sudden jolt, the snap of the bow, and Max hugging his grazed and bleeding body to the rock face. But !Koga's screams went unheard. And it was not Max's struggle to stay conscious that was the cause, it was the quaking tremble of the ground and the roar of air coming up from the devil's lair.

!Koga peered over the edge, down into the face of evil. A malignant stench and the first spray of water and vapour barrelled upwards, concealing the huge tide of water charging behind it.

The mist billowed towards him; a few more seconds and the fog would envelop Max and the water would swallow him. Panic blinded !Koga to his own danger. His friend was hurt; in a moment he would die, and he couldn't help him. He screamed Max's name, but his cry was swallowed up in the roar from below; the cloud was almost on him.

In horror he saw Max's hands slip off the wet rock, saw him tumble backwards into space, arms wide, spreadeagled, looking up, straight into !Koga's eyes.

And then Max vanished into the storm below.

Devoured by the monster !Koga had always known existed.

17

For a moment, Max was floating, suspended on a cushion of air. He watched !Koga vanish, felt rather than heard the water pressure roaring below him, and then he plummeted into a grey soup of spume and fog. Darker and darker the funnel grew as a bizarre jumble of thoughts and panic confused his mind.

They had gone to the big swimming baths in town and the fifteen-metre board was a test of nerve. There were a couple of boys who could dive from up there, but most found an excuse to not even climb the three-storey platform. Except that Max could not turn away from a dare, particularly when it came from Baskins and Hoggart. It was sheer bravado, and he swore he wasn't ever going to do it again. If they did it, he'd do it, he had responded to Hoggart's challenge.

As it was, Baskins was nursing a bruised shoulder from a rugby game, which let him off the hook. So Max and Hoggart had made their way up to the top. He was surprised when he got up there to find just how high fifteen metres was. It didn't look that bad from poolside, but now that he stood on the two-metre-wide board, gripping the handrail – God, it was a long way down. A hell of a long drop. Further than he imagined. His knees felt a bit wonky and his knuckles whitened. He could see that Hoggart was probably more scared than he was, because his jaw had slackened and his eyes were screwed up, as if trying to shut out the distance. Thankfully Max had kept his fear under control.

These two senior boys were always going to give him a hard time, it was in their nature, so by taking this leap of faith, literally, Max reasoned he would get them off his back once and for all.

He let go of the rail and turned to Hoggart. He remembered saying, 'Last one down's a sissy!' And without allowing himself to think any more about it, he stepped into space.

His arms flailed, his feet pedalled, and he kept falling and falling, his stomach lurching over and over again until he hit . . .

The water sucked him under. The Devil's Breath was now a seething turmoil. He fell through the surface and kept going down. He remembered seeing the entrance to the tunnel and even more rock face below that, so he must have fallen twenty metres or more, but his descent was stopped by the upward surge.

Instinctively he had held his breath the moment he sensed the fingers of water reaching at him, but the sucking water seemed to go in different directions and the pressure was crushing him.

Fragments of light from above splattered across his vision as he was tossed this way and that, as if by a giant washing machine; after a few seconds his brain told him that there was no way he could fight this kind of underwater turmoil. He had to let the water take him. He had to stop fighting.

The more he struggled, the less his chance of survival.

What survival? Already his lungs were bursting, his ears hurt like hell from the pressure and he was being tossed around like a rat savaged by a terrier. He curled up in a ball, hoping that might reduce the thrashing from the water, but it only made matters worse; by trying to hug his knees he squeezed his chest and there was precious little air left in his lungs. Clamping his jaws even tighter, he tried to swallow, simulating a breath, but that was a momentary distraction from the pain in his chest. This was the end now. He could swim the length of an Olympic-sized pool underwater by taking time to build up the amount of air in his lungs and then taking a strong dive for momentum. That was right on the edge of his endurance. This was like being smashed, time and again, by a tidal wave. The pounding water was pulling him this way and that. His legs felt as though they were being wrenched out of their sockets and his arms were stretched like a contortionist's.

Blackness. His mind or the pit? He didn't know. His last fragments of consciousness called on God, his mother, his father, and settled finally on a desperate internal cry for help to anyone who was listening – as long as they helped him. And behind it all was the glimmer of thought that tried to make him fly. As he had before. If he could just burst through the surface and fly, he would be free. He could breathe again.

But the power was not there.

He had to open his mouth and suck in the water. He would choke and vomit, and he would die but he had no choice, his burning lungs were going to explode anyway.

The sensation altered. There were flecks of foam close to his face – that meant there was air. It was almost completely dark, but now there was some grey light above his face and he reached out through the frothy water. He was sure he felt cold air. Kicking and twisting, he arched his back, forcing his head upwards. His head broke the surface, his ears thundered with the sound of something like a waterfall, and he was barrelling along, but his face was clear of the water. He gulped, the pain in his ribs eased, but his lungs felt raw. Time and time again, he kept gulping.

As he gobbled up the air, he could see he was being pushed along as if he were on a water slide. He was inside a vaulted cave, half-filled with the water that forced him along. Paper-thin beams of light, deflected from fissures in the roof, gave just enough illumination to see by. He was travelling fast on a white-water ride, and if he could keep his body in a fairly stable position he might be able to keep himself from being pulled under again. How fast and how far he had gone he couldn't even guess, but the white water reflected what little light there was, enough for him to see a couple of hundred metres ahead.

The roar of the water, magnified by the tunnel's walls, dulled his thoughts, but his mind was clearing sufficiently for him to realize what had happened and where he was. The surge had taken him into the very entrance he was trying to climb down to. Pushed up by the water into the fluted walls, he was being washed along the channel that would eventually smash into the churning blades of a generator. Even if he had not fallen and had clambered down here, the unexpected surge of water would have caught him. In fact he would probably have been crushed by the sheer weight and power of the water as it forced its way into the tunnel. By falling into the upward surge, he had become part of the mass, and that had cushioned him.

As quickly as possible he took in as much of his surroundings as he could. Vaulted cave – possibly twenty-odd metres high to the first rocks? Then broken layers that kept going up and up – slabs of uneven rock that became cracks and slits for the deflected light from somewhere, way, way above. The walls were smooth because of the thousands of years' worth of water travelling through them, and he hadn't felt anything like a river bed beneath his feet yet, so the water was probably pretty deep. Must be, to have this power.

He was being pushed past a cave system. Cathedral-sized chambers went off to the left and right, but they only sipped away the overspill from the main flood that carried Max along. This wasn't a sightseeing trip. As amazing and awe-inspiring as these underground caves were, he was still fighting to stay alive. His brain was back in gear, so he tried to alter the course of his journey. By dropping a leg down he could steer his body slightly, and if he combined that with an arm-dragging movement he could almost spin himself around in the water. More confident now that he had at least some control over this pell-mell ride, he peered forward into the half-light.

Sooner or later he would have to make a life-saving decision, because wherever this water went and whatever it went into, he would have only a hundred metres or so before he saw it. And judging by the smooth walls, there seemed little chance of clambering out of this underground river, especially at this rate of knots.

He tested the strength in his arms and legs, each one in turn. Sore and strained but still working OK. Nothing broken, nothing torn. Aching muscles he could deal with. He had been lucky.

The roar of the water had diminished, the deeper underground he had gone, and he realized he was not travelling in any kind of downward direction, so it was the sheer weight and volume of water that carried him along. It still ran deep – no bottom to reach down and touch. His breathing had steadied, the giddiness was gone. He was alert, but he gulped more air when the river took him into a black spot, where no light penetrated from above. That was scary, until the opaque glow picked up the rocks and white-flecked water again.

There was a different sound now: a hum – a deep, low resonance that intruded on the water's gurgling. Max peered ahead anxiously. The walls obviously were throwing the sound, so it was impossible to tell how close he was to the source of the hum. But he knew the generator had to be at the end of this tunnel, and hydroelectric blades spinning at the rate needed to generate enough power for Skeleton Rock were going to be the equivalent of him going through a juice extractor.

A bend ahead in the tunnel's wall, like a fast curve on a race track, swept the water in and around, changing its direction completely. Max went with the water, trying to keep himself above the surface as the speed churned the torrent over itself. Now he faced a black tunnel – a green-hued light in the distance. A blinking eye. The water reflected no light from above; the green tinge barely registered at the end of the tunnel, and the sound was now a deep-chested hum. This was it. That fast-approaching green light must be from the machinery. He had to get off this ride in the next thirty seconds.

He pulled and pushed himself from one side of the water to the other, but all he managed to do was bump into the walls. The channel narrowed, creating extra power to hit those blades at the end. Max tried desperately to gauge the size of the generator sitting at the end of the narrowing tunnel, hoping there was a gap, a crevice, anything he could try to aim for, but the blackness was swallowed whole by the green monster.

As he sped closer, the blinking eye became more obvious; it was the blades rotating so quickly, they flickered the light. It was mesmerizing. Not only were the blades spinning at a blurring speed, but the size of the machine filled the whole cavity. It was as big as a shipping container. The light settled in a sickly reflection from the walls on to the water, rivulets of green picking up its currents like strands of weed.

There was no way for Max to fight the force of water behind him. He had only seconds left, and his brain could not comprehend that he had absolutely no chance of survival. Then he saw one of the green strands slither away to the right, as if going straight into the wall, barely four metres before it met the churning blades. Was it only a reflection? A trick of the water and light? No, the tendril of light was being snatched away into a crevice that ran from top to bottom – a tall, narrow canyon, barely wide enough for his body to fit through, but it was a chance!

He jammed his right arm into the water, felt the tug of

resistance, urged his body to fight the grasping current; tried to ignore, unsuccessfully, the smashing blades that sounded like a huge ship's propeller threshing water, and yelled as loudly as he could, sending a bolt of energy into his body. He spun crazily, felt the sharp, jarring shock of impact on his shoulder as he collided with the crevice's wall. Then he was through.

Within moments the water calmed. The sounds behind him were blanketed by a wall of rock as the torrent became a meandering stream, and he felt, for the first time, coarse sand and gravel beneath his feet. The water became as placid as a village pond.

He scrambled on to what felt like a small beach. There was no light here, only the dull glow that barely reached him from the main tunnel. But he was out of the water. The place had a dank, wet-cellar smell but, compared to the smashing sounds still going on twenty or thirty metres back, it was a haven of peace and quiet.

He stood shakily on the crunching gravel, but his legs wouldn't carry him. The spasm in his stomach made him retch, then he puked, mostly water. He must have swallowed litres of the stuff, at least that's how it felt. Better out than in. He sank down, rubbed warmth and circulation back into his legs and then, finding a boulder for support, pulled himself upright. This time his legs held. His shoulder hurt, but that would only be a hefty bruise. He waited, his eyes trying to penetrate the darkness, but it was almost pitch black in there. The pool of water settled like oil once it had escaped the flowing main channel, from where the threshing sounds still reached him. The air barely moved; although slight, it was obviously the result of those blades causing a backdraught.

He looked harder into the darkness, desperately trying to pick up any fragment of light reflected from the main tunnel. Something which looked like the sharp, curved branches of a tree protruded from the narrow opening. It was obviously something spewed up from the belly of the pit he'd fallen into that had been swept along with the tide of water, finally getting snagged and jammed at the entrance to this side pool. Maybe he could use a branch as a support and probe the water for a way out. Edging around the wall, he waded back into the water. He had not noticed these branches as he was being funnelled into the chamber. Had one of the tree's points snagged him – because he could now see it was claw-like, as big as a barrel – it could have speared him right through. He grabbed hold of one of the branches and realized that the smooth surface was not actually wood but bone. He was grasping the stripped ribcage of a big animal, something like a wildebeest or a gemsbok. Obviously the animal had fallen into the Devil's Breath and endured the same terrifying journey as Max, ending up jammed and drowned at the entrance. Only the ribcage remained, and most of the ribs were shattered into ragged points, lethal spears which would have killed him if he'd struck any of them. They might still be of use. He yanked hard at the rib with the least curve to it. It came away and, using it as a bent staff, he made his way back to the shore.

What to do now? He should explore the cave and its pool further, but the more he thought about that, the less appealing the idea became. There was no shred of light and if he fell and injured himself he was finished. His right shoulder already throbbed from the impact with the wall, and his back and side were grazed from being bounced down the tunnel.

His original idea had been to climb down to the tunnel and try to gain access to the fort. And that was still his objective, but, as long as the water turned those lethal blades, he had no chance. Well, the water had to stop at some stage because the Devil's Breath erupted at different times, so the water surge would stop and probably leave only a shallow level of water in the tunnel. He would move back into the main tunnel and see if there was any way through the blades. Satisfied he had some sort of plan, however risky, Max was suddenly very thirsty, but the brackish water smelled too off-putting; besides, he had already vomited everything he'd swallowed, so he would just have to sit tight and wait for the water to stop flowing.

The green light weakened to a barely luminous glow. The threshing calmed, though it still continued, and the hum subsided. The whole place suddenly became still. The whooshing tide no longer slapped the tunnel's walls and the river became as fearsome as an English canal on a beautiful summer's day.

Now he noticed for the first time how humid the cave was and he heard the splash of condensation dropping into the quiet water. He dare not stop and rest now. Not only was he afraid of falling asleep in that darkness, but he knew that unless he used this adrenalin to carry him onwards, sleep would seize up his muscles. He'd be as stiff as a board and would never manage to crawl through anything. No, the blades had to be confronted, because behind them must be a generator room and above that the fort . . . and in there, his father.

He was about to ease himself back into the pool when he sensed a movement in the water. Barely a ripple at first, then it became obvious. Like the effect of a stone being tossed into a pond, this undulation signalled something in the water. Something pushing the water ahead of itself, and it was coming towards him.

His eyes strained, peering into the cave, following the curve of the small beach as far as he could, but he saw nothing. Then the faint light caught a movement. Something slithered. Like a giant white slug. And then another. The water ripples increased. Whatever the creatures were, they had sought refuge further back from the noise and turmoil of the channelled water and, now that everything had fallen quiet, they had returned from the blackness and the depths.

He stared as hard as he could, straining to see what the creatures were. Only when he heard a heavier splash of another giant white grub entering the water did he realize what was coming towards him.

Albino crocodiles. Blind, never having seen daylight, the offspring of ordinary crocodiles swept down here who-knows-when. They had survived and bred, their bodies adapting to their dark environment, gradually losing their sight and colour, living on carcasses washed down the tunnel.

They didn't need to see; they could smell meat and they could sense movement of a distressed animal.

And Max was both.

18

!Koga froze in fear as Max fell into the bottomless mouth of the monster, but he did not run in panic. Instead, he gripped the edge of the boulder and hunched down as the roaring spume soared upwards and splattered him as it fell back. He imagined the bile from the devil's belly would spew Max out; that he would lie on the sand, flapping like a fish out of water. But Max did not appear, and when the surging water subsided he bravely ran to the edge of the devil's mouth.

Gazing down, all he could see was the last of the white water slipping down the monster's gullet. And then nothing. Desolation squeezed his chest as he sank to his knees. His fear of the monster was pushed away by his anger, an emotion he was unused to and uncertain of. 'Max!' he screamed. But his voice was taken by that frightening place and tossed back and forth like a morsel until it too disappeared.

He picked out the place that Max had shown him – the entrance to the tunnel – but there was no sign that Max had survived. There was no miracle, no smiling face that peered back at him and said something about the explosion of water being scary, or a near miss, or anything. Please, Max, say anything – say you are there; say you have changed into that bird which grips the rocks and pecks at the insects or the snake that slithers from under the rock. But there was only silence. And although there was no body to show that Max had died, he accepted that his friend must surely be dead – taken beneath the ground and devoured while the monster lay in wait for other victims.

!Koga had seen hunters gored by gemsbok, or crushed and ripped apart by lions, but this emptiness he felt was a strange experience. Once the anger subsided and his mind cleared, he stood and gazed at the place where the boy from a distant country had died. !Koga had no power to bring him back from that place, nor could he jump into the gorge and fight the monster with bow and arrow, or knife, or his hands. He was helpless, and he had failed to protect Max.

The boy and his father had given their lives trying to help !Koga's people, so now he would take the paper with the lines on it that told where others had died, and find the girl Van Reenen. He should wait for nightfall, so he could travel fast without needing to seek cover, but the time for waiting was over. He would run all day through the searing heat and risk everything. This time he would not fail.

Turning his back on what he believed to be Max's grave, he began to run steadily towards the shimmering horizon, making sure he never looked back.

Mr Slye did not like Skeleton Rock, for it reminded him of the time he had spent in prison in Mongolia, where he had survived on yak fat soup, yak fat gruel and yak fat tea, in an underground cavern of a cell so huge it echoed even when he breathed. That was some years ago, but the darkness here reminded him of his own dim incarceration, where the light fell less than a metre from the iron-bound door, outside of which an oil lamp burned, not for his benefit but for that of his guard. That guard – shudder and horrors! Unwashed, squat, hairy, bow-legged, probably from spending his life riding yaks, and totally illiterate, so any chance of discussing the finer points of the Bolshoi Ballet were completely out of the question. And Slye would hear him farting as he walked down the steps to his cell. Like a horse walking and breaking wind, Slye had decided, because he had never heard a yak fart, but Shaka Chang's string of racehorses created enough methane to destroy the planet. Mr Slye didn't like horses either. There were no yaks in Namibia, but, as he descended into the darkened bowels of this huge fort with its sheer slabs of rock, its cavernous rooms and the depths of its foundations, other unpleasant memories were aroused.

Like a tear down a cheek, the glass-panelled lift slid noiselessly as the supporting cable guided it down the rails in the rock face. A barely audible ping, and then a gentle, almost loving whisper from the automatic voice, told him he was at the lowest level. 'Basement. Hydroelectric unit to the left, seismic recording instruments straight ahead and torture cells to the right. Have a nice day.'

Shaka Chang had transformed this place into hi-tech usability, but privately Mr Slye thought that the woman with the butterfly voice was just a bit too . . . nice was the only word he could think of. Nice. An awful word. A bald word without energy. Boring. And irritating. Not very nice, he supposed.

He followed the row of lights in the floor, similar to those used on an aircraft to show the way to the escape hatches in the unlikely event of the aircraft experiencing any technical difficulties. Such as crashing. But there were no escape hatches down here. This was where Mr Chang sent you when he wanted you one step away from death. A place where no one would ever find you, where you could be easily forgotten.

Slye gave an involuntary shudder as he went further along the corridor. The air-filtering system functioned only in selected areas down here, and he could taste the seeping smell of river water that lay pooling in the hydroelectric chamber, waiting for the next surge to sweep it away. He pressed his hand against a palm-recognition panel and a glass doorway opened, giving him access to the next corridor. Once again the woman's gentle voice oozingly announced his arrival: 'Mister Lucius Slye has entered the controlled area.'

A white-coated man, whose legs were so short that the white coat almost covered his feet, stepped into the corridor and nervously stroked his beard as he waited for Mr Slye to reach him. Mr Slye's daily visit irritated Professor Doctor Illya Zhernastyn. Despite his best efforts and despite his ongoing reports to Mr Chang, it was always this shadow of a man who was sent to speak to him and assess his patient's condition. Patient, not prisoner. How ridiculous words can be sometimes. He was a doctor and the man in his care was being tortured. Nothing physical – no blood, no violence – only drugs. But these drugs could be as punishing as any severe beating. Chemicals that would seep into the cells, find hidden pathways into the brain, and alter consciousness as they mined for the truth.

Zhernastyn had never forgiven himself for the mistake he made thirty years ago. He was then the brightest star in the Russian medical firmament, a doctor who had sold nano-cellular secrets to a woman he craved. He betrayed his profession and his country, all for the love of a woman who turned out to be an American spy. Had it not been for Mr Chang, the Russians would have put him in a meat grinder and fed him to the dogs. He regretfully owed Shaka Chang his life, a life Zhernastyn believed had yet to reach its full potential – so Chang was a conduit to his own ambitions. Zhernastyn knew the influence Mr Slye held, so he was always polite. 'Comrade Slye. Welcome.'

Mr Slye ignored him, flipped open his personal organizer, and ticked his daily schedule, noting the exact time of his arrival. Slye liked to know where he was even when he was already there. He looked at Zhernastyn. There was no need for words; his gaze was command enough. Zhernastyn nodded and turned on his heel. He pressed his palm against a panel and a stainless-steel door slid open, revealing a room of unyielding spartan facilities which reflected the icy determination of the man in charge down here – Zhernastyn. There was a bed, a steel toilet, a sink, and a man, unshaven from his imprisonment, but dressed in clean overalls. The whole thing gave the unmistakable impression of a con-demned man in a death-row cell.

'Progress?' Slye demanded.

'Slight,' Zhernastyn said.

'Slight is not an answer. It is not defined by any qualitative analysis or quantitive measurement. Progress?'

Zhernastyn grimly controlled his desire to spit in Mr Slye's face, grab him by the neck and shake him until the blood spurted from his eyes and his tongue turned purple. And to scream that he, Zhernastyn, was a scientist, not a lowly minion who emptied bedpans and changed the sheets. He needed time to analyse and compute what was happening inside his patient. The elaborate pathways of the neurological system were not as simple to understand as a map of the London Underground. But he showed no sign of his thoughts and simply nodded.

'Of course, Comrade Slye, forgive me. His blood pressure is now stable and his cognitive ability has increased by thirty per cent, given that he was in an almost vegetative state for two weeks, that he could not walk, that whatever drug he had taken to effectively block out his memory was in complete control of neurological functioning, that . . .'

'I know what happened to him,' Slye interrupted. 'He's a scientist. He took a memory blocker that shut him down like a bank vault so we could not get any information from him. Do not state the obvious. We need to find out what he knows. Do we know anything more than we did then?' Mr Slye asked emphatically. 'That is the progress Mister Chang seeks. Progress?' he repeated.

'None.'

'Ah.'

'But he is standing and walking, as you can see.'

'Yes, I can see him leaning against the wall, but he does not speak, he shows no sign of hearing, he seems to be a dead man propping up a corner of his cell.' Slye looked at Tom Gordon, who was gazing at the far wall: a blank, uncomprehending stare that reflected the drugs which had closed down his mind. Zhernastyn gasped as Mr Slye made a sudden move to strike his patient but pulled up short just before contact. Tom Gordon did not even blink.

Mr Slye looked at Zhernastyn. 'Time is now extremely short. If he has passed on what he has discovered, Mister Chang could be destroyed. Increase the dosage of the drugs.'

'That could destroy his mind forever. He could die,' Zhernastyn said, seeing his experiment being suddenly taken away from him, caring less about the man than the possibilities of scientific exploration.

'Then he will die – and we will be forced to run the risk of not knowing whether anyone else has the information.'

Slye turned away. He needed to escape the cloying hospital smell that lingered down here and the doctor's sour breath that betrayed his gum disease. Perhaps Zhernastyn's lack of dental hygiene was just another of the weapons he used to destroy a prisoner's mind.

The heaving stench of the crocodile's breath had an even more repellent effect on Max than its teeth. The crocodile lunged, its jaws open, sheaths of skin at the side of its mouth stretching to accommodate the size of the bite. If those teeth snapped shut on an arm or a leg, the crushing power alone would sever the limb. Or – the worst nightmare scenario – it would drag him from where he perched between the massive blades, twist and spin him around, tearing him apart as this blind, scaly reptile's mates scrambled for a piece.

Max yanked his leg back just in time. The circular blades were big enough for him to almost stand inside them, but there were two sets, one behind the other, which meant that each blade within this huge, fan-like mechanism was slightly out of line with the other. When water slammed into these front blades, they would whirl into life, forcing the driven water to spin the second set of blades. A mighty big egg-whisk. Max wedged a shoulder against one of the front blades, his feet within the flattened rim where the blades spun.

The crocodile's chest struck the base, halting its attack. Max's adrenalin-charged body flooded with relief.

The dead animal's splintered rib, which Max still held firmly, was of no use in this fight. The crocs were already blind, so he couldn't go for their eyes, and the rib wasn't strong enough to use as a spear against their tough hides. Right now it steadied him as his feet floundered in the knee-deep water that lay beneath the turbine blades, but he continued to jab at the crocodiles' snouts in a futile attempt at self-defence. The blades themselves still turned slowly, and Max had to negotiate one set while trying to synchronize his escape through the second. There was no room to manoeuvre, no second chance. Beyond this, stretching as far as he could see, was an overspill room where the water lay, barely moving, in a tank. Impossible to tell how deep it was, or whether any machinery lurked beneath the surface. Worse still, what if any of these crocodiles had got through this blade system and lay in wait in the gloomy water?

The others were now surging forward. Like a savage pack of dogs, these blind prehistoric killers had his scent and they were frenzied enough to clamber over each other to reach him. If they did, they would have a firm purchase for those clawed feet, would miss the rim and lunge straight through the blades. He had to get out now.

Between the two sets of blades there was just enough space for him to stand – his back towards one set, his face towards the other. It was like flattening himself against a wall, except that this wall might spin and chop him into pieces. There seemed to be only one option. The water was churning, the crocodiles in their blood lust were blocking each other's passage towards him, and Max could feel the water was getting deeper. He'd have to turn his back upon the horror, face the second set of blades and then judge his moment, before jumping through. Turn his back. Go on! Turn! His mind yelled at him. Then another question forced its way through his desperate fear. Why was the water rising? Why were the blades moving that bit faster? *Whoosh, whoosh.* They were cleaving air and water now. Max stared into the darkness. Something was coming. He could feel air pressure on his face. It was another flood! The surge of water would lift and push these crocodiles right on to him or the blades would blur and he'd be mincemeat.

Jamming the piece of bone into the groove that guided the blades, he turned his back to his attackers. There was a horrible splintering crunch. The bone had shattered, unable to slow the fan for more than a second, but he used that time to step forward, stretching out his arms sideways for balance. The whooshing of the blades increased, water pushed against the back of his legs. The big wave was coming! If he didn't get through now, the weight and power of the coming water would slam him into the blades.

Another tearing, squelching crunch and half a crocodile, cut in two by the blades, writhed beside him in a welter of blood, its jaws still snapping. Max recoiled involuntarily from the horror and felt the back blades brush his hair. He jerked his head forward and was nearly hit by the ever-increasing rotation of the front blade. He had to jump. He couldn't gauge it now. It was going to be sheer luck.

Max did not even have time to make the decision. The wall of water hit the hydroelectric turbine blades behind him and they churned into action, the force of air and water thrusting him forward.

He fell headlong into the blades.

His yell was munched by the slashing metal and water, but the space he tumbled into was enough for his body to get through. Plunging deep into the murky water, he flailed desperately for anything that would help him clamber out on to dry land.

His fingers touched steel. Coarse and broken, it crumbled in his fingers. Rust. Thrashed around by the turbulence, he held on tightly, his legs floundering behind him as the full power of the water fought for release through those blades. He'd found iron inspection rungs that went down into this overspill tank.

With the sinews in his arms stretched like bow strings, he pulled himself upwards, hand over hand, until his face broke the surface. He sucked in air and looked back over his shoulder. The frothy, turbulent water in the holding tank was only the aftermath of a surge from the Devil's Breath, like the one that had carried Max down the tunnel, only a couple of hours previously. Now the blurring blades whispered a fan-like hiss. There was a bloody froth on the surface – crocodiles forced through the blades into this tank, churned and blended like a fruit smoothie.

Once he'd reached the concrete platform that surrounded the tank he saw the huge pipes that cut away upwards through the rock face. They must go to the generating room, he reasoned. Above him was an iron grid with what looked like a walkway of metal plates across it. The grid mesh was wide enough for a man to crawl through, and anyone inspecting the area from above would be able to check the tank and blades quite easily. Spotlights were strategically placed at each corner so the area would be illuminated at night. Up there was the way out, but the grid was three metres above his head.

Max huddled in the corner; the air vibrated from the whirring blades and he was desperate for rest. Since falling into the chasm he had had no time to think about !Koga, but now he wondered what the Bushman boy had done. Whatever happened to Max, everything might depend on !Koga finding Kallie, delivering that hydrology map, and bringing help. Would anyone come? Would any of those marks on the map convince anyone that poisoned water was killing people and that their bodies were being hidden?

He was shivering violently. The time spent in the tunnel and the encounter with the crocodiles – as well as almost being scalped by those blades – had taken their toll. But to stay in this chamber would only lead to being discovered. He hunched up, pulling his knees to his chest, making himself as small as possible, trying to stop any more heat escaping from his body. He let his gaze roam over the walls, the grid, the floor, the water, but there were no clues as to how he might escape. The noise from the blades grew distant and less intrusive, and the constant churning of the water settled into a kind of white noise in the background.

Concentrate. What can you see? Stay awake! Look! Come on!

He uncurled himself. Sitting down wasn't going to solve the problem. The lights, the power, there had to be a feed somewhere. He skirted the chamber, his hands feeling the wall, searching for something his instinct told him must be there. A bulge in the corner of the wall, a narrow pipe, plastered and painted over so it couldn't easily be seen, but his fingers found it, and he could tell that it ran from top to bottom of the concrete platform where he stood.

He needed something to cut away the covering, but his knife and all the weapons the Bushmen had given to him at their camp had been swept away by the Devil's Breath. He searched around for anything that might help him, and found a square piece of metal, about the size of a cigarette packet, with a hole in the middle. It was probably a retaining washer for one of the big bolts holding the support plates on the hydraulic pipes. As Max scraped its edge down the corner of the bulge, the plaster and paint fell away, and a few minutes of diligent gouging created enough space to bare the metal behind the conduit. Moments later there was enough room to curl his fingers between the narrow pipe and the wall. He yanked, and a metre-long length of pipe came away. He pulled again, using his foot against the wall for leverage, and the plastic conduit cracked. He fell back, losing his grip and balance, but now he had a means of escape. The split piping held electric cable. With both hands wrapped around the rubber-coated cable, as thick as a broom handle, he heaved again, and the cable ripped free of the brittle plastic pipe.

This was all he needed. He pushed his feet against the wall and climbed upwards, hand over hand. The heavy-gauge iron grid above his head, each bar as thick as his arm, was old and rusted, but had stood the test of time. It was probably built into the original construction. That made sense. If this area had been the dungeons and the crazy German aristocrat knew there were crocodiles down here, then having a huge caged floor built into the rocks would serve as a threat to anyone dragged down here. Not that the history of the place mattered now, as Max hooked an arm through the grid and pulled himself up.

The area he now stood in was quite bare. There was a stainless-steel door to one side, and another in the opposite wall. He could hear the steady hum of machinery, muted by the thick walls, so he guessed that all the fort's power and utilities were located down here. He had visited a German castle in Bavaria on a school trip and wished he could remember more of the layout. That would have helped him get a clearer picture in his mind of where he was within the fort's structure. Wherever it was, he was at the bottom, so the only way out was up. But how? Air ducts were fastened to the walls and the roof, more piping, but no way out. What was it he had seen and heard when he whirled through that darkness? Max ran his hands over the door's dull sheen. Next to it, on a slender column of the same brushed steel, was a square of glass, the outline of a spread hand etched into it. Max hesitated, his hand hovering over the lines. Obviously it was a coded access, a palm-print recognition terminal, but would it set off every alarm bell in the castle if he tried it, or would it simply deny access?

He looked above the door. Between the wall and ceiling was a glass panel, running the whole length of the room. Below it a smallish pipe ran, suspended from sturdy-looking brackets. He could reach that. One good jump and he'd get a grip, then he could see what lay on the other side of the wall. He flexed his knees, feeling the strain on his thigh muscles. Forcing his legs upwards from a squat position, he threw his arms as high as he could. He grasped the pipe, but his hands were sweating and he didn't have a strong enough purchase – the pipe was just that bit too wide. Focusing all his attention on the strength in his wrists, he curved his hands as tightly as he could. Shaking with effort, he pulled the weight of his body up, feeling his biceps bite, but he was losing his grip.

No sooner had he tried to lift his knees to swing a leg on to the pipe than the door hissed open. 'Johnson Mkebe has entered the hydroelectric area,' a woman's voice murmured gently.

A slightly built African, wearing a baseball cap and blue overalls with 'Maintenance' printed across the back, stepped through the doorway. Three things happened in quick succession: the door closed, Max fell, and Johnson Mkebe was knocked unconscious as Max crunched on top of him. After a sudden grunt as the wind was knocked out of him, the maintenance man lay silent. Max rolled free, immediately alert for the sound of running feet. He held his breath, heart thumping, muscles tense. There was nowhere to escape except back into the overspill tank. And that was not an option. He would barge into anyone who came through that door and take his chances with whatever lay on the other side of the wall. But nothing happened. Max waited another few seconds, and still no one came to investigate. Max heaved the man over, unzipped his overalls and yanked them down over his legs, then climbed into the one-piece boiler suit. With a couple of turns on the sleeves and ankles, it fitted. Jamming the cap on his head, he turned for the door but realized that there was only one way to get out of the room. Dragging the unconscious man's dead weight as close to the security palm-reader as he could, he stretched one of his arms out until it rested on the glass plate. 'Johnson Mkebe has left the hydroelectric area,' the voice told him. Max didn't wait to correct her.

As the sliding door swished closed behind him, he moved into an area that was as boxed as the room he had just left. An open steel structure rose upwards to the right; it was the lift shaft. Ahead of him was another closed, brushed-steel door. What next? No choice really. Press the button, get into the lift, find a floor where he could hide until he could see the lie of the land and then he would look for . . .

The door ahead of him slid open. Along the corridor, a man in a wheelchair, his shoulders drooped, his face unshaven, eyes gazing down at the floor, drugged into semi-consciousness.

'Dad!' Max yelled. But Tom Gordon did not even raise his eyes.

At the sound of Max's voice, a malevolent-looking man in a white coat stepped into the corridor, shock registering on his face at the unexpected intruder. He lunged for the fist-sized red alarm button on the wall. In a second, wailing sirens would bring armed men storming in. Max had to stop him.

But he knew he would never reach him in time.

19

'Run, !Koga. Run! Run faster than the shadow that races across the earth when the sun dies.'

Max's words stayed like a mantra in !Koga's head, and he did run. Faster and further than ever before. The sky changed colour, the land grew cooler and the animals hunted, but !Koga stopped only to sip water. He ignored the growling challenge of the lions as they feasted on a buck, he scattered the herd of springbok and irritated the elephants who trumpeted his arrival and departure.

Finally, as the sun's rays brought their nourishing warmth, !Koga stopped. He smelled the wood smoke before he saw it curling from the police outpost's chimney. A square, two-room bungalow with a red tin roof and dust-stained walls sat perfectly in the centre of the arid area designated as its domain. A chain-link fence boxed it in and a flagpole stood rigidly to attention with a limp Namibian flag hanging like a scarf from its neck.

He waited for an hour, until he saw movement and identified the two policemen as they woke to start their daily routine. A needle of steel pointed to the sky, a radio antenna that would summon help.

He moved cautiously towards the policemen, smelled the

coffee being brewed and the meat being cooked. A growl from his stomach reminded him how little he had eaten in these past few days. The police would probably be from the Herero tribe, but he would speak to them in Afrikaans, the common language of the once-oppressed people of Namibia. A cop wearing a vest and boxer shorts was cooking on a gas-bottle stove outside the bungalow and he saw !Koga before he could say anything. !Koga stopped in his tracks. This might be a hostile reception. The authorities weren't always friendly towards the Bushmen.

Like a man enticing an animal to approach closer, the man gestured with the frying pan. *You want to come and eat something, boy?* !Koga's mouth watered, he could see it was a thick steak, its juices basting the meat. He shook his head but moved closer. Perhaps this friendly gesture was a good sign. The cop didn't smile, but he didn't look aggressive either. He turned the steak over, and the second man came outside, a towel in his hand, wiping away remnants of shaving cream from his face. The two cops looked at each other for a moment and the cook shrugged.

'You all right, boy?' the shaven man called. Neither of the cops seemed too concerned; !Koga stepped closer. Lifting his wrist, he showed them the watch.

'The white man who is missing, I have been with his son. He sent me to you. For help,' he added.

The men became more alert. 'We know about the missing man and his son, headquarters have been looking for him,' said the cooking man.

'My people have died; many of them. And this boy. His name is Max and he is my friend, he is also dead.'

The two men looked at each other again. Here, in the middle of nowhere, was news about the very people their boss in Walvis Bay had signalled. Handle this right and they'd be promoted, for sure.

!Koga, still a couple of metres away from them, undid the watch and threw it to them. 'This is his father's watch, to prove I have been with his son. His name is on the back.'

The cook caught the watch, checked the inscription and handed it to his partner, and again they looked at each other. This was for real, all right.

!Koga held the hydrology map in his other hand. 'I must speak to Kallie van Reenen. She is at the farm called Brandt's Wilderness. Only she can help now. This is a paper which shows where the people died.'

The two cops muttered something to each other, then nodded.

'Where's the boy's body?'

'He fell into the monster and was swallowed. The monster took him beneath the earth.'

That was the trouble with these Bushmen; they had crazy ideas about places out in the wilderness: haunted places; places where men changed into animals; places where the ground could swallow you. Being rational wasn't one of their strong points, which was why the government had problems with them about where they could and couldn't hunt. Better for everyone if they just came in and lived in a resettlement area.

!Koga was more tired than he had ever been before. The food and coffee made his mouth water. Now the cops smiled and the cook hooked the steak from the pan with a fork.

'Come on, son, we'll deal with this now. You need some food, *ja?*'

Yes, !Koga needed food and sleep, though the grief he felt for Max still sat on him like a heavy rock. He stepped forward, he had done what Max had asked, perhaps now there was a chance to save Max's father. He squatted in front of the men as they placed the steak on a plate in front of him.

'You'd better give me the paper for this Van Reenen person, then I can tell my people to find her.'

'I can't do that, I have to give it to her, that's what Max told me.' He reached for the plate of food but the cook grabbed his wrist.

'Give me the paper,' he said coldly, no longer smiling. This kid or his people may have killed the white boy, perhaps even his father as well. The watch was evidence, and the paper might prove to be vital.

!Koga twisted in the sand, but the grip was firm and the second cop had moved quickly to hold the wriggling boy down, a knee in his back. !Koga grunted in pain, his fist still clutching the map, but the man was too strong and unfurled the boy's fingers with ease.

The cook seized the map and stepped back. 'All right, put him in the cell until we sort this out.'

!Koga twisted like a snake under the man's weight. His hand found the fork and he stabbed it down into the man's bare foot. With a scream of pain the second cop released his grip, but in an instant they both lunged for him. !Koga was too quick. He ran through the gate and made his escape. The men gave up after a few metres, there was no way they would catch the boy judging by the speed he was running, and even if they got their 4x4 pick-up truck and gave chase, he'd merge into the landscape. It didn't matter, they had the map and the watch, and their boss, Mike Kapuo in Walvis Bay, would be very pleased.

The men weren't so happy, though. One limped, his foot hurting like hell, and they were both hungry – the Bushman boy had stolen their steak.

Max ignored the impossible distance and hurled himself at Zhernastyn – he had to try. Somewhere in the background, an animal snarl reached his ears. Then Zhernastyn caught his white coat on the handles of Tom Gordon's wheelchair. It snagged him and spun the wheelchair, which tripped him up. As he recovered and reached for the alarm, Max pounded into him. The man was terrified. Max felt so focused, so determined to stop him, that everything else was forgotten. It was like tunnel vision. And the snarling sound he'd heard came from his own lips, which were drawn back across his teeth. Zhernastyn fainted.

Max was on his knees in front of his father.

'Dad, it's me. It's Max. I found you.'

He could feel the tears sting his eyes and he wiped them away roughly. Tom Gordon gazed down at his son for what seemed an age in time, and then he smiled.

'Max?' His voice was barely a whisper.

'Yes, Dad, I'm going to get us out of here. And help's on its way.' However, the last bit didn't sound too convincing, even to his own ears.

'Max?' said Tom Gordon as he tried to comprehend that his son was somehow with him. 'What are you doing here?'

'I got your message, and I found the signs you left for me.'

'Max . . . I don't understand.'

Max touched his dad's arm, frightened at how weak he seemed. His dad had always been so strong and full of energy, and now he was so helpless. Max smiled encouragingly. 'We need to find a place to hide for a while, that's all,' he said as he grabbed the wheelchair's handles. But Tom Gordon reached back and weakly took hold of his son's wrist.

'Not yet.'

'What? Dad, we have to get out of here!'

His father shook his head. 'Not yet,' he repeated.

Max looked where his father's trembling hand pointed. The door had closed when Max had launched his attack. Could he drag this doctor to the security point, use his palm-print to open the door, and then get his father out in time?

'You need him,' his father said, and shook his head, as if trying to remember something.

'Dad, what is it? What have they done to you?'

'Memory,' his dad said falteringly. 'I took . . . I took . . . a potion . . . herbs and stuff . . . Bushmen gave it to me . . . had to . . .'

He fell silent. Max waited, uncertain what to do or say, but he knew that time was not on their side. 'Dad, I don't know what to do, other than get you out of here.'

His father nodded and struggled to string together the words he needed. 'Had to blot out my memory . . . much as I could . . . fooled them . . . listen, son . . . listen . . . they wanted the . . . evidence. Everything. I've hidden it . . . it's here . . . my Land Rover.'

'Your Land Rover's here?'

Max's dad was beginning to lose consciousness. Whatever they'd done to him made the effort of recognition and speech too difficult.

'Dad! Where? Where is it?'

Tom Gordon was sweating, the exertion of staying awake draining away his energy.

'Big hangar somewhere . . . near . . . near a fan . . . may be a generator . . .'

Max knew that had to be on the next level. He remembered the water pipes tunnelling upwards from the hydroelectric tank room. That might make sense. This place had to be below ground, so the next floor up was probably at ground level. That would give access to the outside. If he could get up to that room, hide his dad and find the evidence, they might still have a bargaining tool if they were caught. It might at least buy them some time.

'Where's the evidence, Dad? Where is it?'

'Land Rover . . .'

'OK, I know that. But where? In a panel? Spare wheel? Where?'

His father's head dropped, his lips barely moving. Max put his ear closer. 'Water proof . . . water . . . proof . . .'

Max held his father's face in his hands. 'Dad, I know the water's being poisoned, I found the hydrology map. But where is the proof?'

But his father was unconscious.

So now what? Where to keep his dad safe until he could come back for him? Right here. Right where he's always been, because then if anyone came looking, they'd see he was still in his bed.

He wheeled his father back into the room and with a lot of effort manhandled him on to the hospital bed. Stepping back into the corridor, he saw what was obviously the doctor's office. There was a coffee-maker and a small fridge, which yielded a couple of pots of yoghurt, a tub of something in rice and a carton of milk. Max wolfed the lot in an indecently short time and followed it with a belly-churning belch. Now he had to get out of there.

'Doctor Zhernastyn has left the controlled area,' the woman's voice said.

So that's who you are, Max thought, as he eased the still unconscious man's hand back on to his lap and pushed the wheelchair through the doors, with Zhernastyn secured to it with surgical tape wrapped around his body and across his mouth.

The lift slid down, the doors eased open and Max trundled his cargo inside. The panel showed there were six floors. Those from the basement through to the fourth floor were clearly marked, but there was a button above those that said *Private: Coded Access Only*. That would be where Shaka Chang hung out. Max pressed the second button. The lift moved with stomach-dropping speed. Once again the doors glided open. 'Ground floor. Vehicle Maintenance. If you're driving today, be careful, Doctor Zhernastyn. Goodbye.'

Max eased the wheelchair forward into a hangar-sized cave which had been blasted out of the solid rock and turned into a modern work area. He could hear music playing somewhere, and the clang of a spanner as it fell to the floor. Massive doors had been slid back across the hangar's opening, revealing the glare of the desert that filtered in far enough to create a soft sheen of light across the highly polished floor.

A twin-engined jet sat, parked at the centre of the hangar. Dust bags covered the air intakes. The gleaming black metal sported a thin line of trim that ran like an arrow along the fuselage and up to the tail fin, where it formed the start of Shaka Chang's corporate logo – assegais and a shield. The upturned wingtips gave the plane a cutting-edge look, and Max reckoned the wings must have spanned twenty-odd metres. But there was still plenty of room for all the other vehicles. Skeleton Rock must be like an iceberg, Max thought. There's a hell of a lot you don't see from above. And it's probably just as deadly, looking at that gear.

The wheelchair's tyres squeaked as Max turned to the right, hugging the rear wall and ducking low behind a couple of Humvees, painted black and bearing Shaka Chang's coat of arms. A dune buggy and a sleek helicopter, also black, sat further forward. This looked like Shaka Chang's personal playroom, and his toys were expensive. Somewhere near the front of the hangar, a couple of mechanics wiped their hands and moved away from the open cowling of a small aircraft. It looked as though they were going for a coffee break. One of the men switched off a portable radio and they disappeared into the glare. Max could see that a glider, the tips of its huge wings balanced tenderly on supporting blocks, lay as still as a moth transfixed by light.

Max hugged the wall, seeing no sign of his dad's Land Rover. At the far end of a ten-metre passage cut into the wall

– a corridor big enough to drive a lorry through – Max could see a smaller room, if that's what it could be called.

Edging forward cautiously, he found himself inside a smaller version of the hangar. This seemed a more workaday place, though it was just as immaculately clean as the hangar, containing racks of spare parts, a block and tackle, heavy lifting rigs and a couple of inspection pits. In the opposite corner, fairly well tucked out of sight, an engine diagnostic centre sat gleaming, its various computer screens dark – a purpose-built area that looked like something out of a Formula One garage. A huge enclosed cooling fan was bolted to the wall, and it turned lazily on a low power setting, massaging the room with cooled air. Half a dozen motorbikes and a couple of pick-up trucks stood in a neat row on the far side, in addition to several quad bikes and two very sleek Class 3 sand yachts. These were the ultimate: a steerable front wheel and two fixed at the rear. That single wing-shaped sail could snag a breeze and rocket the slender Kevlar hull along at up to a hundred and twenty kilometres an hour.

One of Max's friends had taken him once to help at a sand race in north Devon, and let him try his hand. The thrill of hurtling along that close to the ground under the power of wind was an experience he wouldn't forget. But those memories were getting in the way now; he had to concentrate on finding his dad's Land Rover.

At the end of this room was another opening, and Max ran towards it – this and the other hangar might be his way out. Keeping in the shadows, he peered out across the landscape. The big hangar opened on to the vast plain, but this corner of the fort was on the edge of a plateau, so the ground dropped away to the river. That would make sense. That river must be fed from the Devil's Breath crater, and he could see the marsh grass and the crocodiles basking on the sandbanks. A narrow set of rails led down a ramp from this opening, where a motor boat was held fast. Matted, tissue-paper-like fibreglass showed a nasty gash below the waterline, and there were signs that someone had been working on the repair. Something sharp and with enormous crushing power had caused that damage. It wasn't too hard to imagine what.

The boat had obviously been hauled back up the ramp for repairs; it was too risky to work on it down there – those crocs could move too quickly. There seemed no way out except across that desert, in full view of the fort.

Zhernastyn was coming round, but the initial shock of finding himself strapped in a wheelchair gave way to immediate compliance when Max pushed his face into his. 'You make a sound, you try anything, and I'll push you down that desert ski ramp and let the crocs untie you.'

Zhernastyn's eyes widened and he nodded furiously. He'd seen the driver, and others, fed to those maneaters. Max pulled the tape from Zhernastyn's mouth, the whiskers tearing away like a Velcro strap being undone. Tears wetted Zhernastyn's eyes.

'What did you do to my father?'

Zhernastyn scrunched his face up and bared his teeth, like a baby about to burst into tears. 'It wasn't me,' he blubbered. 'I only did what I was told to by Mister Chang.'

'Oh, that's all right then, I won't hold it against you.'

'You won't!?' Zhernastyn said, eyes open wide now and surprised at the boy's leniency.

'No, of course not. I'll pin a note to your chest to tell the crocodiles they mustn't hurt you because I said so.'

There was the briefest of moments while Zhernastyn seemed to think about that proposal, but then fear swallowed him again.

'What was the drug?'

'Different ones. He'd taken something from the Bushmen. I couldn't identify it in his blood tests. It seemed to block out parts of the memory. I tried everything. But he was very, very stubborn. So stubborn, I doubled the dose. He was *so* strong-willed, he resisted *so much*, he made me *so angry*, I . . .' Zhernastyn got carried away by the memory of his patient's ability to withstand his efforts. He saw Max's eyes narrow and felt the wheelchair nudge towards the ramp. He sucked in air so quickly he nearly choked. 'No!' he spluttered. 'Paradyoxinalthymiate! It's an experimental drug!'

Max stopped the wheelchair and faced him again. 'There's an antidote?'

Zhernastyn grimaced and cringed. 'I could try and develop one,' he whispered, in a vain attempt to save himself.

OK, if Max could get his dad out, there had to be a scientist somewhere who could help him. 'Where's my father's Land Rover?'

'Through there.' Zhernastyn nodded towards the wall on the far side of the small hangar. The light from outside threw a glaring sheen across the rock face, disguising the next chamber whose entrance, another passage cut in the wall, was engulfed in shadow. These huge underground chambers must have needed tunnel-boring machines to excavate them, but that would have been no problem for Shaka Chang; he had everything he needed for the massive dam project, further north. Max grabbed a roll of gaffer tape from a workbench and wrapped it across Zhernastyn's mouth.

Max had seen photographs and films of air-crash investigators as they pieced together the wreckage of air disasters, and this was exactly how it looked, on a smaller scale, as he pushed Zhernastyn into this next chamber. A Land Rover had been completely dismantled and every piece, every nut and bolt, every panel and welded seam, had been taken apart. As if by a pathologist's post-mortem the vehicle had been thoroughly dissected and lay, spread across the floor, on a massive tarpaulin. The engine block had been cut in pieces and lay at the centre of it all. Max parked Zhernastyn and walked slowly around the dismembered carcass. This had obviously been done by experts, and if they'd found nothing then what could he do? He let his eyes wander over the bits and pieces, then he concentrated on each portion of the jigsaw puzzle. There was nothing that could possibly hold any secret.

It had been picked clean by Chang's vultures.

20

Shaka Chang grunted with exertion. The man had attacked him from behind, taking Chang by surprise as he dealt with another assault from the front. The first man slashed upwards with a knife, but Chang stepped inside the knife thrust, blocked the man's arm in a scissor grip, pushed his shoulder hard into the other's chest and felt his breath expelled. He kept hold of the man's wrist as he fell, twisting it in a swan-neck grip. The knife dropped, the man yelled in pain and, just as Chang was going to use his considerable strength and kick the man hard to keep him down, the other assailant had run in from the room behind him.

Slye stood in the doorway, frozen by the violence. Hating the brutality of it. He could barely move, in case he was somehow caught up in the assault.

Chang took the blow to the back of his neck and it stunned him momentarily. He sagged, nearly going down on his knees, and then the man had an armlock around his throat. A knee in his back and one arm pressed in just the right place to cause unconsciousness and death. And the attacker was as big and as strong as Chang. Chang hadn't heard him approach. But that was exactly why he paid these men so much money to be his bodyguards. They were very good at their jobs, but he wanted to be better than the professionals. He wanted to be better than anyone at everything.

Chang rolled, letting the man's weight carry them, and jabbed him hard with his elbow. It took three or four severe blows, but finally the man succumbed.

The men, now on the floor, groaned, each recovering from the hurt inflicted on him. Shaka Chang rubbed his neck and reached for a towel as he spotted Mr Slye, nervously waiting to be summoned closer.

These weekly workouts in the fort's dojo kept Chang in good shape; he was determined that people should never forget that he came from a warrior breed. Chang dabbed the sweat around the jade and Moldavite bracelet, linked by gold. He never took that off. It was his talisman. Jade from his mother's homeland, China, meant protection, the gold mined from his homeland, its chain forged and crafted so tightly that the bracelet should never break. And the Moldavite droplets held fragments of life – entombed secrets – from before man walked the Earth. Legend had it that the green translucent meteoric glass, fragments from a massive impact fifteen million years ago, carried the energies between those of extraterrestrial origin and those inhabiting Earth. He never tired of gazing at the bracelet's beauty.

Mr Slye tried not to wrinkle his nose as Chang nodded for him to come closer. There was always the smell of sweat. It was pungent, like a dressing room after a football game, or a stable full of horses after a race, or even, he remembered with a shudder, the unwashed, farting guard.

'Mister Chang, sir. Might I have a moment?'

Chang rubbed himself down with the towel. 'What is it? You speak to Zhernastyn? He get anything yet?'

'Most disappointingly, he has not.'

'We're only hours away from opening the control gates of the biggest hydroelectric scheme in Africa; tribes have been displaced, billions of dollars have poured in, and people are going to die when I poison their underground sources of water. I will control the complete water supply for southern Africa. I can hold governments to ransom – diamond fields, goldfields, farming, wildlife, tourism – they all need water! And because one man – one man! – knows my plan, all of this is in jeopardy! I will not be stopped!' Chang's voice had become harder and louder until he was roaring at a quivering Mr Slye, who stood full in the blast, eyes squinting as if facing a hurricane. Which well described Shaka Chang's temper.

And then suddenly the eye of the storm settled as Shaka Chang calmed down, the near silence almost more threatening than the tirade. His face was close to that of Slye, who had somehow managed to hold on to his dignity and remain stoically upright. 'Listen to me, Mister Slye. No man's memory is buried so deeply that it cannot be dug out using crude, painful instruments. I want Tom Gordon's memory of where he hid the evidence, and I want it served up on a plate – and I don't care how bloody it becomes. I like my steak rare. You understand?'

Slye nodded. Tom Gordon would have a great deal of pain inflicted on him now.

'Anything else, Mister Slye?'

'A boy. We've spotted a Bushman boy, heading this way. Directly towards Skeleton Rock.'

'Why would a child do that?' Shaka Chang waited a

moment, his dark eyes seeming to creep into Slye's soul. 'Unless . . .' he said almost tenderly, 'he was the boy who was with Gordon's son. You assured me those boys were dead.' His eyes never left Slye's face as his arm pointed towards the open window and the desert beyond. 'You did make a note in your personal organizer that those boys were dead. Didn't you?'

Mr Slye's Adam's apple made a jerking motion, like a chicken about to cluck. 'The odds I calculated, based on the extreme conditions – the temperature alone was fifty degrees; even a scorpion would think twice about venturing out – indicated certain death. Then there was their lack of food and water, their inability to contend with attacks from wild animals and their complete lack of knowledge of who we are and where we are. All of this, Mister Chang, sir, determined that they died more than three days ago.'

'But?'

'But . . . Bushmen are . . . Bushmen.'

'So they could have survived?'

'The Bushman boy, perhaps. Max Gordon, definitely not. Otherwise, why is the Bushman boy coming towards us on his own?'

Shaka Chang smiled at his factotum. The perfect white teeth glistened like freshly painted tombstones. 'Why? Perhaps because Max Gordon is near here. Because he is alive. Because he has learned the secret we have been so determined to find. Perhaps you have underestimated everything, Mister Slye.'

Slye, a trifle indignant at being insulted by the suggestion of incompetence, was silent.

'Check the boy's father, tell Zhernastyn there are no holds

barred, and capture that Bushman boy. If necessary, bring me his body. I want to see it for myself, this time.'

Shaka Chang threw his towel across Slye's face. Slye nearly fainted from the suffocating, sweaty stench.

Max stepped between the pieces of Land Rover, an ever-increasing sense of panic working away in his stomach, threatening to rise up and take complete control. There was just no way Shaka Chang's men would have missed the evidence, whatever it was, after they'd done this. Maybe his father's memory was completely shot. What if he only thought he'd hidden the evidence here? It was hopeless.

A small bird fluttered in and landed at the edge of the dismantled Land Rover. The radiator, bonnet and headlights, neatly separated from each other, were propped against the wall. Like a disembodied skull, the gaping holes in the Land Rover's front bodywork, and the yawning space where the radiator would have been, stared blindly back at him. The bird chirped, flew up and found a perch next to the hessian water bag, hanging from its original position on the front of the Land Rover. This is what kept water cool in the crippling heat, condensing the seepage from the bag and allowing a fine layer of moisture to form on its rough skin. The bird took some drops in its beak, had its fill and flew back outside.

Max was rooted to the spot, remembering the water bag on Van Reenen's Land Rover that Kallie had given him; the attack and the loss of the water bag and the fear that came with the prospect of thirst in the wilderness. *Water Proof. Waterproof. Proof in the water?*

He picked his way through the Land Rover's remains and lifted the bag from the hook. It was heavy, a belly of water that pressed tightly against the sacking. He twisted open the bag's mouth and sniffed. No smell of anything untoward, so he sipped the cold water. That's what it was: cool, refreshing, life-saving water. But there had to be more than that. He squeezed and felt the bag, and his fingers touched something with an edge to it. He upended the bag to let the water gush out, a silly memory of emptying a hot-water bottle after a freezing night at Dartmoor High intruding into his concentration. When the bag was empty, he could definitely feel a square of something, but there was no way it could have been pushed inside the bag through the narrow neck. He searched along the seam. Underneath the sack, someone had cut the hessian and re-stitched it. The water had stretched the material so there was no likelihood of it leaking.

Max quickly found a knife on a workbench and slit the stitching. Shoving his hand inside, he felt the flat box, cold to the touch and wrapped in something smooth. He eased it out. It was a DVD case, bound in gaffer tape to make it watertight.

He wiped the box dry. The tape's adhesive had congealed and it resisted the efforts of his fingernail to cut along the lid. He quickly found a Stanley knife on the workbench, slid out the blade and slit the tape open. A black marker's indelible ink had scrawled three words on the DVD's shiny surface – *Shaka Chang Evidence*. Max held the disc as if it were the Holy Grail. The secrets of life and death lay captured just below its surface.

Jumbled thoughts fought for his attention. He had to get

the evidence out, at any moment he ran the risk of being captured, and he'd just destroyed the best hiding place ever for the disc. He had to rescue his father *and* get the disc to the authorities. He couldn't count on the cavalry riding to the rescue, not in time anyway, if at all. *!Koga, Kallie, Sayid. Help me. Come on, someone. Anyone. Give me an idea.*

Sayid!

Max pushed Zhernastyn in front of the diagnostic system. It all looked so bewildering. Max was OK with games consoles and his computer, but this had a different, a more formidable look to it. Then he reasoned that every computer works on the same principle: it had to be switched on somewhere. He found a scooped button big enough for the convenience of switching the machine on without thought. He pressed it, and the screens came to life.

A blue screen twisted and twirled, ran a montage of Shaka Chang industries, then two spears plunged by invisible hands formed an X. In each quadrant of the X was a blinking cursor. Blazoned across the top of the spears were eight letters: *PASSWORD.*

Sayid was worth his weight in gold at times like this, but he wasn't there, was he? He was probably sitting, glued to his own computer, playing some game that he always won. Max bent down to Zhernastyn, and caught the edge of the gaffer tape that was stuck to his face.

'I can either tear this off slowly or rip it off quickly – slow pain, fast pain – either way, you're going to lose most of that beard and moustache. You decide.'

Zhernastyn muttered a muffled plea for mercy.

Max waited. 'Nod for slow, shake your head for fast.'

Zhernastyn squeezed his eyes shut, then, in anticipation of what was to come, shook his head. Max ripped the tape free and heard the rasping tear of whiskers separating from half of Zhernastyn's face. His mouth opened to yell, but Max smothered it with a grubby hand. 'You say a word and I'll send you and your wheelchair down there,' he said, nodding towards the railed slipway that swept down to the river and the crocodiles. 'If anyone hears you cry out, it'll be too late. Understand?'

Zhernastyn nodded vigorously.

Max eased his hand away. 'I'll give you one chance, and only one.'

'Listen, my young friend, you are so out of your depth you cannot even comprehend it.' Zhernastyn nodded towards the DVD in Max's hand. 'If that is what we have been seeking, you are too late. You understand? You would be wise to consider your position. You cannot save the thousands of people who will die. You have no comprehension of what Shaka Chang has done.' Zhernastyn enjoyed the status that having access to secrets often gave people. 'You can never escape from this place, you know that.'

'Can you access this computer system?'

'Yes. It's an open system, providing you have the password.'

'And do you have a password?'

Zhernastyn hesitated for a second. Max scowled at him. The not-so-good doctor was caught in a deadly dilemma. If he didn't give Max the password, he would be fed to the crocodiles. If he did, and Chang discovered what he'd done, then Chang would definitely feed him to the crocodiles.

Would this boy really do that? Could he? He was just a boy. He looked at Max. Dirt-streaked, no sign of any teenage fat, no pimples, burnished by the sun, nails broken and dirty, as sinewy as coiled rope, and blue eyes that were unflinchingly crystal-clear beneath the scruffy mop of sun-bleached hair.

Only a boy. But he looked more than capable, and Zhernastyn had tortured his father. No question about it, Max had the look. He would do it. Better the devil you know. 'Aleyssia Petrovna,' he said.

'Aleyssia Petrovna?'

'A woman I loved once. You wouldn't understand.'

'Spell it!'

Zhernastyn spelled out his lost love's name as Max typed in the letters. He hit the return button – and he was in.

'One day, when you are older, you will meet such a woman, she will beguile you with her . . .'

Max wrapped more tape across Zhernastyn's mouth.

'I really don't want to hear about your sad, pathetic love-life, Doctor.'

Frantically he searched for a disc-drawer. There wasn't one, but a cable led to a sleek, snake-mouthed box, a curved, toothless grin that beckoned to be fed. Max slid in the DVD and prayed it wasn't corrupted.

The computer had blitzing power. Images, data charts, photographs, statistics, pictures of dead Bushmen, samples of water with crude, handwritten field data beneath each one, all flashed rapidly across the screen. Snatches of information bombarded his brain: drug companies and money, millions, and his father's face, talking on camera. More pictures of dead Bushmen, twenty or thirty bodies, men, women and children. And then Max's dad filming himself again. Telling his secret.

'Everything I have compiled here is the most damning evidence of multinational companies' corruption and one man's intention to murder thousands of people in his quest for power.'

Max froze the image on the screen and sat for a moment, transfixed by the man he remembered as his father. That strong, softly spoken man looked him directly in the eye, his voice firm and convincing, the words chosen carefully. It was not the emaciated, shuffling man he had held in his arms, minutes before. He released the image on the screen and listened as his father reported, like a war correspondent telling a news camera everything he had discovered. How, for many years, Western pharmaceutical companies had been obliged by law to dispose of all their unwanted drugs. The cost was huge, the quantity enormous, massive beyond belief. And governments still gave the companies millions in tax breaks to dispose of these often toxic drugs in a legal manner.

Max muttered under his breath, 'So how does Chang fit into this?' And, as if in answer, his father's voice continued.

'For years, ever since the dam project first started, Shaka Chang has offered these companies a means of disposal. He buries these vast quantities of lethal drugs by the shipload. As far as the drug companies are concerned, they have delivered the unwanted drugs to someone who can take the problem off their hands. Shaka Chang has fooled the southern African governments. They think he's shipping in materials for the dam project, and corrupt customs officers and government officials are helping him, but they don't know the consequences of their complicity. My field assistant, Anton Leopold, and I discovered his shipping route into Walvis Bay. Chang then has the containers taken to a vast underground site that everyone thinks is part of the dam project. The drug companies pay him more money than it cost to build the dam. Everyone is happy.'

Max's father appeared to be under pressure, he kept stopping and moving away from the camera, then coming back into frame. The next time he appeared, he was more hurried. 'They're looking for me. I left Anton in Walvis Bay to see if he can get more evidence, after we found out why the Bushmen were dying. I don't know what's happened to him, but we do know some of the drugs have seeped into the underground water system and when Chang opens the floodgates it will flush the chemicals through every watercourse in southern Africa. The only clean water will be controlled by him. Everyone, governments and industry, will be at his mercy. But worse than that, he will kill everything that drinks from these natural watercourses, including wildlife and thousands of people. I'll do what I can to get this information out . . .'

Max's father suddenly stopped, ducking in a defensive position. Max saw him reach for an automatic pistol in his waistband, and then he noticed for the first time that he had a roughly tied bandage around his leg. The video must have been filmed after they attacked his plane. His father didn't look at the lens again, his eyes scanning somewhere off-camera. His hand reached out and grabbed it, the picture wobbled, feet running, sky, ground – blackness.

The silent, blank screen sat waiting for a response from Max.

The chill he felt was not fear but an ice-cold anger. He was in the belly of the beast all right, he was right there with the murderer, Shaka Chang. And everything that needed to be done to stop this catastrophe rested on Max's shoulders. This time he didn't ask when he ripped the tape off Zhernastyn's face.

Zhernastyn cried out.

'Is there still time for me to stop Chang?'

Zhernastyn smiled, a macabre sneer on his swollen, half-whiskered face. 'It's tomorrow, my young friend. He's opening the floodgates tomorrow.'

'When!?'

Zhernastyn shook his head. That was the key to Chang's success and if Chang ever discovered . . .

Max snarled at him and heaved the wheelchair towards the ramp. It ran free like a runaway pram, and Zhernastyn screamed. Max had thrown caution to the wind, the threat of Zhernastyn's terror being heard was a risk he had to take.

'AllrightallrightallrightALLRIGHT!' Zhernastyn screamed.

Max grabbed the wheelchair's handles and dug in his heels to stop it tipping down the ramp, barely a couple of metres away.

'Yes, yes, yes!' Zhernastyn gasped. 'Tomorrow at sunset, sunset, that's when he'll open the floodgates . . . it's a week earlier than planned . . . before everyone arrives for the grand opening ceremony.'

Zhernastyn looked desperately at Max. He was teetering on the edge of that slope. If Max had a mean streak in him, Zhernastyn would be torn apart in a few seconds.

'Don't worry, Doctor, I need you for a little while longer. I have to get back through security to get to my father. If you had thought that through, you could have kept quiet.'

Max hauled him back to the computer console and tweaked the mouse, found the email page, knowing that Shaka Chang would have the fastest-ever satellite broadband at his disposal. He typed in Sayid's address and a few words to accompany the contents of his father's DVD: I've found Dad, he's been tortured. Skeleton Rock. Need help. Dam gates opened sunset, local time tomorrow. Max.

He clicked on the *Send* button.

It was gone in a flash. He just prayed Sayid was waiting as he had promised. Now all Max had to do was rescue his father, stop the dam gates being opened and escape.

That's all.

21

'Satan's Angels' Kallie's dad called the Russian attack helicopters when he fought in the war, and now Kallie was convinced that the black, fast-moving helicopter on the horizon might be closely related to one of them. She was certain it was homed in on her.

Kallie had flown a zigzag route, following trucks from Walvis Bay into the desert. Beneath the clouds of dust a dozen containers were being transported every couple of hours, all of them in convoy, all heading south of the dam project, all disappearing into a huge underground bunker, its entrance like the gaping hole of a vast underground parking garage. It was time to get out of there and report to someone. She just didn't know who. Mike Kapuo seemed to be in the pay of Peterson in England, and she couldn't reach Sayid. But her sense of helplessness was shooed away like tumbleweed in a gathering storm when she saw that black bug getting ever closer.

She kicked the rudder pedal and turned the controls into a steep bank, down and away.

Time to hide.

*

Angelo Farentino's cigar burned slowly in the ashtray. Another few minutes and it would go out, leaving only ash, and Angelo, aware of the beautiful hand-woven Persian rug, did not want the ash to fall and blemish the carpet. Hours ago, he had gazed from the window of his town house-cum-office in Soho Square and noticed the subtle shift of people in the street outside. The gas main van that had set up its barriers around a manhole cover was the first giveaway. There were no gas mains here, and the barriers had been placed around a water inspection manhole. A furniture removal van had stood, causing misery for drivers around the square, and showed no signs of being loaded or unloaded. A big mistake his enemies made was to replace the ugly traffic warden, a man notorious for his relentless issuing of tickets, with a very attractive young woman who looked super-fit and who seemed to let drivers stay long overdue, when they should have been towed away. And their fourth and final mistake was to underestimate Angelo Farentino.

His exit strategy had been in place long before anything in this present situation turned ugly. As the gas mains worker gave the 'go' into his radio, and his partner the traffic warden moved quickly to Farentino's front door, half a dozen rough-looking men sprang out of the furniture lorry and covered all the exits. The street was blocked off, the black-gloss front door was smashed open and the gang burst into the beautifully cool, timelessly stylish house. And as the door was smashed open, the last of the cold ash from the cigar fell neatly into the crystal-cut ashtray.

Exactly as Farentino had intended.

*

Several hours before Max managed to send the vital information, Sayid felt as though the can of worms he'd opened had turned into a barrel of snakes. They were in the headmaster's room and Mr Jackson stood, quietly observing from the fireplace, hands shoved into the pockets of his corduroys. Sayid sat with his mother on the creased sofa, with Mr Peterson opposite them. The uniformed village policewoman had been ushered from the room by both a Detective Chief Inspector of the Devon and Cornwall CID and a regional member of Special Branch. The village Special Constable was a speck in the universe compared to the people who now filled Mr Jackson's room.

Sayid watched a couple of men from London: cool-dude number one, in tailored jeans and casual jacket, slightly built but with a look of danger about him; he gazed back without blinking, without a smile on his face – in fact no one in the room was smiling. A scrag-arsed surfer-cool-dude, number two, looked as though his feet should be curled over a long board, not jammed into the very expensive trainers he wore. This unlikely pair was MI6. Not exactly the way Sayid imagined Secret Intelligence Service types would look. *Never judge a horse because he looks like a donkey, there may be an Arab stallion inside*, was one of his grandad's more stupid sayings. Perhaps it made a bit of sense now.

And Mr Peterson, he was the biggest surprise of all.

'Listen, Sayid, what you did was exactly right. A hundred per cent,' Mr Peterson said.

'I'm not in trouble?' Sayid asked.

'MI6 aren't too happy,' Peterson said, looking at cool-dudes one and two, 'but I can square it away. Besides, if it wasn't for you, things could be a lot worse.'

'I thought you were one of the bad guys, and when I listened in on your phone call it sounded as though you were out to get Max, his dad and Angelo Farentino.'

'OK. Briefly, this is how it is.'

Mr Peterson spelled it out quickly and without fuss. He left out a lot of background information, but the important bits fell quickly into place. He had once served in the army, where he met Max's dad. They were both adventurers and became firm friends. That's why he had those paintings of the mountains by Max's dad on his wall. When they left the army, they worked for a government department – not MI6 or MI5, but they were trained by those people and often passed on relevant information to them. The easiest way of explaining it was to say that they were international watchdogs. Anyone – big business, corrupt governments, illegal trading of weapons, destruction of natural resources or threat to endangered species, anything they found that could cause irreparable damage – they tried to stop. But Tom Gordon and his wife, when she was alive, and Peterson with a whole bunch of others realized they could never do their job properly as government employees. So, together with similarly minded scientists, they took on the problems themselves. And there were times when governments used them when they themselves did not wish to be seen to be involved.

It was a win–win situation. And the phone call Sayid heard was Peterson asking for help from MI6 – for favours owed. When Tom Gordon took on the investigation in Namibia, there were already signs that it could be extremely dangerous.

Peterson had only been at Dartmoor High for a few months and he was working there undercover.

To protect Max.

What he didn't have was access to the message Tom Gordon had left Max in the vault or the letters Sayid had delivered privately to his best mate. What Tom Gordon hadn't known was that Peterson had moved in to keep an eye on his son.

'But Angelo Farentino was there to help Max. That's what his dad's message meant,' Sayid said.

'No, it was a message warning him against Farentino. I think Max's dad had realized just who was behind everything – had been for years. A perfect secret life: pretending to be a major environmentalist, but in reality building up a huge power base. I thought Max was really going to Canada, but when I found out he'd gone to Africa, and someone had tried to kill him at the airport, that's when I knew Farentino must have been involved.'

'I warned Farentino he was being watched.'

'It's not your fault.'

'But he got away.'

'We'll find him.'

A scruffy bloke, about twenty-four years old, wearing a V-neck sweater over a T-shirt and ripped designer jeans, flung open the door. Dr Lee Mathews, an IT expert, had been monitoring Sayid's computer. 'Nothing from Max Gordon, but we've had contact from Namibia. Some kid called Kallie van Reenen.' He handed Mr Peterson a printout. 'I patched it through to my guv'nor. UK Eyes Only,' he said.

Sayid stared at the computer whiz-kid. Everyone seemed to be really important around here. And Sayid knew that 'UK

Eyes Only' meant that this message was destined for the top: the Prime Minister, the Foreign Secretary and the Head of MI6.

Then it all happened in a hurry. Everyone seemed to know what to do the moment Peterson said, 'We're going. It's on.'

Cool-dudes one and two had mobiles to their ears in a split second, doors opened, running feet echoed down the corridor. Sayid was almost manhandled by Mr Peterson as he barrelled down the corridor. He'd nodded to Mr Jackson, who had moved quickly to Sayid's mother and put a comforting arm around her as her son was whisked away.

'Mister Peterson! What's happening?' Sayid asked. 'What about Max?'

They were through the doors, and Sayid saw and heard the military helicopter on the school's rugby pitch. A couple of armed soldiers were waiting, and they slid the helicopter's door open as Mr Peterson's voice rose above the sound of the thudding blades.

'We don't know where he is. We've been on standby, waiting to get something positive out of Namibia. Now we have something.'

The two soldiers grabbed Sayid, lifted him into the helicopter and slammed the doors closed as Peterson gave the thumbs-up to the pilot, buckled himself and Sayid into their seats, pulled on a set of headphones, then settled another pair over Sayid's ears. Sayid steadied himself as the helicopter rose and banked sharply.

'We may not be able to help Max and his dad right now, we have to stop Farentino and Shaka Chang. We have to get help from the Namibian government,' Mr Peterson said, his voice scratchy from the microphone attached to the headset.

'How are you going to do that?'

'I'm working with a senior police officer in Namibia. Somehow or other he's got his hands on one of Tom Gordon's maps and, together with what this Kallie girl has told him, we think it gives us enough reason to make a low-profile incursion. Trying to get governments to react in time is like trying to stop a supertanker – it takes too long. Our government won't get involved directly, but they're pulling diplomatic strings.'

'An incursion?' asked Sayid. 'Like an attack, you mean?'

'No, we'll be going in as advisers; only when we hear something more concrete will we re-evaluate the situation. There's an abandoned military airfield in the desert; we're going to help the Namibians assemble a strike force.'

'Who's "we"?'

'Some of these blokes' friends –' he looked at the grim-faced young soldiers, their faces streaked with camouflage cream and carrying foreign-looking weapons '– are joining us.'

Sayid studied them for a moment.

'SAS?'

'A long time ago, before you both were born, Max's dad and I served with them.' Mr Peterson smiled and put a finger to his lips. 'Don't tell anyone.'

Sayid listened to the muted roar of the engines outside the protection of his headphones. The helicopter had flown low and fast across Dartmoor, then swung south towards

Plymouth. Sayid could already see their destination – a small airfield – below them. The local civilian airport was used to seeing Sea King search-and-rescue helicopters landing, so this military chopper wouldn't be out of place. Now the pilot eased the camouflaged beast down towards a hangar on the edge of the airfield.

A civilian twin-engined jet sat waiting. Gathered around it were half a dozen men in civvies; their military Bergen backpacks were being loaded into the hold.

'That's a Citation X,' Peterson told him. 'Flies at just under Mach One. It's available for special ops when they have to keep a low profile. Belongs to a well-known businessman who happens to own hotels in South Africa, so it's a good cover for the time being. One refuelling stop in Lagos, and we'll be there.'

Sayid was beginning to feel way out of his depth. Big adventures and risk-taking were Max's domain, not his.

'Why am I going?'

'Kallie van Reenen.'

'She thinks the policeman over there is working for you, I mean against Max's dad.'

'Exactly. She may need convincing to tell us everything she knows. She'll feel more confident when she sees you.'

'She got away from that copper.'

'Well, he's found her again.'

'How do you know?'

'She told her dad.'

When Ferdie van Reenen got Kallie's radio message, he used his credit card to pay another company to secure his clients' ongoing safari, refuelled the twin-engined Baron and flew by the most direct route to where she had landed. He scorched along low and fast, old flying techniques never forgotten from combat days. On the way, he gave Mike Kapuo an ear-splitting mouthful, using language that was definitely not correct radio procedure, on what he thought was the policeman's damned carelessness and irresponsibility in allowing his daughter to get herself in danger.

It took Kapuo a couple of minutes to tell Van Reenen everything, which made him realize just how precious his daughter was to him. People had to be independent and strong in an environment like the Namibian outback, but maybe he'd left his daughter alone too often. He swore quietly to himself that he would make amends and spend more time with her, but he couldn't help feeling a deep sense of pride at what she had done.

22

Max had worked his way back through security, using Zhernastyn's palm-print, then replaced his father with Zhernastyn in the bed, strapped him down and covered his face with an oxygen mask over his taped mouth. With any luck, that would fool anyone taking a cursory glance into the room. But for how long? Max knew time was against him, but he had to find a way of reaching Shaka Chang's control centre. If that could be damaged or destroyed, it might delay the dam gates being opened.

Max looked instinctively at his wrist. The watch was gone, of course, but the moment allowed him a fleeting thought for !Koga. *Bring help, !Koga, I need as much as I can get.*

He had cradled his father, easing him back into the wheelchair. Tom Gordon drifted in and out of consciousness. Max's mental clock ticked away. There was precious little time to hang about in this hospital. He ran back into the hydroelectric tank room and dropped the vital disc, taped back in its box, through the iron grid into the water. Hopefully, by now Sayid would have the information. Max didn't dare risk being caught with it, because then both his and his father's lives would be worthless.

But where could Max escape to? He tried to reason it out. If the fort had been built in the 1800s, then there certainly wouldn't have been any lift shafts in place, all that came later with Shaka Chang. So, there had to be stairs, especially down to the basement area, where the original old iron grid lay across the water tank. In their day, servants might have hauled water up to the kitchens and living quarters. There must be steps going higher. If there was a way up to that hangar without using the lift, that was his best chance of getting himself and his dad out of this murderous place.

Using screwdrivers from the maintenance man's tool belt, Max had wedged open the doors he needed to get through, but he had to make a move quickly. It seemed likely, he reasoned, that the lift shaft would have been dropped down alongside any stairwell that had been cut into the rock face a hundred-odd years ago. Max trundled his father out into the area where the lift doors opened. Somewhere on one side or the other of that modern glass cage was his way out. He gazed up into the darkening space that would swallow the lift car, letting his eyes search the cables and steel supports. It was open rock at the back of that structure, all the way up, as far as he could see.

He had missed the obvious. He must be more tired than he realized. There was a door with a small danger sign – High Voltage. The door felt as solid as steel and it was locked. The maintenance man was still trussed up – but his work belt sat like a gunslinger's holster around Max's waist. His fingers searched out a screwdriver. He would use it to twist and break the lock, but then he saw the T-bar of a short metal rod, about fifty centimetres long and with a bevelled base, in a small pocket of its own. It fitted perfectly between his fingers, allowing him to grip and turn the T-piece. The angled cuts at the end of the bar slid into the hexagonal lock on the door. A twist of his wrist and the door opened. Just like the gas man opening the meter box, back home.

Half a dozen stairs rose up before him and then dog-legged to the right, following a zigzag path upwards behind the lift shaft. He would never get a wheelchair up there.

A light came on above the lift door. The top floor. Shaka Chang's private domain. Someone was in the lift and they were coming down.

Third floor.

Second.

Time had just run out.

Mr Slye felt uneasy.

Routine was the backbone of his world. A rigid system of behavioural patterns meant people were always doing what they should be doing at the time they should be doing it. But there had been no reply when he phoned Dr Zhernastyn. And the tracking computer had shown that the doctor had left the medical area, gone to the hangar and returned again. That was a break in his routine. Why had he gone there? For what reason? There was nothing there that . . . ah. A flush of relief soothed Mr Slye's anxiety. Zhernastyn was a smoker. That disgusting addiction. It added to the stench of his breath and his rotting teeth, and smoking was strictly forbidden anywhere inside the fort. Zhernastyn had gone to the maintenance area to have a cigarette. That must be the reason. No matter, he was now back where he belonged and he could begin the torture of the captured scientist.

Slye closed his eyes and breathed a meditative sigh, releasing the tension he always kept so tightly entombed inside his cadaver-like body. He caught a brief glimpse of his reflection as the lift glided downwards; the glass darkened as it slipped past the rock wall. His black hair brushed severely back from his long, gaunt face gave him the appearance of an undertaker. Caring for and burying the dead. Yes, that was appropriate, he supposed. He cleared up so many secrets and buried them so deeply, only he knew where they were. If he were less loyal, he could make a fortune. If he were less scared, he would be dead.

The lift stopped. The doors opened. The voice welcomed him.

'Basement. Hydroelectric unit to the left, seismic recording instruments straight ahead and torture cells to the right. Have a nice day.'

'Oh, do shut up,' Mr Slye muttered.

Max had undone the tool belt, lengthened it as far as it could go, then put it around his father. Squatting in front of the wheelchair, he pulled his dad on to his back, hooking the belt's clasp around his own chest. He heaved the weight for balance and gave the wheelchair a shove back down the corridor, then dragged himself to the stairs. There was a light switch, but he didn't dare to use it – he needed the etched darkness to hide them for as long as possible.

His knees buckled, but the steps helped him lean forward and bear his dad's weight. He managed to clamber up half a dozen steps before the glass box that was the lift cage slid down past him. Max saw the back of a man dressed in black, his hair swept back over his head, hands behind him, fingers clutching a personal organizer. The man stepped out into the basement area and turned right towards the medical area. Max had probably less than a minute to get as far away as possible.

Max could hardly breathe because of the belt crushing his chest, sweat greased his body and the fetid air smelled like bad drains. If the slimy-looking man found Zhernastyn, he would know Max was inside the fort. A quick search of the basement would reveal the maintenance man and Mr Death-Warmed-Up would realize that Max could not have escaped using the lift. And he would not fail to see Max through the glass.

Alice Through the Looking Glass, more like – crazy thoughts in a crazy, unreal world – words trying to make light of his predicament. '*Malice* Through the Looking Glass' would be better. *Concentrate! Climb!*

He craned his neck upwards into the reflected light from the lift shaft. The steps went on forever. He was never going to make it. His heart sank. He'd come so far, he'd found his father and the evidence, but this last effort was going to defeat him. A dull sheen on the rock face wall, a couple of metres ahead of him, had a different texture from the rest of the stairwell. He stared at it, trying to make out what it was, and then felt a hand grip his shoulder.

Startled, he tried to turn, thinking someone had sneaked up behind him, but then his dad spoke to him quietly. 'Son, it's OK.'

Max unclasped the belt and turned so he could ease his father into a sitting position, his back against the wall. 'Dad, you're awake.' Max couldn't keep the relief out of his voice.

His father nodded, mouth dry from all the drugs, his voice barely a whisper. 'I'm gonna be OK . . . it'll take time . . . don't think there's much of that though, do you? Where am I?'

'Behind the lift shaft. Dad, I've got to get us out of here, they're checking on you now.'

His father nodded weakly. 'I don't know how you did all this, but you've got to go and find the evidence. You must, son. Leave me here. It's in the Land Rover's . . .'

Max smiled. 'It's done. I found your disc; there's a computer in a huge garage of a place. I got the password and I sent it. It's all gone – everything. Dad, we've just got to hide for a while until help comes.'

'How the hell did you manage all that? Never mind . . . tell me later.'

Max turned his head away, listening to a snuffling, scratching noise somewhere behind him. He closed his eyes in concentration and let his jaw open a little, which would help him hear more clearly. His father, knowing what was happening, stayed silent.

Max touched his dad's arm. 'Dad, I've got to go and find out what's up there,' he whispered.

His father nodded. Max plucked a small Maglite torch from the workman's belt and bounded up the steps, feeling as light as air without his father's weight on his back. As he reached the darkened patch of rock, he saw it was a natural

318

fissure running through the sheet of rock – and something moved inside it.

Max looked up the stairs, to where they disappeared around a bend. That would take them higher, so it seemed the most obvious way to go. He looked at the gap again. It was wide enough for him to walk into, and cables and air duct pipes were fastened to the ceiling. He took a chance and moved inside. After a few steps, something coiled around his ankle. Max jerked back, his heart thumping, and fumbled for the torch's switch. A snakelike black mass encircled his ankle: electrical cable, left behind by workmen.

He swept the torch beam across the narrow passageway. There! Something moved. Something that ran away. He heard snuffling, and what sounded like a dog's whimper. Now the passage turned a corner and ran straight for another fifty metres. At the end, there appeared to be an opening, the light barely reflecting on the rock's curved roof. The pipes in the ceiling ran out into what looked like some kind of generator box. Maybe this was part of the electrical system, but it was completely unimportant in that instant because, right at the edge of the passage, was the shape of a jackal.

It sat, unmoving, facing him, ears erect.

The darkness of the passage and the faint light behind the animal meant that Max couldn't see its features. He stood rooted to the spot; neither he nor the jackal moved. But there was some kind of kinetic connection between them – a wordless communication. The figure of a jackal had been with him from the beginning, but this was the closest he had ever been to it.

He went down on his knees, never taking his eyes off the

dark form. Moving on all fours, he edged closer, carefully and slowly, not understanding why, but knowing he must.

Now he was within arm's reach. He could see its fur, layered into a thick mass, and the dull moisture of its nose. The jackal had not moved; it looked to be barely breathing. Max could smell its musky odour as his eyes searched its muzzle, exploring its features. There were no scars from old fights, only a gentle brush of grey fur suggesting that it was an older animal.

He was so close now, he could have moved a couple of centimetres and felt the wet nose on his forehead. The jackal opened its eyes. Max held his breath, not daring to move, mesmerized. The amber eyes drew him in, their gentleness touching something deep inside him. A rich warmth settled in his chest: a sublime sense of joy. He reached out to stroke the animal's head.

He gasped – the jackal was gone!

Max tumbled into space. There was a drop of about twenty metres down to the floor of the hangar. He jolted to a halt. One of the cables had snagged his ankle. Instinctively he tucked his chin on to his chest and shielded his head with his arms. His curved back slammed into the rock face and knocked the wind out of him. The agony knifed through his body, his senses swirled as he hung upside down, spreadeagled.

At the far end of the hangar, half a dozen men had gathered, their raucous voices whooping with pleasure, but he couldn't make out what it was that held their attention.

He had to get out. Sooner or later one of those men would walk across the floor and see him swaying helplessly. Max bent his knees and crunched his stomach muscles. Rolling himself upwards, he snatched desperately at the cable. And missed! He fell back. Another thump in his back from the rock. Max held back a grunt of pain. If he made too much erratic movement, he would be noticed.

He wiped the sweat from his eyes, dried his hands on his shirt, and focused again through the throbbing blood that flooded his head. Taking a deep breath, he exhaled and lunged. His fingers touched the cable. He curled his hand, grasping the lifeline. Then, hand over hand, he heaved himself back over the ledge. Out of sight, he lay still, letting his breathing settle.

Had his imagination conjured up the jackal? Maybe it had tried to show him the way out and then sat, to stop him falling. He'd been stupid. Trying to reach out and touch it.

There was no sign of the jackal now, just as on other occasions when he had caught only a fleeting glimpse. But this was different – this was almost contact – creepy. So what? So far as he was concerned, it was there. Max was learning not to apply logic to everything that happened. With a silent *thank you* to whoever was listening, he made his way back to his father.

Within a couple of minutes Max had secured lengths of the cable around each of them and quietly warned his father about the men at the far side of the hangar. 'Can you manage to get down there?' he whispered. His father nodded.

The gap was wide enough for only one of them to climb through at a time. Max went first, then waited, feet planted firmly against the wall, to make sure his dad could follow.

With a lot of effort Tom Gordon eased himself next to his son, then together they lowered themselves, feeding out the cable as they walked backwards down the rock face. Four metres from the ground, they heard voices directly below them. They froze. Two men in mechanics' overalls were manhandling a mobile toolbox. How long would the men stay there? Would they notice the cables? He looked at his father, who didn't move, holding himself as still as Max, who knew he couldn't stay like that for much longer. Max was amazed his dad had managed the descent at all, knowing he was operating on sheer willpower.

The men rumbled the toolbox away. Max waited until they were on the far side of the hangar, then he slithered down quietly. He picked up the slack from his father's cable and reached up, his hands ready to take his weight. He kept glancing over his shoulder, but the men were out of sight now, since Max and his dad were obscured by the bulk of the Humvees. Tom Gordon was shaking from the exertion and needed time to recover. Max crept forward and put his head over the door of one of the vehicles. The window was down and a small bottle of water nestled in a bottle-carrier between the armrests. As he reached in, he could see through the windscreen that the men were watching a big television screen secured to the wall at the end of the hangar. It sounded as though they were watching a football game because they were shouting and cheering.

Max let his father drink as they sat, huddled against the wall. The cables they had used still hung down from the crevice-like opening, but Max tied them off at the bottom, and to a casual onlooker they would look like any of the other electrical cabling around the place.

'Dad, I have to leave you here for a bit. I've got to try and find a way of jamming the works.'

His father looked uncertain. 'Why?' And then his ravaged memory returned. 'Oh yeah. My God, Max, this is crazy. You shouldn't have come here. I don't know how the hell you got it all together.'

'Dad, can you remember anything? Y'know, the message you sent me.'

'Message? Oh yes. I sent them to Sayid. Tried to warn you. I thought they were going to try to kill you, cos they thought I'd sent you the evidence.'

'They did try. That's why I'm here. It's a long story, so many things have happened. And I made a good friend, he's the son of the Bushman who took your notes. He's great. Anyway, I'll tell you all about it when we get home.'

'Still the optimist, Max.'

'We'll make it, Dad.'

'Bloody right we will,' his father said, and smiled bravely. 'But I want you to get going, on your own. You'll have a much better chance.'

Max shook his head. 'No way. Not after everything that's happened. You sent for me, you left all the messages in the cave. I came here to help.'

'And you have. And I'm so proud of you. But now you have to get out. Please.'

'No. Drink your water and do as you're told.'

They smiled at each other, and Max felt great being this

close to his dad, a moment of shared happiness amid the danger. There were no keys in any of the trucks, and he still hadn't figured out how to stop Shaka Chang from triggering the floodgates at the dam.

'What cave?' his father asked.

'What?' Max felt confused. Were the drugs muddling his dad's brain?

'You said I left a message in a cave. I haven't been to any caves.'

'You must have. The Bushmen's sacred mountain. There were drawings in there. Pictures of me, your plane's insignia, the dove . . .'

'You found the plane?'

'Yeah. Because of the drawings. Well, partly . . . you drew a picture showing you'd been wounded, the hidden plane, me, the Bushmen. It was all there.'

'Max, listen to me. My memory's in pretty bad shape right now, but I can tell you, one hundred per cent, that I never went to any cave. Anton Leopold and I met up in the desert. We left his Land Rover and I flew him to Walvis Bay – by then we had a pretty good idea of what was happening. I gave him a scribbled note to send to you, I flew back, got wounded, hid the plane and made a run for it in the Land Rover. I knew they'd get me in the end – there were too many of them. That's when I sent my field notes back to Farentino. They were just bits and pieces; no one would be able to make much sense of them. I figured it'd buy me time. But I was in no condition to climb any mountains and paint pictures on cave walls.'

The air in the hangar seemed suddenly oppressive, and

something like a shadow crept over Max's skin. He shuddered. 'The prophecy,' he muttered.

He looked at his dad, a strange feeling flooding his mind, as if a door had been opened in a darkened room and shown him a different world. He relived the kaleidoscope of sensations – of death, the flying, the darkness, the raptor's attack and the presence of the jackal. The *BaKoko*.

The Bushmen had told Max about the legend of him coming to their land to help them, but he hadn't managed that yet, not until Shaka Chang was stopped. And one thing they didn't mention in their prophecy was how he was going to save his own dad.

His father's question snapped him back to attention. 'What prophecy are you talking about?'

Max shook his head. 'It doesn't matter. But things just got a whole lot crazier. Dad, you stay here, I'm going to do a recce and see if I can find a way of shutting this place down and getting us out of here.'

His father nodded, there was no point in arguing with a boy who had managed so far.

A flurry of sand whipped across the open space of the hangar. The wind was picking up. If a storm broke, that could give them a chance to escape. Max scurried between the vehicles, then he heard a terrible cry. It was a boy's voice, terrified and alone – a shriek of fear, forewarning of a terrible event.

It was !Koga and the name he cried out, that echoed around the hangar's wall, was Max's.

The pick-up trucks had searched for the Bushman boy all day. Shaka Chang had given the word that the boy had to be brought in, dead or alive, but that didn't mean they couldn't have some sport before they bagged him. Their blood was up and they hunted !Koga as they would a wild animal. The men's cruel intentions were a product of years of war in which violence and destruction were a day-to-day matter. Shaka Chang's decision, on the other hand, was a more cold-hearted approach. Stop him or kill him. It didn't matter which.

The men in the pick-ups had finally tracked the elusive boy, whose skills were not enough to escape from the number of attackers after him. In the back of each pick-up, one of the men held a live video camera to film the hunt, and it was this dust-laden, terrifying chase that was beamed back to Skeleton Rock.

Max stared at the screen. The horrifying picture stamped itself into his memory.

!Koga was crying in fear, legs pounding through the dirt, arms pumping. Max could even hear him gasping for breath as the men ran him to earth. As one of the killers filmed, the other truck would swoop in. One of the men reached out and clubbed him with a stick. !Koga fell, and the men yelled and screamed – scoring points in a game. The trucks' wheels spun, ready to come around again. They were playing with !Koga's life, and the men in the hangar, and probably everyone in Skeleton Rock, watched the vicious hunt unfold.

!Koga calling his name had seared into Max. He couldn't bear to watch, tears stung his eyes, his clenched fists ached and he wanted to scream at the brutality of what they were doing to his friend. !Koga had come back for him, and now they were going to kill him for it.

Max turned; his father stood at his shoulder. He saw what was happening.

'Is that your friend?'

Max could only nod, but he could see the fury in his dad's eyes. He grabbed his son's arm, deliberately wrenching him away from his agony. 'Help me. Come on, let's make them pay.'

Despite his weakened condition, Tom Gordon grabbed a couple of jerrycans. Max took his lead. Flipping open the lids, his dad sniffed the contents. 'Petrol. Better than diesel for what we need. Check those.' He carried the jerrycans to an inspection pit which was as far as they could go without being seen. Max flinched every time the men roared as the hunt against !Koga continued.

'Max!' his father insisted. 'Don't look. Come on, son, you can't help him. Not now.'

Max took the half dozen cans down into the inspection pit, opening their lids. His dad switched off the wall plug that held one end of an inspection lamp's five-metre-long cable. He yanked the cable free and did something to the end of the wires, then dropped the cable down on to the cans. When that wall socket was switched on, it would ignite the petrol. All hell would break loose and that's when they'd make their escape.

At least that was the plan.

'Max Gordon is here?!'

Shaka Chang stood with Mr Slye in the medical unit. Slye had looked everywhere for Dr Zhernastyn, had double-checked the computer's record of the doctor's movements and then, with a sinking feeling in his stomach, far more sickening than any rapidly descending lift, went into the room and pulled back the bedding. Zhernastyn's terrified eyes were a reflection of Mr Slye's sense of impending doom. How had Tom Gordon escaped? A more frightening question – had anyone helped him? It was not difficult to put two and two together – they always made four in Mr Slye's book, he didn't care how clever mathematicians could be – but in this case it was one and one. One Bushman boy running back towards Skeleton Rock might well mean the other one was already here.

Two boys.

Both supposed to be dead.

Double trouble.

He had ripped the tape from Zhernastyn's face, removing another clump of whiskers, and grabbed the gasping doctor by the throat.

'If you know what's good for both our sakes, you should be extremely careful what you say, Doctor. Was the Gordon boy here?'

Zhernastyn nodded.

'And he used you to go through to the maintenance hangar?'

Zhernastyn nodded again.

Mr Slye's grip on Zhernastyn's throat tightened ever so slightly. 'And did he do anything in there he shouldn't?'

The moment of truth.

If he admitted what had happened, Zhernastyn knew he was definitely for the great cheese-grater in the sky, where all sins would be stripped from his evil soul. Like being skinned alive, it was going to hurt. And Slye would not wish to tell

Shaka Chang that the boy he assured his master was dead had gained access to a computer, using Zhernastyn's love-lorn password. And Zhernastyn was definitely not going to mention the DVD the boy had recovered. Oh no. That meant a double failure. That game was over so far as Zhernastyn was concerned. Given a chance, Dr Zhernastyn would beat a hasty retreat. He needed time. No, he had told Slye, the boy hadn't done anything, he was looking for a way to escape. And that's when Mr Slye patted his cheek and gave him that cold-fish stare which meant he had said just the right thing. By the time Slye got round to telling Shaka Chang, Zhernastyn planned to have his own escape route ready. Rats and sinking ships sprang to mind.

Now Shaka Chang threw the wheelchair through a glass window. 'I'm not very happy at the moment, Mister Slye! In case you hadn't realized.'

'We have no idea how the boy got inside, Mister Chang.'

'Then we'll roast head of security!' He glowered at Zhernastyn. 'You let a fifteen-year-old boy get the better of you?'

'His father made a remarkable recovery – it took two of them to beat me. I'd like to know how he knocked the maintenance man unconscious, stole his clothes and sneaked up on me. I fought like a lion. I'm not that young any more, Mister Chang,' Zhernastyn said.

'And you may not be getting any older,' Chang threatened. He turned on Mr Slye. 'So this is the second time you've been wrong. The-boy-is-dead-you-said,' making it sound like the line of a poem.

Slye knew that if he stayed silent, did not twitch at the fury being visited upon him, but stared somewhere beyond Shaka Chang so there was not the faintest possibility of any eye contact which might be misunderstood as some kind of stupid macho-type challenge, then he might be allowed to live.

'If he survived, Mister Chang, he had help. This is not one boy we are up against, there must be dozens of Bushmen hiding out there, they must have found a secret way in. That's the only explanation.'

Shaka Chang had never lost his cool before. Pressure was what he thrived on. He had always won, by fair means or foul – mostly the latter. Winning was everything. But these past few weeks, since the Gordon boy had escaped assassination and had just kept on coming like a heat-seeking missile, at a time when Shaka Chang was about to seize control of unimaginable wealth, had rattled him.

In a few hours, the gathering storm that now buffeted the mountains would break loose and sweep across the desert, flash floods would appear from nowhere. They wouldn't be enough to dissolve the buried drugs and sweep them into the food chain, but this was when he had planned to open the dam gates. All that water gushing beneath the surface, the unstoppable power of nature, aided by Shaka Chang, would secure him everything.

It was only a few hours away. It demanded patience and a cool head.

'Find them,' he told Slye.

A very simple command; a very definite threat.

*

Max's dad had told him it made no sense to try to knock out any of Shaka Chang's communications, they would be too sophisticated. He just hoped, if any information had reached the outside world, that they could respond in time. If Chang was going to open the floodgates, he could do it with a phone call, though Tom Gordon guessed he would want to be at the dam itself to witness the moment when he became one of the most powerful men on Earth. He and Max had laid the booby trap which might buy them a few minutes. But now his dad lay exhausted, sweat glistening on his face and his body trembling. The exertion had taken its toll.

Max bore his father's weight and helped him towards the second hangar area. If they could find keys for a quad bike or a pick-up, they could make a run for it. The boat at the top of the ramp would still be useless, so it would have to be across the desert.

They made it to the passageway leading to the next hangar. Almost there. But they needed a breather. Max heaved a sigh of relief at this small victory, but a nagging guilt plagued him, wondering if !Koga had survived. His father kept an insistent dialogue going, urging Max to stay alert; to believe that !Koga could still make it; that they had to get out and keep moving in order to give themselves the best chance of survival. That was their responsibility – to survive.

The wind outside was increasing, and Max realized that if too much sand and dirt penetrated these hangars, the men would close the doors and then he and his dad would never get out. He got to his feet and began pulling his dad up, but his father shook his head and pointed. One of the men had moved to a work area; if Max tried to get through, they would be spotted.

It was now or never. He pulled open the door to one of the heavyweight Humvees. There was a key in the ignition. He eased it free and crept out of the cab, turning back to where he had left his father slumped against the wall.

And stopped in his tracks.

Dr Zhernastyn. His face looked sore and the odd residual clump of whiskers made him look silly. Beyond the unsmiling Russian, a man in black stepped out of the shadows, the same man he had seen coming down in the lift. The long, sour-looking face gazed at him with dark, bloodshot eyes, like someone who never slept. Bloody hell, Max thought irrationally, maybe it's Dracula's brother.

No one had said anything in those few seconds as Max instinctively grabbed a hefty wrench from a workbench. He'd fight his way clear if he had to, and these two didn't look as though they could stop him.

But you could drop a steel girder on the third man who appeared, and it would probably have no effect.

Shaka Chang smiled. 'So, you're Max Gordon. You just won't die, will you?'

Max stood his ground, fist clutching the wrench at shoulder height like a battleaxe.

Zhernastyn and the other man had taken a couple of steps back. Chang moved unhurriedly, touching this and that on the workbench, as if seeing things for the first time, and occasionally glancing at the fight-ready Max, who shifted his weight, turning slightly each time Shaka Chang moved, ready for an attack.

'You can put that down, Max. I don't fight boys. I've got a couple of dozen men who can walk in here and take a beating before they truss you up like a turkey. You've done well, I admire you. No, no, I do, don't look surprised.'

Max felt sure he hadn't given away his reaction but Shaka Chang was a man who watched every flicker of emotion in a person's face, and if Max's ego had been stroked then the pupils in his eyes would have enlarged slightly at the subtle shift of pleasure from the killer's comments. Max kept his eyes on Chang as he would a prowling lion. Chang was unconcerned.

'What might keep you and your father, your very stubborn father, alive is whether you have found the information that I need.'

Static electricity seemed to crackle through Max's mind. Shaka Chang still needed this evidence. And he would know if Max lied. He averted his eyes, looking at his father slumped against the wall – a perfectly natural reaction, but also a disguise. Max was really using his peripheral vision to look at Zhernastyn, half hidden behind Chang, who was moving in deceptively languid fashion.

A shadow of fear clouded Zhernastyn's eyes.

Max knew.

Zhernastyn hadn't told Chang about the computer. He was trying to save his own neck.

Max looked back at Chang, straight into his eyes, so he would know the truth. 'I found it,' he said, knowing that if he had denied finding the disc, and with only hours to go before the dam gates were opened, their lives would be worthless, or Chang would torture his father in front of him

333

until he confessed. Telling Chang might buy them only minutes of life, but those minutes gave hope, and if you had hope you could climb out of the darkest pit.

Shaka Chang stopped pacing and looked directly into Max's face, a blast of power from those eyes. Max could see why people were so afraid of him. It wasn't just the size of the man – his eyes were portals into a dark soul.

'Where is it?' The question had no more resonance than a breath being exhaled. But it was like a blade being dragged down Max's spine. Almost supernatural.

Their eyes locked.

Did Shaka Chang see something inside Max? Could he see the shadowed place he travelled to when the *BaKoko*'s spirit entwined his own?

'I put it in the water. In the pump room. I dropped it through the grid.'

Chang didn't have to work too hard to figure it out. 'So that's how you got inside Skeleton Rock. That's admirable.' He paused. 'Why into water? Why would you risk corrupting the disc? Ah! Of course. It had been hidden in water, or something similar. The fuel tank of the Land Rover? My men checked.'

'No, the water bag.'

'The water bag. How clever.' He looked at Max's dad, who managed a smile. A small victory.

But Shaka Chang did not allow victories of any size. In one brutal movement he bent down and backhanded Max's father, slamming him into the wall. In the instant it happened, Max, consumed by a frightening anger, hurled himself at Chang. He saw a blur of jade and gold as Chang sidestepped and swung an open hand, catching Max across the back of his head.

Max felt as though he'd been hit by a cricket bat. Down he went, right next to his dad, who had blood seeping from a split lip.

'Boys and injured men, that's how tough you are, Chang. I bet you were the school bully. We ever square up, even if I'm not a hundred per cent, I'll knock you into next week,' Tom Gordon growled.

'Mister Slye, get one of the men to retrieve the disc.' Slye melted back into the shadows, relieved to escape the turmoil and ugly violence. Better to be out of sight in moments of extreme conflict.

Max helped his dad prop his back against the wall. Father and son looked at each other, a brief, almost sad smile crossed Tom Gordon's face. They were finished, he knew that, and his helplessness to save his son showed itself in his loving look. 'I don't believe in giving up, you know that, but there's a time for everything. Even when it doesn't work out the way you'd hoped. I'm sorry, son. I love you.'

'Me too, Dad.'

Max put an arm around his father and kissed him. He hadn't done that since he was about eight. But it felt right. As he hugged him, he held his father's hand. Tom Gordon felt the ignition key being pushed into his palm.

It wasn't over yet.

23

The wind, roaring its urgency, caught the mouth of the hangar, surged inside, then, beaten by the voluminous space, subsided into a whisper.

Out of the brewing storm two 4x4 pick-ups pulled in. The men, covered in dust, lowered a body to the floor. It was the unconscious !Koga. A line of dried blood was traced across the back of his head – the injury from the blow Max had witnessed on the television screen when they hunted the Bushman boy down. Blood leaked from his right ear.

Shaka Chang nodded to one of the men nearby, who whistled the hunters to bring the boy's body closer.

Tom Gordon put a restraining hand on his son's arm. Uncontrollable anger was a weapon that could work against you.

!Koga's body lay on the polished concrete floor, like a corpse on a mortuary slab. The hunters backed away respectfully as Shaka Chang nudged the boy's body with his foot. 'Doctor!' he snapped.

Zhernastyn, who, like Mr Slye, had tried to keep out of Shaka Chang's line of vision, gasped and made an unconscious gesture of easing his collar's tightness.

'Check him. Is he dead?' Chang asked.

Dr Zhernastyn knelt down and examined !Koga.

'He's alive, Mister Chang, but I would say his skull has been fractured. I don't think he'll live without hospitalization.'

Max could hardly bear it. His friend's crumpled figure lay, only a couple of metres away, but he couldn't touch or help him.

'You can't let him die!' he shouted.

Shaka Chang barely glanced at him. Slye had returned, the sealed computer disc in his hand. 'It's here, sir,' he said.

'Good!' Chang beamed. 'Let's check it. If it's everything we expected, we can destroy it.' He paused, then strode towards the lift and glanced back at Max, his father and !Koga. 'And them.'

Shaka Chang and Slye moved out of sight. Zhernastyn wiped the sweat from his face. He was walking a fine line with Chang.

'Can't you do something?' Max begged him.

'No. I don't have the facilities.'

'You must be able to do something.'

'I can't!' Zhernastyn hissed. 'Another few hours and he'll be dead. Anyway, why should I? He means nothing to me.'

'He's my friend. He's just a boy. You've gotta help him! You're a doctor!'

Zhernastyn sneered as he glanced at Max's dad. 'I use my skills for other purposes.'

He turned away with a nod towards the armed guard, but Max shouted after him. 'I can still tell Shaka Chang that I sent that information. He won't like the fact that you lied to him. There must be a hospital somewhere!'

337

Zhernastyn was back in control of his own life again; nothing Max could do or say now could harm him. 'The nearest hospital is on a military base, a day's drive from here, and Mister Chang is hardly going to let him go there. Besides, you have no means of talking to Mister Chang now, and in a couple of minutes, after he's checked that disc, this man will shoot you. The vultures will pick your bones clean in hours. Why do you think they call this place Skeleton Rock?'

Zhernastyn walked away.

Max immediately slid across to his friend, his father at his shoulder. The armed guard kept his distance; these two were no threat.

Max touched !Koga's clammy face.

'Dad, what do we do?'

His father eased open !Koga's eyelids.

'The pupils are a different size, Max. I reckon that quack was right. His skull is fractured.'

Tom Gordon helped to raise !Koga's shoulders so that they were supported on Max's lap and chest. 'That's it,' his dad showed him. 'Support his head against your chest. Keep it turned away from where the blood's coming from.' As Tom Gordon kept a couple of fingers on the pulse in !Koga's neck, he whispered, 'Is there any other way out of here?'

Max's back was to the armed guard, muffling his own whispered reply. 'There's another smaller hangar, but there's only motorbikes and stuff in there. Dad, we can't let him die.'

The Humvee's key appeared magically in his dad's fingers. 'I don't know how we could get him into that and escape.

It's a fair way to the doors, and they'd stop us as soon as they heard the engine start. Max, think, is there anything in there you could use to get !Koga away?'

It took only a heartbeat for Max to realize what his father meant.

'Dad, we're all getting out of here together. I'm not leaving you. Not now.'

Max felt the warmth of his father's hand on his shoulder. 'Every moment we're alive, we're beating the odds. I can't move fast enough. I'm too weak. If you can think of any way at all to get him out and make a run for that hospital, you have to take it, or he's going to die. He may even die in the attempt. But we can't just sit here and let them kill us. Then it will all have been in vain. Understand?' He nodded at his son, emphasizing the near finality of their lives. 'You have to make the decision. Save him. If you can.'

Max fought the swell of tears. Then he nodded. 'I think there's a way. It's a one-off chance, but I've got to get him to the next hangar, through that passage.'

'Then that's what we'll do.' His father took !Koga's weight, allowing Max to prepare for the most important run of his life. 'This kid's been banged about so much, but we have to risk carrying him. Can you get him there? On your own?'

Max nodded.

'OK. You'll know when to go.'

'I'll come back for you, Dad. I promise,' Max said with a fierce determination.

His father touched Max's face tenderly, then the boy saw his father's expression harden. It was just like the time on the boat when the pirates had attacked. As if another person was in there under the skin. Hard and tough and unyielding.

Before the guard realized what was happening, Tom Gordon heaved !Koga's weight on to Max's shoulder, ready to jump up and make the run. As the guard brought the gun to bear, Max had the horrendous realization that his father could never reach the gunman in time, that he would be cut down in seconds. And his father had only made what seemed to be a feeble lurch towards the guard. But neither Max nor the guard had noticed a mechanic's work trolley, just out of sight under the Humvee's chassis. Tom Gordon's lunge was to reach the wheeled inspection trolley and whip it into the guard's ankles. And that's what happened. The trolley smashed into his ankles, the guard fell backwards, and suddenly his dad's slithering body was across the floor and using the man's AK47 as a club.

He barely looked around as he dragged himself away. 'Go, Max!'

Max snapped out of his stupefaction and pushed his legs upwards, gulping air as he ran for the passageway. !Koga was hardly more than skin and bone, but it was weight to be carried none the less. As he was about to plunge through the entrance, he couldn't resist looking back. He saw that his father had reached the workbench, his hand stretching out for the wall socket that held the cable's plug. Men were shouting now, their voices echoing around the hangar, their shadows making them giants as they ran to attack.

Max's dad looked at him, nodded, and a second later a tremendous explosion erupted from the inspection pit where they had stored the petrol cans. He'd obviously pressed the switch and sent a surge of power down the bare-ended wires.

The vehicle straddling the pit didn't move for a moment as flames surged around it, then it too exploded in a muffled *whooomp*. Metal clattered, smoke billowed, men screamed. It was uproar. And Max's dad had disappeared – consumed by the smoke and flames.

Max ran, !Koga's body already feeling lighter as adrenalin surged through his limbs.

He reached the second hangar, hit the big red button that said 'ON' and heard the whirring blades of the industrial wall fan hum into life. Easing !Koga into the cockpit of the sand yacht, he could already feel the blast of air hitting his back. He climbed in behind him; it was an incredibly tight fit, but he lifted the boy's body on to his lap, stretched out his legs, made sure !Koga's head was still nestled down on its uninjured side, and gathered in the ropes attached to the sail.

Gunfire echoed behind him from the other hangar; heavy black smoke billowed through the passageway into this area, sucked through the vortex of the narrow passage. It swirled like the turbulence behind a jumbo jet as the fan whistled into full speed. Max felt the air punch the sail as with a tremendous surge it hurled the sand yacht clear.

They burst out through spiralling smoke into a face-full of wind-lashed sand. With eyes barely open, Max manoeuvred the sand yacht, filling the sail with the veering wind as he struggled for control. Rope burns already stung his hands, but once he got the yacht on a course that put the wind across his right shoulder, the wheels skimmed over the baked surface.

He dared a look back. There was plenty of smoke, but no

flames. Shaka Chang must have had an extinguishing system that smothered any threat from fire, particularly in those hangars where the planes and vehicles were kept. Max knew he had to sweep around the fort and head back in the direction he and !Koga had come from. Luckily the black smoke curling from Skeleton Rock screened him from searching eyes.

They rattled along, the wind buffeting the lightweight sand yacht. Max almost lost control when one of the wheels lifted clear of the ground, but he leaned into it and it bumped down, spinning for purchase. A plume of sand sprayed behind them as they skimmed along, faster and faster. The speedo needle hovered between 77 and 80 kilometres per hour, and Max could hear the humming of the wing sail, taut with energy. The ropes vibrated between his fingers as he steered for the vast openness that lay before him. His mind raced almost as fast as the wheels. He had to remember where the broken fingers of cracked earth lay waiting to ensnare him – one mistake and he would drive the sand yacht to destruction. And kill them both.

He struggled to keep control. The wind was doing all the work, and he knew he had been lucky so far, but his limited skill could also be their downfall. He trimmed the sail, felt the speed drop slightly. If he could keep it going steadily, he and !Koga stood a better chance of survival. The heat from his friend's body lying against him wasn't just from the cramped conditions, !Koga's temperature was burning up.

The sand yacht shuddered. He was hitting rougher ground. The fixed rear wheels bounced across the ruts, following wherever Max steered the front wheel, which was now twisting out of control. Max edged the yacht first one way then the other, until it settled again.

Now he had it. The harmony of wind and sail joined forces to push him at a steady speed: 80, 85, 87. As straight as an arrow he kept his heading. They were in with a chance. He had already saved thirty or forty kilometres by heading right out across the plain. When he and !Koga had crept within sight of Skeleton Rock, they had taken a roundabout, looping course. Now it was as straight as the crow flies. Or the vulture. And it still wouldn't take much to give the scavengers breakfast.

His brief moment of satisfaction turned into one of fear when he saw the straining black fist that was a wind-filled sail soaring towards him from behind his left shoulder. It was the second sand yacht. But this pilot knew what he was doing. He was nursing the black, bullet-shaped body at an angle that would intercept Max. And it must have been doing over a hundred – its lethal beauty would be upon him in a couple of minutes at that speed.

Max wrestled with the ropes, he was getting it all wrong. The sail flapped as he steered off-wind, then surged as he caught it again.

The hunter was closing.

Max knew he was trying to do too much. He had to hold !Koga close to him, so he only had one hand left to control the yacht. He decided to let the sail look after itself and steer with his right hand. He would keep the wind on the quarter as best he could and try to outmanoeuvre his pursuer.

The wind shifted again, lifting a veil of sand half a kilometre ahead and he realized that, despite his erratic piloting, he knew where he was. The rising land was where he and !Koga had camped before the Devil's Breath sucked him down – and behind that escarpment was where he was heading. That's where the plane lay hidden. And that was his only chance to save !Koga's life and radio for help.

His own thoughts and emotions fought each other. Images of his father, the explosion, the flames, that final look, the moments of danger together and the warmth and love from his dad. Deep down, he knew that, no matter how rugged or tough his father was, he held a powerhouse of love for Max. He'd never felt so close to him as in those last few moments together. But his mind shouted at him. *Don't think about it! Concentrate! You've only got one crack at this! You muck this up and you're dead! Concentrate!*

A quick look behind showed only a wall of sand chasing him. If it overtook him, he would be piloting blind, his sense of direction would disappear. A flurry of rain blown in from the mountain storm stung his face. The rain was still too far away to make any impact, but if the sand cloud was behind him, then whoever was chasing him must be caught up in it.

Like a dust devil the leading edge of the sandstorm raced ahead of him, over to the left, about thirty metres away. Was it veering or was it going to cut back towards him and smother him?

He didn't have time to consider his options.

The gloss-black hunter edged out of the fog of sand, its pilot's head and shoulders just visible above the bodywork. He wore a helmet, its visor closed, giving his face full protection against the glare of the sun and the stinging, penetrating sand.

And then, like a charioteer of old, he swung the sand yacht sideways. Max had to stay on course, there were boulders ahead. Was that what the other guy had seen as well? Was he trying to force Max to pile up and rip himself apart?

Max held his line.

The guy came closer. Ten metres, six, three, two.

They were racing side by side. The man's hand came free of the cockpit and pointed at him. Pointed something black, a dull sheen, an automatic. But before Max could react, the other sand yacht jigged a little. The control needed at that speed was so precise, the man needed both hands.

He dared another look. The pilot wasn't even looking at him. He was concentrating on those rocks. Then Max saw why. The ground became broken; not only were there rocks on Max's side, the other pilot faced the same challenge. They were both heading for the narrow gap. Only one of them could get through.

With what seemed a nervous glance towards Max, the other man moved his hands rapidly on the ropes, and his yacht surged ahead. He'd trimmed everything so quickly and expertly that Max could only eat his dirt.

With seconds to spare the two yachts hurtled through the gap, nose to tail. The other man had reacted instinctively, ensuring he was the one who got through, perhaps hoping the dust trail would blind Max and force him on to the rocks. But it was a fundamental error. As Max went through the gap, he eased the yacht to starboard, that was where he needed to go, and when he did, he stole the other man's air.

As Max kept going, he saw his attacker's sail flap as the yacht faltered. Forced to gibe, swinging the yacht around, he lost time trying to catch the wind and, as luck would have it, the sandstorm now hit the man side on, just as he was turning the yacht. Max saw the mast tilt and the wheels lift. The man couldn't hold it. The yacht turned over.

Even if the other guy could get the yacht upright, Max knew he had gained valuable time. 'Hang on, !Koga, we're gonna make it,' he shouted, although he knew the unconscious boy couldn't hear him.

Then the obvious thought seeped into his mind. He might be the only living witness to Shaka Chang's plan. If the information hadn't reached Sayid, he still held the knowledge of what was planned.

The sand yacht was probably not the only attempt Shaka Chang would have made to stop him. Somewhere out there in the confused storm, others might be searching.

Imagination was a dangerous thing when you're scared. Deal with what you know and try to plan for the unexpected, but don't let your mind make you seize up through fear, the voice in his head urged him.

Max held !Koga tighter across his chest and headed for his dad's plane. Knowing what he had to do when he got there was scary enough.

The sight of the trees encouraged him. The sand yacht had faltered, a couple of kilometres away, when the ground changed into shrub and grassland. He had let it slow, easing the sail so it spilled the air, ensuring they didn't tip over.

Carefully lifting !Koga out of the yacht's cockpit, he carried him at a slow jog, stopping every once in a while to catch his breath. The wind was gaining strength, a more consistent push against his back – the storm building itself, ready to release its pent-up rain. If the storm broke before he could reach the plane, the ground would flood and the wheels would never get through it. Max's heart pounded, not from the exertion but from the anticipation. He *had* to fly the plane out.

His visual memory snatched at images, like scenes from old movies, remembering things Kallie had done when she flew him in; trying to hear her voice as she explained things; but they wouldn't gel. They didn't make sense. Fractured elements of recall made their own jigsaw puzzle.

And then they reached the plane.

Max pulled aside the camouflage netting, climbed into the Cessna, then turned and dragged !Koga in behind him, ever mindful of the boy's injury. It took longer than he wanted, but he couldn't rush this, not now.

With !Koga securely fastened, Max clambered into the pilot's seat. The last time he had sat there, his mind had focused on the opening through the windscreen and a changed consciousness had taken him high up, letting him see the landscape and the way to the Devil's Breath. But not now. Now his hands rested on the controls and he could barely think straight.

The way ahead was clear of camouflage net and branches. He needed to start the plane, roll it forward, and then turn on to the flattened grassland. His eyes glazed over at all the instruments. He chastised himself. *Come on, you do one thing, then something will happen, then you do the next thing, and so on. It'll happen. It'll work. Something will click and you'll do it.*

He pointed at a dial. *What's that!?* 'Fuel gauge,' he answered himself.

And that? 'Airspeed indicator.'

And? 'Altimeter, lights, master switch, ignition and magnetos! Right! OK, got it!'

It came back to him. He pulled down the sun visor and the worn tag that held the key fell into his lap. He put it in the ignition. There were things he should have checked, he knew that. At Windhoek, Kallie had done a complete visual check outside her own aircraft. Well, that took time, which was a luxury; this was time-has-run-out time. The sign on the control panel warned him to make sure there was no water contaminating the fuel – another risk he had to take. This was his main chance. Some things had to be left in the lap of the gods. There was a toggle switch to prime the engine. That made sense. You primed a lawnmower before you started it. How long? Couple of seconds, five, ten? Middle. Five should do it.

Fuel selectors. He fingered the small lever into the 'Both' position. Kallie was a great pilot and she had warned him about getting things wrong. What had she said? It seemed a lifetime ago since he had seen her. He re-ran the video clip in his head. Meeting her, liking her, no, not that stuff, what else? The flying. Leaving Windhoek. The old plane, the . . . saying. There was a saying.

He pictured the instruments in her plane. There was a small sign. *My dad worries. He taught me how to fly.* That's what she'd said. And there was a tattered laminated postcard stuck on the panel. She hadn't remembered what it was called. It was a mnemonic, he had told her. That's right, an *aide-mémoire*, she had agreed.

He could see it. Almost. The words were there, forming in his mind's eye. *Rather Too Many Pilots Forget How It Goes.* That was it. His mind raced with anticipation as his fingers did the work.

Radio and Rudder – check.

Trim Elevator for take-off – OK.

Throttle tension, set for start – done.

Mixture, rich; Magnetos on – got it.

Fuel select, both tanks – already done.

Flaps. Something about flaps.

What else did 'F' stand for? Forgetful.

He couldn't remember what the other letters meant, but he had done what his memory told him and everything had flickered into life. The engine coughed and spluttered, the propeller suddenly spun, and when he released the parking brake the plane moved forward. Max let out a cry of victory. Easing the throttle forward on the instrument panel, the propeller roared louder and they broke free from the safety of cover.

It demanded all his attention. The Flight Simulator game on his computer at school was one thing, but this was quite another, and he was going too fast, like driving a lorry with his foot flat down. He had jammed his feet on the pedals and his hands turned the controls, but he had gone the wrong way. He had to face into the wind for take-off.

Rudder, controls, throttle eased back – the plane turned.

The brakes were awkward, sitting just above the rudder pedals, and they pulled to one side. But he raised his foot slightly, found the right position, and the plane wallowed to a halt. Now it sat, braked, facing the wind. Max could feel it trying to lift the wings – exactly what he wanted – but through the high-speed blur of the propeller he could see the leaden sky. It flattened all the colour of the landscape: the malignant clouds in turmoil, the storm fit to burst. Max had to take off, but he couldn't stay on that heading once he was up there. That turbulence would chew him up and spit him out. In pieces.

He hesitated. The radio had hummed into life once the engine started. He could just call for help, the batteries were charging now, he could simply keep on calling until someone heard him, and then they'd come and rescue them. Maybe.

The decision was made for him.

The same pick-up truck that had hunted !Koga was coming straight for him, from exactly where he had abandoned the sand yacht. Men hung on in the back as it jolted across the uneven ground – they'd obviously seen him, but they couldn't get a clear shot at him yet.

Max scanned the dials and gauges in front of him. What else? Had he forgotten anything? Too late to worry about it; he released the footbrakes, pushed in the throttle, and the plane bucked forward. It veered, lurching because of the propeller's gyroscopic pitch – not that Max knew why it had pulled. Instinctively he tapped the left brake with his foot and it corrected itself. But the plane still swung left and right, the tail wheel bouncing across the uneven ground, causing it to sway. Max didn't know what to do except ride out the problem. Then, as the airflow moved across the wings, it stabilized.

Faster now, trying to maintain direction with the rudder pedals, heading straight towards that heavy sky on the horizon. More speed; fifty knots, he had to go faster. He shoved the throttle all the way forward; sixty, seventy. Bumping badly now, the controls vibrating in his hands; the men less than two hundred metres off; the end of the grass in sight – it had to be now. Eighty.

Max pulled back the controls and the plane lifted its nose – if he went too steep he would stall – he remembered, light touch, nothing too brutal with a plane – nurse it upwards, let it do the work. Hailstones clattered against the fuselage . . . three holes appeared in the port wing – they weren't hailstones. *Come on! Come on! Take off!* The pick-up truck was almost on him. The men's mouths yelled silent curses. The plane soared upwards.

As the wind helped lift the wings, the altimeter told him he was already at three hundred feet. He adjusted the throttle until the air speed indicator showed he was flying at a hundred and twenty knots. Max eased the plane around in a long, sweeping turn, watching to see that the nose stayed up, the propeller tip nudging above what he could see of the horizon – he knew that was the ideal attitude for a plane. Now he had the storm at his back, it was time to call for help.

Taking off was one thing. Landing was a far more terrifying problem.

24

Down in the airfield's bar, Ferdie van Reenen was rolling a cigarette, a cold beer on the counter top in front of him, as Tobias poured himself a mug of coffee and muttered when he splashed some on his yellow T shirt that sported Nelson Mandela's smiling face.

Kallie was sitting next to her dad. 'I thought you'd quit smoking.'

'I did, but you've put me back on to them. I'm too old for all this stress, y'know. Anyway, I haven't lit it yet, have I?'

He emptied the tobacco from the cigarette paper into his hand and began the process again. Ferdie van Reenen was no good, sitting around and doing nothing.

Mike Kapuo came in, closing the door firmly behind him. 'Wind's picking up.' He nodded at Tobias as the barman offered the coffee pot.

'Storm'll break in a couple of hours, then no one will be flying. When are those Brits getting here?' Van Reenen asked.

Kapuo checked his watch. 'About an hour, maybe a bit more.'

Van Reenen had rolled another cigarette. 'And what about your blokes?'

'Bogged down in bureaucracy and in-fighting. Army wants one thing, police commissioner wants another, and the politicians all want to be covered in glory.'

'They'll be covered in something else if they don't get this mess sorted.' Van Reenen moaned as he put the cigarette between his lips.

Kallie gave him an imploring look.

'Go and sit further down the bar. I want a cigarette. I'm a big boy now,' he told her.

Kallie eased off the stool and moved away. 'Don't expect me to look after you when your lungs pack up.'

'What I expect is your antics will have put me in an early grave long before then.'

'Whatever,' she said, and found herself a stool further along the counter. Their chit-chat was a way of relieving the tension because, whatever else was going on, they were being forced to wait and it was driving them all crazy. Kallie stared at the receiver propped behind the bar. Wherever Max was, he might still be able to reach a radio and send a message.

Kapuo lowered his voice as he confided in Van Reenen. 'I sent two helicopters and my tactical team to the underground site Kallie reported.'

'And?'

'They're on their way here. Nothing they could do. It's sealed. Steel doors, concrete blocks. I'd need high explosive or tanks to get in there. There's no sign of anyone. It's just shut down.'

'Then something's due to happen.'

'Which is why I want a couple of dozen of my own men

on hand. I'm not waiting for some pen-pusher to make up his mind.'

'If that place is some kind of underground bunker system, you need to get it blown,' Van Reenen said.

'With what?'

'I dunno.' He lit the cigarette, and coughed. 'These things never taste as good as you remember them.' He stubbed out the cigarette. 'Mike, if this thing is as important as you and I think it is, our Minister of Defence should get on the blower, speak to his South African counterpart and get their air force to put in a strike. They've got bunker-buster missiles. It's gotta be big time if the Brits are sending in a team.'

Kapuo nodded. It was time for his senior officers to pull strings. He needed to do some shouting. 'Bang goes my pension.'

'Ach, it was a rubbish one anyway,' Van Reenen said, sipping his beer.

The storm whiplashed the air. Max was struggling to keep the plane flying on an even keel while it was being buffeted by the violent wind. !Koga was still unconscious and Max couldn't even be sure whether he was still breathing. Flying with one hand, Max checked the radio; it was set to 121.5 megacycles. Was that right? Would that get through to anyone? Why would his dad have had that frequency tuned in? It must mean something. He pressed the handset to his lips. 'Mayday, Mayday, Mayday.' He released the transmit button. Nothing. 'Mayday, Mayday, Mayday. This is Max Gordon. I need help. Can anyone hear me? I'm flying a plane and I need help. Hello? Mayday. Anybody?'

Ferdie van Reenen had scrambled over the counter, spilled his beer, and grabbed the handset. 'Max. We hear you! Over.'

Kallie was right behind him.

There was a garbled response that then was cut off. 'Max, listen, son, this is Kallie's pa. Speak into the handset, release the button, and listen. That's how it works.'

Max's voice came over the tannoy. 'I understand. I need help.'

'I know. Is your father with you? Over.'

There was a pause.

'No,' said Max. 'Dad's at Skeleton Rock. But I've got an injured Bushman boy with me. He's really hurt and he needs a doctor. Over,' Max said, remembering the radio procedure.

There was no doctor. Not in these parts.

'That must be !Koga,' Kallie said.

'All right, Max. Let's get you down first. Can you see any landmarks? Over.'

Max peered down. From the air, the wilderness he had travelled across looked different. A ravine, scrubland, in the distance becoming more obscured by the dust, a straight line that was a dirt road. He clicked the handset.

'Nothing. Just . . . nothing. There's a road, a track, dead straight. Running across my flight path. Bottom left to top right. There's a huge storm behind me. I can tell you that.'

In the bar, Tobias had already unfolded a map. Kapuo and Van Reenen scanned it, trying to get an idea of where Max might be. Kallie gestured for the handset and her father passed it to her.

'Where'd he take off from? What's his compass bearing?' Van Reenen instructed her. 'If the storm's behind him, he's flying in a southerly direction.'

'Max, this is Kallie.'

The plane bellied into turbulence and the instrument panel shook on its mountings as a violent gust made it drop a hundred feet. Despite his seat belt, Max's head hit the ceiling. He dropped the handset, his pulse raced, and the metal structure around him suddenly felt very flimsy. He levelled the plane, the horizon bar on the dial dipping left and right, but finally settling on an even keel. Max pulled back the handset's coiled cable and pressed the transmit button.

'Kallie! Brilliant. I just fell into some kind of hole in the sky. This isn't fun.'

'Max, I'm not even going to ask how you got up there – that can wait. What does your compass say? Over.'

The compass needle wavered as the plane was pushed this way and that. 'Er . . . it's . . . south . . . south-east . . . a hundred and thirty something, hundred and forty degrees. You get that?'

'Got it.' Her voice crackled through the speaker. It was difficult to hear her without a headset, the plane's engine rumbled loudly, its pitch changing as it dealt with the buffeting wind. 'Where did you take off?'

'Dunno. Below the Devil's Breath somewhere. Can't be sure. Must have been south. Must have been.'

*

Van Reenen turned the map, his finger tracing the possible route. Using the edge of a beer mat and a stub of pencil, he drew two intersecting lines. One from Skeleton Rock, through the Devil's Breath, and the other from the approaching northerly storm.

'He's going the wrong way. There's nowhere we can talk him down. He has to turn towards us.'

Kallie pressed the transmit button. 'Max, you have to turn the plane on to a south-west course. Repeat. South-west.'

'Er . . . right . . . ah . . . er . . . turning it . . . er . . . pushing me down!'

'Lift the nose! Lift the nose. Get her level!'

Crackle. Static. Silence.

'Max?'

There was an agonizing pause.

'OK! I did it! Kallie . . . listen . . . !Koga's skull is fractured. He's really bad. Get a doctor and get me down. Can you do that?'

Van Reenen shook his head. 'There's a military hospital at Khomtsa.'

'It'd take him hours at his speed,' Kapuo said.

'You're right. We get him down here, I'll take the boy in the Baron,' Van Reenen told them. His twin-engined plane could make the journey in less than half an hour.

Before anyone could say anything, Max's voice filled the bar. 'Kallie. Bit of a problem, I think. The fuel gauge . . . both needles are below the quarter mark on the dial. I think I might be almost empty.'

Kallie barely hesitated, she shoved the handset into her

father's hand and ran for the door. 'We don't have time for him to find us. Keep him on course. I'll find him.'

Van Reenen didn't have a chance to argue. Kallie was sprinting for her plane.

Clouds snatched at the windscreen as light rain splattered on the plane's skin. Max hadn't realized that by keeping the nose pointed just above the horizon he had overcompensated. The altimeter showed 2600 feet. He must have been going upwards since he took off. He needed to get down to where he could identify features on the ground. No wonder the plane had been gobbling fuel – not that he knew how much he had had in the first place – one of the things he'd forgotten to check. Not that it would have mattered. He'd have taken the chance anyway.

He pushed the nose down gently. No sensation of dropping, just the view through the propeller's flickering shadow. It could be really easy to gaze through that, see the ground coming up, closer, closer, until it was too late to pull up.

He was well below the cloud now, down to about 1000 feet. Still in the middle of nowhere. In truth, he didn't want to land. That was a really scary thought. He was just fine, skimming through the sky. If he had an unending fuel supply he could just keep going.

Wake up! The voice in his head shouted. The hum of the engine, the whirring propeller and the exhaustion that was quickly claiming him had eased him into that strange dream state where he thought he was awake but wasn't. His eyes didn't want to stay open. He needed air. He wedged the side window open and felt the freezing-cold air prickle his skin.

'OK! I'm awake! I am awake!' he shouted to the sky. And then he heard Van Reenen's concerned, insistent voice. Max answered, assuring him that he was OK, but he was frightened that he had not heard Kallie's dad calling him.

Van Reenen's voice kept up a steady stream of instructions, mostly to keep him edging on course and telling him that Kallie was going to fly alongside him. Could he see her? Coming from starboard. Keep your eyes open. Stay on course. Stay level. Keep looking. Keep looking.

And then, like an ageing, overworked angel, the battered Cessna flew into view. A streak of sunshine escaped through the leaden sky, painting her wings a shiny gold. He had never been so happy to see anybody in his life. Except his dad, that is. He waved. She smiled and waved back. Her plane was flying level, not twenty metres away.

'Kallie! Amazing! What do I do? Can you hear me?' he shouted into the handset.

'Loud and clear,' she replied. 'I'm going to fly slightly ahead of you and a little higher. In a few minutes you'll see what looks like a river bed, but it's a crack in the ground, then a couple of lumpy hills and, past that, there's the runway.'

'Understood.' The tone of her voice meant there was no time to talk. She turned, he followed. He was surprised how easy it was to miss landmarks, the whole perspective when flying altered his awareness. He concentrated madly, trying to see where they were going, but the barren land yielded no sign of an airstrip.

'To your right, towards the horizon. You see the airfield?'

Kallie said after about twenty minutes. He looked hard, his eyes scanning the ground.

'No!' he said, feeling the edge of panic in his voice. 'I just can't see it.'

'OK, relax, just follow me,' she reassured him, remembering her first solo flight. She'd thought she'd never find the airfield again – and that was down in Windhoek, which was big enough to be seen from space. She knew the difficulties Max was experiencing. 'Look below my aircraft, let your eyes go to the horizon and then look left. There's a plateau that looks like an upside-down iron . . .'

'Got that!'

'Look to the point of the iron, there's a couple of buildings.'

He couldn't see them, dammit! Yes! The corrugated roofs made a wave of shadows as the light changed. 'I can see it, Kallie. I can see the buildings and the strip. I've got it.' Relief flooded through him and he relaxed his hands that had been gripping the controls too tightly.

'OK, Max. Fuel?'

He looked at the fuel gauge needles. They'd dropped to the bottom of the dial. 'They're in the red.'

She didn't answer. And he realized this was it. One chance at getting the plane down in one piece.

'OK. You don't have to spell it out, Kallie.'

'Excellent. So, normally we'd take a pass over the airfield, check the windsock and get the wind direction, but we don't have time for that. And I know where the wind's blowing from. Trust me?'

He thought she was amazingly calm and promised himself

he'd try to control the anxiety in his voice from now on.

'Trust a girl? I'd have to think about that – if I had the time.'

'Ready?'

'Let's do it.'

The moment he heard the words come out of his mouth, a strange calmness settled over him. The rocking of the aircraft, the uncertain picture through the windscreen – none of it mattered. He was going in for a landing, and when something this big stared you in the face, when there was absolutely no choice left, you faced it with as much calm as you could. Like a man about to be executed.

Kallie's voice sounded gentle but firm, as if she was holding his hand. 'You're nicely established on the downwind, keep it going until I ask you to turn to the left. OK, time to do a couple of pre-landing checks. Don't waste time responding unless you can't do any of them.'

She didn't need to ask him to check that the fuel selector was on the 'Both tanks' setting. It was now or never.

'Check the mixture is on "Rich".' She paused, giving him time. 'Check the magnetos are on the "Both" mark.' She could see his head dipping as his fingers traced her instructions. 'OK, Max. Good. You're doing really well. Now, reduce your power to a steady ninety knots.' She had already cut back her own speed and watched as Max's plane slowed. The boy was getting it right. He was listening and doing what was being asked of him. Maybe they were in with a chance after all. 'Max, find the lever and lower the flaps to ten degrees.'

The trailing edge of the wing showed the gap when the flaps lowered.

'How you doing, Max? Have you done everything?'

'Yeah. Everything. All the checks.'

'Here we go. We're going to make a crosswind turn ninety degrees to the runway.'

Max followed her, and the runway lay to his left. Now he could see everything. The strip was flanked by a couple of buildings: one of them looked like a workshop area, the other was just a tin-roofed shack. There were men standing at the door, one of them wearing a lurid yellow T-shirt and red baseball cap.

In the centre of the field a civilian jet was parked next to a smaller plane with twin propellers. Near the white-painted jet half a dozen men, bare-headed and dressed in black, were gazing up at him. Everyone was looking up at him. He was the centre of attention. All eyes on him. He hoped he wouldn't make a mess of it. He'd never live it down.

If he lived.

'Max?' Her voice tugged his mind back. 'Start to turn for your final approach and line up with the runway.'

He moved the controls gently and felt the plane turn almost gracefully, despite the erratic wind that kept trying to upset things.

'That looks good,' she said. 'Now reduce your power to about seventeen hundred revs and aim the plane for a point about a quarter-way down the runway, keeping the wings level. Keep her level!'

Easier said than done. It seemed he had so many things to do, but her voice wouldn't let him falter.

'OK, lower twenty degrees of flap and adjust the power to maintain seventy knots.'

He fingered the throttle, watched the airspeed indicator needle drop, and realized with a growing sense of finality that he was now much lower than he had believed.

Outside the bar, Tobias's can of beer hovered between his chin and his lips. Van Reenen chewed an unlit cigarette and Mike Kapuo's unblinking eyes were locked on to the two aircraft, now only a few hundred metres away. The one below the other seemed to be wobbling.

'The landing gear on those Cessnas is made from spring steel,' Van Reenen said, to no one in particular.

Kapuo and Tobias dared a glance away from the unfolding drama.

'What does that mean?' Tobias asked.

'Anything other than just about a perfect touchdown, and he'll be bouncing from here to kingdom come,' he said. 'That might just finish off that kid with a fractured skull. And he's too low. I hope she can see it. Come on, Kallie, tell him. Tell him,' he muttered to himself.

Pilots talk in feet, Max thought in metres, but his eyes told him he needed to be higher. Should he pull up? The wind was being difficult, a rush across the ground, a swirl at rooftop height. Whatever happened, Max did not have the skill to start side-slipping the plane. He had to come in dead straight.

'You're getting a little low, Max, apply a touch more power. Keep her level, a little more power, come on.'

That was how you did it. Don't pull up, just 'a touch more power'. That's it.

Max didn't take his eyes away from the ground as he reached out, pushed the throttle in, heard the engine pick up and then her voice telling him that was better, and that he could slowly reduce power again.

Couldn't she make her mind up?

'You're about thirty feet off the ground, Max. Twenty-five. Remember after touchdown to keep the plane straight. Use your rudder, do *not* touch the brakes until you've lost speed and the tail wheel is on the ground. OK, good, twenty feet, lower thirty degrees of flap and try and keep the speed at sixty knots with the throttle.'

Her voice was now a continuous assurance. Calm, even, steady. Almost tender. 'Ten feet above the runway, start reducing power and be sure not to let the nose drop.'

Max couldn't see the runway any more, it had slipped below the propeller, and it felt as though the plane was sitting back on her tail. The bloody wind snatched at him.

'Keep it straight! Don't drop that wing. You are just about to touch down.'

The hum of tyres on concrete vibrated through his seat.

'Great, you're down, keep it straight and close the throttle completely!'

He pulled the lever all the way out. The propeller began to slow.

'Your tail wheel is on the ground, you can apply brakes gently. Well done! Raise the flaps and taxi in. Looks like you've got a welcoming committee.'

Max saw Kallie's plane soar upwards to come around again and make her own landing. Mother Earth. Solid, unyielding. Welcome home, everybody.

The engine died, the last gasp of fuel spluttering, and then silence. For a moment he couldn't move, but then he saw the men running from the jet; they were dressed in assault gear. Then someone yanked open the door and eager hands reached in for him.

'All right, son, bit of a blinder, eh? Good one.'

A cockney accent. What was its owner doing here? He didn't have time to figure it out.

'My mate's in there –' Max began.

Another man. Scottish. 'Aye, don't you worry about him, we know he's hurt.'

The men passed him from one to the other down the line, until he stood clear of the plane and watched as one of them clambered in and began easing !Koga out.

Someone familiar-looking was walking towards him. Max stared. It couldn't be. Mr Peterson!

'No!' Max yelled, turning back to the soldiers who had put !Koga on to a folding stretcher. He hadn't gone through all of this to fall into Peterson's hands.

One of the men grabbed him, not roughly but with enough strength so that Max knew he couldn't compete with him. Everything seemed to give way inside him. He'd lost. Max almost cracked up.

It made no sense.

Kallie's plane landed and stopped in a very short distance; Mr Peterson was standing in front of him, a big smile on his face, and the men in black were carrying !Koga to the twin-engined plane, where a man with a wild beard sat in the cockpit, shouting for them to hurry.

The world had finally gone mad.

Max went down on his knees.

He saw Mr Peterson frown, saw his mouth shaping his name.

And couldn't stop himself falling into blackness.

25

Something moved in the darkness.

He was sitting cross-legged, as if he were a small boy in school assembly, except that there was no one else with him. What he could describe only as a dark wind rustled the blackness, like silk being brushed by air. His father's face became almost visible, yet Max felt no great compulsion to reach out to him. His father smiled, nodded approvingly, and faded back into the undulating night.

A silent streak of lightning tore across the darkness, exposing a massive walkway, like a bridge through the night sky. It was sheathed in dull moonglow, and Max watched himself running along it. He looked strange. Filthy, shorts torn, his hair matted and wild, and he was running harder and faster than he could believe possible. Running towards a gaping hole in the night. A dark cave in a black night. It made no sense. He watched as he collided with a force that repelled him, like a glass door that didn't break, heard his own cry of fear, and saw himself disappear over the edge into oblivion.

And the vision disappeared.

Max sensed another movement.

The *jackal*.

It loped towards him, swaying gently, until finally it stopped, sniffed his face and sat down, as before, on its haunches, facing him directly. Its eyes gazed into his own and, without surprise, Max heard it speak.

'You are Brother of the Night,' it said.

And licked his face like a dog with a puppy.

'Are you all right? Max? Are you all right?' a voice called, erasing the dream, merging the rhythm of the words.

Someone had stuck superglue to his tongue. It felt like Velcro when he peeled it off the roof of his mouth. He opened his eyes.

'Max! You idiot! You stupid idiot! You're alive!'

Sayid?

Sayid jumped up and down like a lunatic. 'I got airsick, I was puking in the loo when you were coming in to land. I had to clean up the mess. You're alive. You're crazy, man!'

Max groaned and eased himself up from the bed someone had put him on.

'Sayid. What the hell's going on?'

Sayid took Max's arm, hauled him to his feet, and dragged him outside. Three helicopters, armed soldiers and the assault troops who had dragged him and !Koga out of the plane stood with Mr Peterson, who seemed to be in charge. And then Kallie stepped out of the other building and smiled at him. That gave Max a really good feeling.

'Oh, so you're back in the land of the living,' she said as she stepped towards him and kissed him on the cheek. Her lips almost touched his, but he reckoned that as his mouth felt like the bottom of a birdcage his cheek was probably her better option.

'Where's !Koga?' Max asked, the fog clearing from his brain.

'I've just been on the phone to my pa. He's in the operating theatre now. We don't know much more. Not for a while.'

Max looked at the gathered men. 'Mister Peterson is in on this?'

Sayid smiled. 'He's been on your side all along. And we got the info you sent.'

'Why don't you get cleaned up and eat, then Sayid and I can tell you everything that has happened,' Kallie said.

Max shook his head. 'Do you mind?' And he pointed to the water bottle in her hand. She passed it to him and he drained it, the water like fuel for a car. 'Look, I can't even start to tell you what happened to me and !Koga, but those men look as though they know what's going on. And I have to get back to my dad.'

Kallie failed to hide her uncertainty.

Max flung the empty bottle down. 'I know he's alive! He has to be!'

'Max, don't. There's gonna be a lot of violence when those blokes attack Shaka Chang,' Sayid said.

'I hope so,' Max told him and walked towards Mr Peterson.

A blast of air pummelled his skin as he sat on the rim of the helicopter's doorway. They were going in for the attack on Skeleton Rock.

Mr Peterson had argued the case for him being present when the soldiers said they didn't want a kid getting in the way. It was Max, he reminded them, who was the reason they were all there, and it was Max who knew his way in and out of the fort. If they wanted any kind of Target Appreciation, then Max was the one who could give it them. And once Max had told them how he got into the fort, through the Devil's Breath, the men smiled. That was too tough, they had laughed, even for the SAS.

Time and weather were against them.

The helicopters flew low and fast, but the rain still stung Max's legs. The Namibian soldiers had told them that in less than an hour the mightiest of storms was going to break over the mountains. The helicopters would be unable to fly, and there'd be flash floods that would swamp the ground. Then there could be no attack.

So, there wasn't going to be time to go in through any back door; they would assault the main building, with Mr Peterson and Max with two of the SAS soldiers and four Namibian desert troops going straight into the main hangar. The other helicopters would have two SAS men in each, leading the local soldiers.

Priority one – stop Shaka Chang.

Priority two – rescue Tom Gordon.

It had to be that way. Thousands of lives were at stake. The Namibian and South African governments had already sent troops to the dam, but nobody knew whether they would get there in time, nor whether Shaka Chang had any kind of remote device to open the dam's gates. And even if he realized his plan had been discovered, he could still commit an act of vengeance and disappear.

The cloud base was down, hugging the top of Skeleton Rock, and as two of the helicopters went straight for the fort, Max's chopper swung low and around. It was a scene he would never forget – helicopters dodging gunfire streaking from the fort, black clouds spitting rain, and the tight-banking, evasive flight of his own helicopter as tracer bullets cut through the darkening sky towards them. And Mr Peterson grabbing him back from the open door, out of the danger zone. Max remembered – a lifetime ago – running across the moor towards Dartmoor High as other bullets cut red through the night and an assassin had tried to keep him from learning the truth. Well, it had been a long journey he had travelled, but the truth was out and the whole frightening episode was almost over.

Dad, hang on. I'm coming. Hang on. Please!

Shaka Chang climbed aboard the black helicopter in the hangar. The fire Tom Gordon had started had caused an enormous amount of damage, but Chang's very expensive fire-protection systems prevented the blaze destroying the aircraft he needed to make his escape and complete his plan. As far as Shaka Chang was concerned, no one knew what he was going to do and, when Skeleton Rock disintegrated, any clues concerning Chang would be vaporized. The destruction of his African headquarters would be put down to a vicious fire that had got out of control.

Mr Slye scurried like a rat behind Shaka Chang. The helicopter's engine hummed and clattered into life.

'The landing strip at the dam! Twenty minutes!' Chang shouted at him as the helicopter lifted away towards the mountains, fighting the ever-increasing wind. Slye watched the helicopter go and made a calculated decision. He knew that damned Gordon boy had got a message out and it was only a matter of time before some prime minister or president told his soldiers to get Shaka Chang. And Mr Slye had no illusions about where he would end up. He felt a wave of nausea as he remembered the Mongolian prison guard. He waved at the helicopter, not that Chang could see him, but Mr Lucius Slye felt it appropriate that all his years of servitude should warrant a goodbye wave. For years he had been squirrelling away funds into a Swiss bank account – and now the time had come to enjoy it.

Dr Zhernastyn ran into the hangar. 'Mister Slye! Wait! What about me!?'

The Learjet's pilots waited for Slye to climb aboard.

'What about you, Doctor Zhernastyn?'

'How do I get out?'

'Is that a trick question? I don't know. How *do* you get out?'

'Help me!'

'No. You're very lucky I didn't tell Mister Chang that you allowed Max Gordon to fool you! You're already playing in extra time, Doctor. Find your own way out. But I would do it quickly if I were you because, within twenty minutes, it won't matter.'

The Learjet's door closed behind him and the plane taxied out of the hangar towards the runway.

Mr Slye liked the smell of leather seats, and the Learjet's comfort was something he could quite easily get used to. He gave the pilots a sheet of instructions.

'There's been a change of plan,' he told them.

He knew they wouldn't dare argue with Shaka Chang's right-hand man.

Max's helicopter hovered beyond the hangar's mouth. The pilot was fighting the storm and he signalled to the men that he couldn't hold it much longer. They had listened to the troops' firefight over the radio as they cleared the main area. Chang's bullies were no match for a disciplined attack. But then, instead of the all-clear, a dreadful warning came over the radio – the place was ready to explode. Clear the area immediately.

The pilot prepared to lift off. 'No!' Max cried and jumped to the ground. Without hesitation Mr Peterson and the soldiers followed him as he sprinted into the hangar. 'Dad! Where are you? Can you hear me?!' he screamed.

A blur of white against the distant wall caught Max's eye. Zhernastyn. He'd know where his dad was, but as he shouted his name Mr Peterson caught up with him and grabbed him.

'Enough, Max! We have to get away! Take him!' Mr Peterson yelled to the soldiers, who roughly grabbed him and pulled him back towards the helicopter. 'Mister Peterson! Dad's here! Right here! Don't leave him! Please! Please!'

No matter how he fought and kicked, he was no match for the tough soldiers.

'The place is gonna blow, mate. You've done all you could,' one of the men shouted as he covered their retreat, his machine gun tucked into his shoulder. Max had never felt such despair. All the fight went out of him. He had lost. And he had used his very last ounce of energy to keep going. There was nothing left inside him now. No matter how much he willed himself, his body had finally failed him.

One last gasp of hope.

The key!

The Humvee.

Where else could his dad be? He would have crawled away from the blaze and the gunfire when Max had escaped. The armour-plated Humvee was the only safe place to hide, but if they didn't get him out he would be burned to death.

'The Humvee!' Max yelled.

He looked into Mr Peterson's eyes and for a brief moment it seemed that Peterson faltered. He did. He stopped as they dragged Max further and further away from finding his father. And then Mr Peterson turned back into the hangar.

Somewhere in there, lights were flashing. Max could barely see now; the rain stung his eyes and the helicopter's noise beat the air out of his ears, but there were definitely orange lights flashing and a siren – a car's alarm. The weight of clouds sat over them now and the wind's unearthly growl cut a frightening wound through the air.

His back scraped against the metal floor of the helicopter.

Voices shouted. *They had to go. Time was up. They had to go now!*

The black shape with the lights flashing and the struggling sound of the alarm was a Humvee. His dad hadn't made it out, but he was in there. Max screamed at the soldiers, but no one could hear him shouting against the storm and the helicopter's rotors that his dad was in there. That his dad must have heard the helicopter, must have heard Max's voice calling to him. That his dad had set off the Humvee's alarms. To alert them. For help.

Strong hands still held him. The helicopter quivered, the skids lifted.

Then one of the soldiers, eyes squinting against the rain, pointed.

From out of the hangar, through the curtain of rain, Mr Peterson was holding his friend, Max's dad, and was carrying him like an injured child towards the impatient helicopter.

Drenched by the rain, but alive, Tom Gordon was hauled into the helicopter. Soldiers yanked Mr Peterson aboard, and the pilot worked hard to get them airborne.

Max's eyes were closing. As the storm snatched at them, he saw a break in the clouds and spotted the figure of a man in a white coat, making his escape in a boat, down the slipway, into the river, where the boat settled for a moment and then began to sink.

In his panic to escape, Zhernastyn had forgotten that the boat was in need of repair.

The clouds closed around the picture of the man in the rain-stung water as bow waves rippled towards him.

Crocodiles don't mind bad weather.

*

375

The wind and rain muffled the explosion, and the clouds shrouded the fort's collapse. It didn't matter any more.

Father and son lay, soaking wet, next to each other on the cold metal floor. Max pulled himself against his unconscious father, lay an arm across him, and put his head against his chest.

He wanted to hear his heartbeat.

Nothing else mattered.

Fading words, snatched through the noise, penetrated his thoughts. *Too late to reach Chang . . . troops can't . . . thousands'll die . . . poison water . . . weather shut down . . . rain cleared at dam . . . but . . . too dark . . . too late . . . too late.*

Carried into a storm-blasted lullaby, the swaying helicopter rocked him this way and that. But the frightening sensation of being at the mercy of a tremendous storm was not what Max felt. Part of him inside had stepped through that place again. His shadow-form had left him on the floor of that bucking helicopter and glided across the darkness that had settled over the land. Now he could feel his feet gripping rock as he ran, hard, unyielding in his determination, and he smelled the musty warmth of another animal nearby.

He ran into the night, instinct guiding him; his lungs burned; his eyes searched for the unseen quarry. Being earth-bound could not help him. And what was less than a thought-beat away became reality. The scudding clouds had taken the rain with them; now there was only the wind, but the wind was second nature to him. He no longer felt the hard-edged stone beneath him, now the sky was his domain.

He saw the steel bird that sheltered in an enclave of rocks, a safe haven from the storms. It sat unmoving, its wings silent. The sword and shield tattooed on its body were defiant in the night.

A movement caught his eye. A blackened shape loped across the rocks where moments earlier he had run, and he heard the familiar whinnying call. The dog-creature stopped. It had gone as far as it could on the clifftop. Max circled. The jackal looked upwards at Max as he heard his own keening call in response.

The lightning that crackled down from its hidden place above the clouds illuminated the mountains – ghostly veils of mist tearing away from the rock face. The concrete bridge between the two mountains. Images repeated themselves from his memory – the dark cave in a black night. He hurtled ever closer. Trying to understand.

The cave was a shape that moved. A man. Big and square-shouldered. He held a dully glowing light in his hand. A control. Some kind of remote device. And as the man held his arm out towards the stone towers that controlled this bridge across the night, Max knew he was at the dam.

Gates in the dam wall began to open. Far below, the white spume of the river's overspill was already hurtling through the valley floor. As the floodgates opened wider, a tremendous force of water spewed out. The power seemed even greater than the storm that now punished the land on the horizon.

Was it instinct that made Shaka Chang turn and look upwards? Was it his unfailing ability to know when danger was close? It made no difference. He spun on his heel as Max fell ever faster, directly at him.

An instant of fear. Of knowing. Of failure and death. It was Shaka Chang's turn to realize he was finished. Whatever it was that screamed out of the night sky in a near vertical dive shimmered through the darkness. His reflexes didn't fail him as he smashed a hand through the air, and he connected with talons. The attack stopped him from completing the code on the remote control that would have fully opened the floodgates. He grappled, felt the bite of claw on his hands and arms. He dismissed the pain, but the attack caused him to drop the device, which arced away from his bloodied hands. How many times in training had he spun like a ballet dancer and struck out? How often had he deliberately failed to pull his punches, as every martial arts expert should, and caused crippling injury or death to his opponent? Such a turn of speed was second nature.

One hand grabbed the safety rail to counterbalance his lunge for the remote control. The blood on the steel barrier was like oil on glass, and his bulk and weight carried his momentum forward. In his moment of disbelief he felt the breath of ice-cold water flare in his nostrils as he tumbled over the edge. Caught by the thundering torrent that he alone was responsible for, he was snatched and pummelled into oblivion. His scream was unable to escape his final gasp for life.

Max had slept for two days and when he woke up had a ravenous appetite. The private room in the military hospital was basic but comfortable, and the food they brought him was enough for two men.

The doctors insisted he should eat before they allowed

anyone to visit him, but they assured him that his father was safe and being cared for and that !Koga had come through his operation.

Once he had scoffed every last morsel, he eased himself achingly on to the cold linoleum floor. His reflection in the bathroom mirror told him that someone had bathed him. His hair, longer than usual, left a pencil line of white between his scalp and a dark brown tan. Now that the dirt and ingrained grime had been scrubbed off, he could see the cuts and bruises he had sustained; some would leave permanent scars. It didn't matter. What he wanted more than anything right now was to clean his teeth. They felt as though they were caked in cement.

No sooner had he got a mouthful of foaming toothpaste than Sayid barged into the room, saw him, and cuffed him round the back of the head. 'You jammy devil! Yeah? You're a bloody hero, mate. I'm gonna eat out on this for a long time to come.'

Max stopped himself from choking and spat the toothpaste out. 'I'm OK. Thanks for asking,' he said.

'Oh yeah. How are you? You were out for the count. Couldn't wake you.'

'I feel as though I've been run over by a steamroller.'

'Yeah, you look taller. So, what do you reckon? Freebies for ever?'

'Odds are, the powers that be will shut the whole thing down and no one will say anything. Imagine the scare stories that could come out of this. No one would ever fill a kettle again.'

Before Sayid could argue, Kallie tapped on the door, more

for the sake of politeness than as if expecting a response. 'Up and about, hey? Next time, go on a guided bus tour, will you, this was too much trouble.' She kissed his cheek, which made Sayid examine the walls a bit more closely.

Max was wearing boxer shorts, but when she looked at him he felt uncomfortably naked. 'They said I could come through. Thought I'd say hi. Feeling OK?'

'OK.'

'Yeah, I bet. You did all right.' She smiled. It seemed a hell of a compliment.

'Listen, Kallie, you did wonders out there. I mean, getting me down on the ground and everything.'

'Nah, it was nothin'. You didn't need me, you'd have sorted it out.' She smiled. 'Even a monkey could fly one of those things.'

He smiled. It felt good to see her again.

She helped herself to one of the apples on the bedside table. 'Pa's got himself in a state. Says I'm not to be trusted flying around on my own, so he's grounded me, literally, for a few days. Just long enough to make sure you Brits leave the premises quietly. Want to see !Koga? He's doing great.'

'Absolutely. Dad first, though.'

'Doctors are doing their rounds, Max,' Sayid said. 'Mister Peterson'll come and get us when they've finished.'

Max grabbed a T-shirt and pulled on a pair of shorts. Everything was squeaky clean. He winced as he tugged them on.

'That cut on the top of your leg will take a while to heal,' Kallie said. '!Koga told us everything that happened. I reckon you must have done it when you fell into the Devil's Breath.'

Max nodded. 'I suppose it'll take me a while to put the bits that hurt together with the time when I did it.'

Something didn't sound right. The cut on the back of his leg was high up. Just below the cheek of his backside.

She smiled as she saw him realize. 'Look, I've got a brother at home, there's only one bathroom. They were *short* of nurses! Everyone was running around, looking after your dad. All right?'

'You washed me? All over?'

She shrugged.

He blushed.

'Gross,' said Sayid.

The military hospital was in a small town where mainly army personnel lived. It was where they took soldiers injured in battle. A quiet, little-known place with an airstrip that seeped out of the desert at one end and disappeared into the trees and scrubland at the other. The perfect place to keep secrets.

!Koga had never worn pyjamas in his life, but the military nurses had insisted. Now he sat with the window wide open, his jacket undone, the heat touching his skin. Anything less would be worse than a prison cell for a boy who had never slept under a roof before. There was little sign of the operation he'd had, other than his shaved head and the dressing that covered the surgical wound, and he looked as skinny as ever.

His face burst into white teeth and laughter as Max came into his room. The two boys hugged each other. 'You saved my life! They told me!'

'You came back for me. What are friends for?' The tensions and danger of their journey were behind them, the freedom from fear gave them a lightness they had not known for a long time.

'Miss van Reenen told me everything, and your friend Sayid, and the man who came from England, and Miss van Reenen's father has taken his plane down to find my family. Then we will go home.' His smile faded a little. 'And you will go home.'

'Yes,' Max said, 'I will.'

Mike Kapuo stood with Mr Peterson at the door. 'I'm Detective Chief Inspector Kapuo. I need to talk to you two boys. That OK? We have to piece this whole thing together from day one.'

'OK,' Max said. 'Where do you want us?'

'Well, I know !Koga's first language isn't English, and I don't speak much of the Bushman language, so I've brought in an army interpreter; he's a Bushman, so we'll talk to !Koga first, and maybe Kallie can stick around to help out.'

Max hugged his friend. 'Don't tell them about the cave paintings and the prophecy. They won't believe you.' He went out, leaving Mike Kapuo and Kallie with bewildered looks on their faces.

'I will tell them because it needs to be told, and it is the truth,' !Koga laughed.

Out in the corridor Mr Peterson shook Max's hand. 'You look OK; doctors have given you a clean bill of health.'

'Thanks, Mister Peterson. And thanks for saving my dad.'

'I didn't – you did. You *knew* he was in there, and I

had to give it one last try. You want to see him?'

Max nodded and swallowed the lump in his throat.

They stood for a moment outside his dad's room, looking through the window at the gaunt figure of his father, who lay in bed, drips feeding into his arm, seemingly asleep. Mr Peterson put an arm around Max's shoulders.

Sayid pulled a face. 'Sorry, Max, I tried to cover it over. I didn't know how to tell you.'

Max nodded. ''S OK,' he answered quietly.

Mr Peterson stepped away, allowing Max to go into the room when he was ready. 'This is going to take a very long time to try and fix, Max. He's going to be all right physically, but they hurt his mind – we don't know how long it will take.' Mr Peterson hesitated. Max looked at him, seeming to hear the unspoken words – *maybe he'll never be healed.* 'You understand, Max?'

'Yes, sir. I understand.'

'OK. We're flying back to England tonight. The government has laid on a plane and a doctor. You, me and Sayid, with your dad. No sense in hanging round here. He needs specialist care now.'

Sayid gave an encouraging smile to Max, ready to leave.

'Sayid, thanks for everything.'

'I didn't do anything.'

'I bet you did.'

Sayid nodded. There'd be time enough later for talking the whole thing through.

'Anyway. Thanks for being here. For being my mate,' Max said.

*

Max stood for a couple of minutes, watching his father. There were so many things he wanted to tell him, but perhaps that didn't matter too much right now. They had shared such intense moments these past few days, each of them had told the other how they felt. There was no more awkward father–son thing. They had come through, and they were both alive.

Max went into the room and sat next to his father. His eyes opened and he smiled, his hand reaching out to touch Max. 'Hey,' he whispered.

'They said you're gonna be all right, Dad,' Max said.

'Oh yes.' He frowned slightly. 'Thing is, my brain's a bit like scrambled eggs. I know there're a lot of pieces missing. Lots I can't remember.'

His dad smiled. 'I remember you, though.'

Night comes quickly to that part of Africa, and today was no different, but it was too soon for Max. Everything was drawing to a close. The sun was retreating and Max hovered, uncertain how to say his goodbyes. His dad was loaded into the plane, Sayid had got aboard and Max waited with Mr Peterson as Kallie pushed !Koga out in a wheelchair.

What was it about Africa that seeped into your blood, like the sunset caressing the sand? Whatever it was, he envied the people staying behind. There was no place on Earth like it.

'What happened at the dam?' he asked.

'We're not sure. Shaka Chang died there, we know that much. He didn't have time to open the floodgates fully,' Mr Peterson said.

'When I was in the chopper, with Dad, just before I blacked

384

out, I thought I heard someone say that the storm had stopped the soldiers getting there.'

'That's right. The rainfall was torrential. It cleared over the dam briefly, but it stopped the ground and air assault. He'd have poisoned thousands. He had no idea you were alive and had got the message out.'

They watched the darkening sky as Kallie and !Koga got closer. Mr Peterson shrugged. 'Strange place, Africa. Things happen. Things you can't explain. Shaka Chang's pilot had landed the helicopter at the dam site; he was waiting for Chang to come back, then they were going to fly out to an airstrip, an hour away, to link up with his private jet. That's disappeared somewhere. Anyway, he said he saw a hawk, well, he insisted it was a peregrine; he seemed to know what he was talking about. Said it came out of the sky and attacked Chang. He tried to fight it off, but it clawed at him and he lost his footing. They'll never find his body.'

Kallie and !Koga had reached them. 'OK, Max, five minutes and we're off. 'Bye, Kallie, thanks for everything. You too, !Koga. You're two of the bravest kids I've ever known.'

'And Max?' Kallie said.

'He's the bravest, just don't tell him I said that or I'll never get him to do homework again.'

Mr Peterson walked off towards the waiting aircraft.

'I'll stay in touch, Kallie, if that's OK?' Max said.

'Sure. Whatever. Hey, I might be coming to Europe. Dad's agreed to let me go to college – tourism degree or some such. Thinks I need educating. It'll help the business. I'll look you up.'

'I'd like that.' And she knew he meant it.

He looked at the Bushman boy who had not only saved his life but also shown him a different way of living it. 'You be careful, !Koga. I will think of you and I will seek out the morning star – the Dawn's Heart – and always remember.'

The boy nodded. 'Remember, Max, this is all a dream.'

He embraced them again and turned away. Kallie called after him. 'Max! I almost forgot!'

She pulled out a folded envelope and emptied its contents. 'Your watch. You gave it to !Koga, remember? The police gave it back to me. I said I'd make sure you got it.'

His dad's watch. In his heart he wanted !Koga to keep it, but he knew with equal certainty that the wild and free boy had no need for the confines of time.

'And this,' she said, spilling out a jade and gold bracelet. 'You were holding this when they pulled you out of the chopper. You wouldn't let go for ages.'

Max turned the jade and Moldavite in his fingers. 'This is Shaka Chang's,' he told her.

She looked puzzled. 'How did you get it?'

'I don't know. Maybe I picked it up in the hangar when we went in with the soldiers. I'm not sure.'

The quickening sun warmed the gold bracelet and touched the Moldavite pearls, reflecting infinite years of trapped light.

And from within the bracelet Max thought he saw a fleeting image of Shaka Chang's hand clawing at the sky, as a pair of talons raked his wrist.

*

The plane lifted off just as the edge of the world turned red. Max gazed back at the darkening ground and saw a shadow move into the last ray of broken light.

The creature looked over its shoulder at the departing plane.

And then the jackal loped away into the night.

Acknowledgements

A number of people helped me with the writing of this book. Keith Chiazzari, pilot and adventurer, has flown the world from the frozen north to the Namibian wilderness and he guided me through the critical stages of flying in this story. My good friend James McFarlane, whose eagle eye for details about all things African (and much more besides), made invaluable suggestions for the manuscript.

A huge hug to Puffin Books' team for the creativity and enthusiasm from Francesca Dow, Kirsten Grant, Emily Cox, Jodie Mullish, Sarah Hughes, Sarah Kettle, Wendy Tse and the brilliant Tom Sanderson for his magic. Thanks, Yvonne, for your first 'nod' and a very special thank-you to my editor, Lindsey Heaven, champion of champions, whose enthusiasm inspired everyone.

Thanks to Conrad Williams, my film agent, for his ever-present encouragement, and to my tireless book agent, Isobel Dixon, who has found so many wonderful homes for Max Gordon and his adventures.

Most of all, my love and gratitude go to my wife, Suzy, who knows what it means to be married to a writer.

*

Finally, if anyone wishes to learn more about the Bushmen, and other hunter-gatherers, an excellent place to start is Survival International's website: survival-international.org